He lifted her ha
her wrist one l
with a soft kiss.

"I would never call a woman a trophy. A gift, perhaps, but never a trophy." He spoke softly, his lips brushing her wrist. "Women aren't meant to be fought and won. They should be seduced."

Stella's lips parted ever so slightly as she drew in a deep lungful of air. He knew her jaguar side would scent his desire for her.

"Is that what you're doing? Seducing me?" She had been trying for snark, but the words came out as a breathy whisper.

"Yes, but if you have to ask, I must be doing it wrong." He flashed her a grin and winked, releasing the building tension in the room, more out of self-preservation than anything. His cock was hard enough to hammer nails and his tiger side was ready to pounce. "So why don't you let me try again?"

...and brought it to his mouth. Then he gave
...st caress with his thumb before replacing it

# PRAISE FOR CELIA KYLE'S SHIFTER ROGUES SERIES

## *WOLF'S MATE*

"Nonstop action, lots of explicit sex, and smart banter add snap to this rough-and-tumble adventure that nicely launches this series."

—*Library Journal*

"Celia Kyle's my go-to for sexy alpha shifters and fast-paced, delicious storylines."

—Jessica Clare, *New York Times* and *USA Today* bestselling author

"I had a blast reading this. It was so freaking fun! A lighter paranormal romance with really likable characters. It was fast paced, kept me on my toes, and left me excited for the next book…This was just super entertaining to read and left me with a smile on my face."

—*About That Story*

"This book was amazingly written and had the best character interaction and dialogue I have read in a long time."

—*Novel Reads*

# ALSO BY CELIA KYLE

## Shifter Rogues series

*Wolf's Mate*

# Tiger's Claim

Shifter Rogues Book #2

# CELIA KYLE

**FOREVER**
*New York   Boston*

Copyright © 2018 by Celia Kyle
Cover illustration by Kris Keller
Cover design by Elizabeth Turner Stokes
Cover copyright © 2018 by Hachette Book Group, Inc.

Forever
Hachette Book Group
1290 Avenue of the Americas
New York, NY 10104
hachettebookgroup.com
twitter.com/foreverromance

First Edition: November 2018

Forever is an imprint of Grand Central Publishing.
The Forever name and logo are trademarks of Hachette Book Group, Inc.

The publisher is not responsible for websites (or their content) that are not owned by the publisher.

The Hachette Speakers Bureau provides a wide range of authors for speaking events. To find out more, go to www.hachettespeakersbureau.com or call (866) 376-6591.

ISBNs: 978-1-5387-4456-7 (mass market); 978-1-5387-4454-3 (ebook)

Printed in the United States of America

OPM

10 9 8 7 6 5 4 3 2 1

*When life gives you lemons, you can always count on your best friends to make you lemon margaritas. To my three besties—Flora, Jill, and Marina. Thank you for being there to listen to my doubts, my fears, and always having that margarita ready when I need it most.*

# Tiger's Claim

# CHAPTER ONE

$C$ole lifted the glass of champagne to his lips and pretended to take a sip. The sparkling Armand de Brignac Brut Gold was a cliché cake topper to the torturous night. He'd been served more of that champagne at more parties than he could count. The elite rich assholes needed to find a new "classic" drink.

Cole voted for Heineken, but his oldest brother said he was an "uncouth asshole who wouldn't know the difference between hundred-year-old wine and shit wine out of a box if his life depended on it."

Cole's big bro wasn't wrong.

Big bro also wouldn't consider an evening surrounded by beautiful women in gowns that cost more than a Porsche cruel and unusual punishment. He'd enjoy being in a room lit by glittering chandeliers while background music provided by a string quartet filled the air. He'd revel in schmoozing with the other rich dicks and dancing with ladies who asked about his bank account first and his hobbies second.

Then there was the penguin suit Cole had been forced to wear.

*Mmm...penguins.* His inner tiger purred in the back of his mind, the feline licking its chops. The little shit. They *were not* going to think about hunting penguins. Especially since it wasn't like he could sate his craving anytime soon. They were in South Carolina at a Southern plantation, not Antarctica.

The cat padded forward and nudged his mind, wanting to know if they could borrow his brother's jet for a quick trip south.

Damn but it was tempting. Both halves of him—human and tiger—wanted out of this mansion. He hated being surrounded by people who'd rather turn his kind—shape-shifters—into fur rugs than friends.

Well, he'd rather blow up the mansion—and its inhabitants—than spend another moment in their company. His inner tiger purred at the idea of destroying every bit of wood, drywall, and marble flooring. *Then* they'd go to Antarctica.

The damn beast had a one-track mind. Too bad his boss wouldn't appreciate him screwing up the operation. His employer—Shifter Operations Command—frowned on unauthorized bombings.

Not that he normally cared, but he was the only one uniquely qualified to infiltrate this millionaire crowd. Blending in to get intel took priority over watching things burn. He mentally sighed. It'd been too damned long since he'd watched anything be destroyed in a wave of fire and concrete. He missed seeing the air clouded with smoke and powdered drywall.

Cole lowered his glass as two women wrapped in sequins and glittering jewels strolled near. Their gazes stroked him from head to toe, and his lips tilted up in a practiced panty-wetting smirk. He knew how to play the high-society ballroom games even if he hated every minute of his time among the rich.

The brunette licked her red-painted lips and gave him a look that said she'd give him a good time, while the blonde hung back. Not quite standoffish, but not inviting, either.

No bother. Cole was on the hunt—for information—and the brunette would be easy prey. He focused on the woman, giving her the full heat of his stare, and the warm scent of her arousal teased the air.

He tipped his head to the women. "Ladies, good evening."

The brunette wetted her lips in an age-old attempt to tease him. The blonde's mouth tipped up in a small smile, though it almost resembled a grimace. He could sympathize with her hatred of these affairs. He returned the heat in the brunette's stare, forcing himself to appear interested when all he wanted to do was toss them both through the nearest window. He wasn't normally a guy to abuse women, but . . . they wouldn't hesitate to kill him if they knew he was a shifter.

Hell, everyone in the mansion would want to kill him. It was a Unified Humanity party, and that was the thing about the world's largest anti-shifter organization—they wanted his kind dead.

"I don't think we've met before, Mr. . . . ?" The brunette's voice trailed off in obvious question.

"Turner." He pulled his lips into a welcoming smile. "Cole Turner." Neither caught his James Bond impression. "And you lovely ladies are?"

He already knew the answer to his question. His SHOC team had done their homework, and Cole had memorized every file the team had prepared. He knew all about this deliciously deadly human woman.

The brunette held out her hand first. "Olivia Walters."

He gently grasped her fingertips and brought her hand

to his mouth, brushing a soft kiss to her knuckles. "It's a pleasure."

In more ways than one. She was beautiful to look at—even if her father was an evil monster. More importantly, she was the first step in getting close to said evil monster. It'd taken him four months of coming to blasted hoity-toity parties—rejoining the old-money class he hated—to finally get invited to a Walters gathering.

Cole released Olivia's hand and turned to the blonde. She was pretty in an understated way, and her hand trembled as she held it out for his.

The daughter of the notorious Richard King—rich genius, shifter hater. And she was a *nervous* murderer. *Interesting*.

"Charlotte—"

Olivia nudged Charlotte away, the woman's hand dropping from Cole's before his lips had a chance to brush her skin. "Cole..." She purred his name. "Can I call you Cole?" Olivia didn't wait for a response. "Are you associated with the Turner Group?"

Cole parted his lips and drew in the surrounding scents. His tiger padded forward even further, anxious to help so they could get the hell out of there. He tasted each flavor and easily identified them. Excitement. Anticipation. *Arousal*.

Gross.

"I am." *Unfortunately*. He flashed her his most disarming grin and fought to suppress the churning in his gut. He hated his connections to the Turner Group, but they were undeniable and—right now—useful. "I'm the youngest of the Turners. My older brother is the president. The rest fall in line after him."

Olivia giggled as if he'd said the most amusing thing

in the world, and he fought the urge to roll his eyes. "And what do you do for the company?"

Cole winked at her. "I'm the independently wealthy black sheep of the family."

Even if he had black and orange fur instead of wool.

"I've always enjoyed spending time with the naughty ones." Olivia eased even closer, her large breasts brushing his arm.

"Olivia," Charlotte broke in, and Olivia shot a glare at her friend. "Your father is looking for you."

Olivia gave him a strained smile—Daddy's little girl didn't like being summoned by Papa. "I'd love to finish this conversation later. If you're not here with anyone, perhaps we can find each other again. Somewhere a little more private."

"The night is, happily, my own." He winked, using the charm he'd perfected during his own family's shindigs over the years. Parties Cole had attended before he'd decided a life of violence was better than one spent in the boardroom.

Olivia stepped closer, fingers skating down his lapel. Her touch left a trail of her scent on the fabric, and he decided he'd burn the damn thing rather than have it cleaned. Dry cleaning could only do so much, and removing the stench of evil mixed with a bit of Chanel No. 5 was beyond most cleaners.

"Excellent." She ran her tongue along her lips. "I'll see you later this evening, then." With that, Olivia slowly turned away, giving him a nice view of the long line of her bare back and her heart-shaped ass. "Come along, Charlotte."

He kept his gaze on the two women, watching Olivia slice through the crowd with practiced ease while Charlotte King scurried in her wake. A waiter drifted past, and Cole reached out, snagging another glass of champagne while leaving his empty one in its place.

He slowly made his way along the outer edge of the crowd and turned to face the wall, gaze on some overly expensive—probably priceless—piece of shitty artwork. His beast lent its help to amplify his hearing, making him even more sensitive to the world around him. He listened to the murmured conversations in his immediate vicinity before moving on. He drifted past one group after another— each little clique whispering gossip while plotting another's downfall.

He hated the entire scene—trophy wives, pompous executives, and bratty daughters hunting for a rich husband. More than one sugar baby wannabe looked at Cole like he was rich-husband material.

Rich? Yes.

Husband? A mate, maybe. Someday. A day far from right now and only after he found someone exactly like… exactly like a woman who was already mated to one of Cole's SHOC teammates, which made her off-limits.

Cole was an asshole, not a homewrecker. Even if he did feel a pull toward a certain cougar shifter.

Cole listened to the discussions with half an ear, gaze traveling over the people he neared. He knew everything there was to know about rich shifter families, but these guys were all human. He'd had to study up before the op began. He mentally went through the research, identifying the humans he came across.

The balding man in the corner had a net worth of forty million. The guy who'd had a little too much to drink and slurred every other word only had twenty-eight million in cash and assets. There was a woman in a skintight, midnight-blue dress with a net worth of fifty million. Her husband had died early in their marriage under *suspicious* circumstances. At the moment, Olivia's father—James Walters—was closing in on her.

Walters needed money—a lot—and it was only a matter of time before the human realized Cole was the one to give it to him.

Olivia wandered up to her father, Charlotte on her tail, just before he reached the widow, and the two exchanged a few whispered words. When James Walters cut Cole a quick glance, Cole knew he was their topic of conversation.

*Time to play hard to get.* There was no sense in making this game easy on Walters. Rich men were used to having to pander to *richer* men. Cole's net worth was at least triple of anyone else's in the building.

He changed direction and carefully cut through the crowd, passing off easy smiles whenever someone looked his way. He lost himself among the suits and glittering dresses, allowing the humans to swallow him with their presence. He kept a sedate pace while he wove between people. He didn't want attention for any reason *other* than the size of his bank account. His assets alone should draw the right kind of attention.

He definitely didn't want stares because he made a fool of himself, but that was exactly what he did. He froze mid-step in the center of the room—at least on the outside. In his mind, the tiger snatched control and forced his gaze to remain on the woman who'd captured his attention. The woman with hair the color of wildfire. The woman with curves he ached to trace with his palms. The woman whose pale skin reminded him of moonlight.

She turned her head, giving him a glimpse at her profile. He traced her face with his eyes—the delicate slope of her nose and the soft line of her jaw. He spied the fullness of her lips and wondered what it'd be like to taste her—explore her.

Cole remained her captive, unable to overpower the cat so they could continue the operation. It urged him to go to her, pull her into his arms and never release her. Beauty like that should be worshipped.

"Another glass, sir?" The intrusion tore him from fantasizing about the flame-haired beauty. The spell she'd woven around him shattered, and he looked to the waiter.

"No." He shook his head. "Thank you."

He stepped around the server and returned to his wanderings, ignoring the occasional confused glance from guests who'd obviously seen him staring. They'd get over it. He had enough money that others were willing to overlook eccentricities.

He finally reached the other side of the room and turned and leaned against the cream-colored wall. He took another sip of champagne and forced himself to swallow. The shit was nasty. What he wouldn't give for a beer.

Cole watched and waited. He'd stay put for a little while. Just long enough for James and Olivia to catch sight of him before he changed location once more. A game of cat and mouse. Or rather *big cat* and crunchy humans.

The tiger didn't want to stay put. Instead, it wanted to hunt a specific female. He tried to remind the cat that they were at a Unified Humanity party and had a job to do. Besides, only UH members were at the party, which meant their redheaded vixen wasn't a fan of shifters. Did the beast want to seduce a woman who would love to see their kind eliminated?

The beast hesitated, and Cole sensed the feline weighing its options when its choice should have been obvious.

Crazy cat.

He spied Olivia and James in his periphery, the father's and daughter's attention on him. He should push away from the wall, find a new location to wait for the duo. Except *she* demanded his attention once more.

The tempting woman cut through the crowd, a flash of deep red as she wove her way past guest after guest. With every step, more of her was revealed—sparkling green eyes, those lush lips, the soft glow of her cheeks. Then there were her curves. The curves taunted him, the bodice of her dress snug over her large breasts to her nipped-in waist before flowing over the plump line of her ass.

And now she was close—so close he could almost reach out and touch her. The hem of her gown ghosted over his shoes, and her delicate scent teased his nose.

She was gorgeous.

She was tempting.

She was... Cole drew in a deep breath, savoring her natural flavors... a shifter?

## CHAPTER TWO

Stella's attention drifted across the ballroom, and she handed out polite smiles anytime one of the guests happened to glance her way. The humans didn't meet her gaze that often. One sweeping glance was all it took for them to decide she wasn't worth their time. Which was all the better for her since she had a bomb in her boobs and a destination in mind.

God willing, Stella's boobs wouldn't explode. She was attached to them—literally—and they were her best feature. In her opinion, anyway. As far as Stella's inner jaguar was concerned, *its* existence was the cherry on the "Awesomeness of Stella Moore" cake.

She continued her slow glide through the crowded space, her first goal within sight. She planned to silently exit the ballroom and turn left, sticking to the shadows until she reached the servants' stairs at the back of the house. A lovely little source had told her they were no longer in use, which meant she could reach her final destination without risking her perfectly spotted jaguar tail.

Her footsteps remained silent on the thick carpet, heels sinking into the plush flooring. Her ankles wobbled, and she reached for the wall to steady herself so she wouldn't end up sprawled on the ground. Why had she thought four-inch heels were a good idea? Normally, she was a barefoot and jeans-cutoffs kind of shifter. Not eight-hundred-dollar Louboutin shoes paired with a vintage Dior ball gown.

Not that the shoes and the gown coordinated well, but she'd always wanted a pair of those red-soled stilettos. What better reason to buy them than for Operation: Kill the Asshole?

She pushed away from the wall and quietly made her way along the corridor until she reached the dead end. In truth, there was a door hidden by the wainscoting, making it invisible to the casual visitor. A soft press of her fingers against a particular spot on the wall had the door swinging open and granting her entrance. She carefully crept into the dusty passageway. The only light in the tight space came from the hallway itself, filling the area with impenetrable dark shadows.

Goose bumps rose along her bare arms, over her shoulders, and then darted down her spine. She shuddered and battled against the irrational fear of creepy crawlies that attacked her nerves.

The she-cat snarled inside her mind, spitting a long, drawn-out hiss. It reminded her she was a *jaguar shifter*, for goodness' sake. What could bugs or mice do to *her*? Stella took a deep breath, then immediately fought the urge to sneeze. *Focus*. She had a goal, and panicking wasn't going to help her accomplish it.

Stella turned left and climbed the aged wooden steps in the hidden passage. The barest snippets of light crept through the cracks in the wall. She kept her fingertips on the uneven surface, while her other hand rested beneath her breasts to hold the most important part of her plan in place.

Carrying a bomb tucked just beneath her boobs had

sounded like a good idea at the time. Now? Not so much. Who knew explosives could be so heavy?

Soon she'd climbed high enough in the mansion's hidden walls that no sound from the party reached her, and she knew she was close to her goal.

Stella stood before the door at the top and took a deep breath, breasts—and bomb—straining against her bodice. Could she do this? Plant an explosive that...

That would kill the person who'd ruined her life and the lives of so many others?

The jaguar snarled and curled its lips back to bare its fangs. *Yes*, it assured her. Yes, they could. It did, however, remind her claws could do the job as well and it'd happily step up to the plate and get the job done.

Not gonna happen.

Stella opened the creaky door and slipped into the hallway, thick carpet meeting her feet once again. She nudged the door to the hidden entrance closed with a soft *click* before she moved on.

The moon's glow illuminated the hall, and she made her way toward her destination—second door on the right. One of James Walters's most private areas.

Now or never, right?

Her hand trembled as she grasped the polished brass doorknob. She could do this—get in and get out with no one the wiser. She could also ignore her prodding conscience. Was this the kind of person—shifter—she'd become? One who could plant a bomb and hope for the best? Er, worst?

Her jaguar assured her she *was* that type of shifter and it was James Walters who'd made her that way. He had no one to blame but himself.

The past threatened to rear its ugly head, the dark brown of Walters's evil stare overtaking her every thought. She'd never forget his face. She'd never forget the way he'd looked at her as he'd grabbed Madeline. It hadn't taken him long to ruin Stella's life.

Every day her mind was pummeled with loneliness and grief, which never seemed to leave her be. They ebbed and flowed, occasionally softer before growing in strength once more. But they never disappeared. They'd been her constant companion for so long...

Those memories had her straightening her spine, and a new determination pushed her onward. Walters had almost destroyed her life once. She wasn't going to give him the chance to continue his "work" and hurt so many others. She twisted the knob and opened the door, quickly entering the dark study before she lost her nerve.

She moved through the room from memory, not risking a light to guide her steps. She strode past the rows of crowded bookshelves and toward the far side of the space to the massive desk—ornately carved, highly polished, and bigger than a twin-sized bed. She wondered if what they said was true. Were men with big desks overcompensating because they had little...?

Her jaguar snarled at Stella. She needed to focus on the task at hand. She could ponder the meaning of life and micropenis sizes later.

Stella rounded the desk and went to the leather executive chair. She gathered layers of her dress and pulled the fabric aside as she lowered herself to her knees.

Now she focused on her task. She tugged on the neckline of her gown, jiggled her breasts, and reached past a boob in search of the package she'd tucked away. She grunted and pulled, her breast nearly popping out of her bodice. Her fingers brushed the outer wrapping of the bomb, nails scraping the taut fabric wrapped around the deadly bundle.

"C'mon, dammit," she grumbled, and switched hands, trying a different angle. She wasn't going to have her plans fall apart because of her chesticles. "Why are you being so difficult?"

"My mother often asks me the same thing." The deep timbre of a male's voice vibrated through her body.

Stella whipped her attention to the intruder, her gaze meeting a pair of intense blue eyes across the polished wood desk. Blue eyes, light-brown hair, wide shoulders...

He leaned forward, the rest of his body hidden by the furniture, but there was something he *couldn't* hide. Not from her and not from one of her kind. *He* was one of her kind.

She inhaled, drawing in the scents around her...Fresh rain, damp earth, crisp sun, and a natural musk that sank through her pores. The scents consumed her, wrapped around her in a cloak of deliciousness that she could easily become addicted to. Her jaguar urged her to keep taking in more of his aroma until it told her to stop. Which would be never.

She ignored her cat and continued to stare at the stranger, gaze taking in every detail from the light scruff on his cheeks to the small bump on his nose. There was only one word to describe him, and it wasn't "gorgeous" or "sexy" or "sensual." It was...

*"Tiger."*

# CHAPTER THREE

*N*ormally Cole was an ass man, but standing above this curvy little female and staring into the deep V of her cleavage, he decided he preferred tits. Or at least, *her* tits.

The way she cupped one of her breasts was even sexier, and the tiger purred inside his mind. It wanted him to get up close and personal with the... He carefully drew in a lungful of air, seeking out her scent to confirm the suspicions that'd driven him to follow her.

"And you're..." he whispered, sorting through the sweet, sensual warmth that came from her. The flavors made his cock hard and his tiger purr, and his body reacted in an instant even while he sought her species. Unfortunately, another familiar smell—C4—crowded the air, making it difficult. Cole frowned and narrowed his eyes as he tipped his head to the side. "What are you?"

Other than perfect. She had those gorgeous curves, alluring green eyes, and long softly curling hair. The cherry on top was the fact that she carried explosives. A woman after his own, bomb-loving heart.

She licked her lips, pink tongue darting into sight for a split second. "Uh..."

Cole dropped his voice and added a rumbling purr from

his tiger. "Cat got your tongue? Is there something I can do to you?"

"You mean *for* me?" The words came out in a sensual, breathy whisper.

Cole winked. "That too."

Her face flushed pink in the moon's glow. Cole gathered more of the scent in the room, his beast pushing aside the tar-like smell of the C4 to identify her. He captured evidence of Walters and sweet cigar smoke, but that was to be expected since they were in his house. Then more of the woman's scent filled his lungs as well.

Staining that aroma were two other warring flavors— fear and arousal. He scared the shit out of the redhead, but he stirred her desire, too. Then there was the slightest brush of something feral and wild—her inner beast. Her inner *feline*.

He should run her off, pat her on the ass and tell her that the big kitty didn't need anyone else intruding on his undercover operation. It was dangerous enough without having her around as a distraction. One wrong word, one small slip, and he'd find himself chained deep within one of Unified Humanity's bases. Not something he wanted to experience anytime soon. His tiger agreed—in principle.

But, dammit, she came in such a curvy, sexy-as-hell shifter package. Then there was her natural scent hiding beneath the floral notes of her perfume. She made him want— made him *crave*. And it went deeper than just her body. The tiger wanted more than a quick one-night stand with this lush kitty. Much more.

Then his question about running her off was answered for him. Based on the noises filtering down the hall, they had only a few minutes of privacy left. He couldn't send her on her way just yet.

*Just perfect.*

His tiger didn't appreciate Cole's sarcasm.

"What are you doing here tonight, sweet?" Cole's voice remained low, too low for a human to hear.

"I . . ." She shook her head. "It's Stella. And, uh, I'm not doing anything. Nothing at all. I—I—I got lost and—"

Cole lifted an eyebrow and drawled, "Uh-huh. I get it. Why bring a bottle of wine for the host when you can give the gift of C4?"

Stella gasped, her green eyes widening while a tremble shook her body. A flicker of yellow tinged that startling green for a split second and then vanished.

He didn't take his eyes off her, which meant he saw the moment she realized others approached the study. The resulting blatant fear sparked his tiger's protective instincts.

His inner animal huffed and nudged his mind, drawing his attention away from the woman and back to their surroundings. The cat was interested in the sexy little pussy just as much as his human half, but it didn't want to lose its dick because of a woman.

"C4? I don't know what you're talking about." Stella pushed to her feet, hands tugging her bodice back into place. *Too bad.* "I have to go. People—"

"Will walk through that door in the next sixty seconds." Cole straightened and rounded the desk, not stopping until mere inches separated their bodies. Now Stella was caught between him and the leather executive chair—his prisoner. His cat purred at the thought and wondered what she'd look like wrapped in rope and tied to his bed.

"Did you rig the desk?" He lifted a brow with the question.

"Uh . . ." Her skin rippled, and his curiosity about her inner animal was sated with that small movement. Golden fur

with hints of dark rosettes danced into view and then immediately disappeared.

Aha, his little kitty was a jaguar.

"I guess we'll find out." He shrugged and gripped her
waist, plan solidifying as he lifted her, turned, and sat her
on the desktop.

Cole's tiger wouldn't let him sit idly by while the
woman blew his cover *and* potentially blew up a handful
of humans. He'd worked too damned hard to gain access
to James Walters and the upper echelons of Unified
Humanity. He wasn't about to have his work ruined before
he'd accomplished his goal. Stella was tempting, but not
tempting enough to risk the lives of so many. He refused to
acknowledge that his actions were spurred by his need to
keep Stella safe more than completing his mission.

"What the *hell*?" she whispered with a hint of her cat's
snarl.

Her golden fur and those black spots flowed into sight
once again. Shit. The returning spots showed she didn't
have the best control. He just hoped the intruders didn't turn
on the lights and catch her covered in jaguar fur.

"You need to work with me, Stella, or we're both gonna
have a bad night."

An even worse one if he didn't get her—and her cat—
under control. The best he could do right now was distract
her from the humans and their impending intrusion. With
luck, his next act would snap her out of her rising panic and
get her to focus on him.

Though he knew he was destined for hell with his next
move. The most he could do was beg for forgiveness
later.

Once he'd saved both their lives.

Cole wrapped his right arm around her, palm settled on

her lower back, and pulled her butt to the edge of the desk. He gripped the curve of her hip with his left hand. The tips of his fingers burned as his tiger eased forward, transforming human nails to claws. They pierced the smooth fabric at her hip with ease. He anchored her in place and stepped closer, forcing her legs to part and make room for him until their bodies were aligned.

"I'm sorry," he murmured, his stomach churning with his every move.

Cole's fangs descended, slipping through his gums with sharpened points. He lowered his head to her bared shoulder and scratched her flesh. Not enough to break skin, but enough to show Stella's jaguar who was in charge. The she-cat froze in place and sucked in a quick breath, holding it for one moment and then another, before releasing the air in a whooshing gust. He expected a scream. Or maybe frozen silence with an edge of the cold rage females tended to favor. He didn't expect...

"Did you just fucking *rip my dress*?" Stella shoved his shoulders, but he wouldn't be moved. Not when he had her in his arms. Even as his conscience beat at him, cursing him for the act they had to perpetrate, he had to admit that she felt too good, too right in his arms. "I can't *believe* you ripped my dress."

He lifted his head and met her glare, Stella's golden eyes reflecting what little light filled the room. She jabbed a claw-tipped nail at him, the point a handful of inches from his nose. Yes, she was all pissed-off kitty now.

"You're paying for this."

Cole smirked. She was fucking gorgeous when she was mad. "Am I?"

"Yes," she snapped. "*And* you're—"

"Don't have time for this, sweet," he murmured. "Put the

kitty in her place. Company is close, and they're not fans of shifters. I need you to play along."

"I don't have to—"

"We're on the knife edge of life and death, Stella. You work with me, or they're going to use that C4 on *us*. Make your choice."

And damn him to hell for making her choose. For making a civilian join his op when she was anything but trained.

He stared into her eyes and watched the gold of her cat bleed away to reveal emerald green. The light dusting of fur retreated as well, milky-white skin dominating her body once again. The pale tips of her fangs disappeared, withdrawn into her gums. To the casual observer, she was 100 percent human. To Cole's tiger, she was five feet nine inches of "belongs in my bed." The cat curled its lip, snarling because he'd misinterpreted the feline's desire. Stella didn't just belong in his bed; some part of him said the kitty *belonged to him*.

And that scared the fuck outta him.

The study knob turned, and Cole jolted into action. He covered her mouth with his and pushed his way past her lips. He explored her depths, gathered her sweet taste, and then delved deep for more. Hot and sweet and so damned delicious. Strawberries with a dash of honeysuckle, followed by the delicate undertones of watermelon. He'd never been a fruit guy—tigers were all about meat—but *damn* she tasted good.

*One ticket to hell, please.*

The door swung inward, and light from the hall burst into the space. It bathed the room in a soft glow, destroying some of the shadows.

It also revealed them to the visitor.

The sharp edge of her fangs emerged from her gums

and scratched his lips. He doubted she knew that his tiger liked a little bit of roughness. It made him crave her even more. The pain turned sharper, no longer luring his tiger forward, but he wasn't about to give up and put them at risk. Not while they hovered between leaving the mansion alive or succumbing to death via torture from Unified Humanity members.

If he couldn't bullshit his way through the next few minutes, his little jaguar would likely end up in one of UH's very nasty shifter prisons. As for Cole...he'd be at her side.

With the intrusion, Stella seemed to fully grasp his motivation and threw herself into the kiss. Her tongue stroked his, her growl transformed into a deep moan, and she pressed her breasts into his chest while she wrapped her arms around his neck.

Cole pulled back and nipped her lip before taking more from her sweet mouth, drawing a whine from her throat. She tugged on him, fighting to increase the pressure between their mouths, and he leaned into her hold. He needed her closer. He needed more. He wanted to rip the dress from her body, lay her out across the desk, explore every inch of her, *devour* her from head to toe, and—

And he needed to remember she was playing along—not really aching for him as he ached for her.

"Cole?" The deep voice, the sharp snap edged with a hint of scandal and interest. Then came a fresh wave of *that* scent.

Human. James Walters. President of Apex Industries. A man who believed Cole was a human interested in funding Unified Humanity. A sliver of unease snaked its way down his spine, something akin to fear attempting to enter his blood. Not fear for himself, but for Stella. He could withstand anything UH threw at him, but a civilian like Stella...She wouldn't be able to survive.

Cole eased from their kiss—slowly, carefully, *regretfully*—and dropped his head to nuzzle her neck. Just enough of a caress to whisper without being caught. "Showtime, sweet. Hopefully you can turn on the charm."

# CHAPTER FOUR

Showtime? *Charm?*

With his few words, his sensual spell dissipated, like a cloud shoved across the sky with strong gusts. Somehow, she'd allowed herself to be seduced by the tiger shifter. What had begun as a way to cover both their asses had turned into Stella losing herself to the stranger's seduction. Stella shuddered with his low whisper, the roughness of his voice. It was gruff and deep and sank into her in a way her jaguar enjoyed a little too much.

The cat liked it enough to get them into the "bend me over the desk while I lift my tail" kind of trouble. Her inner bitch no longer cared about their goal—ridding the world of James Walters. It was all about the cocky shifter.

Horny little cat. It didn't deny Stella's accusation.

Yeah, it'd been a while, and this stranger—this *tiger* was...A tremble of need skated down her spine. This male was all big cat—dominance and feline strength. Two traits that appealed to her jaguar.

His human form appealed to Stella's other half as well. Like other shifter males, he was covered in hard muscle and imbued with overwhelming power. Shifted he'd be nearly eight hundred pounds of fierce beast—more than four times her jaguar's bulk.

The perfect big cat package.

The sexy stranger eased away, his warmth disappearing as he put distance between their bodies. His breath gently fanned her cheeks, and he brushed his lips along her jaw as he withdrew. He gave her one last nibble on her lower lip before he pulled back enough to meet her stare.

"Turner?" A new voice—male, insistent and sharp—acted as a reminder that they weren't alone. They had a human audience.

And their kiss had been nothing but a performance—a play—for this human. She swallowed hard, pushing down her disappointment at the fact that their passion hadn't been "real." Even if it wasn't real, she'd still enjoyed the feel of his lips on hers, his firm chest pressing against her breasts.

His lips curled into a smile, wide and welcoming, but the grin didn't quite reach his eyes. They settled into a cold flatness, not revealing the thoughts whirling in his mind. His scent was an enigma, too. It remained hot with the tempting musk of his desire and ... nothing more. There were no hints of surprise or anger over being interrupted. Literally, *nothing*.

Which was odd considering that shifter scents—like humans—were an amalgam of flavors. She wondered why he was the exception to the rule. Was he a sociopath who lacked *any* emotions, or did he just have that much control over himself?

"Mr. Walters." Cole's attention slid from her to the doorway. "Good evening."

Stella followed the direction of Cole's gaze and recognized her target for the evening. Behind him stood his spoiled daughter, while two other humans remained in the shadows.

But she didn't care about Walters's daughter or those other humans. Stella's focus was on the man himself. Fire burned in her veins, muscles tensed, and adrenaline flooded her body. Fight-or-flight instincts kicked in, but her only natural instinct was to *fight*. Fight him for what he did. Fight him for what he *would do*. She remembered the C4 still tucked within her dress, and her fingers tingled with the need to move. To wrap her fingers around the bundle and set off the bomb. She'd die, but she'd save others. So many others.

"Mr. Turner." Walters growled what she assumed was Cole's last name, but it was a pale imitation of a shifter's growl. Her jaguar would show the human what a true shifter growl sounded like. Just before she got her jaws around his head and cracked it like a coconut.

"What are you doing in here?" A small wave of fury from the human stung her nose. Walters wasn't happy. Stella wasn't happy, either. She wouldn't be happy until the human was six feet in the ground. Forever.

Cole stepped back, his large hands grasping her wrists to untwine her arms. Then he gently gripped her hand, and she used his hold to maintain her balance as she lowered her feet to the ground. Next time she infiltrated a rich-boy party she'd wear flats. But first she had to get out of this situation with her tail intact. The kiss had been a nice bit of quick thinking on Cole's part. It'd also been more than a little nice. More like delicious.

"We wanted a little privacy." Cole slipped his arm around her waist and squeezed her side, his hold firm as he forced her to turn and face Walters.

Walters had a stiff smile on his face. Oh, he tried to hide

his emotions with that feigned grin, but there was no hiding the stink of his suppressed irritation.

He looked like she remembered. There was a little more gray and a few more lines on his face, but the cold look in his eyes was familiar. He'd looked the same on *that day*. Her own personal apocalypse and he'd been the catalyst.

It'd be so easy to get the job done. There were only four humans, and they weren't carrying weapons. She hadn't caught a hint of gun oil or gunpowder in the air.

"In my *private* study?" Walters quirked a brow. "And with Miss—" He turned his attention to Stella, eyes narrowed as he looked her over.

Those eyes raked over her, and her panic changed. The longer his stare remained on her, the more her body's desires altered. It went from "fight" to "flight" in a blink. That dead gaze was edged with suppressed violence. Was there a hint of recognition, too?

No. No way. It'd been more than twenty years since she'd last seen him in the flesh. He'd kidnapped Stella's fraternal twin. The two of them hadn't looked anything alike. Madeline had taken after their father—pale blond hair, blue eyes, and upturned nose. Stella was a miniature of her mother, her fiery coloring nothing like Madeline's. But maybe there'd been something in their appearances that they'd shared. Did he see it? Did he know who she was? Did he . . . ?

*Fuck.* Now wasn't the time to debate. She'd maintain her identity and act as if she'd never met the despicable human.

Stella drew her lips back into a wide smile and was thankful the cat hadn't decided to "help" her. If the jaguar had its way, she'd be baring fangs. "Stella Moore. We've never met, but it's an honor."

She held out her hand and took a step toward the man—

or tried—only to have Cole's firm grip stop her. She forced a laugh and turned into his embrace. She gently tapped his chest to draw his attention, and he met her gaze with those cold, flat eyes.

"Darling, I'm trying to say hello to your friend. He's not going to steal me away with a handshake." She returned her focus to Walters and rolled her eyes. Part of her died at having to smile at the human who'd caused her so much pain. "Excuse him. He gets *so* jealous."

"Does he?" James turned his suspicious stare on Cole. "Funny, he failed to mention your existence." The human wasn't done. "You didn't RSVP with a plus one, Cole. And you informed Olivia you were alone for the evening. I don't like surprises."

She didn't like that James Walters still breathed, so they were even.

Cole shrugged as if Walters's anger didn't matter. "I don't like being predictable. Besides"—a grin teased the tiger's lips—"I wanted to test your security before I considered investing in your *business*."

There was extra weight on that last word. Cole wasn't speaking about Walters's company, but something *else*. Stella's heart raced, thumping harder and harder while she fought to understand why the *ever-loving fuck* a shifter would do any business with Walters. Period.

Did he not know the depths of Walters's depravity? Did he not know that the human helped run Unified Humanity? Did he...?

"I see." A speculative gleam sparked in Walters's eyes. "You thought to bring a stranger into my home? To my private study? To test my *security*? And you thought that behavior would make me eager for your investment?"

"I think you can't afford to turn me away if I choose to

offer my backing. Not after your recent loss." Harsh. Flat. Cocky as hell with a dash of "I don't give a fuck."

Stella wondered when James would lose his patience and they'd be surrounded by security and executed. Maybe Walters would do it himself. He seemed furious enough to pull the trigger—more than once.

She'd lose her chance then. All of her plotting and planning thrown out the window. The years of saving enough money to make her old self disappear so Stella Moore could be born—a new identity wasn't cheap. Definitely not something she could have afforded on a paralegal's salary. She'd paid off student loans, worked three jobs, and studied all the ways a human could be killed.

Then she'd watched and waited for the perfect storm of events—a gathering with all of the top players in attendance.

Tears burned her eyes, but she blinked them away, unwilling to cry in front of the piece of shit. Later...Later she'd sob over her failure. Then work on another plan to kill the man who'd destroyed her life.

"Of course, now that some of your vulnerabilities have been pinpointed," the tiger inserted smoothly, "the Turner Group would be happy to provide a detailed list to your security staff. Free of charge, of course."

Walters shook his head. "Apex Industries doesn't need the interference of the Turner Group."

"You just need our money," Cole drawled.

"My secondary business needs people I can *trust*. You've already proven you aren't a person worthy of my faith. I don't even know what kind of *person* you brought into my home," the man volleyed back.

Cole stiffened. "You're showing your paranoia, Walters. Do you think I didn't have her tested?" He shook his head.

"She's not a *furry*," he sneered. "We're in this room because she enjoys a hint of danger. I indulge her when it's convenient."

Stella's stomach churned, and she swallowed the bile that rushed up her throat. Her body's reaction wasn't caused by fear. It wasn't. Though Walters's doubt was enough to spur her to join Cole's game. She joined him in pandering and charming James Walters.

She gasped and clutched invisible pearls. "He thinks...?" She turned a wide-eyed, hopefully innocent-looking stare on James Walters. She'd rather glare at him. "You think I'm a...?" She shook her head, wrinkled her nose, and shuddered. "Absolutely *not*. I can understand your worry, though." She nodded. "First Cole doesn't talk about me or tell you that I'm attending." She threw him a feigned glare. "That wasn't very good of you, darling. Now here I am crashing what is *obviously* a private Unified Humanity event."

"What do you know of our organization?" Accusation filled Walters's voice, while a craving for violence consumed his scent.

She should have taken drama instead of an extra foreign language class in high school. She could count to ten in Japanese, but that wasn't going to get her through this confrontation. She had to act innocent and sweet when she just wanted to see James Walters die.

"I know only what little Cole has shared with me. Pillow talk about the good the organization can do with proper funding. Of course, I don't know of everything Unified Humanity has accomplished to clean the world of its unnatural taint." Stella quoted UH's own language and added a shudder. "I'm only thankful you stand up for what's right and pure."

"I...see." Walters was still skeptical, but that edge of suppressed viciousness had retreated.

Cole spoke up. "I'll call for my driver and we'll leave immediately. I'd hate to ruin the evening."

"The evening isn't ruined," Walters told Cole, but that narrow-eyed stare remained on Stella. "You'll both stay and enjoy the rest of the party." It was a statement, not an invitation. "And you'll bring her with you tomorrow. Serene Isle can always use another beautiful face." Walters flashed a charming smile, but the edge of suspicion lingered in his eyes. "Though you'll be searched upon your arrival."

"Of course," Cole murmured.

No. Not of course. Never, ever, of course. She'd rather *die*.

Except she was certain that if she didn't, she *would* die.

# CHAPTER FIVE

$C$ole preferred Stella's spurts of anger and the fire in her eyes over the placid she-cat who'd been at his side all night. He understood why she'd adopted the polite grins that never reached her eyes while she exchanged boring chatter with other guests. In truth, he should be thankful she'd gone along with his act and hadn't blown his cover.

Though he hadn't blown *hers*, either. What had pushed the pretty kitty to breach Walters's home and try to kill him? One look into those green eyes, one glance at her face, and he knew everything he needed to know. Stella wasn't a killer. She didn't have that stain of death and blood on her soul. Not like Cole. Not like the rest of his Shifter Operations Command team.

So why? He hadn't had the opportunity to ask…*yet*. They'd been surrounded by guests for the remainder of the evening, which didn't give them a chance to discuss the situation. Though Stella's scent told him more than words ever could. Her natural aroma changed with her every emotion—betraying her true feelings.

Jealousy when another woman looked at him with desire in her eyes.

Anger when one of those women "stumbled" into him, requiring him to catch the guest before she fell.

Utter fury when she was forced to speak to James Walters. She'd craved blood and death, and Cole's tiger wanted to grant her every wish. The cat didn't want her tainted by committing murder. It would happily take on the job for her.

Then came the wariness, the fear—of him. He hated that emotion—it appeared only when they were left alone. Anytime they stood along the wall, drinking champagne while others danced, the sticky scent would fill his nose.

His beast hated her fear. It wanted to kill everything that scared the sweet jaguar. Unfortunately, *he* was the one who frightened her, and he wasn't about to commit suicide.

Three hours later, as the party ended and guests drifted from the overwhelming mansion, Cole escorted Stella to the front steps, her arm twined around his as they descended. He had James on his left, the man's daughter on Stella's right. Cole fought to keep up with both conversations while also ignoring the heavy scent of her terror.

Walters asked about recent investments while Olivia questioned Stella's outfit.

Shit. He hoped to hell it was nice enough—expensive enough—for this crowd. Cole had bought his way into the party with his bank balance. He couldn't have his date dressed in something off the rack. It looked fancy and slinky, but what the hell did he know?

Then Stella's softly murmured "vintage Dior" drifted his way, followed by a sharp snap of jealousy from Olivia. Well, it was good enough for the man's daughter to covet, so Stella must have passed muster.

They reached the bottom of the steps, and Walters's

valet stood beside Cole's low-slung sports car. The valet held the door open for Stella while Cole took his time helping her into the vehicle. She'd already almost tumbled once because of those sexy shoes. He didn't want her breaking an ankle before he had a chance to feel those pointed heels digging into his back.

The moment the door thumped closed, he turned to face his hosts once more. "James." He gave the human a firm handshake, stopping short of breaking his fingers. "Olivia." He released James and gave the man's daughter a whisper-soft kiss to the back of her hand. "The evening was lovely. Thank you for tonight's invitation. We both look forward to this weekend."

He hated all of this bowing and scraping crap—his tiger even more so—but it was necessary bullshit. He had to play nice and pretend he didn't ache to rip the pair's heads from their shoulders.

He left the two humans, strode around his vehicle, and slid behind the wheel. The valet nudged the door closed, and Cole dropped the car into gear. A touch on the gas had them moving, the smooth ride over the well-cared-for driveway silent. He gave the wheel a gentle pull, navigating around the path's arch, and then straightened again to follow the long exit.

Cole reached for Stella's hand. He wrapped his fingers around hers, grip firm as he drew it to his mouth. She pulled against him, eyes nearly glowing with the combination of anger and uneasiness. Well, he was going to win *this* fight. Though he had no doubt he'd lose one or two in the coming hours.

"Tired, sweet?" He pressed a kiss to the back of her hand. His cat urged him to steal a taste of her skin, flick his tongue over her silken flesh and savor her sweetness. But he managed to control himself. Barely. "Maybe you should lean back and rest for the ride to my apartment."

Green changed color and eased toward yellow. "*Your*—"

"We have plans for the weekend, remember?" He dropped his voice and pushed his next words through gritted teeth. If there were cameras spying on them as they left, they wouldn't be able to read his lips. "Keep playing along. We're still on Walters's land." He wished he knew what kind of monitoring devices Walters used. Then he spoke normally. "It would be easier to spend the night at my place since the party ran so late. We'll swing by your apartment in the morning, on the way to the airport."

"Oh, *right*," she drawled. There was no missing the anger in her stare. The scent of her fury scorched his nose. "I'd forgotten. It looks like I'm more tired than I realized."

"Just close your eyes, sweet. We'll be home soon." Though Cole wasn't looking forward to arriving at his place. Stella had been all smiles and easygoing laughs during the party, but none of that remained. Now he faced one pissed-off, glaring jaguar shifter who looked like she wanted to turn him into a scratching post.

Cole's tiger was fucked up enough to be intrigued by the idea. He wasn't normally a masochist, but Stella was one sexy package. The cat was willing to give it a shot if it meant he got the little feline naked and beneath him.

He whipped his car onto the highway, merging with the sparse traffic. He hit the gas as soon as he broke free of the small crowd, shifting gears and revving the engine while he picked up speed. His tires clung to the curves—right and then left.

"Are you crazy?" she shouted above the roar of the engine, and he glanced at her, grinning when he caught her smile. Nah, it wasn't a smile. She bared her human teeth in a clear threat. "What were you doing back there? Hell, what am I doing *here*?"

"Having fun." He gave her a wink and returned his attention to the road.

"Pull over and let me out. Now." The sticky burnt scent of her tingling fear filled his nose. She sounded tough, but fear clung to her. He couldn't blame Stella. He'd essentially kidnapped her. For the greater good, sure, but it was still kidnapping.

"Unfortunately, I can't." He grimaced and pressed his lips together, swallowing the rest of his words. Like apologies.

"Look, we both have an agenda. We used each other to get out of a difficult situation, but now it's time to part ways."

"Eventually." Cole couldn't say much else. Not while he had to focus on navigating the streets.

A deep growl came from Stella's side of the vehicle, the rumble accompanied by the tempting scent of her jaguar. When she spoke, the words came out in a mixture of growls and snarls. "Let. Me. Go."

"I'll explain everything when we get to my place." He spared a look for her. "I swear."

Once he got them home, he'd just need to convince her to trust a complete stranger. *Easy*. He wasn't sure why—maybe his scent told her he spoke the truth—but she calmed with his promise.

They hadn't been driving long, but they were already close to his place, the car eating up the miles. Ethan—one of his fellow Shifter Operations Command agents—had turned Cole onto the low-slung, whip-fast sports car. Ethan coveted his Porsches—many. Cole preferred Jags—the engines tuned until they could outpace Ethan's vehicles without breaking a sweat.

"Cole..."

He wondered if chicks went to school to learn that tone. Every woman he'd had in his bed had pulled off identical hints of warning while they said his name.

"Stella?" He mimicked her pitch, only half paying attention to her while he worked at crossing the highway. He whipped across four lanes, sliding from the far left to the right and onto the exit ramp in a single fluid move.

He ignored her screech.

Chicks *had* to go to school for that sound.

Cole took his foot off the gas, letting the vehicle coast as he approached the green light. A quick right and he joined the late-night traffic along the Port St. James, South Carolina, coastline. Last time they'd been in the area, Eric Foster of FosCo—the primary financial support of Unified Humanity—had ended up dead and one of Cole's teammates had gotten mated to a sweet little cougar shifter.

This time their target was the brawn of Unified Humanity—the man responsible for arming and organizing UH's unending violence. He'd been working on infiltrating the group for months—black-tie events, high-priced sports cars, and the beachfront condo they now sped toward. A place that few could afford. It came at a premium— beautiful views with the right address for James Walters's circles.

Too bad it was so small. Two thousand square feet wasn't enough for his cat's liking, and it wasn't looking forward to sharing its territory with yet another person—even for one night.

Stella wiggled in her seat, the brush of fabric on leather followed by a creeping tendril of her scent into his lungs. One that beckoned his beast closer.

Okay, maybe he could share his space with *her* for a night.

The cat wondered if several nights would be enough. Nights when they weren't worried about being outed as shape-shifters to Unified Humanity. Cole reminded the animal that was a lot of nights. They weren't into long-term relationships.

It seemed too pleased with the idea of holding Stella close for days.

He slowed the car as they drew near their destination—his high-rise on the right. He slipped down the private drive, and the security system scanned the bar code on his car. The gate parted to grant them entrance and then immediately dropped back into place. The security wasn't the greatest, but then again, it was created by humans.

They rolled into the underground parking garage. He navigated the darkened space, soon finding his spot, and then they were on the move once more.

Cole helped Stella out of the car, escorted her to his private elevator, and finally they rode up toward his apartment.

Stella stiffened more and more the higher they rose. Layer after layer of her "delicate female" mask peeled away until he was left with a furious feline. She was spitting mad by the time they reached his floor, her eye color wavering between human green and jaguar gold. Her pale skin darkened the tiniest bit, her fur making her appear tan instead of milk white. Each time she fisted her hands, her muscles grew, thickening as her inner cat pushed forward. If she'd shifted, all her fur would be standing on end and he'd be facing a hissing, spitting cat.

The idea of seeing her that way—all fire and fur—made his dick hard. Probably not the best time to become aroused, but he was a guy. Shit happened.

The elevator *ding*ed, announcing their arrival at his apartment, and the doors parted to reveal his temporary residence.

"Home sweet home," he murmured, holding out his hand and gesturing for her to go first.

Stella stomped into his condo and he kept pace, doing a bit more ogling since she was too pissed to pay attention to him. If she knew how much he appreciated the way her ass wiggled with her heavy steps, she would probably walk softer.

Well, he wasn't gonna tell her.

The elevator doors slid shut, cutting them off from the outside world, and Stella spun on him. "Well? Is it safe for me to rip you a new asshole *now*?"

He wanted to tell her no just so he could postpone their argument, but he didn't make a habit of lying unless necessary. The tiger snorted in disbelief, reminding him they lied all the time. Okay, *with her* he didn't want to make a habit of lying unless necessary. He sure as hell wasn't going to try to figure out why. Or admit the she-cat made him *feel* things. Not just his cock—it wasn't all physical—but something in the area of his heart. Not that he had much of one, but what little was there ached for the jaguar shifter.

"Safe enough." Especially since the guys on his SHOC team shared the apartment with him. He had two thousand square feet of privacy from the world, but not from the rest of his Shifter Operations Command team. Bastards.

"Good. That means I can ask *what the ever-loving fucking fuck?*" She had a set of lungs on her—her words echoing off the walls by the time she reached that last *fuck*.

"I could ask the same," he drawled. "What's a pretty kitty like you doing breaking into James Walters's home?"

She licked her lips, and panic filled her eyes. His tiger lent its assistance, and he heard the racing *thump* of her heartbeat.

"Nothing." She managed to keep her voice even despite her swirling emotions.

"Uh-huh." He quirked a single brow. He flicked his gaze to Stella's bodice, the explosives she'd snuck into the mansion concealed in her dress. "I always bring explosives to a party when I'm doing 'nothing,' too. Try again. 'Cause looking at you, sweetheart, you aren't a bomb and bounce kind of girl."

He didn't want her to ever become that woman, either.

"I…" She swallowed hard, and he followed the delicate line of her neck, stroking her body with his gaze until his attention moved to the valley of her breasts. It'd take only one little tug to bare those beautiful tits.

Which… wasn't going to happen. At least, not while he had his team staying in the apartment with him. They'd remained out of sight so far, but he didn't think that'd last for long.

"You…?"

She shook her head, red curls brushing her moonlight-pale chest. "I had my reasons for being there tonight."

"Business? Or personal?" Cole voted personal. Stella had been caught—by him and Walters—too easily. Then again, she could be new to the murder game. A game he didn't want her to play.

"That's not important."

"It is, considering I need Walters alive"—for now—"and you tried to kill him tonight."

"The man doesn't deserve to *breathe*," Stella hissed, her jaguar's fangs peeking past her upper lip. Her hot fury burned him, the strength of her anger telling him that taking out Walters wasn't a job. It was *personal*.

"Why?"

She snorted. "Seriously?"

"Oh, he needs to be six feet under, but why do *you* want him gone?"

She shrugged. "Like I said, he doesn't deserve to breathe."

"Tell you what..." He dropped his voice to a soft murmur. "You help me and I'll help you."

"No." She shook her head, speed picking up with each whip from side to side. "I'm a one-woman show."

"You just gained a partner."

"Cats are solitary." She pointed at him, and he wanted to nip her finger. She'd probably rip off his balls if he tried.

"Aw, sweet..." He poked out his lower lip like he'd seen so many women do. "You don't want to play with me anymore?"

Her eyes flashed gold, her inner cat rushing forward. "Stop calling me 'sweet.' Instead, call me a cab. I'm out of here."

"If you're not on that plane to Serene Isle tomorrow morning, we're both dead." Cole had seen it in Walters's eyes—the suspicion, the promise of what'd happen if Cole was caught in his lie. "I saved you by claiming you're my girlfriend, but that didn't do anything for his suspicions. One word from him"—Cole snapped his fingers—"and it's over."

"Look, thank you for helping me out, but sucking face to pull one over on Walters and flying to a tropical island are two totally different things."

Cole wouldn't mind sucking face a little more, but that was a discussion for another time. "Do you even *know* who James Walters is?"

Stella's eyes hardened. "He's the president of Apex Industries—premier supplier of guns and ammunition to the United States government. He's also a high-ranking member in Unified Humanity."

"Exactly."

"Which begs the question... What was a big bad tiger doing at a Unified Humanity party?" she snarled right back. Feisty. He liked it. He also knew she was trying to distract him.

"I like to live dangerously." He grinned and beckoned his cat forward until his fangs dropped as well. He eased closer, placing his hands on the wall near her head, bracketing her with his arms. He leaned in, not stopping until his lips brushed her ear. There was no missing the delicate shudder and shake of her body. "It's exciting, isn't it? The chance of being caught?" He nuzzled her neck and breathed deep, savoring her scent. "Why did you risk your life, Stella? Business or personal? Is there someone pulling your strings? Is that why you were at the party tonight?"

"I've got no strings."

From deep within the apartment, a low tenor followed Stella's statement. "'To hold me down...'" *Grant.*

*Pinocchio?* Seriously?

Cole sighed. It seemed his bit of privacy was at an end. It also meant he'd have four single shifters—thankfully the fifth member was mated—crowding around Stella at any moment. His tiger pushed him to rub all over her and cover her with his scent.

Weird cat.

*Possessive* cat, the tiger countered.

Well, he was a *possessive* cat dealing with a *pissed-off* cat, because the sound of those voices was enough to flip Stella's "take a bite out of Cole's throat" switch.

And she tried. Hard.

# CHAPTER SIX

Stella went for his throat first, arm pulled back, hand curled into a fist, and then she swung. But the tiger was fast, his larger hand grasping her wrist before she hit him.

"That's not very nice." Cole's eyes flashed amber, his tiger peering at her through his human eyes.

Instead of replying, she tried with her left this time, only to be thwarted once again.

He clicked his tongue at her. "Didn't your parents teach you any manners? It's rude to punch your host."

Maybe it was rude, but at the sound of several deep-voiced men singing a Disney song, her jaguar had flipped into fight-or-flight mode and settled on fight.

The heavy *thump* of several sets of booted feet filled the apartment, those unseen men closing in on them. Held captive by Cole, she only had one option left.

Stella eased her weight to her right leg and jerked up her left knee, right into his ...

Cole wheezed and then grunted, releasing her so he could cup his balls. Now it was time for her to skedaddle. Stella spun in place and took off down the hallway. Her soles slipped on the smooth tile and her pointed heels wobbled, and it took everything in her to remain upright. Her fingernails transitioned to dark claws, and she scratched the wall, using it to steady herself. Tips dug into the paint and drywall beneath, and crumbling Sheetrock fell to the ground in her wake.

Stella drew closer to the elevator, now mere feet from the shining silver doors. She focused on the call button, the round disk her key to freedom. Intent on escaping, she hadn't paid attention to the chaos she'd left behind. Or the flesh and bone barrier who obviously didn't want her to leave. A stranger stepped into her path, a breathing wall of male who didn't touch her—didn't say a word.

She risked a quick inhale to identify him. Not just a male, a *shifter* male.

She slid to a stop, arms flailing and feet sliding in opposite directions while she tried to remain upright.

Unfortunately, she still ended up flat on her ass, cream and red dress billowing around her. Dammit. She looked like some sort of smooshed strawberry shortcake that'd been rode hard and put away wet.

The man who'd blocked her—more than six feet of muscular, dangerous-looking shifter—remained in place. He crossed his arms over his chest and braced his legs shoulder-width apart. He stared down at her, dark brown eyes transitioning to black, and his expression said more than words ever could.

She wasn't leaving the apartment. At least, not through the elevator.

Through the window? That had to be a dozen floors from the ground. Plus, there was the fact that it'd kill her.

"Aw, Birch, did you break her?" Movement to her right drew her attention, and her heartbeat doubled as another man approached. He appeared just as dangerous and deadly as the guy in front of her. Except Stella got the feeling he was more dangerous to the sandwich in his hand than to her. Or was that just the impression he wanted to make?

"Really, Grant? You couldn't put your food down before you came after her?" That voice came from her left, and she whipped her head around to watch a third male approach. This one was equally tall, blond hair and blue eyes giving him a boy-next-door appearance.

"Fuck off, Ethan," the guy at her right—*Grant*—grumbled.

So, she was faced with Ethan to her left, Birch up front, and Grant on her right. Cole was behind her, and she heard two other men near the wheezing tiger shifter.

Six men total. *Goody.*

Her jaguar did not appreciate her sarcasm.

Stella decided the jaguar could suck it.

"He okay?" Birch looked over her head, but she didn't turn to see Cole's condition for herself. She needed to focus on leaving the condo, not on what she was leaving behind.

"Eh, he'll live." Dark, a hint of a rough rasp. "It's what he deserves if he's gonna let his guard down."

A low grunt followed those words. On its heels was the distinct sound of flesh hitting flesh and Cole's low wheeze. "Fuck off, Pike."

A snicker from a different man. "Poor Cole. Don't be mad a woman handed you your ass. Don't you remember when Abby took out a Unified Humanity goon with a fucking *calculator*? Made my dick hard."

"Seriously, Declan?" Annoyance filled Cole's voice.

Yeah, Stella wasn't sure what she was supposed to do with that information, either.

"Tighten up." Birch drew everyone's attention. "Let's figure out what to do with this one."

Her human eyes remained locked on Birch's while her jaguar kept track of the rest of the group. The men at her left and right remained in place, stares intent on her. Two behind her moved in her direction—Pike and Declan. They were followed by Cole's slower shuffle.

Cole was a tiger. What about the others? Her cat pushed forward a little more, and Stella parted her lips, drawing air across the gland in her mouth. She tasted the air and tried to pick them apart, identify the different scent strands that belonged to the men in the condo.

Except her fear overrode the feline's abilities. The stench of her own panic filled her nose, blinding her to the others. There was the familiar musk of shifter, but nothing more. All she was sure of was that they were dangerous men who wanted something.

From her.

That was never good.

Two more shadows loomed over her. Pike and Declan had finally arrived.

"What to do with me?" Stella swallowed hard. "You could let me go?"

She hated how timid and unsure she sounded, but it couldn't be helped. The cat recognized a pointless fight when she saw one. The knee to Cole's balls had been luck. A single woman—shifter or not—against these six . . .

Stella didn't pause to think. If she had, she might have realized her next action was stupid. She shoved her hand down her bodice and nudged her boobs aside as she sought her prize.

"Strip show. *Nice*." Grant punched the air with his non-sandwich-holding hand.

"I'll show you nice," she grumbled, and curled her lip to expose a lengthening fang.

She yanked her hand out of her dress and held up her prize, the bundle of wires and C4 clutched tightly in her fingers.

*"Yes!"* Stella waved it in the air. "Now back off. All of you. Or I'll blow this place sky high." Nobody moved. "I mean it." She shook the bomb again. "Seriously."

"Ooh, Birch, she means it," Ethan drawled, not a bit concerned she could kill them with the press of a button.

"Are we supposed to be scared?" That rasp sounded just as emotionless as Ethan. "I didn't study drama, but if chicks can fake an orgasm, I can handle this." Pike cleared his throat. "Oh no. Stay calm. Think about what you're doing. Have you thought about what this will do to your *soul*?"

That was followed by a deep sigh and a low grumble from Birch. "Pike, why did I think adding you to the team was a good idea?"

"Because he's an upstanding citizen?" That one was Declan.

Birch just grunted. "Cole, you about done being a pussy?"

Stella snorted. He was a pussy *acting* like a pussy. She shoulda stayed quiet though because that small snort had everyone staring at her. Again.

"There are more bombs where this one came from." She waved her arm again. Which was a lie, but she wasn't above bluffing.

Their attention dropped to her chest, and more than one set of eyes darkened. Now pure, masculine appreciation filled their expressions.

Well, except one. Declan or Pike—she wasn't sure—but that man's stare was on the ceiling and *not* on her tits. Ah, right. He had to be the one who'd mentioned Abby.

"And why are there more bombs? Why do you have bombs at all?" Birch's tone was mild.

"Uh…" Her mind spun, trying to come up with a way out of her situation without revealing anything about herself.

"My presence at James Walters's home isn't up for discussion, and I don't care why Cole was at the mansion. I don't care who you six are." She sought out Cole with her gaze. "I'm really sorry I messed up your little… whatever."

Ethan snickered "*Little whatever*." A smartphone cradled in his hands, he tapped and swiped the screen, his gaze not straying from the device. "I'm telling everyone a chick said you were little."

Stella ignored him. "I'd like to go home."

So she could plot and plan another way to get to James.

No one said a word, but that didn't mean they were stationary. Cole—still as sexy and seductive despite her attack—moved through the group until he crouched in front of her. Blue eyes with a hint of tiger's gold collided with hers—intent, determined… seductive? Her jaguar purred and padded forward, anxious to rub against the big cat.

Nope, nope, Nope-ville in the land of Not Happening.

"Let me break this down for you." Cole ran a finger along her jaw, the touch gentle despite his dark stare. "We've been working on this for a long time and wrapping the operation hinges on this weekend. You want Walters dead. We want Walters dead—*eventually*—but we need something from him first. I was supposed to go in alone, but now James thinks we're together, which means you're tagging along. We're going to get the data we need while on Serene Isle, and you're going to help us. No negotiation. It's done."

"Us?" she whispered, barely able to push the question past her dry lips.

The low murmur from behind raised the hairs on the back of her neck. "Shifter Operations Command."

# CHAPTER SEVEN

$S$tella was gorgeous even when she glared at him with those narrowed golden eyes, pursed lips, and furrowed brow. Her cheeks were flushed pink, her eyes flashed with her inner cat's fury, and her body was stiff, with her back ramrod straight. "Shifter Operations Command?"

"Yes," Cole confirmed. "Welcome to the team."

The guys were quiet while he and Stella had their little stare-off, their silence a fucking miracle in and of itself. He held out his hand, palm-up, and waited for her to take it so he could help her off the ground. She'd fallen in a heap of sequins and shiny material, and he didn't imagine she'd manage to climb to her feet too well. Not with all that fabric tangling around her legs.

Stella's glare remained while she placed her palm in his and he helped her to stand. The glittering dress slid over her curves. The woman was made to be worshipped, and he was more than ready to apply for the job.

He'd start with her lips and gradually work his way down, lingering here and there—tasting every part of her he could reach.

When she was steady on two feet, she snatched her hand from his and turned that penetrating glare on the rest of the group. "I appreciate the *invitation*, but I already have a job."

Cole quirked a brow. "If your 'job' is to destroy James Walters and the rest of his merry band of psychos, I'd say you're failing."

"Only because you interrupted me," she snapped back at him, and he grinned.

"Feisty. I like it," Pike commented, and Cole fought the urge to punch the wolf. Just a quick jab and Pike would be a crumpled heap on the ground.

Punching Pike was tempting. Very, very tempting.

Stella's snarl redirected to Pike for a split second before returning to Cole. He liked it better when she hated on one of the others instead of him.

Cole resumed criticizing her. "I *caught* you because you're a piss-poor—"

Birch clapped his hands, grabbing their attention and silencing them at the same time. "Enough arguing. It's time for bed." Birch pointed at Cole and Stella. "You two have an early flight." Then he pointed at Grant. "And you have to get set up on the island before they arrive."

Grant grunted. The wolf wasn't one for early mornings.

Stella tried speaking up again. "I didn't agree—"

Birch focused on Stella, bear peeking out past the man's eyes. "They've tried to play nice"—their team leader gestured at their group of unrepentant psychopaths—"but I'm telling you that helping us is your only option. The situation is bigger than you—one person wanting revenge. You'll get what you want, but not before we get what *we* want."

The scent of Stella's trepidation, laced with hints of fear, teased Cole's nose, and his tiger didn't like that one bit. He opened his mouth to tell Birch to back the fuck off, but a sharp glance from the grizzly had him snapping his teeth together. Sure, Cole Turner was a highly skilled SHOC operative who knew more than a hundred ways to kill a man, but he also wasn't an idiot. He had no intention of tangling with a grizzly, and that'd be the only outcome if he objected to Birch's actions.

Cole slipped his arm around Stella's waist, secretly pleased when she didn't attempt to jerk out of his hold. "C'mon. I'll show you where you can sleep."

*In my bed.* Though he doubted Stella would let him join her. Not that he could blame the she-cat—they were strangers—but that didn't mean a guy couldn't dream.

There were enough beds in the place for the team to double bunk, and Cole had the master bedroom. It was his money paying the mortgage, after all. But there were *only* enough beds for the team.

He pretended not to see the smirks the team tossed his way. Group of high school assholes. If Birch wasn't around to make them behave, they would already be teasing him about sharing a room with Stella. Not that she knew they *were* sharing a room. He figured they could argue about that privately.

*"Cole and Stella sitting in a tree . . . "* one of the dicks singsonged after them.

*Teenage punks.* Though when 90 percent of their time was spent hunting, maiming, and killing, they had to blow off steam some way. Their team just happened to enjoy acting out like a bunch of immature teens.

Stella remained quiet while he urged her to turn and head down the hallway to their left. They strode past Ethan, the tech-obsessed lion not glancing at them while he tapped at his cell phone. Cole always wondered if the lion was working or playing Farmville. With the kind of men on their team, it was a toss-up.

He and Stella left the guys behind, turning a corner at the end of the hallway and walking another handful of feet before pausing just outside the master bedroom, the door ajar. He nudged it open and let her move past him into the space he'd claimed as his own. His tiger paused long enough to enjoy the view of Stella in their space—their temporary den.

He followed, closing the door behind him and locking it with a soft *click*. The low sound had her whirling, dress flaring with the rapid spin.

"Why'd you lock the door?"

He huffed out a chuckle. "I'm not big on midnight visitors. I wouldn't put it past one of the guys to think pranking me—*us*—is a good idea." He strode past her, fingers going to his bow tie, and he tugged on the choking bit of fabric. He hated this kind of clothing, necessity or not. "*And* I don't feel like searching for you if you disappear in the middle of the night." Still fumbling with the tie, he tipped his head toward the door. "I'm a light sleeper and that lock is loud. You try escaping and I'll hear you before you take one step out of the room."

Cole ignored yet another glare tossed his way. He also ignored her mumbled "Escape implies I'm a prisoner" comment. He was too busy fighting with the damned piece-of-shit bow tie to care if he angered her further. He toed off his shoes to the right of the door and padded across the carpeted floor to the nearby dresser with attached mirror. He leaned forward, intent on his reflection while he pulled and tugged.

Stella sighed and grumbled, the swish of her skirts the only hint that she was in motion. She soon came into sight, and he met her gaze in the mirror's reflection. The harsh edge of her anger had softened a little.

"Turn to face me." She sighed, rolled her eyes, and shook her head. "You'll just keep making it worse."

Cole angled his body toward hers, standing still while those delicate fingers went to work on the silk. This close, he was able to see the smattering of freckles across the bridge of her nose and the various shades of red in her hair. It wasn't a single color, but made up of strands that ranged from the deepest maroon to an almost pale blond. Her hair color was as varied as the facets of her personality.

"Had a lot of practice with bow ties?"

Stella smirked, a single brow rising with that tiny grin. "Enough."

Cole grunted. He didn't like that she'd had "enough" familiarity with men's clothing. He also didn't like that he didn't like it.

"My father has"—she coughed and cleared her throat, falling silent for a moment before speaking again—"*had* a hard time with them. While my mother got ready, I'd help him." She tugged one last time, and then silk slipped against cotton as she pulled the tie from around his neck. "There you go." She patted his chest with the hand still clutching the silk. He imagined the heat of her skin sank through his dress shirt, her warmth causing the frozen shell of his heart to thaw. Just a little. "You're free of the big bad bow tie."

The weight of her touch lessened as she withdrew, fingertips trailing over fabric. Cole snatched her wrist before she could retreat, engulfing the fine bones in his grip. He stroked her pulse point with his thumb, the rapid flutter of her heartbeat telling him even more about the jaguar shifter. She put on a brave front, hissing and spitting at him while maintaining that glare, but it was a front.

Stella was scared.

His tiger told him that was unacceptable. Well, shit. It

wasn't like Cole's human mind reveled in her fear. But it *was* his human mind that'd have to deal with soothing her. They had to work together, and being at odds wouldn't help their cover story.

"Had?" Cole rubbed small circles over her silken skin. Her breath caught. From his question or his touch?

"It's not..." Stella licked her lips, pink tongue making a quick appearance, and he swallowed the growl rising inside him. He wanted to follow her tongue with his own once again, explore her hidden depths. The kiss they'd shared in that study hadn't been nearly enough. "There's no reason to share life stories."

And didn't that stab him in the gut. It felt like a knee to the balls and a swift uppercut to his chin. Stella whooped his ass with those few words, telling him exactly what she thought of him—them.

He mentally shook his head, trying to banish the pain that came with her denial. Why the hell should he be hurt? She was no one. *Nothing.* A woman who'd help him get a job done. Right.

Besides, he wasn't a "sharing" kind of guy. Pouring out secrets was a chick thing, and Cole was anything but a chick. They didn't need to get to know each other to complete the mission. They didn't need to braid each other's hair or paint each other's nails—chick shit—to dig up the dirt before the end of the weekend.

His tiger snorted, tail flicking in agitation. Yeah, he didn't believe himself, either.

Then the AC kicked on and he was assaulted by a new wave of flavors. He drew in a deep breath and sorted through them, ignoring those from his team. He singled out Stella's emotions. He found her anger and frustration, but there was something hidden just a little deeper.

Pain. Not physical pain. This was emotional pain.

Cole didn't release her, choosing to continue stroking her in small circles in what he hoped was a soothing motion. "We need to share some things. No one will believe you're my lover if we know nothing about each other."

It was an underhanded way to learn more about her, but he didn't care.

Stella's breath hitched when he said "lover." That was followed by an increase in her pulse and a change in her scent. He caught a hint of musky sweetness—the beginnings of arousal shoving aside her emotional pain. His tiger purred, encouraged by the subtle change. It wanted to hunt for more of that aroma. Hunt it to its source and lap up every drop.

She jerked against his hold, but he held fast. He wasn't ready to release her. He enjoyed the feel of her skin too much.

"I'm meant to be your little trophy this weekend. Since when do rich assholes know anything about their trophies?" Stella quirked a brow.

He gasped and pressed his free hand to his chest. "You wound me. I'm not just a rich asshole. I'm an *obscenely* rich asshole."

He gave her a teasing smirk, one that usually made women whimper and swoon. He lifted her hand and brought it to his mouth. Then he gave her wrist one last caress with his thumb before replacing it with his lips.

"I would never call a woman a trophy. A gift, perhaps, but never a trophy." He spoke softly, his lips brushing her wrist. "Women aren't meant to be fought and won. They aren't meant to be purchased like a toy. They should be seduced."

Stella's lips parted ever so slightly, her chest expanding

as she drew in a deep lungful of air. He knew what her jaguar would find in the myriad scents surrounding them—his desire for her.

"Is that what you're doing? Seducing me?" She had been trying for snark, but the words came out as a breathy whisper.

"Yes, but if you have to ask, I must be doing it wrong." He flashed her a teasing grin and winked, releasing the building tension in the room, more out of self-preservation than anything. His cock was hard enough to hammer nails, and his tiger wouldn't cease its unending roars of encouragement. It was ready to pounce. "Why don't you let me try again?"

Stella shook her head, silken curls swaying and sliding over her exposed shoulders. Hints of her natural scent drifted from her, spurring his tiger's wants to a fever pitch. The asshole urged him to throw Stella over his shoulder and haul her to bed. It didn't care about the possibility of her still being angry over the whole kidnapping and recruiting her for SHOC thing.

"Let's not and say we did. How about that?" She gave him a smile, though it was more like she bared her teeth, lips only slightly curled at the corners, while she glared.

"It could be fun." He slipped his arm around her waist and gave her a quick tug. She fell against him, free hand coming to rest on his chest and body flush with his. "I can show you all the wicked things I can do to your body."

"Just my body?" She quirked a brow. "You don't want anything to do with my mind?"

"Hmm…" He pretended to think on her question, but what he really did was draw in more of her addictive scent. He didn't want to delve back into asking her questions about herself. He'd finally gotten rid of the stink of her pain. He didn't want it coming back. "That's something we'll have to discuss. At length. In *intimate* detail. I want to know everything about you—body *and* mind."

Stella rolled her eyes and shook her head once more while a change in her scent filled his nose. She wasn't enjoying his game any longer.

"Not happening." She pulled away, and this time he let her go. There was no pleasure in playing with a woman who didn't enjoy the game. Except hadn't he just told her it wasn't a game? "This weekend isn't happening, either."

Cole huffed out a laugh. "We're back to this argument again? Really?"

"You can't just kidnap—"

"You need to understand that I can. *I did*." He sighed and stepped away from her, putting distance between them while he continued to undress. He worked on his cuff links next, dropping the bits of diamonds and platinum in the shallow bowl on the dresser. "We just went over this. The situation is bigger than you." Then came his dress shirt. Damn the tiny buttons down the front. He tugged and pulled, his thick, blunt fingers having trouble with the small things. He growled, attention on his chest while he continued talking. "It's bigger than me and my team. This is about our kind."

Stella sighed and came to him, the rustle of her dress marking her approach. "Bow ties are one thing, but you can't even undress yourself?"

Cole dropped his hands and shrugged. "I never wear a tux. I can't even remember the last time I wore a business suit." He stared at the top of her head, her red hair looking like fire in the room's soft light. "I'm a soldier. You'll find me in camouflage and war paint before you'll see me in a tailored suit."

She slipped the last button free and moved away once more, gaze pointedly *not* on his body. Though her scent told him she'd like to stay close. "Even though you're *obscenely* rich?"

"I have money, but I don't spend every waking moment making that money. That's my family. I save lives." He forced himself to move, to ignore the message her musky scent broadcast. He'd never earn her trust if he tried to seduce her now. He had to give her time to get to know him. Her scent said one thing, but her body language said another.

Cole eased away from her and shrugged out of his dress shirt, white, crew-neck undershirt clinging to his upper body. If he stayed close, he'd take her up on the invitation she posed—conscious or not. He fought for self-control, unwilling to frighten her with his burning desire. Even when she glared at him, she was perfect.

He reached behind his neck and grasped the thin cotton, gathering it in his hands before tugging it over his head. Leaving him bare from the waist up.

He fought to ignore the way her gaze caressed him. How her eyes touched on every part of his chest and abs. She didn't want to want him, but she did. And fuck if that didn't make him crave her even more.

Instead of seducing her, he focused on what he needed to accomplish before morning. Like sleep.

He dug in one of his drawers and pulled out one of his favorite T-shirts. It was old, torn in several places, and it'd seen better days, but it had a lot of good memories woven into its threads. His tiger wanted to add Stella to those good memories—to draw her into their life.

"Save lives?" Doubt filled her tone.

"And end them when needed." He nudged the drawer

closed and turned to face her. He leaned against the dresser, not speaking until he had her full attention. "By the time me and my team are sent in, 'upper management' has decided that the only answer is death. We may be tasked with gathering intel first—like this weekend—but the eventual end is always the same."

Stella paused in the middle of the room, arms wrapped around her middle, and he was reminded she was a civilian. Despite her attempt at killing James Walters, she wasn't a killer at heart. "Do you enjoy it? The... the killing?"

Cole frowned and stared at the beige carpet for a moment while he organized his thoughts so he didn't sound like a psychopath. Which wasn't as easy as some might think. "I enjoy saving our people. Shifters aren't 'out,' and the work I do with Shifter Operations Command ensures humans don't find out about our kind. The council handles small one-off issues, like when a cub mistakenly shifts in front of a human. But SHOC protects shifters from the larger threats like Unified Humanity. We discredit them and we attempt to *end* them.

"No. I don't enjoy taking a life, but I enjoy saving a shifter in the future by killing someone today. If that someone has done harm to one of our people... Well, I enjoy their pleas for mercy." He lifted his head and met Stella's stare. Might as well get it all out there. Give her the truth and let her realize the kind of male she'd be spending time with over the next few days. He could experience her reaction here, in the privacy of his room and without an audience.

Then the guys couldn't ride his ass about having *emotions* and shit.

"I enjoy killing, but I enjoy seeing others live even more. I do what I have to do for shifter kind, and if others fear me because of it..." He shrugged and pretended others' fear didn't hurt. Pretended that most of shifter kind rejected him simply because he was an agent. That he was a threat merely because he breathed. "...then they fear me. I have my team, and I have the satisfaction of knowing I'm doing the right thing no matter how many people disagree."

"Who disagrees?".

"We're getting awfully close to sharing life stories, you know." He lifted a single brow and got a perverse pleasure out of watching her squirm before he got on to answering her question. She might not want to tell him about herself, but he'd lay it all out for her. He didn't have personal secrets. "You mean, other than you?" She opened her mouth to reply, but he continued. "My family." He shook his head and copied his father's usual tone. He pushed away from the dresser, clasping his hands behind his back as he strode across the room in equally spaced steps. "The Turner tiger pride doesn't get their hands dirty. They don't *work*." He sniffed and looked down his nose at Stella like his father had looked down on Cole so many times in the past. "They hire people."

Her lips twitched, and she pressed them together, as if she fought the urge to smile. "'They hire people'?"

Cole chuckled and nodded. "Yeah, my dad isn't usually such an elitist asshole, but he has a hard time understanding this—my choices." He waved his hand, encompassing the room. "He wants to throw money at Shifter Operations Command so they can just 'deal with the problem.' I have three older brothers, and they always wanted to follow in our father's pawsteps while I was driven to do more than sit in an office pounding on a keyboard. My parents and brothers hate the way I live my life, but they deal with the choices I've made."

Though the holidays always ended up a clusterfuck of silent disapproval.

"Do they know about this weekend?"

He shook his head. "No one outside the team and our chain of command is aware of the op."

"And me." Stella hugged herself tighter, her gaze leaving him to focus on the far wall. She curled in on herself, as if making herself smaller would somehow change things.

"And you," he agreed with a tip of his head. "I need your help, Stella. If we work together, we'll both get the results we want. SHOC gets whatever intel we can find. The quicker that happens, the quicker James Walters will die by my claw. It's a win-win. Your participation will help bring down the rest of the organization. This op will have far-reaching consequences. You'll contribute to the end of Unified Humanity."

He padded to her, and when he got close enough, he held out the shirt. "Go ahead and change. Take tonight to think about it."

"Birch made it sound like I don't have a choice."

Cole shrugged. She didn't, but if she truly opposed the situation...he'd figure something out. Even if it meant going rogue like Declan had for his mate, Abby. "I'll deal with Birch."

"Okay. I'll...I'll think about it." Stella turned her attention to the shirt, her fingers twisting the fabric. The flavors of her unease scraped his lungs, and his tiger snarled with the scent. It didn't like upsetting Stella. At all.

# CHAPTER EIGHT

$J$ust because Stella said she would think about Cole's proposal didn't mean she *wanted* to fill her head with thoughts about the weekend. Or thoughts about Cole's hands on her. Beyond that, she didn't want to remember the taste of his lips or the snippets of flavors that still lingered on her tongue. Her jaguar nudged her, wanting Stella to pounce and claim more of his essence. If she went to James Walters's island, maybe...

She sighed and dropped the T-shirt on the counter, then placed her hands on the gleaming granite surface. Now wasn't the time to ponder all of the wicked ways she could enjoy Cole's body. This wasn't about Cole. It was about ridding the world of James Walters and his twisted organization.

Stella stared at herself in the large mirror, the reflective surface taking up one entire wall of the massive bathroom suite, and finally admitted the truth. She couldn't say it out loud—sure as hell wouldn't admit it to Cole—but the knowledge was undeniable.

She'd failed in her mission. She'd failed to take vengeance.

Just...*failed*.

Her throat tightened, old emotions rearing their poiso-
nous heads and attacking her heart and soul. She'd made
a promise—to herself, to...*her*. A sob crept up her throat,
but she pushed it down, unwilling to let it have free rein.
Now wasn't the time. This wasn't the place. Later...Later
she could think about what'd gone wrong.

Sure, she'd failed because Cole had interfered. But if
he hadn't intruded, she probably would have been caught
by Walters and his group. Caught and then interrogated by
some of the best.

Was that what *she'd* endured all those years ago? God,
Stella hoped not, but she was a realist, too.

One who knew it wouldn't have taken much for him to
identify her as a shifter—a blood test took no time at all.
Then she would have been in for hour after hour of torture
before he finally killed her.

Or they would keep her around long-term. A plaything
he could revisit again and again. She'd heard that some
shifters were used that way. Though she wasn't sure how
reliable those whispers were. A friend of a friend of a
friend...

Stella's eyes stung, moisture filling them, and she took
a deep, cleansing breath while her mind spun through
memories. Memories intermixed with imaginary "what
ifs" that always stabbed her in the heart. Long ago she'd
lost loved ones to Unified Humanity. Since then, every
time she let her thoughts drift to them, her mind filled
with disturbing dreams of blood and pain that eventually
led to death. Except that death always took so, so long to
come.

She wasn't sure if her nightmares were anything close to
the truth, but that didn't stop them from coming.

Stella wanted to kill James in retribution, yes, but also

to end those tear-jerking, agonizing dreams that chased her when she closed her eyes.

Helping Cole would give her peace with James Walters's death. If they acquired the intel SHOC needed, it would lead to the end of Unified Humanity.

All she had to do was put her trust and faith in Cole. But could she?

Stella stared at her reflection and whispered, "Can I?"

She wanted to shout an unmistakable *yes* to the world. She *would* put her trust in him. She *would* risk everything in the belly of the beast for the good of shifter kind. She *would*... admit to herself that facing the human she hated most in the world for a full weekend scared her shitless. If she had Cole at her side though...

Two quick knocks broke the silence in the bathroom, followed by Cole's voice booming through the door. "You okay in there?"

Not really.

"I'm fine."

She pushed away from the counter and stood tall, reaching behind her for the dress's zipper. She couldn't stand around in the bathroom thinking all night. Morning came early, and she'd either be dropped off at home or hauled away in a private plane.

"All right. Let me know if you need anything."

As if. The man was way too tempting. She wasn't about to ask for anything from him. At least, not until she'd made a decision.

Stella stretched for the hook and eye just above the zipper, straining and pushing to reach the stupid loop. She squirmed and wiggled. Even did a little shimmy and shake with an added twist at the end while her fingers scraped the sequined fabric. When her left arm wasn't successful, she tried grasping the closure with her right. Of course, that didn't work, so she went back to her left. Then right. Then...Dammit. She'd gotten the dress *on*. Why couldn't she get it *off*?

She dropped her arms to her sides and let her head fall forward, chin to her chest. She closed her eyes and huffed, accepting defeat no matter how much she hated having to ask for help.

She turned to face the door, licking her lips and swallowing hard, her nerves making her mouth dry. His presence had taunted and tempted her jaguar before. Now she'd be half naked with the tiger shifter, and she wasn't sure she could resist him.

"Cole, I could use a little help with my dress."

The door whipped open so fast she knew he had to have been standing on the other side, waiting for her to ask for something. And that grin on his lips...It should be outlawed. The way the corners of his mouth curled up combined with the blatant desire in his eyes...Way. Too. Sexy.

"I'm happy to do *anything* for you."

The cheesy line stomped down some of her craving for him, so that was a plus.

"Yeah, okay." She turned and presented Cole with her back. "Can you unzip me, please?"

He eased closer, his warmth bathing her shoulders and the skin above her dress. He ran his fingers over her bare flesh, sliding down to the edge of her dress. He teased her with the softest of touches, caress not ending until he reached the zipper. It took him no time to unhook the small hook and eye, and then he focused on the zipper. On taking his time as he drew the slider down to expose more of her.

Stella shuddered as the bathroom's cool air kissed her newly bared skin, causing goose bumps to rise along her arms. Cole continued to lower the zipper, revealing more and more of her, and she fought a battle inside herself. Her human mind urged her to rush him along and change already. Nothing good could come from being half dressed in Cole Turner's presence.

The jaguar wanted to shred her dress and dance naked for the tiger. It seemed her jaguar was a bit of a whore.

The longer he worked, the looser her dress became, and she hugged the bodice to her chest, saving herself from flashing the dangerous tiger. She clutched the fabric, clinging to the sequins and silk like a shield, while he drew the slider down the last few inches.

Cole didn't move and neither did she, frozen and engulfed by the sensual tension bouncing between them. Her jaguar wanted to shred his clothes along with her own.

"No bra?" he murmured. "Naughty kitten."

That squashed her human half's arousal. "Kitten?" Holding the dress in place, she spun to face him. "Really? You don't have anything more original?" She snorted. "'Sweet' is better than *kitten*." She shuddered. "Gag me."

That was about the time she realized that facing him was a mistake. A huge one. Because Cole Turner in a tux was hot, but Cole Turner in nothing but a pair of baggy shorts that barely clung to his hips... Sexy. As. Hell. She got to see all of those delicious lines of his abdomen as well as the deeply carved V at his hips. Her fingers twitched and her mouth watered. She ached to stroke and lick every one of those muscles.

"Need me to help you out of anything else? Maybe keep you steady while you step out of that dress?" He licked his lips, his gaze sliding up and down her body, and she swore she could feel his stare as if it were a physical touch. Warm hands, calloused palms, and a seductive pressure that was just enough to send tingles down her spine.

"No, I think I've got it," she drawled, and rolled her eyes, pretending she didn't want him doing more than helping her undress.

She hadn't taken time away from Cole to focus on how good sex between them could be. She was supposed to be making a decision. Was she going to help Cole—and SHOC? Yes or no?

Her hesitancy didn't come from the ultimate goal—they both would eventually get what they wanted. But the trust it'd take to put herself at his mercy... Her stomach churned, twisting while indecision battled it out in her gut.

Cole would give her what she wanted, but he wanted something in return—her. Could she trust him? She swallowed hard and took a deep breath, releasing it slowly as she searched for calm once again.

Could she *trust* him? Could she trust SHOC? Could she—

*Fuck*. She didn't know, but she needed to. Soon.

Stella snared the T-shirt Cole provided and shook it out with one hand. She grabbed the bottom hem and tugged and nudged the cotton top until it worked its way over her head. She managed to get one arm through an arm hole, quickly followed by the other. With a few more wiggles, she was able to drop the dress while remaining hidden from Cole's intense stare.

She let the gown slump to the ground in a heap of cream and red and then carefully stepped out of the ruffled pile. Once she was alone she'd deal with her Christian Louboutin's, La Perla garter, and thigh-high stockings.

After she'd rejected his assistance, Cole hadn't said a word. Even after she'd escaped the vintage Dior dress, he remained silent. His mouth hung open while he stared at her legs, and she glanced down at herself. There didn't seem to be anything out of place.

When she refocused on him, she realized that the amber of his tiger had overtaken the blue in his eyes.

"Cole?"

He didn't say a word. Just kept staring.

Stella tried again. "Uh, Cole?"

Nope. That got her nothing.

She leaned forward and snapped her fingers near his face, a quick *snap, snap, snap* inches from his nose, which finally grabbed his notice. He shook his head as if breaking out of a trance.

"Hi." She grinned. "Nice of you to join us." She took a breath and released it in a quick huff. "I've thought about it and—"

He dragged his attention to her face. He moved slowly, almost as if he fought himself to stop staring at her legs and meet her gaze. "Promise you'll always wear thigh-highs and those heels." He pointed at the wide expanse of her thighs that the shirt didn't quite cover. At the lace that peeked from beneath the thin fabric. "Swear it."

"Seriously?"

Cole shook his head. "Usually I'm an ass man, but your legs..." He shook his head harder this time, blinking quickly to clear his head. "What were we talking about?"

Stella wasn't sure if he was pretending to be awed by her legs to break the tension between them or if he'd really lost himself to the beauty that was Stella Moore's thighs. She mentally rolled her eyes at herself. *The beauty that was Stella Moore's thighs?* Really? Sometimes she was super lame.

"You want me to go to James Walters's island and help you, right?"

"Right." He nodded, but he still seemed a little dazed.

"I've thought about it, and I'll join you this weekend. Willingly." Mostly, anyway. She still voted for killing James Walters immediately, but Cole's—and SHOC's—approach made sense.

Cole's gaze drifted back to her legs, and he nodded. "Right. Yeah. But you'll bring the shoes, right? And the thigh-highs?"

# CHAPTER NINE

*E*arly the next morning Stella made sure she was as quick as promised when it came to grabbing a few things from her apartment. From there they went directly to the airport to hop onto Cole's private plane.

Walters met them on the runway after they landed and oversaw the unloading of their luggage before it was hauled to their private bungalow. Then he'd handed Stella off to some overly perky "island secretary."

Island secretary? What the fuck? Seriously?

Cole must have realized Stella was two seconds from asking the question aloud because he'd given her the stink-eye. She'd snapped her mouth closed and swallowed her words. She'd reluctantly allowed herself to be hauled away by the bubbly woman and then dragged across the island from one end to the other. She'd seen the spa, the pools, the beach, and then her eyes had sort of glazed over while the chick continued to prattle about the other amenities.

Thankfully Stella had only had to listen to little Miss KillMeNow for two hours before she'd been deposited in front of the bungalow she'd share with Cole for the weekend. The woman had given Stella a big smile, a small wave, and assurance that Stella had *plenty of time* to get cleaned up before Cole returned.

She had to look her best for her lover after all.

Where was the equality, dammit? Maybe he was the one who should get prettied up for *her*. He was the one who should slip into something silky and lacy. How about a jaguar-spotted "banana hammock" with bows at the hips for easy access?

She'd tug a dangling string and then *pop goes the weasel.* Er, tiger.

Since she sure as hell wasn't going to get prettied up for Cole's arrival, she could at least be useful. Cole needed intel and, at minimum, she could do a little recon. There'd been several buildings Miss KillMeNow hadn't identified during their tour. Those had piqued her inner kitty's interest, and now was the perfect time to investigate while the "menfolk" enjoyed drinks and cigars.

Was Stella a Shifter Operations Command agent who had been trained in bad-assery? No. But that didn't mean she'd sit around and do nothing while Cole interacted with the humans. There were two of them, which meant that together they could do twice the work.

Eh, who was she kidding? This was probably a dumb idea, but everything from the moment she'd snuck into James Walters's home the previous night had been a dumb idea. Why stop now?

Stella went to her suitcase and unzipped the bag, delving into its depths for the perfect outfit. A combination that balanced between "thief in the night" and "butter wouldn't melt in her mouth."

It didn't take her long to find what she sought— adorable, high-waisted floral shorts in shades of pink, orange, and burnt yellow on a white background. Then she pulled out her contrasting light-blue, spaghetti-strap bandeau top and ballet flats that matched the shade perfectly. She tugged her red hair into a high ponytail and then added light-pink, semi-translucent sunglasses.

Instead of exiting the front of the bungalow to the paved path, she snuck out the back door to the sandy beach. With all the new arrivals, she was sure the "island secretary" and her staff would be busy with orientation. Stella didn't want to chance running into them. She was supposed to be getting pretty for her lover, after all. *Yuck.*

She carefully made her way across the wood porch and down the worn steps. At the bottom, she toed off her shoes and gathered them in her hand before stepping onto the white sands. The cool, fine grains felt almost like silk against her soles. She padded across the beach and closer to the edge of the waves, walking easier on the damp ground.

Stella scanned her surroundings as she moved along the island's edge, her jaguar on alert for any others nearby. She kept her lips tilted in a small smile to appear happy and carefree as she took a stroll. Soon the coast curved left, curling inward into a small, natural bay. A handful of docks stretched into the water, their tethered sailboats swaying with the gentle waves and the cool breeze.

The long stretch of beach remained empty, and Stella decided now was her chance to duck out of sight. The vegetation grew thicker the more inland she moved, thin grass turning into low bushes that were eventually replaced by overhanging trees. Then she reached the asphalt pathway.

Traveling parallel to the path, she finally reached a fork in the lane. The right would take her back toward the main buildings open to guests. She went left, to the portion of the island off-limits to visitors and separated by an eight-foot concrete wall.

With her kitty already imbuing her with its abilities, she
bent her legs, arms raised, and hopped up to scale the wall.
Nothing too big just in case someone managed to catch her
on videotape. She was "human," after all.

She grasped the edge of the fence and swung one leg
up and over. She used her weight and momentum to pull
the rest of her along and rolled across the wide ledge. She
landed on the ground in a crouch, feet hitting the grass with
a soft *thump*. She remained in place, scanning her surroundings and watching for any guards, but none came into view.
No alarms were raised to announce an intruder. Nothing.

It remained quiet. Too quiet?

She darted across the walkway and moved deeper into
the vegetation on the opposite side. She made a beeline for
the nearest building, careful to keep her steps silent as she
moved.

Adrenaline coursed through her veins, fine-tuning her
senses, and she paused near the next pathway. She remained hidden and scanned the area once more, cataloging
the building not more than twenty feet away. A sign above
the door labeled it as BUILDING A.

She mentally snorted. *Super* inventive.

Security cameras panned across the area in a slow arc,
and she knew their gradual progress was easily avoidable.
The front entry was nothing more than a single glass door
with two windows on either side. Access seemed to consist
of both a keycard system and a numbered keypad. Or
maybe they could crack one or the other? They might not
need to disarm both.

Unless... She recalled that statistics showed that even
though people paid tens of thousands for security systems,
they also then tended to leave them unarmed. Would James
Walters be that stupid? Well, she'd find out.

She kept her gaze on the slow-traveling cameras and timed her movements, striding across the asphalt and up the narrow sidewalk to the door without being seen. She ducked beneath the overhang and completely out of the camera's view.

Now for the fun stuff.

She nibbled her lower lip and wrapped her fingers around the handle, giving it a soft tug until she came up against the lock. Unfortunately, James Walters *wasn't* that stupid. Dammit.

Stella turned her attention to the numbered keypad. She searched for extra wear on any of the buttons. *The one looks rough. And the five. Maybe the nine…*

"What are you doing here?"

She froze, shoulders twitching as she winced and scrunched her eyes shut. If she couldn't see them, then they didn't exist, right? At least, that was the game she'd played when she was little.

She slowly turned to face the human. Or rather, human*s*. Two bulky men stood nearby—paunch hanging over tight belts and buttons straining to keep their shirts closed over their bulk. The word "security" was embroidered near the collar, and a small badge was pinned just beneath the stitching. As if they were *actual* cops.

One of the men placed his hand on the butt of the gun in its holster on his right side. The other actually drew his weapon. She narrowed her eyes, giving the firearm a hard look. What were they carrying? A nine-millimeter? A forty-five caliber?

*Ha!* She swallowed her snort. What she'd thought was a gun was a Taser. It'd hurt, but it wouldn't slow her—or her jaguar—down, and it sure as hell wouldn't kill her. Not like a carefully placed bullet.

"Lady!" The man on her left shifted his weight from one leg to the other, his grip tightening on his Taser until his knuckles turned white.

Stella slipped off her sunglasses and hooked them on her top between her breasts, drawing their attention to her cleavage. She wasn't a fan of distracting men with her body—she had a mind, dammit—but she'd do what needed doing.

Their gazes followed her movements, eyes widening when they focused on her chest. She breathed deep so her tits strained against her top and put her hands behind her back. God had given her boobs, and she'd use them.

"Hi." She brought one arm around to give a small wave and immediately tucked it back in place while she pasted a wide—utterly fake—smile on her face. "How are ya?"

Her grin remained strained while her mind spun, trying to think of a way out of this mess. If it were Walters, she could pull off one of those bimbo schmoopy routines like she had last night. Rich guys like him were familiar with the dumb trophy-chick type and never expected for there to be a brain beneath the beauty.

"What are you doing here? This half of the island is off-limits to guests. How'd you break in?" He still had his weapon drawn, fingers tightening and relaxing in a steady rhythm. The look in his eyes said he'd love nothing more than to hurt her. *Creepy human.*

"Break in? That seems a little excessive, don't you think? How about *wandered*? How did I *wander* in?" *I hopped but not like a bunny because...jaguar.* "The, uh, usual way."

Mr. Doubtful Asshole on the right scoffed and shook his head. His gaze slid over her body from head to toe, lingering on her chest. "Uh-huh, sure."

She threw up a little in her mouth. "I really was just—"

"Cover me." Doubtful holstered his Taser and looked to the other guy. She'd name him Idiot Asshole.

"Cover you? What?" Idiot frowned and furrowed his brow in confusion, but he did as ordered. He slid his glorified cattle prod out and pointed it at her.

Then Doubtful reached behind his back and pulled out a pair of zip-tie cuffs.

"Do we really need to cuff her?" Idiot frowned some more. "It's not like she got into anything. She's a *guest*."

She was beginning to like Idiot Asshole. As for Doubtful Asshole...

Oh. Hell. No. She wasn't going to let some shifty-eyed asshole with a superiority complex incapacitate her, *thankyouverymuch*.

There was a definite twinkle of lust in Doubtful's eyes as he crept forward. "Ma'am, please turn around."

Stella shook her head and backed away. She held her hands up, palms out to stave off his approach. Her cat yowled and snarled, pushing to be set free. If some human thought he could tie them up, the jaguar would be more than happy to show him the error of his ways. *Violently*.

"Yeah, not happening." She shuffled backward, putting more space between them. "I'm gonna *wander* back to my bungalow and leave y'all to do what you do."

"We have to take you in for questioning and—" He darted forward, meaty hand reaching for her, and she ducked his grasp.

Stella popped up on his other side and jerked out of reach once more. "You're not taking me anywhere. I'll leave and go find my ma—" Okay, it was odd that she'd almost called Cole her mate. Weird, right? Eh, it was because of their charade. That was all. "My boyfriend."

She spared a glance for Idiot and was relieved to see that he hadn't moved. He wasn't stopping Doubtful, but he wasn't helping him, either. Good enough.

Doubtful snarled at her. "All you're gonna find is your ass cuffed."

"That's rude."

Another quick snatch and he failed once again, Stella using what little space she had to avoid him. Mostly. Because then he grazed her arm, the human's soft fingernails scratching her skin, and her kitty...sorta lost it.

Stella grasped the human around his throat and squeezed his vulnerable neck. A quick twist of her hips, and she used her body weight to throw the man to the ground. She followed him down, still choking him while she lowered herself until they were nose to nose.

Through every movement, she fought her cat. With every flex of muscle, she battled the feline for supremacy. The beast wanted to sink her nails into his flesh. It wanted to rip out his throat for even *thinking* about restraining her. Her bones ached, the jaguar straining against its leash. It attacked her from inside out, the cat rippling just beneath the surface of Stella's skin. But she kept it at bay. Barely.

The jaguar needed to stay under wraps. There was no coming out to play while they still had a job to accomplish. She couldn't allow herself to ruin this chance at ending UH. She'd already fucked up enough by being caught. She wouldn't make it worse.

"Like I said, *I* want my boyfriend," she growled in the man's face, swallowing the instinctive hiss that traveled up her throat. "If I let you up, are you going to try to cuff me again?"

"You're in an unauthor—"

"Your mother dropped you on your head a lot, didn't

she?" The cat pushed forward, wanting to *bite* the human's head. The jaguar decided he'd make a lovely snack. If the cat didn't stop, she'd upchuck all over the security guard.

Not waiting for an answer, she snatched up the guard's discarded zip-tie cuffs and shoved the human this way and that until she had them secured around his wrists. Stella gave the ends one last tug and then straightened. She propped her hands on her hips, Doubtful bound at her feet, and met Idiot's gaze.

"You got something to say about this?" She huffed and blew a puff of air at an errant lock of her hair.

Idiot wasn't as big of an idiot as she thought, because he quickly shook his head. "Nope. Not at all."

Thank fur for small favors.

# CHAPTER TEN

*A*greeing to test SHOC's new com device—designed by his teammate Grant—had been a mistake.

Pro: he didn't have some shitty piece of plastic shoved in his ear anymore.

Con: the com was buried under his skin.

Before letting them insert the small disk beneath the skin behind his ear, he'd asked for one promise. Nothing big. His demand wouldn't make the team or SHOC vulnerable. His only request: don't contact him unless it was absolutely necessary.

Grant had sworn he wouldn't abuse his electronic power. Then Birch had sworn he'd keep the wolf under control.

They'd lied.

Grant didn't only like to munch in Cole's ear. He also liked to identify any animals he saw outside his hideout, give weather reports, and recite random facts he discovered while surfing the Internet. The asshole needed to find something else to do before Cole put him down like a rabid dog.

"Hey, did you know that an octopus has three—"

"*Enough*," Cole growled softly, thankful that human hearing was far inferior to a shifter's.

"No need to get pissy."

Cole snorted. No need? There was an "hours of listening to the wolf ramble" level of need.

"You're not the one locked in an empty, boarded-up bungalow."

No, Cole was the one surrounded by humans who deserved killing. He mentally sighed, but he couldn't do anything. Yet. Hopefully soon, though.

His tiger perked up at the thought, tail flicking and ears swiveling as if listening for permission to go on a rampage. When he denied the animal, its ears drooped and it curled its lip in a silent snarl. Yeah, his human half was just as disappointed.

"Besides, I'm just doing my job."

"Your job?" Cole scoffed.

"I'm trying to keep you from slaughtering everyone, and you haven't killed anyone yet. You're too busy trying to figure out how to take me out without getting caught."

"Quiet," he snapped.

The fucker was right. Not that Cole would agree with the wolf. Instead, he refocused on the world around him.

Nearly twenty human men occupied the bar area, the dimly lit room filled with groupings of heavy leather chairs and couches, low tables, and unobtrusive waiters that seemed to anticipate everyone's needs. The servers swapped out empty glasses for full, swept away used ashtrays, and remained at attention to meet any comfort.

Walters's guests congregated in the area, raucous laughter occasionally overriding low murmurs. Cole chose to relax by the bar, one elbow on the aged, polished wood and a lowball of scotch in hand. He sipped, ignoring the sting as the alcohol slithered down his throat. He preferred bourbon, but Walters was a scotch man and Cole's job was to get close to the human.

Cole called his tiger forward, but the cat hissed at him and gave him its back with a flick of its tail. Apparently, it didn't want to cooperate.

This time he gave a yank on its mental leash, tugging hard until it was forced to slide closer. The little shit was going to help so they could do their job and leave. He wouldn't admit that his motivation wasn't so much about getting intel as getting to Stella's side. She'd felt so right—so damn perfect—in his arms, and he wanted to experience that again.

The tiger grumbled, its version of *Why didn't you say so?*

The animal padded forward so he could better overhear the humans.

Gossip. Mentions of who was fucking whom and murmurs about who was next to claim bankruptcy. Two men farther down the bar discussed whose boat was bigger, and another handful of humans chatted about their recent car purchase to the tune of two million dollars.

From what he could catch, no one discussed Unified Humanity. Dammit.

"So, Cole..." Grant. Again. He'd thought he'd get a longer reprieve.

He sipped his scotch, swallowing quickly so he didn't have to taste the drink for long.

Cole used the glass to shield his mouth. It was easier than keeping up with the ventriloquist crap. "What?"

"Do you happen to know where your girlfriend is?"

"In our bungalow." He wouldn't admit that thinking of her as his girlfriend felt too damn good.

Then Cole sighed, sure Grant was about to tell him he was wrong. The wolf had *that* tone. The one that conveyed he knew something Cole didn't.

"Eh, not so much," the other shifter murmured, and Cole noted the tension in Grant's voice.

Cole pushed away from the bar and straightened, then downed what remained of his scotch in a single gulp. Connoisseurs would call it a travesty—scotch should be savored—but he had a feeling he'd need to slip away soon.

He turned and placed the lowball glass on the smooth bar, his back to the room. Adrenaline crept into his blood while his tiger padded forward, the beast recognizing that something was wrong. "Where is she, then?"

*Please, dear God, let her have not been caught by Unified Humanity.* His tiger released a low rumble, adding its agreement. If Stella had been captured...he'd destroy the island.

And that reaction scared the fuck outta him. He didn't have a problem with fucking shit up, but it was the *reason* that had his breath hitching. It wasn't about getting into her panties. There was something...more that drove his actions.

"North side of the island. You know, the portion that's off-limits to guests. You might have seen the eight-foot walls and the security cameras positioned every five feet."

Cole figured the "every five feet" was an exaggeration, but probably not by much. The most pertinent portion of Grant's message was the fact that Stella had broken into a restricted area. Was she trying to get their asses killed?

He clenched his jaw and took a deep, calming breath. She probably thought she was "helping." She didn't realize that it was more like "scaring the living fuck" out of him. He'd rescued too many shifters from UH, had seen too many shifters broken and beaten. The mere thought of her being in that kind of situation drove his tiger to the edge of insanity.

Cole wasn't going to examine the level of fear that struck him with Grant's message. Or the fierce reaction of his cat as it learned Stella's location. Because acknowledging either would say a little too much. Too much about him. Too much about his feelings for Stella.

The bartender whisked his glass away and asked him if he'd like another. *Not just no, but hell no.*

With a shake of his head, he turned and made his way toward the exit. He kept his steps slow and loose, no tension filling his body. He couldn't let his body language betray him. Not when he was desperate to hunt Stella down. "She got any company?"

"Yup."

Fuck, fuck, *fuck.* His tiger roared and then snarled, batting at his mind with a massive paw. As if it were Cole's fault she'd wandered into the situation. As if Cole's human half wasn't just as panicked as the beast.

"Direct me." He stepped into the blinding light filling the lobby. He hoped he got there before she blew everything. Even more, he hoped he got there before she got hurt.

"Mr. Turner." Walters's clipped voice echoed in the open room, words bouncing off the marble tile walls.

Biting back his annoyed sigh, he turned to face the approaching human. He pulled his lips into a half grin with a touch of a smirk. "Walters. I thought we had dispensed with formality."

Walters *harrumph*ed and ignored Cole. "It seems your guest has been seen in a restricted area."

"Has she?" Cole jolted back, opening his eyes wide while also parting his lips. He shook his head, continuing to feign surprise. "I can't believe it."

He took a moment to survey the room behind Walters, attention flitting from one person to the next. It didn't take him long to locate the security guard—a hulking human— lingering in the shadows. His cat allowed him to get a clearer view despite the darkness, and he took stock of the guard's weapons—shoulder, ankle, and lower back based on the way his pants hung on his hips.

"Do you know why?" Walters's voice held more than a hint of suspicion.

"Of course not. I admit that Stella is a little flighty and tends to wander, but... Was the gate left unlocked?"

"No."

"Hmm... I can't imagine her breaking in anywhere. That's just not her."

*Liar, liar, liar*... But why the hell did the woman have to get caught? *Why?*

"Right," Walters drawled.

Cole parted his lips and inhaled, drawing in the scents around him. The disbelief was expected. As was the anger. But there was something else there... Fear? What did Walters fear?

"Will your security personnel lead her to our bungalow, or...?"

"Security reported that she's been detained. We'll meet them in the field." Walters made a sharp turn on his heel and strode toward the exit.

"Of course," Cole murmured, following. His long strides allowed him to easily catch up to the human.

The crisp *clicks* of men's dress shoes announced that they were being followed, and he glanced over his shoulder. A quick count had him mentally groaning—six plus Walters and then whoever else they came across while searching for Stella. Not the greatest odds if they decided to get violent.

Cole remained at Walters's side for the ten minutes it took them to reach a large, locked gate. Cole let his attention wander, taking in the security measures in place and counting the cameras. A handful of beeps came from Walters's direction as he disengaged the locks and then the gate swung wide, granting their party entrance.

"Got into some of the cams and found Stella." Grant's voice was low. "Shit, Cole, this isn't pretty."

A soft beep followed the wolf's words, one of the human's own com devices sounding an alert.

A voice followed—muffled by a man's ear and poor electronic quality. "Intruder outside Building A." Then a series of huffs and then a groan. "Hurry."

Grant's voice came to his ear again. "The kitty just... *Ouch.* Now she went and...*Dayum.* I wonder if she'd show me how to do that. *Ooh*, that had to hurt." The play-by-play would have been more helpful if it weren't just announcer commentary.

"Mr. Walters." One of the security guards behind Cole spoke up. "Just received a notice that an intruder is outside Building A."

That news earned Cole a dark glare from Walters.

He just grinned in return, pretending he had no reason to be worried about what they'd find when they arrived. Yet inside his stomach churned. Inside his tiger roared and scraped at Cole's mental bindings. Adrenaline flooded his veins, muscles tense and body preparing to fight his way free of the situation. He hadn't liked the odds he'd face with so many trained humans around, but that didn't mean he'd lose in a fight. It'd simply take longer to win than he preferred.

They'd all regret touching Stella.

"I had no idea chicks could bend that way," Grant murmured. "*Shit*, she almost got his dick with her *teeth*."

Walters took a sharp right at the next intersection, and their group followed. The farther along the path they walked, the louder the sounds of a fight grew. Male shouts were accompanied by the occasional feminine yell and screech.

This time he sighed aloud. That had to be Stella.

When Walters paused to address the guards, Cole broke into a jog toward the battle. He had no doubt the others followed, but he wanted a head start to get the jaguar under control. He hoped.

He rounded the next corner and had to fight the smile that teased his lips. Stella in all her enraged glory stood above a human security guard, the large human bound with a pair of zip-tie cuffs. Him being incapacitated didn't stop her from kicking a man when he was down. She punctuated each word with a hit.

"I. Can't. Believe. You. Would. Hit. A. *Woman*." The guard tried to crawl away, and she dragged him back. "Oh, hell no. You started this. I get to finish it. I'm not done yet."

The sound of the approaching guards reached Cole, and he rushed forward. He wrapped an arm around her waist and lifted her away from the human with ease. She struggled against his hold, legs kicking at the air while she dug pointed nails into his forearm.

She tried to hurt him. All it did was make his dick hard.

He laughed at her struggles, the chuckle so loud it scared a few birds from the trees.

Stella's wiggles had her ass caressing his dick, and she froze. "Cole?"

"Hello, sweet," he murmured, nuzzling her neck and nipping at her exposed flesh.

"Gag." Grant followed that with the sound of dry heaving. Bastard.

"Whatcha doing?" Cole asked.

"Uh... The thing about it is..."

And then Walters and company arrived. "What is the meaning of this?"

Cole looked past Stella's shoulder and gave the man a fake-as-hell smile. "It seems Stella had a little trouble with a couple of your men."

Really, she seemed to have had trouble with *one* of the two guards. The other stood nearby, his hands tucked in his pockets and expression a combination of fear and awe.

Walters quirked a brow and turned his attention to the guards, nudging the one on the ground with the toe of his shoe. "What happened here?" Then he looked to the other human. "Well?"

The one on the ground, one eye swollen shut and blood dripping from his split lip, spoke first. "Sir—"

"Mr. Walters—" The other guard spoke up at the same time.

"She was trying—"

"She just flipped him over—"

They tripped over themselves to explain.

At the mention of Stella's strength, she tensed and Cole growled, the sound echoed by Grant in his ear. Dammit. Did they know she was a shifter? Fuck him sideways.

He carefully set her on her feet and tucked her into his side, arm slung over her shoulder. He frowned at her and inserted a hint of chiding in his voice when he spoke. "Sweet, what have I told you about giving people a chance to talk before you pounce?"

Stella shot him a glare that said she wasn't happy about playing the idiot, but he knew she would. She poked out her lower lip with a small pout and added a delicate sniffle. "I was just so scared and they're so *big*." Her voice wobbled. "I panicked."

One of the assholes tried to interrupt again. "Sir, she—"

"Enough." Walters sliced his arm through the air, and the burn of his anger scorched Cole's nose.

Then the human turned to them, his gaze on Stella. "Miss Moore..."

"Stella," she purred, shrugging off Cole's arm. She delicately padded forward. "Please call me Stella."

Cole didn't like her getting close to Walters. At all. His tiger prowled just beneath the layer of his skin, the cat's claws pressing against his nails. He didn't miss the way Walters's attention flicked to Stella's cleavage. He also didn't miss the way his cat yowled in denial and demanded the human's blood for touching what was *theirs*. The beast was ready to burst free and protect her from Walters. It'd kill for her.

He tried to remind the beast that she was a temporary distraction. She might be theirs, but only for this op.

The cat *harrumph*ed and growled at him.

Cole wasn't sure why he even tried reasoning with the tiger.

"I am *so* sorry for the trouble I caused." If he scented any hint of fear or unease from her, Cole would jump into action. The only aroma coming from the jaguar was annoyance. "I didn't mean to hurt anyone."

Cole almost snorted. Almost.

As for Grant, his snort filled Cole's head. "She's kidding, right?"

Cole clenched his teeth, ignoring the wolf.

"I was attacked once, and Cole taught me to protect myself." Stella wiped away an invisible tear. "So, when your guard came up behind me, I overreacted." She sobbed. "I'm...so..." She wheezed. "Sorry."

Then she collapsed against Walters, crocodile tears sliding down her cheeks. She was good. He almost believed her tears were due to fear, but he knew better. Her scent was clouded with annoyance and anger mixed with the smallest dash of distress. Probably from when she'd been caught.

As for Walters... The human's anger bled away to be replaced by a bland mask, hiding his emotions. Stella clung to him, and he simply stood there, allowing her to lean against him, but he didn't try to wrap her in a comforting embrace. He didn't push her away, but he didn't attempt to console her, either.

Walters turned his head, that blank stare settled on Cole, and the human lifted a single brow. He didn't say a word, but the question was clear—was Cole going to get his woman under control?

"Come here, sweet." He reached for Stella, peeling her away from Walters, and shot a dark glare at the two guards. "I'm sure they didn't mean to frighten you."

"She..."

"Body slam..."

Cole's glare darkened, and both men stopped trying to talk and simply shook their heads. At least they weren't bleeding anymore.

Walters snapped his fingers, and they fell silent. "Of course not. They apologize." The human lowered his gaze to Stella and Cole, and the burning anger in Walters's gaze forced him to fight the growl traveling through his chest. "Just make sure you remain on the public paths going forward. This is a restricted area, and I wouldn't want something *unfortunate* to happen if you wander over here again."

There was the threat Cole had expected.

"You're going to gut him for threatening Stella, right?" Grant's growl filled Cole's mind.

Hell yeah he was.

# CHAPTER ELEVEN

Six hours later—after a dinner that hadn't garnered any intel or insight—Cole's heart rate still hadn't slowed. James's threat hadn't been subtle, and Cole's tiger bounced between wanting to eliminate the danger the human posed and abandoning the op and getting Stella to safety.

Fuck, was this what Declan had felt when Abby was in danger? What the wolf experienced just before he'd told the team to fuck off and gone rogue to keep Abby safe? Because Cole was prepared to do the same. Prepared to snatch her close and run as far and as fast as needed to keep Stella safe.

What the fuck was this? Cole was experiencing *feelings* that had nothing to do with bombs, sex, or food. A mix of anxiety, need, and possessiveness consumed him. And fear. He'd never reveal his fear to anyone, but he could at least admit it to himself. Stella had scared the hell out of him. From the moment he'd realized she'd gone and broken into somewhere she shouldn't, he'd been fucking *scared*.

Not scared of his cover being blown. Fuck that. He couldn't have cared less. No, it was panic for Stella. His tiger growled, the passing thought bringing the cat forward to hiss at him. The cat blamed his human half for letting Stella stumble into danger.

And Cole...yeah, he blamed himself, too. She was too precious to risk, and he'd left her alone. She wasn't a SHOC agent. She was...Cole's chest constricted, while his mind flipped through the different words he could use to describe the jaguar.

Stella was annoying, gorgeous, maddening, sweet, irritating, and beneath all of those conflicting emotions, he figured she was damn near perfect.

What the hell was wrong with him?

Sure, there were things in his life that he liked. He loved his brothers even if they were a group of rowdy assholes. And his parents even though they weren't fans of his job. But someone else...

Maybe he was getting sick.

He shook his head. Shifters didn't get sick. Ever. So, what was this? He sighed and leaned forward, forearms braced on the porch's railing. The sea air ran its invisible fingers through his hair and pulled his clothing tight against his body. He was thankful their responsibilities toward James were done for the night and he'd changed into a worn T-shirt and frayed, equally ragged shorts. The fabric was faded and lived in, not the fitted suits he was forced to wear when schmoozing with Unified Humanity.

Now they could settle in for a calm night before facing the evil humans once again in the morning. He'd planned on sitting on the porch and kicking back with a beer while watching the sunset. He had the chairs and the beer on hand, the cool glass bottle now covered in condensation.

Unfortunately, Stella hadn't quite agreed with his plans.

Her version of unwinding involved padding across the sand and diving into the waves.

"Cole!" Stella sang his name, drawing his attention. "Come on!" She hopped in place with the two syllables, red hair up in a bouncing ponytail. That wasn't the only part of her that bounced. Her breasts jiggled as well, teasing him, and the cause of his increased pulse changed. Now his heart thumped because of the curvaceous jaguar asking for his attention.

Stella had also changed when they'd returned to the bungalow. She'd tossed aside the dress she'd worn to dinner, replacing it with a swimsuit and a thin, nearly see-through dress/cover-up thing. Hell, he didn't know shit about women's clothes. He just knew that she had a bikini under that lacy fabric and he wanted to see it without obstruction.

*"Daaarrrling!"* Her voice reached him once more. She reached for the hem of her cover-up and slowly inched it up, revealing more and more of her thighs. She wiggled her hips side to side, doing a little shimmy.

As if a striptease would get his ass in that ocean.

The tiger told him a striptease from *Stella* sure as hell would get his ass out there. Now. Besides, just because Cole's human half didn't want to get in the water didn't mean his cat didn't. The feline loved swimming, and it informed him it'd been too long since it'd gotten to experience water on its fur.

He reminded the feline that they couldn't shift.

It told him to shut up and move his ass already.

Stella continued to pull that cover-up higher as he mentally argued with the animal. She exposed more of her milky-white thighs and then the curve of her hips and the dip at her waist.

Cole's body reacted to the sight, cock slowly hardening while arousal thrummed in his veins. Damn she was gorgeous—all lush lines, pale skin, and a hint of wickedness that called to him like nothing before.

In a final rush, she whipped the cover-up over her head and tossed the flimsy fabric aside, revealing all of her.

Damn. His dick throbbed, and he ached for her. *Ached.* He'd stolen a couple kisses and had felt her body against his, but he never could have imagined her clothes hid so much perfection.

And she was all his for the weekend. Sure, there was danger surrounding them at every turn, but nothing said they couldn't steal a few moments of joy here and there.

Stella spun in place, giving him a damned good look at the back of her bathing suit. As well as everything it left uncovered. The tiny triangle of fabric on her ass covered so little it might as well have not been there at all. He imagined himself peeling the bit of nothing from her body, leaving her bare for him and...

Stella flashed him a wicked smile, a hint of teasing and desire filling her expression. "You coming?"

He hadn't yet, but the moment he got inside her...

Cole shook his head. That wasn't the kind of "coming" she meant. But he couldn't do *that* kind without being with her. He pushed away from the railing and placed his beer on one of the deck chairs.

Barefoot, he thumped down the few steps to the ground and made his way across the pale sand. Her joyful shout filled the air, and then she was off, racing toward the rolling waves. She dove beneath the surface only to pop right back up to face him. A wide smile split her lips, and her eyes danced with happiness.

Something so simple as a swim in the sea made her happy. He shook his head. Not money or gifts. Just a swim.

Cole tugged his T-shirt off, not missing Stella's appreciative stare, and jogged to join her. Hungry eyes caressed his body, her gaze stroking across his chest, down his hard stomach, and finally settling on the bulge of his shorts. There was no shame in her seeing what she did to him. With any luck, they'd take care of both their needs before the night was through.

He reached the tide line, took another few steps, and then dove into the cool waters. His tiger purred with the feel of it against his skin. It whined that he wasn't wearing fur, but this was enough for it for now. Though Cole did have to promise they'd go for a *real* swim once this business was handled.

He sliced through the water with firm, quick strokes and broke the surface right in front of the beautiful jaguar.

Cole wrapped his arms around her waist, tugged her close, and spun her in a circle. "Got you."

Stella's tinkling laugh filled the air, and she clutched his shoulders while they whirled and whirled. He slowed and spun the opposite way, reveling in her happiness.

He gradually brought them to a stop, but he couldn't find the strength to release her. Not yet. So he kept his arms in place, palms flat against her slick skin. He held her around the waist, but he took a moment to reposition his hold. He slid one hand farther south, caressing her ass with a gentle touch. Fabric soon gave way to heated skin, and he squeezed her ass cheek.

Stella squeaked, and he grinned, giving her another squeeze before tugging her thigh and encouraging her to wrap her legs around his waist.

"Hold on to me," he murmured, nearly groaning when she lifted her other leg as well. She crossed her ankles at his lower back, clutching him tightly.

While also bringing her pussy so damned close to his cock.

She twined her fingers behind his neck, holding him

tight. "You got me." She grinned, green eyes twinkling. "What are you going to do with me?"

"I know what I want to do." He lowered his voice, the words coming out with a rasp.

She squirmed in his hold. "Yeah? What?"

If they were on land, he was sure he'd scent her arousal. He'd smell her body preparing for him, and he'd be powerless to resist her.

"I'd..." He brought his head closer to hers until their lips were an inch apart. "Spank this pretty ass until it glowed red."

Then he did a little of that. He lifted his hand and popped her butt. Not hard—the water slowed his movements so a spank felt like nothing more than a nudge—but the intent was there.

"What?" She pushed away, but he tightened his grip.

He repeated the pop. "I'd spank you for doing something so *stupid* as to try to break into a secured building."

That earned him a glare. He wasn't sure if it was for the spanking or for calling her behavior stupid. Eh, he deserved a glare for both, but he sure as hell wasn't about to apologize.

"You're saying I'm stupid?"

Ah, it was that comment, then. Which meant she didn't seem to have a problem with a spanking. Huh. His little kitten had a hint of kink.

Cole's dick twitched with the thought. He could spank her until her ass glowed red, and then he'd slide behind her and pound her sweet pussy until...

He couldn't let his mind get away from him.

"No. I said what you *did* was stupid. There's a difference."

If her darkening glare was anything to go by, Stella disagreed. "I can't believe you're not more appreciative of the risk I took—"

"It wouldn't have been a *risk* if you'd kept your ass in the bungalow. But *no*, you had to go—"

"It wouldn't have been a *risk* if you hadn't stopped me from doing what I wanted to do last night. But no, *you* and *your team* had to play things your way." She sneered at him. She pulled away, wiggling her ass.

"Nuh-uh." He shook his head. "This talk ain't done."

"Yeah." She pushed at his shoulders. "I think it is."

Fuck, but Stella was beautiful. Happy, sad, or so pissed she wanted to rip his balls off, she was flat-out gorgeous. Her struggling against him reminded him of those first few moments when they'd met. Which had him thinking about what'd happened just *after* they'd met, and...

"No, it's not."

Before she could say another word, he moved his hands. One remained cupping her ass, but the other rested between her shoulder blades. He increased the pressure and pulled her closer. Close enough for him to capture her lips with his own. He didn't start out soft. There was no slow seduction. It was all need and want and a craving he couldn't deny.

He slipped his tongue between her lips, flicking hers and gathering the sweetness of her flavors. They slid over his taste buds, and his tiger purred with that small sample. It wanted more, though. It wanted everything.

Cole's human half did, too.

He caressed her mouth, delving in search of more of her natural strawberry sweetness. His dick turned rock hard, aching to sink into Stella's soft, welcoming body.

Fuck he wanted her.

Stella whimpered, and her hold changed. She went from pushing him away to tugging him closer. Her arms wrapped around his neck and pulled until their fronts were flush. He felt the tips of her nipples harden against his chest, more proof of her desire.

She wiggled her hips, gradually moving until her hot center came to rest along the hard ridge of his dick. He shuddered as the heat bathed him. She rolled her hips, and he echoed the move, rubbing his cock against her pussy. She moaned with each thrust, whining and twitching each time those parts of them met.

His balls drew up tight, throbbing with the need for release. He'd fill her until there was no telling where Cole ended and Stella began.

Stella's nails pricked his neck, small, sharp points digging into his vulnerable skin. He growled with that jolt of pain, his body reacting to the snippet of hurt. It bolstered his desire, ratcheting up his need for the delicious jaguar.

Their tongues twined in time with the roll of their hips, mouths fucking while their bodies remained separated by cloth. What he wouldn't give to strip the fabric away and sink into her silken heat.

A tremor overtook him, and his balls grew firm and drew up close to his body. Need pulsed in his veins. Pleasure gathered and coalesced around his cock. He shuddered and groaned, a hint of a growl joining in the closer he drew to release.

"Stella," he rasped, fighting for air. "Fuck, Stella."

Stella whimpered and then whined, diving back into their kiss the moment her name left his mouth. As if she couldn't bear to be separated from him.

As if…

The loud rumble of a motor cut down his arousal in an instant.

Cole snarled and jerked his mouth from Stella's. He scanned their surroundings for the source and spied a Jet Ski hauling ass away from the dock.

*"Fuck."* Piece-of-shit humans. Didn't they know he was trying to get laid?

Not that he should. They were near strangers, and he still had a job to do.

Oh, and they were in the middle of Unified Humanity territory.

* * *

Stella wasn't sure whose ass she wanted to kick more—the fuckhole on the Jet Ski or her own.

*Stupid, stupid, stupid Stella.* Yeah, it was dumb, but it felt oh so good. His kiss, his touch, his hard—

She cut off that thought before it could get her in trouble. Again.

While Cole focused on the view behind her, she dropped her head to his chest and closed her eyes. She swallowed the groan that threatened to escape—no sense in letting Cole know her level of disappointment—and focused on calming her heart.

Gentle waves nudged them, sending their bodies swaying back and forth, and the evidence of Cole's arousal teased her center. His grip tightened on her hips, sharpened nails pricking her skin, and a low growl vibrated through his chest and into her.

Okay, at least she wasn't alone in the sexual frustration department.

He pushed her away from him, forcing their bodies apart until their hips no longer touched. He kept up the constant pressure until she lowered her legs to the shifting sands on the ocean's floor. Then he took a giant step back, putting a few feet of seawater between them.

Stella stared at him, secretly pleased by his heaving breath and the subtle hint of amber in his eyes. She'd brought his tiger out while they'd kissed, his beast lured by her touch. Then she realized he'd done the same with her. Her jaguar had altered her vision, and she still had trouble breathing.

She closed her eyes once more. Maybe if she didn't look at him, she wouldn't want to jump his bones.

"Stella?"

She shuddered, and a new sliver of arousal slipped into her bloodstream. His deep voice, the dark rasp and that hint of a growl in his tone... Her pussy clenched, and her body begged to be filled by the big bad tiger.

Apparently closing her eyes wasn't enough to thwart Mission: Tiger Dick.

Distance. Distance was what she needed.

"I'm fine," she rasped. She coughed and cleared her throat, then turned her attention to the shore. "I'm good. Maybe we should..."

"Head in," Cole finished, a deep roughness tinging his voice.

Stella nodded, and a part of her was happy she wasn't alone in her continued suffering. "Yeah."

Neither of them moved. Instead, they remained in place, gazes locked as the world continued to move around them. The waves gently buffeted them from side to side, and the wind whipped at their hair. The rumble of Jet Skis was joined by high-pitched laughter, and the cries of island birds warred with the mechanical sounds.

"We should..." Cole tipped his head to the left.

"Yeah." She drew in a deep breath and pushed her jaguar

back. It fought her nudge, the cat wanting to remain present. It wanted to pounce on Cole and take every bit of pleasure he could give.

Which seriously wasn't happening. *One weekend, remember, asshole?*

It hissed at her.

With a sigh, she slowly went into motion. She moved with the rolling water, fighting the sea when it withdrew from the shore. Her feet sank into the silky sand, and she trudged onward to shore and back to the bungalow.

Stella followed the porch to the left side of the house and the outdoor shower. "We can rinse off the worst of the sand over here. There's a door that leads into a bathroom, too."

She kept her eyes on her destination, still too buzzed with desire to trust herself. She was strong in many ways, but when it came to Cole it seemed she was the weakest woman to ever walk the earth.

Stella thought Cole might have grunted in response. Or groaned. Regardless, another small tremor sizzled down her spine.

And to think, they still had a couple of days left in each other's company. Sure, they'd have to deal with the mission, but otherwise they'd live in each other's pockets.

She paused by the shower, and a quick turn of a knob had the water flowing from the showerhead. Cold water rained down, and she stepped beneath the spray, goose bumps forming along her skin.

The moment she felt clean enough, she slipped from beneath the raining water and went to the side door. Her teeth chattered as she spoke. "I'll get the hot water started for showers."

Cole didn't say a word, so she glanced back at him.

And then wished she hadn't.

He had his fingers at the button of his shorts. He tugged his zipper down—all beneath her watchful gaze. The deeply carved lines of muscle at his hips were revealed, and she wondered what that part of him would taste like. Hell, she wanted to know what *all* of him would taste like.

"See something you like?" he murmured.

Jolted, she squeaked, spinning to face the door once more. Yes, yes, she did like it. A lot. Hadn't she been two seconds from getting naked when they were in the water? It hadn't taken much to spark her need—a few touches and soft whispers—and then she'd been ready for him. Not that taking Cole for a sexual spin was a good idea.

Because it *so* wasn't. He was a violent badass agent, and she...was not.

"Uh..." She'd just had her tongue down his throat and now she couldn't talk to the man? Really, Stella? Really?

Yes, apparently. *Really.*

Cheeks burning, she rushed into the sparse bathroom, tugging the door firmly closed in her wake. She quickly had hot water flowing and was soon stripped and luxuriating beneath the warm spray. She washed away what little of remained of the salt water and made use of the small bottles of shampoo and conditioner for guests.

And it was during those few minutes that she let her mind drift—to Cole, to their argument, to that damned building on the other side of the island. Getting caught was stupid, stupid, *stupid*. Not that she'd been willing to admit it to Cole. She might have been scared shitless, but a girl had her pride. And when she had nothing else, pride was the only thing she could cling to.

She left the water running and poked her head out, unsurprised to find a blatantly nude Cole staring back at her.

*I will not look at his body. I will not look at his body. I will...*

She looked at his body.

*Dayum, he's got some muscles.*

No. Bad Stella. Bad.

She closed her eyes, and her cat whined. It wanted to keep ogling the sexy tiger. Yeah, that wasn't happening.

She held out a hand. "Can I, uh, have a towel?"

Cole chuckled, the deep laughter vibrating through her, and she wondered if she could come from just listening to him laugh.

Probably.

Especially if he laughed against her clit.

Dammit, couldn't her mind stay away from sex for a second?

A fluffy towel appeared in her hand, and she quickly wrapped it around her body before stepping out of the shower.

"It's all yours."

He took a step forward, and then another, closing the small distance between them. "Are you all mine, too?"

Yes.

She mentally shook her head and lifted her gaze—meeting his stare. "For the weekend. That was the agreement, right?"

He narrowed his eyes but didn't say a word. Instead, he stepped past her and climbed into the shower. The tension that'd crowded her left in a rapid rush, and her shoulders slumped with the sudden loss of anxiety. The spell he'd woven around her broke with the separation, the shower curtain acting like a shield against his sensual magic.

Stella snatched another towel from the linen closet and

got to work on her hair, taking out the bulk of the moisture in the strands. "Cole, I'm going to—"

"Stay right there." He spoke above the patter of water against tile.

"I just want to—"

He jerked the curtain aside, and she met his stare in the bathroom mirror. All hints of sexual interest had fled, as if the warm water drove out his desire for her. "Stay right there. I don't want you running off while I'm not looking."

She rolled her eyes and turned to face him. "You're acting like that's a habit."

"For all I know, it could be," he grumbled. Then he retreated, tugging the plastic back into place. "Do you want to tell me what the hell you were thinking?"

"Not really." The words left her mouth before she could stop them. She glanced around the bathroom, eyes scanning the ceiling and walls. "Should we be talking about this, you know, *here*?"

"We're clear. Now, don't try to change the subject. What were you thinking?"

"I just wanted a look around." She tightened the towel wrapped around her body and tucked the ends between her breasts to secure the terry cloth. Fairly covered, she hopped onto the counter and got settled. "I thought I'd take a peek, maybe get the lay of the land and wrap up your side of the mission so we could get on to the fun stuff."

She managed to keep the rest of her thoughts under wraps. The ones that agreed with Cole. The ones that said she shouldn't have gone off on her own. The ones that still caused her heart to race and adrenaline to flood her veins.

He stuck his head out once again. "Sex?"

Stella glared at him. "Torture and killing."

He disappeared once more with a grunt. Sort of a "too bad; it would be awesome."

Yeah, she could imagine it would be if his kisses were anything to go by.

"Stella." That was it. Her name said in a tone that told her he meant serious business.

Well, good for him. He might want to talk about her field trip, but she wasn't addressing the "breaking and entering" elephant in the room.

"It was nothing, Cole."

"Nothing?" His voice barely rose above the patter of the shower. Then there was a metal squeak and the water ceased, leaving silence in its wake. Cole gripped the curtain and wrenched it aside. If cold fury didn't cover his expression, she'd steal another peek at the business he had going on south of the border. *"Nothing?"*

All right, "nothing" obviously wasn't the right answer.

Cole stepped out of the shower, droplets of water clinging to his skin and sliding down his tanned body. He moved closer, crowding her against the counter until she was forced to part her legs. But he didn't stop there. He leaned into her, hands flat against the counter, and she eased back until her shoulders touched the mirror.

"You entered a secured area—"

"—it was only a wall. It wasn't even topped with razor wire."

Based on the way his eyes flickered amber for a moment, her words hadn't helped her situation.

"—and then tried to break into one of the buildings without any tools or backup." Cole tapped his neck just below his ear. "You don't even have one of these. How could you have been so stupid? You were alone and—"

"Hate to break it to you, but I've been alone for most of

my life. I've never had a 'partner in crime.' There has only ever been one person I could trust—me," she snarled right back at him.

"There's a fucking reason SHOC has us running in teams." His eyes no longer bounced between blue and amber. They were now fully tiger yellow. The scent of his beast swirled in the damp air, amplifying the hints of damp earth, crisp sun, and Cole's natural musk. It was tinged with his anger—the taint of burning wood.

"The shit we do is dangerous. *This op* is dangerous, and you just..." He sighed, and his shoulders slumped as he lowered his head, chin to his chest. "You can't pull shit like that."

He stayed in place, his breath coming in deep, even intervals. She lowered her head slightly, just enough so that her nose tickled his hair. She breathed deep, testing his scents while trying to pick apart his emotions.

The anger was easy to find. It overrode everything, running roughshod over all others. But her cat was tenacious, and she dug deeper. There had to be more.

And then she found it.

Her breath caught in her chest, heartbeat stuttering for a moment as her mind processed what she'd discovered. She lifted her hands and placed them on his arms, sliding them over his wet skin, up his biceps, over his shoulders and along his neck until she cupped his face. A small hint of pressure had him lifting his head, and she didn't stop until his gaze met hers.

"You were scared."

"I..." He swallowed hard, the sound audible in the silent bathroom.

"For me."

Cole shook his head, denying her, but she saw the truth

in his eyes. She'd worried him. Something she hadn't ever thought twice about—doing recon and breaking into a building—had frightened the badass tiger.

That...touched something inside her. Something deep that she'd hidden long ago. A part of her she'd tucked away out of sight so it couldn't ever be hurt again—her heart.

"Cole..."

He shook his head again. "You can't pull that shit, okay? You can't..." He clenched his teeth, jaw working while he fought to keep silent. "Running off half-cocked will blow the mission."

"Right." She didn't believe a word of what he said. Somewhere between a quick grope in James Walters's study and this moment, their odd acquaintance had turned into something else. She didn't have a name for whatever they'd become, but it was different. New. Odd. And...welcome.

"You like me a little bit." Stella grinned, and he glared. She darted forward and pressed a kiss to his nose. "I promise I won't tell anyone." His narrow-eyed stare remained. She rubbed the pad of her thumbs along his cheekbone, his afternoon scruff scraping her skin. "No one's ever been worried about me before."

Stella wasn't sure where that admission came from—it wasn't usually something she talked about with anyone—but there it was.

"Your parents..."

She shook her head. "No. I was little when..." She swallowed past the knot in her throat. "You're the first in a long time." *Ever.*

Stella held him steady while she brushed her lips across his. Just the tiniest of caresses. "Thank you." Then another. "Thank you." And yet another, though this time she added a hint of tongue. "Thank you..."

# CHAPTER TWELVE

## GRANT

*G*rant was bored as hell and tired of listening in on Cole's bullshit conversations with smarmy Unified Humanity–supporting assholes. And he sure as fuck wasn't listening to Cole *fucking*.

Grant pushed to his feet and bent side to side, cracking his back with each tilt. Damn he was getting old.

He padded through the bungalow, thankful it'd been emptied in anticipation of the construction work to come. There were no pieces of furniture to trip over. Unfortunately, that also meant he didn't have a couch or a coffee table to prop his feet on.

And *no* refrigerator. How the hell did a male survive without cold beer? He was a shifter—it wasn't like the alcohol would impede his mind or body—but sometimes a man just wanted a cold one after a long day of listening to assholes.

He'd have to settle for a nice breeze and crisp ocean air instead. *Gag.*

He went to the back of the bungalow and into the kitchen nook, pausing to peer through the window and into the darkness beyond. He beckoned his wolf from the back of his mind, and it readily came forward, eager to do *something*. The beast was just as bored as his human half.

This late at night, the moon hung high above the ocean, light glinting off the dark, gentle waters. The sea lapped at the pale beach, and the murmur of the waves beckoned him to leave the small building. The bungalows on either side of him hadn't been assigned to any guests for the weekend, which meant they were empty as well.

The wolf nudged him, urged him to at least open the back door and test the wind. If they didn't scent anyone nearby, then maybe...His animal whined and prodded him again.

It wasn't like it asked to run. It simply couldn't remain cooped up any longer.

They'd had enough of that in their life. More than enough. Five years too long in the hands of—

An echoing snarl reverberated in his mind, Grant's beast cutting him off before his thoughts could travel back to that time. He still suffered from those years in captivity, but there was no reason to dwell on it now. Not when SHOC— his team specifically—was so close to finding and destroying the organization responsible for his lingering agony.

He went to the back door and flicked the dead bolt, then silently twisted the knob. The door swung open on silent hinges, and the sea air swept in and washed away the stagnant smell that pervaded the bungalow. He stepped onto the back porch, weathered wood firm beneath his bare feet. Sand scratched his soles and beat at his exposed skin, the wind whipping the small grains through the air.

He tugged the door closed just as quietly as it'd opened

and silently made his way across the patio. He slowly tromped down the creaking steps and breathed deep, letting the briny air fill his lungs. Fresh air—of a sort—filled him, and his muscles slowly relaxed. Being cooped up really had been hell. More so than he'd realized.

Grant followed the worn, sandy path to the expansive beach and glanced to his left. In the distance, bright lights shined and broke up the darkness. In that direction lay the occupied homes, now sparkling with activity. To his right, the beach remained dark—empty. Just the way he liked it.

He moved toward that darkness, letting it swallow him whole. If he shifted, he'd easily blend with the shadows— his near-midnight coloring hiding him from human sight. His wolf wagged its tail and nudged him in encouragement, wanting to feel sand beneath its paws.

Eh, his wolf wasn't the sharpest crayon in the box sometimes. It didn't seem to care that they were on a Unified Humanity–owned island and that every single person on the island would happily kill them.

It chuffed and reminded him of Cole's and Stella's presence.

He rolled his eyes and continued his walk. Okay, everyone but *two* people would happily kill them.

The breeze tugged at his dark hair like insistent, determined hands. Like fingers demanding he tilt his head back and stare into the bright light as doctors checked his eyes. He shook his head, reminding himself he wasn't strapped to a stretcher and beaten half to death.

The beast snarled and scraped him from inside out, sharp claws dragging along his forearms. Ripples traveled beneath his skin, the animal making its presence known.

It didn't want his mind going there, dammit.

Yeah, well, it wasn't a picnic for Grant's human half, either, but it knew what happened when Grant was alone. When he didn't have the distraction of his teammates and the frenzy of training or a mission to keep him occupied.

Grant followed the coastline, the sand gradually giving way to rougher pebbles, then rocks, and finally a stone cliff. Aerial imaging showed that this area remained uninhabited, while the rest of the island had been developed. Leaving a barren outcropping of stone. No trees, either. Just some random bits of undergrowth that managed to cling to the rough ground.

Stubborn bits of grass.

Kinda like him—determined to survive even when he was told he should be dead.

He followed the next bend, his attention on the water, when he heard a gasp barely louder than the waves. A woman was sitting nearby.

Eyes wide, he froze in place and flared his nostrils as he breathed deep. His wolf fought past the scents of the sea and nature. It sought the natural aromas of the interloper and found sweet merciful deliciousness.

Honeydew with a hint of bright citrus on a hot summer's day.

Dayum.

Grant's wolf whimpered and chuffed before giving his mind a soft prod. For once the animal didn't make a demand—it begged.

He stared at the stranger—the delicate female looked as if a strong wind could send her tumbling over the cliff. The pictures he'd compiled as part of the mission profile hadn't told the full story. She'd appeared slight in the surveillance photos, but this...She looked like an ethereal fae— otherworldly despite her humanity.

Pale blond curls were snared by the breeze, long golden tendrils flowing behind her. Shining blue eyes met Grant's, and he waited for sexual interest to fill her gaze. He wasn't an arrogant bastard, but shifters weren't exactly hit with the ugly stick. Combine that with being shirtless and in a pair of jeans that hung low on his hips?

Yeah, he was sex on legs. At least, that's what he'd been told in the past. Now he wanted to hear those words fall from the blonde's lips.

Of course, that required talking to her first. Something he hadn't done quite yet. Instead, he'd stood there and stared at her. He panted like a pup looking for a scratch behind his ear.

"Good evening," he murmured, just loud enough to be heard over the rolling waves and rustling wind.

"Uh…" Her eyes widened, and her small pink tongue darted out to wet her plump lips. "Hi."

Grant took a step forward and then another, gradually closing the distance between them. The nearer he drew, the more her fear seemed to grow, until the next gust filled him with the overwhelming stink.

He froze in place and softened his expression. The smell was enough to banish his growing interest. His growing *sexual* interest anyway.

He'd give the elfen woman a moment to get used to his presence while he…tried to reconcile his desire with the identity of this alluring woman. The profile contained page after page of intimate details, but not a one said that she'd steal Grant's breath. That her beauty would make him consider getting involved with someone connected to Unified Humanity.

She didn't look like her father, but Grant knew the truth. This woman called Richard King "Daddy."

"I'm Grant." He tipped his head toward the water to his left. "Nice night, isn't it?"

"Yeah, it's..." She turned her attention to the sea once more, giving him a look at her delicate profile. Her focus remained split between him and the water—watching him as if he was a dangerous predator. Which he was.

She must have decided he wasn't *too* dangerous because she finished her thought. "It's beautiful."

He tucked his hands into his pockets and followed the direction of her stare. "It is." He nodded. "The sea is hard and soft at the same time. She can be forgiving but just as quickly turn around and kick your ass."

That had her looking at him again, her lips tipped up in a teasing smile. "She?" She quirked a brow. "What makes the ocean a 'she'?"

She was calming but still uneasy. With any other woman, his wolf would cut its losses and tell Grant to move on. They shouldn't bother with a skittish female. But with her... the wolf urged him to stay.

He lowered himself to the ground in a single fluid move. He leaned back on his palms and forced his body to relax— to convey that he wasn't a threat. Yet anyway.

The wolf reassured him he'd never be a threat to this delicate female. Ever.

The wolf, apparently, didn't recall exactly *who* she was—Charlotte King, daughter of Richard King, the suspected brains behind Unified Humanity.

His inner beast chuffed and rolled its eyes. Apparently, her father didn't matter in its opinion. It wanted to lick Charlotte from head to toe. Twice.

"What makes the ocean a 'she'?" Grant repeated the question and winked at her, smiling when those pale cheeks flushed pink. He didn't miss the way her gaze strayed, sliding down his toned body. He didn't have to work too hard to get his muscles, but he liked being appreciated. "Well, men aren't exactly soft and gentle."

She tipped her head to the side. "Some are."

He raised his eyebrows. "Most aren't."

"Point conceded." She'd used one of those two-dollar words, and damn that was sexy.

"Men are rough and hard. Obstinate as hell and just as stubborn. Most of us take a stance and there's no give." He patted the ground. "We're like this cliff. Solid and unmovable through and through."

Charlotte's lips parted, and she gave him a wide smile. "I can agree with that."

"The ocean there"—he tipped his chin toward the waters—"she's soft and sweet when the weather's nice, but you get her mad..." He shook his head. "Whoo boy, you better watch out. She gets a storm raging, and then she's stronger and meaner than anyone you've ever met. Those waves will kick this cliff's ass from one end of the island to the other and still be ready for more." Charlotte snorted, and he winked at her, matching her smile. "Nothing I fear more than a pissed-off woman...or a storm on the sea."

"So, you'd be afraid of little old me?"

"Absolutely." He gave her a straight face, eyes wide while he nodded.

"Now I know you're full of shit."

"Honey." He couldn't help but call her that, her honeysuckle scent urging him to get closer. "I'm more afraid of you than *anything* in my life."

Charlotte rolled her eyes. "Unlikely. And it's Lottie, *not* 'honey.'"

"Lottie? Short for Charlotte?"

She curled her lip. "There are only a few people who call

me Charlotte, and they're . . ." She shuddered, and the sweet scent was replaced with something like disgust. "I prefer Lottie. My friends call me Lottie."

"We're friends?"

"Well, we're not enemies."

As far as she knew, anyway. He wasn't about to correct her.

Their status as enemies couldn't be determined until Richard King discovered he'd been infiltrated by a few shifters and Grant discovered whether Lottie harbored the same level of hatred as her dear old daddy.

"Or are we enemies?" She lifted her eyebrows in question. "I don't remember you at the reception or dinner."

Grant shrugged. "Don't like parties. Don't like people, really."

"Don't like . . . *them*?"

The way she said that word—*them*—told him who she referred to, and she wasn't talking about rich assholes. *Them* as in, shifters. Her tone didn't tell him how she felt, though. There was no heat or coolness in her voice. He couldn't figure out whether she hated shifters, liked 'em, or flat-out didn't give a fuck.

Now he had to craft a response that didn't get his ass exposed. Maybe leaving the bungalow had been a mistake. But then he never would have gotten to meet this little package of near perfection.

"Like, dislike . . ." He shrugged. "Life sucks all around. Only difference is that we're in a position to know that sometimes the reasons for shitty situations aren't always laid at the feet of a human. Some can be attributed to *them*."

Lottie's voice trembled when she spoke. "What if it's rarely—hardly ever—shitty because of someone who isn't quite human? If they're not always at fault or dangerous no matter what others say? What if they're not totally...?"

"Evil?" Sure, his kind had evil-as-a-motherfucker shifters. His team was made up of 'em, after all. But they were mostly good. Sometimes. More so now that Declan was mated. No one on the team wanted to call Abby to get bailed out of jail. Especially since she was pregnant.

"Yeah. What if they're not evil like they say?"

Grant leaned forward and propped his elbows on his knees, staring out at the rhythmic waves. He appeared relaxed, but he remained tense and on alert. "Then that needs some thinking."

"Thinking that ends in opening a checkbook for Unified Humanity?"

She was testing him, and he couldn't exactly say *hell no*. Instead, he shrugged. "We'll have to see." As in, he'd have to see how quickly he decided to kill the bastards who wanted to kill Grant and his kind. "We'll just have to see."

# CHAPTER THIRTEEN

$O$livia Walters wouldn't quit looking at Cole as if he were a wagyu steak and she were a starving woman. It made Stella want to release her claws and slit the woman's throat. Not that she was bloodthirsty. Much.

Stella sighed and stuffed her jealousy aside. After getting caught yesterday, she needed to prove more than ever that she was nothing more than pretty arm candy. Like all the other women on Walters's yacht. Every woman was dressed up in tiny little skirts, tight tops, and utterly inappropriate shoes. Heels on a *boat*? Stella, at least, sported sparkly ballet flats.

Olivia's friend—Charlene. Or Cheyenne? Wait, it was *Charlotte*—stared at the passing waves while Stella pretended not to notice Olivia's presence. Mainly because if she acknowledged the chick, she'd be tempted to cut her into tiny pieces.

Stella leaned against the railing and turned her head, letting the breeze brush her hair from her face. She closed her eyes and breathed deep, letting the clean air fill her lungs. She couldn't deny her cat's happiness at being outdoors. Even if they were on the water and she spent her time alternating between puking and wanting to gut Olivia.

The jaguar purred at that thought, already imagining the human woman's blood dripping from her claws. *No. Bad kitty. We have to help Cole.*

"I was surprised to see you with Cole." Olivia's voice remained low, but she was still able to hear the words.

Stella opened one eye and quirked a brow. "Oh?"

Olivia shrugged. "You don't seem like the type of woman the Turners prefer."

"Really? Do tell. What makes me so different?" Stella bit her tongue and swallowed the rest of her words, though she did let them dance through her mind. *And so unlike you, Miss Fornicatress of Babylon?*

Stella wasn't a big fan of the word "whore."

A waiter strolled past, and Olivia lifted a glass of champagne from his tray. If only the glasses were filled with whiskey...

Olivia toyed with her glass, one finger tracing the rim in a slow glide. The human woman's eyes remained on Cole as if she attempted to seduce him with the subtle movement.

Stella thought Olivia would have been better off deep throating a hot dog to get his attention. Cole didn't seem like a "subtle" kind of guy.

It was fun to watch the woman make a fool of herself though.

"You know." Olivia turned her gaze to Stella, smirk in place and her eyelashes fluttering. "Our set focuses on making connections, forming bonds, that sort of thing. You are simply"—her gaze scraped over her from head to toe—"different."

"Olivia," Charlotte murmured in warning.

"Hush," Olivia snapped at the blonde before returning her attention to Stella. "I'm simply saying you have no ties to the corporate world. You aren't involved with the movers and shakers." She shrugged a shoulder. "You two don't exactly share a common background."

*But we share a bed, don't we?* As for bonds...Stella wasn't opposed to bond*age*.

Again Stella kept her mouth shut. Her jaguar snarled at her, the beast furious when she didn't defend her claim on Cole. It didn't give a damn about James Walters, the mission, or keeping a low profile. It was focused on the bitch who wanted what belonged to them—Cole.

"What do you bring to the table?" Olivia tipped her head to the side.

Stella was glad she hadn't bothered snaring a drink. She clenched her fists so hard she would have snapped the stem of a glass in half without a thought.

Then she'd stab Olivia in the eye with the broken end.

Her jaguar purred. It liked that idea.

Stella sighed and shook her head. There was that bloodthirsty attitude again.

"See, Charlotte? What did I say?" Olivia clucked her tongue. "It's not what she brings to the table, but what she brings to the bed."

Stella rolled her shoulders and tipped her head side to side. Her cat prowled just beneath the thin surface of her skin. It bared its fangs, long teeth more than ready to tear into Olivia's flesh. She'd show the human woman *trash*.

Her fingertips burned, the cat's nails pressing against her thinner human ones, fighting to be free. Her bones ached as well, the feline battling to come out and face off against Olivia.

Stella was ready to do some disposing of her own.

"Olivia, stop," Charlotte hissed. "She's a *guest*."

Oliva snorted. "Cole Turner is a *guest*. This one"—she used a finger to gesture at Stella—"is something else."

Cole had ordered her to be good. No drawing attention to herself. Especially not after the drama in the restricted area. Just play well with others for an afternoon.

One. After. Noon.

It'd sounded so easy when he'd grumbled and growled at her. But real life was hard. And not in a fun "hard-on" way.

"Jealous, sweetheart?" Stella smirked and shook her head. "It's not a good look for you." She reached out and tapped the area between Olivia's eyebrows. "It'll give you wrinkles." She gasped and covered her mouth while widening her eyes. "Oh no, it's too late."

Olivia leaned close and hissed, "Do you know who you're talking to?"

Stella eased forward as well, meeting the human's fury with a wide smile. "A daddy's girl with an Oedipus complex?" She turned her attention to Cole and tipped her head. Cole and Walters stood together on the opposite side of the deck, the two men schmoozing. "Cole doesn't look like your papa, though. Is it just the money with him? Get married, give Cole a kid or two, and give your father's charity a few hundred million."

Okay, based on the fury that filled Olivia's eyes, Stella *might* have gone a step too far. Perhaps a dozen steps too far. It was obvious Stella had difficulty following directions. Cole's order of "play nice" had somehow turned into "antagonize the bitch until Olivia tried to throw Stella overboard."

Not that Olivia had tried. Yet. But the way the woman formed a tight, white-knuckled fist with her hand, Stella figured it was only a matter of time.

Charlotte moved closer, wrapped her arms around one of Olivia's, and tugged. The blonde held Olivia back when she would have launched herself at Stella.

"Olivia, calm down," Charlotte pleaded. "Your father—"

"Wouldn't want anyone around who would *dare* insult me," Olivia hissed back.

Her jaguar purred, loving the way Olivia's face burned bright red. Pure fury was etched into every line of the human woman's body. It was only a matter of time before she popped and went after Stella. That might be fun for a few minutes. At least until Stella threw Olivia overboard or knocked her out. Either sounded fun.

Sadly...

"Ladies, good afternoon." A familiar, thick arm slid around Stella's waist, his large hand settling on her opposite hip while he pulled her to his side. He pressed a soft kiss to her temple and then rubbed his lips over her skin as he breathed deep.

Stella suppressed a shudder, memories of his hands and mouth all over her body sparking her arousal. Playing at a relationship didn't diminish the passion they'd shared last evening. If anything, the short-term aspect of their involvement made it even better—hotter.

"Are you enjoying yourselves?" Cole's deep baritone slid through her, his voice vibrating against her nerves and stoking her growing need. The man was sex on two legs and he knew it.

Stella tipped her head back and grinned at him, pulling her lips wide until she was sure he could see the sharp points of her fangs. "Of course, sweet. I was just getting to know Olivia and Charlotte. They're both just the *nicest* people I've ever met. They're making me feel right at home." She fluttered her eyelashes. "Isn't that wonderful?"

# CHAPTER FOURTEEN

*C*ole chuckled and flashed a smirk at Stella. One of her fangs lengthened slightly as he stood there, staring into her green eyes. A flow of her jaguar's yellow teased the edges of her irises, but the hue vanished as quickly as it'd come. If he hadn't scented her annoyance, that little display would have told him she was *not* a happy kitten.

His tiger flicked its tail and padded forward, torn between wanting to kill whoever upset her and the desire to antagonize the angry she-cat. Like his human half, his inner tiger enjoyed angering a female . . . and the makeup sex that came after.

Makeup sex with Stella? His cock twitched and hardened. At the same moment, he caught the scent of another's arousal. Or rather, more than one person's. Stella's drew his beast forward with her delicate, musky aroma. She was wet, wanting, and Cole's tiger wanted him to sate her desire. As for the other . . . *Olivia.*

Cole swallowed hard and fought not to heave all over the deck. He also suppressed his animal, the tiger surging to scare away the other woman who desired him. The cat didn't want anyone but Stella, and it ached to make that known.

He warned the cat to back off. It was getting a little too attached to the jaguar. This was an op, and—no matter how sexy—Stella was an asset.

The tiger tried to tell him that she was a *partner*.

He shoved the cat back. "Partner" had a sound of permanence that he refused to acknowledge. His cat's definition of "partner" felt a lot like "mate." Just because he'd enjoyed what they'd shared didn't mean he had "keeping her" kinds of thoughts. That was crazy.

Cole was occasionally unhinged with a penchant for blowing things up, but he wasn't *crazy*. He had a report from a psychiatrist. There were a shit-ton of diagnoses, but none of 'em said "crazy."

"That *is* wonderful, sweet," he murmured. "I'm so glad you're having fun." He lowered his head and rubbed the tip of his nose against hers. His cat wanted to get a full-on nuzzlefest going so she'd wear his scent, but now wasn't the time to act like a feline. "*And* staying out of trouble."

She poked out her lower lip, pouting for their audience's sake. He nipped her lower lip and then stole a kiss, caressing her mouth with his. Her sweetness teased his nose, and he wished they had some privacy. Privacy so he could show her that this growing thing between them was more than a job.

Stella spoke as soon as he retreated. "I never get into trouble."

"Uh-huh." He winked, still playing the part of indulgent lover. This *coo*ing crap wasn't for him. Not in public anyway. If they were alone, a locked door between them and danger, he'd nuzzle her neck and give her those gentle kisses.

Cole spoke to the other two women, eyes still on Stella. "Olivia, Charlotte, you both look beautiful this afternoon."

He turned his charm on the ladies, focusing on Olivia. "The sun and fresh air suit you."

Olivia tittered, the sound high pitched and piercing. "I think it's the company."

Her eyes remained focused on him, and a gust of wind brought him the stomach-churning aroma of her desire. Once more he was glad he hadn't eaten a big lunch. "You flatter me." He made sure he flashed a dimple. "Or are you teasing and there's another gentleman that's caught your eye?"

"Hmm…" She tried to mimic Stella's pout, but it didn't work. She looked more like a fish than a seductress. "If you can't tell, I must be doing something wrong."

Tension radiated through Stella's body, but he pretended not to notice. Instead, he remained focused on the human woman. He'd smoothed over yesterday's events with Walters, but he wanted to get closer to the man. If that required being friendlier with the daughter… so be it.

He noted the tension between Olivia and Stella. Jealousy bounced between the ladies, and "stealing" him would be a nice feather in Olivia's hat.

"Sweet." He lowered his gaze to the she-cat in his embrace. Tension vibrated through her, but there was now outward indication of her growing anger. Damn, jealousy looked good on her. "Didn't you say you had a bit of a headache? James mentioned there's a nice, quiet sitting room just beyond that door." He gestured to the left. "Why don't you rest for a few moments?"

"I'm happy to keep you company while your"—Olivia's emotions burned his nose, a combination of hate, jealousy, and desperation for violence warring with one another—"*girlfriend*," she said, practically spitting the word, "takes some time for herself."

"Perfect." He smiled wide and gave Stella a quick kiss. "Run along, sweet."

Cole released her and gave her ass a nice little pat as she walked by. She shot him a glare over her shoulder, and he knew he'd pay for that later.

The moment Stella disappeared, he had a human female invading his space, a thin arm wrapping around his while her overwhelming perfume filled his nose.

"I know Father had that dinner last night, but he's always so stuffy." Olivia fluttered her lashes. "Let me introduce you to some of our greatest supporters. We're a tight-knit group, you know. Contacts are—"

"Olivia," Charlotte hissed, reminding him they weren't alone.

"Oh, hush." Olivia waved her friend off and rolled her eyes. "Cole isn't some upstart with new money. He knows how the games are played." She turned her simpering gaze on him. "Don't you? There's a little back-scratching between friends and associates with similar viewpoints." Olivia turned back to the blonde. "It's not a new concept. This"—she waved her hand to encompass the group—"is simply a way to make new friends who have complementary interests."

"Exactly." Cole rested his hand atop Olivia's. "And I'm thankful for the introduction to these fine men"—he let a little heat enter his gaze, pretending he stared down at Stella instead of the human woman—"and beautiful ladies."

"Olivia, Mr. Turner hasn't—"

"It's fine," Olivia snapped. "My father has looked into the background of everyone present. Cole wouldn't be here if he wasn't loyal to the cause."

Charlotte wasn't giving up. "*My* father—"

Olivia pulled out of his grip and stalked to her friend.

She lowered her voice, but Cole still managed to catch her words. Thank goodness for shifter hearing. "Needs money. Cole has it. He has more than *anyone* here."

Cole snatched a drink from a passing waiter and brought it to his lips. He spoke to Grant. "Take a hard look at King for brains of the op."

"Been on it, but it's not easy finding intel."

He snorted. "For you?" There wasn't anywhere Grant couldn't hack. "Slacking, puppy?"

Grant just grunted and fell silent, no witty retort. "I *said* I've been on it."

Cole kept an eye on the arguing ladies and slowly moved to lean against the railing. "Did someone forget to feed you?"

"Fuck off."

All right, then. He ignored the wolf's bad attitude. "Report what you find."

Then he returned his attention to the two women, the whisper fight continuing.

"...security staff said she—"

The words "security staff" and "she" were words Cole didn't want to hear together. Since, as far as he knew, there was only one woman who'd tangled with Walters's security—Stella.

"Ladies? Perhaps I should go find Stella and leave you two—"

Olivia whirled, one of those feigned smiles politicians had perfected now firmly in place. "Of course you shouldn't." She stepped close, placing one hand on the railing and the other on his chest. He nearly gagged, hating the fact that her scent now coated his clothing. "Charlotte and I can finish our conversation at another time."

"If you're sure..."

"I am." Once more Olivia's arm slipped around his. She led him away from the railing, and they both disposed of their glasses on a nearby tray. "Let me introduce you to Trevor Stedham. He's the president of Signet Coms and works closely with my father in developing field communications when outfitting soldiers."

"For the military or...?" He let the sentence trail off, telling her without words who he referred to.

"Both, though we know who gets the best." She flashed him a grin and winked. "Let's speak with Trevor and see what his group has been up to lately." Olivia led him onward to the other side of the yacht. "Oh, Trevor, *darling*."

An older man turned to face them, excusing himself from a conversation with his own woman. "Olivia, how are you? Your father sure knows how to treat us, doesn't he?"

"Always, Trevor." She stepped forward and kissed the man's cheek before returning to Cole. "He always takes care of his friends. Old"—Olivia glanced at him, the smile that attempted to be sexy but failed directed at him—"and new."

"New, eh?" Trevor accepted a glass of scotch from an attendant.

Walters really wanted them drunk, which Cole could understand. A drunk man was more likely to empty his pockets.

"What's your name, boy?"

It'd been a long time since Cole had been called "boy." "Cole Turner."

"Of the Turner Group," Olivia cut in. The woman was more excited about his connections than Cole himself.

"Ahhh..." Trevor nodded. "Good work, those Turners."

"I told him the Turner Group could be better if they worked with Signet Coms. What do you think, Trevor?"

Olivia squeezed his arm. "Since he's practically one of the family now."

"Practically?" The older human man quirked a brow. "So, you talked things over with your father and King, then? Because I don't recall being included in any conversations."

Cole decided he'd add Stedham to the list of likely suspects as well.

She rolled her eyes. "Not you, too." She sighed. "The organization is going to fail if they continue to move at such a slow pace. The infection isn't going to slow just because the men in charge drag their—"

She paused and cleared her throat just before she cursed. The woman could make a sailor blush and *now* she censored herself? Because of Trevor in particular, or was it simply a rule among the men running the show?

"The longer we go without, the stronger *they* become." Olivia squeezed his arm. "I'm simply showing Cole the benefits he'll receive by joining our little group."

Trevor clicked his tongue and shook his head. "You're still the same headstrong little girl."

Olivia smoothed her dress, hand tracing the curved lines of her body. If she wasn't a shifter-hating piece of shit, he'd think she was hot. "Not so little anymore."

"No." The human man's gaze heated as he caressed the woman's body with his gaze. Stedham was old enough to be her father. "Not so little, but you're still overstepping, like you always have."

Trevor tipped his head toward him. "It was good meeting you, Cole. I hope that after you make up your mind and there's been some discussion among the others, we can work together."

"I do as well."

"Olivia, I'll find your father later and we can talk about this." Trevor's expression said that the *talk* wouldn't be a good one.

Olivia's face flushed pink, and the stink of her anger—burning wood—drifted over him. She didn't like being put in her place.

"Of course," Olivia murmured, her smile turning hard and brittle. "Enjoy the rest of the cruise."

When Olivia moved, Cole allowed himself to be drawn over to the next grouping and then the next. No more business offers were made. Only bland conversation was exchanged, with the occasional subtle question about his feelings toward *them*.

The lies he had to tell tasted rank on his tongue. Once more he sought out a drink, glancing around in search of an attendant but found none.

Dammit.

Cole placed his hand on Olivia's lower back and leaned toward her, whispering in her ear, "I'm going for a drink. Would you like one?"

"Aren't you just the sweetest?" She turned her head, their faces so close it wouldn't take much to make their lips touch.

If she managed to kiss him, he'd gag and his tiger would lay the woman out in a single punch. He wasn't one for violence against women, but he'd just spent hours listening to her spew hate about his kind.

"Thank you, but I'm fine." Her breath fanned his face, and he held his breath. "Hurry back."

"Of course." He couldn't wait for the op to be over. If it wasn't soon, he couldn't be held responsible for his actions. One way or another, every person on the yacht had participated in the ending of a shifter's life. He should blow the yacht and be done with it. He mentally groaned. He couldn't destroy them all. Yet.

*Integrate, gather intelligence, extraction, elimination.*

He was still on the "gather intelligence" step. Though he and Stella were about to have some fun prepping for the elimination portion of the plan.

Cole forced himself to smile and tip his head to acknowledge those he passed. He traveled along the railing of the deck, searching for an entrance. Sure, he wanted a drink, but he needed to check on Stella, too. He hadn't spied her on the deck, and no one had screamed after being pummeled by the tiny woman, which meant she was probably still inside.

Causing trouble? He hoped not. He'd spent all this time endearing himself to the assholes. He didn't need her destroying that progress already. He'd let her kill whoever she wanted as long as she played nice through the weekend.

Maybe he should remind her that her homicidal urges couldn't be sated unless the op was a success. Yes, that was a good plan.

He finally located a side door, a glass window inset allowing him to peer inside, and he spied Stella. The area was empty of humans, a sitting room with no television or other entertainment, so passengers had avoided the sparse space.

Except Stella.

She stood near a window overlooking the stern and the churning waters the ship left in its wake. The sun had gradually crept toward the horizon as time passed, changing the angle of its rays. Rays that now danced over her fiery hair and milk-white skin.

Gorgeous couldn't describe her. It wasn't strong enough.

She lifted a champagne glass to her rosy lips and sipped at the bubbling liquid. He watched the ripple of her throat as she swallowed, and his mind immediately went to the gutter. To wondering what it'd feel like if she swallowed *him* down.

Now wasn't the time, and in the middle of the ocean on a yacht filled with Unified Humanity members wasn't the place. That knowledge couldn't stop his mind from wandering though.

Cole grasped the door handle and turned the lever, swinging the door inward the moment the lock disengaged. He stepped into the quiet space and closed the door with an audible *click*. Stella breathed deep, her breasts straining against her top, and his mouth watered with the need to taste her. To lick her from head to toe and everywhere in between.

Cole resorted to talking to himself. *You're on an op, man. Keep that shit in your pants. At least until we're in our bungalow, all right?*

"I found you," he murmured, and strode forward, stalking her like a cat would stalk its prey. Which wasn't far from the truth.

"You did." She glanced at him, smirk in place, then swallowed another mouthful of champagne. "Though unless you're here to tell me I can pounce on Olivia..."

He snorted. "No pouncing." He continued on his path, not stopping until mere inches separated them. "And jealousy doesn't suit you."

Stella rolled her eyes. "It's not jealousy. It's that her father—"

Cole couldn't risk Stella speaking against Unified Humanity. Not when he hadn't had a chance to scan this room—any of the yacht really—for bugs.

He reached for her, slid his hand into her hair and fisted the silky tresses. He urged her head to move, to turn so their gazes met. Then he could do what he truly ached for—kiss her. He captured her lips, tongue sliding into her mouth with a sensuous stroke. He repeated the move, tasting her and exploring her depths. Rocking forward and back, mimicking what he ached for most. His cock hardened, shaft lengthening with each breath as he sought out more and more of her flavors.

This. This moment, this rising tide of desire and want, was real and true. It wasn't part of the op, wasn't a game of pretend to fool the humans. They'd do that later. *This* was because he couldn't keep his hands off her. Because the sound of her voice made him crave her and even the lightest touch made him feel...things. Emotions he'd buried when he'd decided working for SHOC was the right direction for his life. An agent drowning in guilt, regret, and sadness couldn't do their job properly, so he'd pushed them aside.

Then he'd met Stella, tasted her, and damn near fell in love with the woman with that first glare. Love? Fuck that.

Cole threw himself into the kiss. Savored the slide of their tongues and the sweet flavors as they danced across his taste buds.

At least until the familiar sound of the door latch disengaging intruded. He slowly pulled out of their kiss, brushing his lips across hers with one last sweeping caress before separating entirely.

"See? No reason for jealousy at all," he murmured. "I have what I want."

Stella's lips were pink from his kiss, her cheeks flushed and her eyes still closed. Her eyelids fluttered as she forced them to part, and she met his stare with drowsy eyes.

"Oh," she whispered, clearing her throat and then licking her lips.

The appearance of that pink tongue made him ache for

another kiss, but they still had work to do while out at sea. Sure, they had to get to know the other passengers, but Cole had one other task to accomplish.

A task that—luckily for him—included quite a few more of those kisses.

# CHAPTER FIFTEEN

Stella's knees were weak, her heart rate thundered in her veins, and her body ached for the fierce tiger that held her. He remained near, scent enveloping her in a sensual embrace, and her hands tingled with the need to pull his head down to her. She wanted more of those kisses. Many more.

Except the soft shuffle of feet over carpet and the *clink* of a glass placed on a table reminded her that they weren't alone.

Cole had told her that there was no reason to be jealous of Olivia Walters. She cleared her throat and shook her head, trying to banish the lingering remnants of passion clouding her mind. "Like I said, there's no jealousy."

"Uh-huh." His voice was low, for her ears only. He leaned down and nuzzled her neck, brushing his lips over her skin before withdrawing. "I see. Of course it's not jealousy."

Yeah, it looked like he *so* didn't believe her.

Cole wrapped his hand around her champagne glass and pulled it from her loose grip. He drank what remained in a single gulp and released her long enough to place it aside, then returned to her. One around her waist, the other resting on the windowsill.

"Since James was kind enough to invite us on his yacht, let's go explore."

"Explore? I'd rather…"

He brushed a kiss across her cheek. "We're here to meet others, sweet. Let's mingle."

Stella threw up a little bit in her mouth, bile burning her throat. Right. She'd forgotten about the real reason they'd willingly walked into the lion's den. "Of course. I can't wait to meet everyone." She gestured at the nearby door. "Lead the way."

His smirk told her that he didn't believe her for a minute. Good, he shouldn't. But he didn't call her out in the tiny lie. Can't wait? How about "I'd rather die than mingle with these assholes"?

Instead of saying that aloud, she let herself be led from the room, Cole's left arm around her waist, his right tucked in his pocket. The perfect look for a relaxed millionaire with nothing but vacation and spending money on his mind.

Stella returned smiles when necessary, tipping her head in acknowledgment whenever Cole stopped to speak.

They paused near a nameless couple, Cole tightening his grip on her hip, and she tipped her head back to meet his gaze. At least for a moment. The next instant, his lips were on hers, tongue lapping at the seam of her mouth. She leaned into him, hands on his biceps, and fell into the kiss. She didn't care that they were surrounded by UH members. Not when he smelled and tasted so damned good.

He shifted in place, muscles of one arm tightening and relaxing as he moved his arm. Then came a soft *clink* when he braced himself on the rail, Cole moving as if Stella had given him her weight, nearly knocking him over the edge.

*What the hell?*

Then it came to her—the plan and the part she played in

its completion. So this kiss was 100 percent work related. The low *clink* was him placing one of his magnetic disks, which were meant to go boom. No bigger than a quarter, each one was a destructive party waiting to happen.

Cole gradually ended the kiss, pulling away before she melted into a puddle of sexual need.

"Mingle," he murmured, and kissed the tip of her nose.

She released a low growl. One so soft that no one but Cole could hear. "Fine."

*The job. Focus on the job.*

Next he drew her to a set of stairs, leading her down the steps to a massive lounge—one with several seating areas.

Cole pulled her into the first conversation they stumbled across.

"Trevor." Cole held out his hand to one of the two men. "I forgot to give you my card." He withdrew from Stella and reached into his inner jacket pocket, producing a rectangle of thick white cardstock. "Regardless of this weekend's conclusion"—he waved the card, gesturing at their surroundings—"I'd still like to speak with you about some business."

The human stared at Cole as if he were no more than a bug beneath his shoe, but he did manage to suppress the sneer that lingered just below the surface. "Of course."

"Excellent." Cole smiled wide and nodded. "Excellent." He repeated himself and then turned to the other man. "I don't believe we've met. You are?"

"Turner, this is Armstrong of Strong Tech." Trevor stepped up and performed the introductions, though the stink of his reluctance swirled in the air. It didn't show in his face, but Trevor found Cole *wanting*.

Well, Stella wanted to throw him overboard.

"Strong Tech is involved in—"

Cole didn't let Trevor continue. "Space technologies. You originally worked with NASA, correct?" Armstrong nodded. "But now you also distribute to the civilian sector."

"Yes." Armstrong didn't look like he wanted to speak with Cole, either. "And you're Cole Turner of...?"

"The Turner Group. A little of this, a little of that." Cole reached into his jacket and produced another business card. "Here's my card. My interests are varied, and I'm always looking for a good opportunity."

Cole's free hand braced his weight on an end table for a moment—just long enough to place another of those small, deadly disks—before he bounced back. "I hate to chat and run, but I'd like to show Stella a little more of the yacht."

Both men murmured "of course," and Cole drew her away from the duo and back to moving through the room at large.

He leaned over and kissed her temple, a soft caress of his lips. "You're perfect."

She smiled and glanced at him. "Because I stand here and look pretty while keeping my mouth shut?"

"Exactly." That earned her another glancing caress.

They didn't speak to anyone else as they traversed the room, Cole pausing only to inspect this piece of furniture and the next. Each time, his hand disappeared into his pocket before dropping another disk in couch cushions or behind a piece of furniture.

And Stella played her part—getting cozy and stealing kisses whenever she could, acting like a possessive bit of fluff. She wanted to yell at the men. She was more than a sexual object, dammit. She had a brain!

They stepped onto yet another deck, Cole encouraging her to twine her arm with his. They traveled closer to the edge of the large deck overshadowed by the level above.

They paused on the side of a column opposite the door they'd used. At the back of the yacht, they weren't far from the propellers. Oh, they were hidden beneath decking, but there were also plenty of nooks and crannies in the area.

"Your turn," he murmured, and then his mouth was there again.

A seductive kiss that went all the way to her toes. It slithered throughout her body, sliding over her nerve endings and setting them all on fire. She wanted him oh so bad. Wanted to be taken and filled by him. Wanted to spend days in bed with nothing to do but eat and make love.

Not that she expected that to happen—what with all the Unified Humanity members nearby—but that didn't change her cravings.

He had his arms wrapped around her waist while she laid her palms on his hard chest. She stroked the thick muscles beneath her hands and let her touch wander. Her left hand delved beneath the lapel of his jacket, and she dipped her fingers into a hidden pocket. With a deft touch, she withdrew a few of Cole's party favors and palmed the explosives.

Stella opened one eye and peered through her lashes, searching for any observers. Coast clear, she performed her task. One disk held between her forefinger and middle finger, she made a short flicking motion and it went flying. It quietly clinked and bounced off the sharp angles before settling in a seam. She repeated the motion, aim true as she sought out destructive homes for Cole's toys.

The final piece tossed away, she refocused on the tiger's kiss, sinking into the mating of their mouths. It was mostly for show—a way to distract anyone who glanced their way—but that didn't change her body's reaction to him. Hot. Delicious.

Cole adjusted his position slightly, pressing his hardness into her lower stomach, and she moaned into his mouth.

Then the ass pulled away, leaving her breathless and needy. She whispered a single word when she finally caught hold of herself. "Tease."

He smirked. The asshole. "Not if I plan on delivering."

Stella was overcome by ethereal tendrils of desire sliding through her blood. *"Cole."* She couldn't hide the whine in her voice.

He squeezed her hip. "Patience."

Yeah, not something she'd been born with.

Cole led her onward, bypassing a few other lingering groups. He'd stopped attempting to join conversations after pausing to chat with Stedham and Armstrong. Now he simply tugged her along, nudging her toward a set of steps at the end of a long exterior deck. He gripped the doorframe and swung her around until her back met the solid structure.

Then she had his lips again. In truth, it was his lips and more. His hard body flush with hers, proof of his arousal cushioned by her curves while his mouth plundered hers. His passion rose higher, dragging a moan from deep within her throat. She grasped his lapels and pulled him closer, needing the weight of him. He was so much larger than her, so much stronger. He could overwhelm her in an instant and yet…he was gentle, not demanding. Or at least, deliciously demanding in all the best ways.

She nibbled his lower lip and caressed his tongue with her own, taking more of what he offered. If they could only find a bedroom.

When would she remember that they were on the job? Distraction was the reason Cole had caught her at James

Walters's mansion. Being distracted now could mean their lives.

Cole fumbled in his pocket; then he gathered her hands and pinned them above her with one large hand. The pressure against her wrists increased the tiniest bit as he placed a disk against the wall above them. She tipped her head back and watched its color morph until it matched its surroundings—hidden in plain sight. He ran his fingertips over that spot one more time, and that's when he eased their kiss, slowly withdrawing from her mouth.

Cole gave her another few chaste presses of his mouth, trailing them along her jaw until he reached her ear. "You're so fucking tempting. You make me want."

She wanted him, too. Desperately. But heading to bang-town in front of one and all was a step too far for her. The kisses had done their job, distracting other passengers.

*"Look at the new couple. Look at how uncouth they are to act that way in public."*

Then they'd all looked away or left—blatantly *not* looking at them.

He nuzzled her neck, and she forced herself to remain still. This sensual haze could leave anytime now. His touch, his kisses, were driving her crazy, and she was two seconds from losing it and climbing him like a tree.

"Let's finish this." And not even think about wanting and banging.

He just grunted and eased away, his attention flitting from side to side as he ensured they were alone. Then she had one hand captured by his again. He led her to a nearby door, this one plain and white. Obviously not an ornate entry meant for guests.

"This way." He tugged again.

"What's this way?"

"Privacy."

Stella rolled her eyes. "We don't need privacy. We needed the engine room."

He glanced at her, smirk in place. "Conveniently, they're one and the same."

# CHAPTER SIXTEEN

*C*ole grasped the door handle and pushed it down before giving it a nudge. It didn't budge, the lock holding it securely in place. Yeah, he wasn't dissuaded by a little lock. He tightened his grip and gave it a hard shove, his cat adding a little of its strength to the movement. The handle popped, lock breaking in an instant, and he carefully eased it open.

He paused just inside the dim hallway, stepping forward enough to let Stella follow him and then closing the door behind her. The rumble of the yacht's engines was louder in the narrow corridor, padding not a necessity in this type of pathway. One meant for the staff, not guests.

Cole led them onward, pulling the yacht's layout from memory as he led her down the hallways and stairs. There was no *easy* way to get to his destination, the path taking him up and down different levels until he reached his target. The whole while, Stella remained behind him, a curvy temptress that called to both man and beast.

They took one of the last turns, heading down the final hallway that would take them to their goal. Only to spy one of the staff heading in their direction.

Cole dove for a nearby doorway, shoving hard against

the handle. The door swung open without protest. He pulled Stella after him, spinning her around until her back was flush with the closed door, and as for her front... He took advantage of the situation and left no distance between their bodies. Her lush body was snug with his once more, all of that softness cradling his hard body.

She somehow cradled his hardened soul as well. Some gentle part of her that managed to ease the tension and rough edges he'd formed over the years.

"Hello, again." Cole spoke loudly, lips next to her ear so she could hear him above the cacophony. He drew in her scent, using the sweet tones to suppress the overwhelming stench of fuel and grease. The ship's aromas permeated everything in the area, coating it all on a layer of the disgusting smell.

*Five more minutes down here. Ten, tops.*

Cole's tiger was right on the edge of his control, the beast snatching power now and again. As for Stella... she was all woman. No hint of her jaguar in sight. The anger she carried came from her human half. And her human half was a little more than just pissed.

He listened to the action in the hallway, the staff member tromping by and his footsteps finally retreating fully. He eased back and kissed Stella on the nose. "Lovely conversation, but we have to move."

"Cole..." She growled his name, and he had to suppress the full-body shudder that rose along his spine.

"Almost done." He pulled her away from the panel and opened the door once more, carefully peering out. He looked both ways and forced his cat to diminish the sounds of the engines. That left him with their surroundings, and he took his time listening for others.

He found no one.

"C'mon." Another pull and he was striding down the hallway, his destination fifteen feet away. Then ten. Then five. Then...

Why the hell did everyone lock their doors?

A rough yank on the door handle and slam of his body against the door had it wildly swinging open. Once more he dragged Stella along, releasing her after ensuring the door remained closed.

The ongoing rumble of the engines traveled through him, shaking him like a woman's vibrator on high.

Only not as fun.

Cole delved into his pockets, pulling his toys of the trade free. He squatted and laid them out on the floor, separating the different pieces and organizing them for easy construction.

"So, what are we doing?" She crouched beside him.

He pointed at the three piles, beginning from left to right. "A, B, C. Mix A with B, and then form a small ball and press C onto it. Then we'll take the—"

"What are you doing?" He frowned and stared at her. While he'd spoken, Stella had grabbed an item from each pile and done as he'd advised. Except once she had C stuck on the mixture, she'd kept poking and prodding her A/B.

She pressed her thumb to the ball and then turned it to face him. "A little man in a hat."

Cole sighed and dropped his head forward. She'd added a face to the small explosive.

A. Face.

He closed his eyes and pinched the bridge of his nose. "I've got enough for thirty small explosives. Scatter them around the left half of the engine room. I'll take the right."

She didn't reply, just reached for more and carefully created her small bombs. Grabbing a couple before leaving to perform her task. He mindlessly assembled his own, half of his attention on his task and the other half… on the jaguar shifter helping him.

Dammit, he wanted another taste. Another sip of her mouth and the feel of her skin beneath his palm. Next time he told her he wanted her, he'd make sure she knew it had nothing to do with the mission. It had everything to do with the softness of her skin and the sweetness of her lips.

Ev-er-y-thing.

Cole mirrored her actions, reading pipes and applying the explosives where they'd do the most damage. When all was said and done, he wanted this bitch to go *boom* in a big way.

*Big*.

It didn't take long to finish their task. Hell, it had taken longer to *get* to the engine room than to plant the devices. So far he was calling this objective a win.

He drew Stella back to the door and peeked out before he pulled her into the hallway. She'd just closed it behind them when a familiar person turned the corner.

*Fuck*.

Cole didn't have time to say anything. He whirled and wrapped his arms around Stella, his hands moving to her ass. "Wrap your legs around me."

Thank fuck she didn't even question him. She did as he asked without hesitation. The perfect partner. Partner on the *job*. Not in life or anything. Because… Yeah.

The moment her legs lifted, he had his mouth on hers. He delved into her mouth, reveling in the taste and feel of her lips and tongue. So sweet. So hot. He wanted all of her, and he didn't think he'd ever get enough.

Ever.

He squeezed her ass and rocked his hips, pretending they

weren't about to get caught by one of the most evil humans on the planet. Instead, he acted as if he were wholly focused on the woman in his arms. He brought one hand to her chest, cupping her breast and kneading the plump mound. Her nipple hardened against his palm, proving her arousal.

He rocked his hips again, taking pleasure in the heat of her pussy. She whined and gasped in response, speaking against his mouth. "*Cole* ..."

He couldn't speak. Could only moan deep and continue teasing her—them.

Until the rushed, sensual passion he'd sparked was doused with cold water. Or rather, the sound of James Walters's voice.

"What are you doing here?" James had to shout over the engine sounds, though Cole's cat allowed him to easily hear.

The woman in his arms squeaked and stiffened, pushing against his shoulders while unlocking her legs from around his waist. He slowly lowered one leg and then the other, not fully releasing her until she stood on her own two feet. He took a small step back to give himself room to straighten his clothing and then turned to face the intruder.

"James, fancy running into you here."

"What?" James yelled in response, one hand cupping his ear. "I can't hear you."

"I *said* ..." Cole actually yelled the second time, loud enough for James to hear, and then he simply mouthed the rest of his sentence. He needed James to get them out of the staff area before the man saw what he'd done to the engine room's handle.

It'd seen better days.

"Come with me! We're going outside!" James spun on his heel and stomped past the other person who had accompanied him. Based on the man's uniform, Cole identified him as security.

The security officer stared at Cole, his narrowed eyes speculative, and Cole just shrugged. He tucked his hands in his pockets and stepped forward, making it only a couple feet before he realized that Stella hadn't followed. He went to her, grasped her wrist, and forced her to hook her arm through his. "Come along, sweet." He wasn't leaving her to suffer behind him. Wasn't allowing the security personnel to frighten her in any way. He wasn't sure what the guy had done, but her fear was enough for Cole to justify acting. "It seems James wants to have a chat."

He led her onward, not stopping when they reached the end of the corridor and continued to retrace their steps. It seemed like it had taken forever to get to the engine room, yet it took no time at all to return to the public area. They stepped through the broken door they'd used such a short time ago and came face-to-face with James.

A very, very unhappy James.

Which just made Cole smile.

Cole wrapped his arm around Stella's shoulders, pulling her close. His tiger purred when she leaned in to him, palm lying over his heart. Sure, she was probably pissed about the games he'd played, but she still touched him.

"James." Cole tipped his head toward the human. "What can I help you with?"

The guard stepped onto the deck and tugged the door closed, remaining in front of the entry with his arms crossed over his chest.

"My security"—James gestured at the guard—"was notified that there was an incursion in the staff areas."

He quirked a brow. "And?"

The number one rule of outlaws—admit nothing.

"And when we go to investigate, we find you and your"—James looked Stella up and down—"friend. Once again in a restricted area."

His face didn't betray his feelings, but James's scent told its own story. The human was disgusted. Because Cole and Stella had been caught where they didn't belong? Or because he just didn't like Stella? There was something else under there... Anger? Hate? No, that wasn't quite right. This scent had a smoky hint of burning wood.

*Suspicion.*

The next question was—what did he suspect?

Cole squeezed Stella's shoulder. "I'm sure you've had friends in the past, James. Sometimes privacy is necessary."

"With her kind?" James's lip curled ever so slightly. Just a twitch, as if he attempted to hide his reaction.

The human could hide nothing from a shifter.

"And what 'kind' is that?" The wind whipped at them all, clothes flapping against their bodies and hair flowing on the breeze. The boat rocked, the occasional large wave making them shift with the uneven surface.

But Cole remained motionless, his body tense and his tiger waiting for the human to insult Stella. It felt extremely... proprietary when it came to the little jaguar shifter. Insulting her was unacceptable.

Instead of James responding, it was the security guard who'd brought James Walters to find them. "A shifter."

Stella chuckled and shook her head as if that were the most ridiculous accusation ever. Cole was the only one who could feel her trembles and scent her fear.

Cole quirked a brow. "Really?" He looked to James. "We're back to this? I thought you and I settled this question the other evening."

"My employee assures me that Miss Moore is too strong

to be purely human. I discounted his report because you and I had already spoken." James stepped closer, his chin slightly raised so he could meet Cole's stare. "Now I find you both in a restricted area in the engine room."

"Near," he corrected.

"What were you doing in the engine room?" James pretended he hadn't heard Cole.

"Exactly what you saw. We were *near* the engine room and used the area for both privacy *and* the 'benefits' to be found."

"Benefits?"

Cole grinned wide. He reverted to the uncaring playboy Walters expected while he internally cringed at what he was about to say. Stella deserved better, but they both had their parts to play. "The walls vibrate."

# CHAPTER SEVENTEEN

## GRANT

*T*he moon taunted Grant, tugging at his inner wolf. The beast wanted to drop to four paws and run across the sand. It wanted to play in the waves until it was exhausted and then fall into a dreamless sleep on the shore.

At least then he wouldn't be thinking about her—blond hair, blue eyes, and five feet seven inches of fragile human female.

Lottie King.

He refused to admit that he'd been thinking about her all day. While Cole and Stella were risking their lives on a boat surrounded by Unified Humanity members, Grant had been hoping to hear Lottie's voice through the tiger's com.

He'd heard a little, at least. Just a few murmurs from the woman, and that'd soothed his wolf's sharp edges. Long enough for him to design a modified subdermal com for himself. One that made Cole's look like a play toy and enabled Grant to escape the bungalow for a little while without worrying he'd miss chatter from his teammate.

Between the modified software he'd installed on his computer and the upgraded com beneath the skin behind his ear, he was good to escape without worries.

All worries but one, anyway. Leaving his post to spend time with a woman—one tied intimately to Unified Humanity—stabbed him in the gut. Guilt ate at him, but it wasn't so strong he turned back. His need to see her overrode his hesitation. His need to see her smile and revel in their mutual attraction. Her scent, her shy glances, and her teasing told him that she was drawn to him as much as he was lured by her.

Grant wondered where his loyalty had gone. When had he turned from a dedicated SHOC agent to whatever he was now?

Grant padded through the bungalow to the back door like the previous night. Only difference was that it was earlier, just past sunset, with night settling in for the next ten hours. He gripped the knob and turned it, anxious to see if Lottie had decided on another walk. Except his wolf pulled him back, mentally gripping Grant with its teeth to keep him from leaving.

The beast was good with going to see Lottie again, but Grant had to grab something first. Something he *literally* couldn't live without.

But fuck, he hated the shit—hated that he needed it.

Unfortunately, the animal wasn't letting him leave without bringing a dose along.

He wondered if the beast remembered what a dose did to his human half.

The wolf snorted. He'd been taking meds for his "condition" in one form or another for eighteen years. It remembered.

Unified Humanity had taken Grant as a young wolf

and performed experiment after experiment on him—attempting to rid him of his inner beast. To "fix" him. Eventually, Grant had escaped, his wolf intact. Except, he hadn't gotten free, had he? Not really. Even after leaving the UH lab behind, he was still forced to deal with the genetic changes the organization had forced on him. Each dose was a reminder of what he'd endured.

With a sigh, Grant snatched what he needed from his duffel, ignoring the animal's smug chuff as he exited the home. Asshole.

He retraced his path from last night, taking his time as he walked along the coast. The waves ebbed and flowed, washing over his feet and cooling the heat in his blood. Anticipation warred with his dedication to his pack. Not a real werewolf pack, but the team was a pack of sorts. The only one a mutt like him deserved, anyway.

The wolf told him he was a dumbass, and Grant couldn't exactly disagree. Which just annoyed the beast even more. He mentally shrugged. Not much he could do about that.

He followed the bend in the shore, his inner animal's enhanced vision allowing him to see every detail of the world around him. Including the lone person standing at the edge of the cliffs.

The wind picked up, laying the person's clothes flat against their—*her*—body. Her skirt waved and flapped in the breeze, the swirls of air catching her hair and making it dance. She was a lone stoic sentry on the cliff, and he wondered what she was thinking.

Not because of the mission. Just…because.

His mind should be all about the op, but it wasn't, and that was some fucked-up shit right there. He knew it, but he couldn't seem to make himself care.

Another gust brought a new wave of scents to him, the

briny sea now tinged with the sweetness he associated with Lottie. He didn't catch a hint of any others, so he continued his approach. He was practically on top of her before she finally noticed his arrival.

His movement must have caught her attention, and she jumped with a squeak, followed by a growling chuckle. "You scared the hell out of me!"

Her laugh smoothed something inside him, and he smiled. "Keep those eyes open, sunshine." He reached up and brushed a tangle of strands from her face, tucking them behind her ear. "And then I wouldn't."

That single touch was enough to have his wolf straining against its mental leash. When she shut down in front of him, unease and wariness suddenly emanating from her, the wolf fought even harder.

Grant snatched his hand back and tucked his fists in his pockets, restraining himself the only way he could without her thinking he was into something kinky. He was, but he also had a thing for willing women who didn't stink of fear.

He took a step back, searching for anything out of place. There was no hint of disturbance in the trees and grasses, and the sand at the edge of the rocky cliffs held only their footprints. The pebbles and rocks marring the cliff looked exactly the same as last night. The one thing that hadn't been there when they'd last met was the basket at Lottie's feet.

He nudged it with his toe, causing the wicker basket to scrape against the rock. "You brought dinner? Did the rich guys not shell out for food on your field trip today?"

Lottie flicked her attention to the woven carrier and then refocused on him. She snorted and rolled her eyes. "Let's not talk about *today*. It was . . . Never mind." She sighed and shook her head. "I thought we could eat over on the sand."

His stomach growled, and she glanced at his midsection, quirking a brow. "Hungry, are we? I figured I could feed you since you're saving me from"—she waved at the trees and the people beyond—"*them*."

Grant ignored her jab at his grumbling stomach. Instead, he picked up the basket with one hand and then bent at the waist while he gestured toward the nearby sand with the other. "After you, milady."

Lottie remained silent while she padded across the rocky ground. He kept his eyes on her, his stare drifting down the long line of her back to the dip at her waist and the roundness of her ass. He had to admit that the enemy was sexy as hell.

If she was the enemy. Something inside him said she wasn't.

She didn't stop until she reached a wide swath of sand, and he paused at her side, placing the basket down. She reached in and tugged out a blanket she'd dragged along. He helped her spread it out before joining her on the checkered fabric.

"I have to admit"—he flicked open one half of the lid— "I've never had a woman cook for me before." He grinned and gave her a wink. "I could get used to this."

Lottie's face flushed red and she glared at him, but he knew she wasn't angry. It was a show to cover the flavors of her embarrassment. Apparently, she wasn't one to cook for a male.

She sniffed and sat up straighter. "It was the kitchen staff. *I* didn't do anything."

Yeah, she'd done something. She simply didn't want to admit it. Which was fine by him. He still got fed.

"The kitchen staff gives out picnic baskets for the guests?" He raised his eyebrows in question and worked on plucking containers from the basket.

"It depends on who you are and who you know." Her

voice was soft, almost stolen by the sound of the rolling waves.

"So." He lifted a plastic lid and sniffed the contents. Ham sandwich. *Score.* "You are someone important or know someone important enough to get a picnic basket? But you still couldn't get out of the field trip?"

Lottie sighed, and the wind brought him her scent. Sadness. Anger. Frustration. Defeat.

The defeat killed him. No one should feel beaten down and without hope.

"No." She took the container he handed over and toyed with the top. "In this case, who I know is *too* important. I was stuck." She shot him a glare, but there was no heat behind it. "Unlike some of us who didn't attend."

Grant grunted, shrugging.

Lottie brushed sand off the blanket, not looking at him. "No one at the party has mentioned your name."

He didn't comment. He didn't exactly have a cover story prepped since he wasn't supposed to do anything but sit in that damned bungalow and observe.

"And the island secretary doesn't have any record of a 'Grant' scheduled for this gathering." Lottie's eyes remained downcast.

Yeah, he didn't have anything to say to that, either.

A soft tone *ding*ed in his ear, the sound inaudible to anyone but him since it transmitted through his new com. Time to take his medicine like a good boy.

He dug into his pocket, searching out the small plastic capsule filled with the one thing that had kept him sane through the years.

"Grant?"

He wrapped his fingers around the pill and tugged it free before looking to Lottie.

"Are you going to tell me who you are? Why you're here?" She shook her head. "Are you squatting or something? Is that what this is? Because the men who own the island…" A wave of pure fear and heartache filled his nose. "They're not good people."

He ignored most of her questions. "Yeah, I've heard rumors about the owners."

He placed his container on the ground and brushed off the capsule.

"Whatever you heard, however bad it sounded, it's worse." She tried to warn him again.

"Some rumors are that they're crazy. It's a big delusion. Too many people with too much money buying into shapeshifter bullshit."

"And if I told you it's true?"

He finished brushing off the rest of the fuzz from his nightly dose. "I'd wonder if you forgot to take your meds or something. People don't believe in…*you know*."

"Some do. They do. Not because they're delusional but because it's true."

"You've seen evidence? Of shifters?" Maybe he'd get some intel out of this, after all. He might not have his ass handed to him when the team found out what he'd done.

Lottie rubbed her arms, but he didn't sense that she was cold, merely overwhelmed with emotion. "I have. I've also heard what the owners can do. You're right about them, but it's more like too much money and not a rational thought between them. Or a conscience."

Grant nodded and stared down at the dose in his palm. The hard, outer shell held his salvation. The liquid inside would stave off the symptoms and pain for another day. "I think that's pretty common. It doesn't seem reserved to the people on the island. The question is: do you agree with them and what they're doing? Or are you drinking the water?"

He placed the ampoule between his front teeth, lips peeled back. He bit down and sucked in a rough breath as if he'd used an inhaler. He gently exhaled and sucked in another lungful of air, draining the last of the ampoule. Once empty, he drew it into his mouth and swallowed the outer casing.

Lottie didn't answer his question. "What was that? That thing?"

He opened the container he'd claimed and pulled out the sandwich, taking a big bite. The worst of the hunger would hit any second. It was best if he started feeding that beast now instead of later.

"Sometimes crazies with too much money make mistakes." He shrugged. "They might want to test a new treatment without going through the proper channels. They might be willing to steal people who fit the patient profile." Specifically, shifters. But he didn't tell her that. He was already risking enough. "That was my own personal fix for what was done to me when I was younger. It's most effective when inhaled. Unfortunately, I can't always carry an inhaler, so I developed a different delivery system that's easier to transport."

"Did you report them? Whoever experimented—"

"Can we go back to my last question? Are you drinking the water around here? Are you okay with people being taken—tested on—and destroyed unless they manage to escape?"

He'd said enough. If she was smart she'd connect the dots between the crazies she talked about and the people who'd fucked with his genetics so bad he had to take drugs every day.

"Sometimes there's no choice. You might not drink it, but that doesn't mean they can't drown you."

"No?" He tipped his head to the side, staring at her. "You can't leave? Run?"

Lottie chuckled. "Who'd take me? Or even believe me? Better yet, who would protect me once they found out?" She shook her head, the heavy scent of her despair encasing him. "I'm alone in the middle of a crowd of crazies, Grant."

"You're not alone."

And if he had his choice, she never would be again. He just had to make sure she wouldn't happily gut him for being a werewolf first.

# CHAPTER EIGHTEEN

Stella should have blown Walters's mansion sky high when she'd had the chance and fuck the consequences. He deserved death, and if she'd been taken by the explosion, too...At least his reign of terror would have ended.

She'd looked into James Walters's eyes twice now—been the sole focus of his hate-filled gaze—and still couldn't shake the fear he caused. It taunted her while in his presence, and the moment he was gone, it invaded every part of her body. It reminded her of those years she'd watched her parents waste away. It tormented her with ghostly remnants of agony.

She'd let Cole and his SHOC team talk her out of her plans for vengeance. Then she'd let them talk her *into* helping them. Now she was on an island with Walters and he suspected she was a shifter. Fear threatened to strangle her, wrapping around her and tightening with every heartbeat.

"Stella?" Cole called out to her, and she sighed.

Last night they'd shared kisses—and almost more—but their night had ended with nothing more than cuddling. Bastard. He'd gone on and on about the mission and blah, blah, blah...Maybe it was for the best. Both halves of her wanted to be near Cole, but they also knew he'd simply lead them into danger once more. They'd be shoved into James Walters's path again.

Not a pleasant place to be.

"In here." She raised her voice and called out for him.

She returned her attention to the landscape before her. The rolling waves formed small whitecaps before caressing the coastline and soaking into the sands. With the sun now beneath the horizon, the crystal-clear waters had turned midnight black—a swath of darkness that seemed to absorb the moonlight. Like a black hole just waiting to swallow the world whole.

No, not the world—just her. If James got his hands on her...she'd pray for death and throw it a party when it finally came.

Cole's approach was near silent, the soft *whoosh* of his bare feet on carpet the only warning of his arrival. "What are you doing in here?"

*Here* was the bungalow's spare bedroom, curled up in a plush chair set before a bay window that faced the beach. Feet tucked beneath her and knees to her chest, she'd formed a small ball. As if she subconsciously tried to make herself the smallest target she could.

Did her body know something her mind had yet to accept? Was her capture imminent?

Stella shrugged in reply. "Watching the waves."

"We have to be out of here in thirty minutes."

"Yeah." She sighed. "I know." She had thirty minutes to get her shit together, put on a pretty face, and be prepared to flash sparkling smiles to a bunch of shifter-hating humans.

All without showing fear.

"Stella?" True worry filled his tone, and a hint of unease slithered into his scent.

She took a deep breath and released it slowly before tearing her attention from the ocean. She turned her head and practiced one of those smiles. "I'm fine."

Cole narrowed his eyes and tipped his head to the side. "You're lying."

Now that she looked at him, her banked desire sparked to life. The man was sexy as hell in ragged jeans, but in a tux...His hands rested on the doorframe, pulling his button-down shirt taut across his muscles. The top two buttons remained undone, his bow tie draped across his neck. The pants hugged his waist, and the legs hinted at the power hidden just beneath the fabric. He hadn't pulled on his shoes, feet bare.

A disheveled millionaire.

Stella swallowed hard and refocused on their conversation. This wasn't the time for sex thoughts.

Another shrug. "Does it matter?"

Cole moved away from the doorway and came to her, a tiger prowling across the room. He circled her chair and crouched in front of her, blocking her view of the world outside the bungalow.

"What's going on?"

She shook her head. "Nothing. Give me a few minutes and I'll be ready to go."

She could give herself a pep talk and get through the night. Maybe.

He gripped her ankles and tugged, forcing her to uncurl and let them hang over the front of the seat. Then he tugged and pulled her to the edge of the cushion. "Try again."

Stella pressed her lips together, gritting her teeth while she tried to think of something to say. Something that wouldn't be a lie but wouldn't be the full truth, either.

"I'm just tired. I'll be fine." She *was* tired after a night spent filled with sexual frustration. And as soon as she got off the island, she *would* be fine.

Two truths and not a lie in sight.

"Uh-huh." He squeezed her knees, and his hands moved to skate along her outer thighs, then hips, and on to trace the dip in her waist.

Her simmering desire warmed further as he eased closer and closer to her breasts. Would he finish what they'd started in that bathroom? Or would he call a halt—*again*?

Except he kept going, calloused fingertips skating over her skin. One hand moved to curl around the back of her neck. He gave her a gentle squeeze, and a tendril of calm crept into her body. It stroked her nerves and soothed them just a bit. It was as if he'd scruffed her cat while she remained in her skin.

The other hand cupped her cheek, and his warmth sank into her flesh.

His closeness gave her more of his scent, a mixture of his unease, and those flavors of fresh rain, damp earth, and crisp sun invaded her. She breathed deep, drawing the aroma in, and her cat chuffed with his nearness—his scent and touch. It wasn't enough to banish what plagued her, but it took the sharpest edge off of her emotions.

"What's going on, Stella?" he murmured, and she dropped her eyes to his mouth, remembered the feel of his lips on hers.

So soft. So sweet. So hot, before he'd stepped away and told her to put clothes on.

"Noth—"

Cole placed his thumb on her lips, silencing her with the gentle touch. "The truth."

She closed her eyes and shook her head. She'd revealed enough yesterday. He had enough "truth" as far as she was concerned.

"I can't help you if—"

She snorted and jerked away. The hand on her cheek fell away, but he still held the back of her neck. "This isn't about helping *me*, Cole. It's about helping you and SHOC. The fact that we want the same things is a happy coincidence."

"That's what you think?"

Tears stung her eyes, and she squeezed her lids shut and then relaxed them before focusing on him once more. She wasn't gonna cry. Period. No matter how hard the next few hours—days—were going to be, she wouldn't cry.

James Walters had caused enough tears.

"It's what I know," she whispered.

"That's what you think after yesterday?" A growl tinged his words—his tiger joining their conversation.

"It was a few kisses." She huffed. Kisses that meant more to her than just tiny pecks. "Then today you used me to accomplish your goal. You've proven that they don't mean as much to you as they may have meant to me."

"Stella..."

She gave him a sad smile, unwilling to get in an argument. "Look, let me shower and shake this off. I can get through tonight. I'm fine." She wasn't sure if she was trying to convince Cole or herself. *Probably both.*

"It was more than a few kisses. And I should have told you the plan instead of tricking you." The words were garbled, more tiger than man, and the hold on the back of her neck tightened. "Tell me what has you here sitting in the dark. Why do you smell like pain? Misery?"

Yeah, the beast was in control.

Stella shook her head. "It doesn't matter."

Cole leaned forward and pressed his forehead to hers. Their gazes met, and amber eyes clashed with her green-eyed stare. "It matters *to me*. Every thought, every emotion, every breath, every*thing* about you matters to *me*."

She snorted. "You want to know what's got me tied up in knots? What's making me wonder if it's better to face James Walters—again—or take my chances swimming to the mainland?" He opened his mouth to speak, but she didn't want to hear him just yet.

"I was a twin. Or am a twin." She frowned. "I'm not sure if I should use present tense or not because she's..." She swallowed hard, old pain making itself known once more. "She's dead."

"Tell me what happened."

"It hurts." She hadn't told anyone about Madeline. Ever. Even thinking about that time brought forward agony. What would she feel talking about it all?

"Tell me," he demanded again.

"We lived in this little house. It looked like a cottage with wood shutters and a cute little porch and a white picket fence." She remembered the two of them playing in the front yard, running in circles, screaming their heads off and driving her mother crazy. Hair in pigtails, a cute summer dress, and more energy than the average eight-year-old. It was like they fed off each other, excitement constantly doubling until their father put his paw down.

"We had this huge tree in the front yard that we'd climb and hide in the branches until my dad came home. Then we'd leap together and he'd always catch us."

Always. Not once had he let them fall.

"We were happy."

Until they weren't.

Cole stayed quiet. If he'd spoken, she wasn't sure she could have gone on.

"She was my best friend. We did *everything* together.

And then one day I lost control." She shook her head. "I partially shifted at the playground. I didn't think anyone saw, but two days later it happened."

Her throat burned, closing up and strangling her. "We were playing. Then there was a van and Madeline was screaming. I was crying." A tear slipped down her cheek, followed by another. "She told me to run. She didn't ask for help. She didn't beg for me to save her." Her chest ached, and a sob ripped from her mouth. "She told me to run and I...ran."

"You were a child."

"I'm a jaguar. The ones who stole her were human. I should have—"

"They easily outweighed you, and I'm sure they had weapons." When she didn't speak right away, Cole urged her on. "What happened next?"

"My mother heard my cries and came out just as the van pulled away. And that was it. Madeline was gone. My other half for eight years just...gone." Another tear streaked down her cheek. "My parents blamed me."

Cole caressed her cheek with his thumb, and a damp coolness trailed over her skin.

She sniffled and pulled away, rubbing her cheeks to wipe away those tears. "Sorry. I didn't mean to cry on you." She cleared her throat. "We should stop. I need to get—"

Cole wasn't having it. He stayed silent but rose to his feet, scooped her into his arms, and took her seat. He sat her across his lap and cradled her close. "Finish it."

"I..."

"Now, Stella."

Bossy asshole.

"There isn't much else." She shrugged as if it didn't matter, but it did. It *so* did. "They kidnapped Madeline. Life went on. That's it."

"Stop lying to me."

"I could be telling the truth."

He propped his chin on her shoulder and then nuzzled her neck. "I can sense there's more there."

"God you're an asshole." He just chuckled but didn't deny her accusation.

So she picked up where she'd left off. "My mother called my father. She called the council. Anyone, everyone. Phone call after phone call. My father came home and hugged my mother." She wiped away yet another tear. "No one said a word to me. People—shifters—in and out of the house at all hours. No one said a word. I..." She swallowed hard. "I think they forgot I existed."

She let her mind drift through those years. Creeping into Madeline's bed after her parents went to sleep. Needing to be close to her sister. Her parents not talking to her—or each other. Food would appear in the cabinets, but no one cooked except Stella.

Eight-year-old Stella burning herself on the stove. Neither of her parents cared—too lost in their grief. They blamed her for some of that grief. Hell, most of it. It was *her fault* that Madeline was gone.

It'd taken her a long time to get over that. The guilt hadn't truly left until her parents died. Dead of a broken heart. They shared a house, but never spoke. They brought home food when they remembered Stella existed, but never ate themselves.

"Then they died. They let their grief kill them. They let their grief blame me. They let their grief abandon me." She forced herself to continue. To reveal the depth of her need to take revenge on Walters himself. "James Walters put his hands on my sister, Cole. He snatched her off the street while I watched. The last time I saw her, it was in that human's arms. My parents let James Walters kill them, and now he's going to get me."

"I won't let him hurt you."

"Just being near him hurts. Breathing his air hurts." She rubbed her forehead. "I want to forget, but I can't."

"You shouldn't forget. You should let those memories fuel you."

Her chest squeezed and stole her breath. "They bury me. Just seeing him..." She stared into Cole's eyes, hating how weak she was but unable to do anything about it. "I thought it'd be easy. I hated that you wanted me to wait, but I thought this weekend would be a piece of cake."

"But it isn't."

"No," she murmured. "I'm forced to talk to him. To flirt and smile and..." A tear trailed down her cheek. "And pretend I didn't have to experience my family crumbling in front of me. Pretend he didn't take the other half of my soul."

"There is no doubt in my mind that he's going to die, Stella. He is going to know pain." Stella's jaguar purred with his words. "And I'll make sure he knows that you helped. That the family he destroyed is the reason he's going to die."

She couldn't miss the promise in his words—his tone telling her that he'd keep his vow no matter the cost.

"Stella?"

She swallowed hard and nodded. "Okay."

Cole leaned forward and pressed his lips to her forehead, his warm breath fanning her skin. "I'll protect you."

She leaned into him, taking comfort in the chaste kiss. If only she didn't want more from him. Because as stupid as her desire was, she craved Cole Turner—his touch, his kiss, his heart.

* * *

Fire scorched Cole's soul. A fury like he'd never experienced burned through his veins. His fingertips throbbed with his rapid heartbeat, his tiger's nails pressing against his human flesh. His gums ached with the push of his fangs, and his skin felt stretched thin, the cat struggling for release. It yowled and roared, furious that Cole wouldn't let it free. It wanted to hunt and pounce, take down its prey and then present the kill to Stella. It wanted to show her there was nothing left to fear. He'd rip James Walters into tiny pieces and it would be done.

If only it were that easy.

They stayed silent for a while. Only the rhythmic sounds of their breathing and the gentle mumble of the waves filled the air. And he was content to stay that way. He drew in more of her scent and held that breath in his lungs. He tasted her flavors, her sweetness tempered by pain.

He wanted to take that pain away. He knew he would—eventually—but he wanted it gone *now*.

Patience, cat.

It curled its lip, flashing a fang, and followed that with a long hiss. His cat wasn't known for its patience. Ever.

"We should go." Stella's voice was strained, the teasing lilt and tinkling laughter no longer present. It was more of a rasp that scraped his nerves.

"You sure?" They *needed* to go to the party, but he'd figure something out if they skipped it. "We can…"

Stella shook her head. "No. We're doing this. I…" She took a deep breath, the inhale hitching as she tried to fill her lungs with air. "I can do this." She pulled back, and he let her retreat. Now wasn't the time to crowd her even if he wanted nothing more than to haul her close. "I'm sorry—"

Cole darted forward and snared her lips in a quick kiss, their mouths touching briefly with a hard press. "No apologies."

She blinked at him and then blinked again, eyes open wide with surprise. "But I..."

He shook his head. "I don't want them. Don't apologize for your feelings. We all have shit that drives us to do what we do. Sometimes it rears its ugly head and catches us when we're least expecting it."

"And you have something like that?"

He nodded. He'd never quite figured out what to say when someone offered condolences. "I got my vengeance. When this is done, you'll have yours. I swear it."

"I believe you."

He scented the truth in her words. Their conversation had taken painful twists and turns, but now she believed in him. He wanted to be worthy of her trust. He *would* be worthy of it, dammit.

"Let's get you dressed." He pushed to his feet and held her steady while she rose from the chair.

Not releasing her, he led her through the bungalow—across the open living area and into the room they shared. The bed remained unmade, their scent still clinging to the fabric. His cock throbbed, remembering the feel of her in his arms as he slept.

The cat hissed at him, snarling that he hadn't taken her last night—claimed her. He rolled his eyes. Dumb tiger. They weren't the claiming type.

It snorted. He would have continued arguing with it, but he and Stella had reached the walk-in closet.

He pulled her in after him and then released her hand. "Clothes?"

"Uh..." She didn't move, but that was fine. He didn't

need her help. He was a master at undressing. How hard could dressing be?

"Top first," he murmured, reaching for the hem of her tank top. "Arms up." He tugged. She didn't move. "Stella? Need some cooperation here."

"I can dress myself."

"Uh-huh. Arms up."

"Cole, seriously?"

He stopped and cupped her cheeks, drawing her closer while he took a step forward. Less than an inch separated them, and his tiger urged him to close that remaining distance. They'd never leave if he got his hands on her fully.

But maybe a kiss was okay...

Cole lowered his head and brushed his lips across hers. Just a careful tease once, twice, and then he lingered. He lapped at the seam of her lips, tasting her natural flavors. He nibbled and nipped her lower lip, then soothed the sting with his tongue. He alternated between chaste pecks and more passionate caresses until...

Until Stella opened for him.

He delved into her mouth, gathering her delicious taste and hording each snippet of flavor. Strawberries and honeysuckle drifted over his taste buds, and he swallowed every drop. He explored her mouth, taking more and more from the seductive jaguar. Her tongue twined with his, and he mimicked what he ached to do to her body.

His body thrummed with arousal, pleasure thumping through his veins. The tiger drove him on, demanding he *finish* this.

But not yet.

Stella was the one to lean against him. She was the one to twine her arms around his neck. She pushed to her tiptoes and increased the pressure between their mouths.

And Cole took advantage of the new position. He changed his hold, abandoning her cheeks to instead wrap around her waist. He pressed her hips hard to his own, his cock cradled by the softness of her lower stomach.

Fuck, but she made him *want*. She made him willing to throw it all away for a night in her arms. No, more than a night.

She wiggled and then whimpered, and a tremor shook her smaller frame. Then…then came a scent so addictive he didn't think he'd ever get enough. Salty musk teased his nose—Stella's arousal now filling the air. His own joined hers, his body and beast craving her.

Cole tightened his grip, squeezing her even tighter, until he knew she'd never get free unless *he* allowed her. She was his sensual captive. One he wanted to fuck for hours.

He shuddered, and his balls drew up tighter against him. Pleasure wrapped around him, cupping his balls and stroking his cock with invisible hands. He could come this way—with nothing more than Stella's lips on his.

It wouldn't be nearly as much fun as sinking into her silken wetness.

Stella moaned again, and she scratched the back of his neck, sharp fingernails digging into his skin without breaking the thin tissue. That was followed by a soft whine, one he wanted to echo and—

"Sorry to interrupt you two lovebirds, but you've got less than ten minutes to get pretty." No better way to kill a hard-on than to hear Grant's voice in his head.

# CHAPTER NINETEEN

*C*ole couldn't tear his attention from Stella. Even if she wasn't within his line of sight, his tiger managed to track her through the room by scent and sound. The beast knew she mingled with the guests, pausing to speak with others—both men and women. It had no problem with her chatting with the ladies, but the males were another story. Especially when more than one hit on her.

Yet he was stuck speaking with Richard King in a secluded corner while Stella interacted with others. Being pulled aside by King was good for the mission. It was not all that good for his jealousy, though.

Plus, King was so. Fucking. Boring.

The man had the personality of a rock with the intelligence of Stephen Hawking. Thankfully Cole had Grant in his ear so he could at least follow *some* of the conversation. The wolf was smart as hell.

"With an influx of funding…"

"…to begin immediately."

"…appropriate test subjects."

"…recently acquired."

The acquired part snared his attention. "Acquired?"

Grant echoed Cole, albeit a little more colorfully. "Mother*fucking* acquired?"

Richard adjusted his glasses, pushing them up his nose as if it was a nervous habit, before answering. "Yes, as I'm sure you're aware, this disease is an epidemic of global proportions. Steps must be taken, Mr. Turner. Steps that require funding from like-minded individuals such as yourself."

"I'll give him like-minded. I'll rip his mind out through his nose and fucking like it," Grant growled, and the sound vibrated through Cole's mind. Almost as if it were his own beast.

"I see." Cole paused to take a sip of his drink and calm his raging tiger. "I have to admit that this is the first time details have been provided, Richard." He tilted his head to the side. "I'm not sure I understand where this sudden openness and bout of trust comes from."

Richard pressed his lips together until they formed a white slash beneath his nose. The burning flavors of anger assaulted him, coating his tongue with the sour taste. "We all have our specialties. Some people involved in this venture are more intelligent than others." The way Richard preened told Cole that Richard believed he had a useful mind.

Grant snorted, and Cole echoed the sound. Richard King was an idiot.

"You're one of the smart ones." A question and a statement in one. Cole tipped his glass toward the human with a smirk.

"The King Institute boasts some of the most gifted minds in the world." Richard wasn't bragging. The institute really was one of the world's greatest think tanks. Unfortunately, it was associated with Unified Humanity.

He wondered if the employees knew about shifters and believed his kind needed to be eradicated or "cured"?

"That's never been in question. I believe my father has benefited from your services in the past." Until his father had learned of King's extracurricular interests.

"Hmph. The *past* is correct. We haven't participated in any research or development with the Turner Group for some time."

"Uh-oh," Grant singsonged in Cole's ear. "The evil man is cranky because he's *poor*."

Though "poor" wasn't really the word Cole would use. King Institute still pulled in billions annually. Some of it simply no longer came from his family.

"Yes, well, the Turner Group is in the hands of my brothers now. I have no control over operations." He flashed the human a feral smile. If he had any sense of self-preservation, he'd be on edge. "I'm simply the playboy who reaps the financial benefits."

"And with your participation, the world can flourish in the grip of our kind once more."

"Everyone in attendance supports this endeavor?" Cole gestured to their gathering.

"Of course." King squared his shoulders and straightened, giving his jacket a slight tug. "Our guests have been meticulously screened and researched."

"You can appreciate my worry, though. Not everyone believes in Unified Humanity's mission." He shook his head. "And it's not as if a clear board of directors is revealed to potential investors. I have a hard time parting with millions only to discover they've disappeared into someone's pocket." Cole shrugged. "You understand, of course."

"Mr. Turner—"

"Cole, please. There's no reason to be so formal when

nine-figure investments are involved." There. Let the human chew on the idea of a donation of one hundred million dollars or more.

King's eyes widened slightly, and then Cole was bombarded with the human's anticipation and excitement. He listened to the rapid thump of King's heart and the hitch in his breath. *Greed.* Greed was a great way to destroy a person's hesitation.

Unified Humanity was very greedy.

"Are you two hiding and talking shop when you should be mingling?" Olivia's overwhelming perfume preceded her arrival.

The stink of heavy sandalwood clouded the air, and Cole fought against the sneeze that threatened.

"Olivia," Richard King snapped, glaring at the young woman. So, all was not well in the UH world. Between Richard and Olivia directly, or were King and Walters having problems? "Hasn't your father taught you not to interrupt?"

The brunette pouted and seemed to ignore King's snarl. "I was just going to introduce Cole to a few of Father's closest friends."

"Olivia." King's tone silenced the woman in an instant, earning a glare from his daughter.

"Here you are, darling." Stella's voice stroked him with an invisible sensual caress down his spine. The scent soon followed, the peculiar hints of human and feral beast that wrapped around his cock like an ethereal hand. "I've been searching for you everywhere."

She cuddled against his side, arm wrapping around his waist while she leaned into him. She formed a physical barrier between him and Olivia, forcing the human woman to take a step back.

"Who's this? I don't believe we've met." Stella held out her hand to King. "I'm Stella—"

"Moore." Richard grasped her hand and brought it to his lips. "We haven't met officially." The human's mouth lingered. "I did, however, have the opportunity to get a glimpse of your"—his eyes dropped to Stella's cleavage, and Cole wanted to behead the man for looking at what belonged to him—"assets at James's get-together several days ago."

Stella tittered. Honest to God, she *tittered*. Not a sound he'd ever expected to come from her. "Oh, *you're* that shadow from the hallway. Naughty, naughty for spying."

His teammate snorted in his ear. "I wouldn't have just spied. I would have gotten comfortable for the show."

Cole's tiger surged, snarling in his mind. It pushed a growl up his throat, one that couldn't be suppressed. It caused his vocal cords to vibrate, and the nearly inaudible grumble transmitted over the com.

"Tou-chy." Grant's reply coincided with Stella's twitch.

The humans couldn't hear his jealous rumble, but the jaguar sure did.

"Cole, darling." Stella turned in his embrace and laid her hand over his heart. She petted him with gentle strokes, and his tiger gradually calmed. "I'd love to dance." She looked to King. "You won't mind if I steal him for a moment, will you?"

"You'll have to excuse me, Richard." He pushed the words past gritted teeth. "A beautiful woman can't be denied."

"Of course. Of course." The human waved him away, and Cole ignored the heated glare from Olivia.

If he didn't get out of there, he'd pluck King's eyes out. Then the man wouldn't be able to see anyone's "assets."

Cole grasped Stella's hand and drew her away from the secluded corner. His tiger relaxed more and more with every step he took away from the lecherous bastard. Though that calm didn't last long. The farther they walked, the more attention Stella drew from others, which brought his possessive instincts raring to the forefront of his mind.

He'd blind them *all*.

They reached the outer edge of the dance floor and insinuated themselves among other couples drifting across the square. He placed one palm at Stella's lower back and cradled her hand with the other. In sync, they danced to the slow tempo, bodies moving as one.

Stella stepped closer until their fronts touched. "Discover anything interesting?"

"Possibly," he murmured.

"*Definitely*," Grant added.

"She can't hear you, asshole."

"Your lovely neighborhood trash compactor?" Stella's teasing lilt filled his ear.

"Yes, and he won't shut the fuck up," Cole growled.

"If you'd tell her—"

"I'm gonna tell her, asshole." So much for trading intel with the wolf. "Fuck off."

"No, *you* fuck off, you pussy."

"Pussy? Did you just call me a—"

Stella slid her hand from his shoulder to the back of his neck. She toyed with the long, slightly curled strands. "Pussy *is* another name for a cat." Cole growled, his tiger annoyed with Grant *and* Stella. "Oh, hush. I'm a pussy, too."

"I bet she has a nice pussy." The wolf just couldn't keep his mouth shut. Grant obviously had a death wish. "Is it sweet and—"

"One more word." Cole dropped his voice to a rumble that only shifters could hear. "One more word that doesn't have to do with this mission and I'll gut you myself."

Stella caressed his neck once more, fingers trailing along the column of his throat. "You know Birch wouldn't like that."

"What she said." Grant chose to speak despite Cole's threat.

And now he hated Grant a little more just because he knew Stella was right. His team alpha really wouldn't like it if Cole killed the wolf. Something about each of them being an integral part of the team or some shit.

Cole called bullshit, but since Grant was his closest backup, he'd force himself to play nice a little longer.

"Now, ignore him and tell me what you found out."

Cole tried to do what she asked. His tiger was already wrapped around her little finger, and it wanted to give her whatever she desired. "I spoke with King alone. I've got him at the top of my list as the brains behind UH, though Stedham is still included because of something Olivia said."

A low growl, the tone different from Cole's, vibrated in the air. It took him a minute to pinpoint the source, and it hit him that now it was *Stella* on the verge of causing a scene. Well, well, well ... maybe he wasn't the only jealous one.

"What did the bitch say?" Stella's words came out in a garbled mess, but he got the gist.

"I believe Trevor Stedham sits at Walters's left, and King is either on Walters's right or very close to the man. Unless you've heard otherwise, our target is one of those."

"And Walters." Her voice remained rough and grating.

Grant spoke up, but Cole ignored him. "You know that Birch wants to keep Walters alive for—"

Instead, he answered Stella. "Yes, but at the right time."

"Which is after I get all of the information we need and make sure he's answered all of your questions. Then I'll…"

"He's already suspicious of you, Stella. *You're* not doing anything but staying out of his way." Cole would stand firm on this one. Even if she glared at him until the end of time. He couldn't risk her—his tiger wouldn't allow her to be threatened. And Walters? He'd do more than threaten if he discovered she was a shifter. He'd kill.

"Cole…"

"No. Do you know how dangerous he is? If his suspicions are confirmed, he'll take you. He'll—"

"I know what he'll do," Stella hissed, but thankfully her cat's appearance didn't overtake her human features.

Cole eased them off the crowded dance floor and cupped her face, gently tracing her cheek. "No, I don't think you do, Stella. I can't risk you. I won't. You have a personal interest in Walters, but *I'm* the one who's trained for this. You don't have the heart of a killer, sweetheart. I swear, you'll get what you want."

*Eventually*. The team might keep the human around for a little while, but Cole would keep his promise.

"Cole…" He ignored Grant's warning tone, too.

"Good." Stella gave him a blinding smile. "But I can—"

"Cut in?" That wasn't Cole's voice, and it sure as hell wasn't Grant's.

No, it was Walters's, and he was looking at Stella like he wanted to devour her.

Over Cole's dead body.

# CHAPTER TWENTY

*C*ut in? Over Stella's dead body. Walters couldn't cut in, but Stella was willing to cut *him*. Or the man's cuntalicious daughter. Ooh, how about both? Both would be good. Cole would probably tell her she wasn't allowed. Why the hell had she agreed to work with him again? Oh. Right. No choice. Bastard. Sexy bastard, but a bastard nonetheless.

"Of course," Cole murmured, his deep tenor vibrating through her chest, but his expression told her more than words. It was a silent communication, an expression of worry and warning. He didn't need to warn her. Fear—her constant companion—was sitting in the front row of her emotions.

But despite that fear, she pushed on, refusing to back down and ruin the operation when they were so close to the end. She could be strong. For SHOC. For Cole. For her sister.

Cole loosened his hold, stepped back, and turned her over to James Walters. "Though I will expect her back at the end of the song."

"I don't know. I may decide to keep her." Walters grasped her hand gently. "She is gorgeous."

"Flattery will get you everywhere," she purred even as

her cat gagged. Being told she was beautiful was nice. Touching the man who wanted to destroy her people...not so much.

"Everywhere?" Walters smirked and placed his hand on her lower back. His clammy fingers rested on her bare skin, sending a shudder up her spine. Revulsion churned in her stomach, the emotion warring with the terror that consumed her blood.

She really shouldn't have gone with a backless dress. Really.

Walters pulled her toward him until their fronts were flush. She could feel every line of his pudgy, soft body, and her cat recoiled. It wanted the firmness of Cole, not this Pillsbury-like human.

"Be good, you two." With that, the tiger turned and left her with Walters, disappearing into the mingling guests.

"Dance with me." James tightened his grip and swung them into a slow dance across the floor. "Tell me, Stella, will flattery get you in my bed?"

"First a dance and now you want me in your bed? You do move fast." She struggled not to let disgust overtake her expression.

"You have to move fast in business. Options are presented, and I make a choice. If I wait too long, I could lose."

His life if she was lucky.

"You're willing to risk Cole's anger by stealing me away?" She *tsk*ed. "I thought you were recruiting his bank account for the cause." She eased away so she could meet his eyes. "They have to be stopped, you know." She traced his neck once more, smiling when he shuddered in her arms. "Cole's money could help."

"Hmm..." He gave her a noncommittal hum and then smirked. "There are things you could do to...*help*."

Her stomach churned. His innuendo wasn't lost on her. He was thinking with his little—bow chicka wow wow—head.

"Me?" She lifted her eyebrows, eyes open wide. "What could *I* possibly do?"

*Please don't say fuck. Please don't say fuck.*

"I think the answer deserves private discussion." He traced her thumb with his own and pulled them into a turn with ease. "Don't you think?"

No, she didn't think. Being alone with Walters hadn't been part of the plan. She was meant to be arm candy. A silent listener while Cole did everything else. Getting private time with James *was not* silent snooping. It was going against every order Cole had given her.

"When were you thinking about sneaking away?" She had to tease him, keep their chat going and hope he wanted to disappear later. After she had a chance to organize things with Grant and Cole so she wouldn't really be at risk. Except...

"There's a door in the south corner of the room. We can slip away and talk about how we can help each other." He caressed her with small circles of his thumb.

She'd need to bathe in bleach at the end of the night.

"Each other?" She caressed his lapel. Her jaguar wanted to sink its claws into his chest. Stella's human half recognized that the situation was getting out of hand. "I assume I'm supposed to help you by delivering Cole's checkbook, but what can you do for me, Mr. Walters?"

"Anything you want? Diamonds? Cars? A vacation home?"

She quirked a brow. Really? If she was Cole Turner's trophy girlfriend, didn't James think she'd have more than enough material gifts? "The only problem is it'd be paid for with Cole's money, and Unified Humanity would be back where it started—with a cash-flow problem."

James didn't like *that* pointed out to him, and his next spin was quick and hard. He glared, and his jaw flexed as he gritted his teeth. "A few trinkets won't harm the cause."

"I can get trinkets from Cole now." Her dress swayed with their steps while she tried to think up a demand that would make Walters balk. "I want to be more involved."

"Involved how?"

"I want to meet them—the men behind the curtain who work so hard to get rid of that disease. I've always dreamed of shaking the hands of the people determined to save us."

"You've already met a few, kitten, and they've all taken a moment to appreciate what they've seen." His voice turned husky. "They'd all appreciate a moment to get a closer look, too. Is that what you want?" James murmured.

He wasn't supposed to sound intrigued. He wasn't supposed to look at her like what she asked for was possible—within her grasp.

*Fuck, fuck, fuck.*

Stella matched his volume, adding a hint of desire to her voice. It wasn't easy—James made her want to vomit as if she'd been on a two-day bender—but she managed. "Yes, that's what I want."

"Then come with me." James released Stella and stepped away.

He snatched her wrist and began to stride toward the back of the room. His pace was slow but determined. Several guests attempted to stop him, but he waved each one away. He didn't allow himself to be distracted from his goal.

Her wrist was locked within his grasp, and his hold remained firm but not painful.

No. No. *No*. God, she was a fuckup. Stella kept up with James's strides while she scanned the room. She hunted for any sight of Cole, silently praying he'd stop them before James got her out of the ballroom. This wasn't right. Not just because it went against Cole's orders, but also because... it felt wrong. There was an oily tang to James's scent. He was too happy. Too excited. Too...

She struggled to keep up with his strides, pausing only when they'd reached Charlotte King's side, where she spoke with Trevor Stedham.

"Apologies, Stedham." James tossed out the words, but they seemed perfunctory, not sincere. As if Trevor wasn't worth James's notice. "Charlotte," James murmured low, but Stella still heard him thanks to her inner kitty. There wasn't a conversation in the room that she couldn't catch with her jaguar's hearing. "I need a meeting with your father." He tugged and drew her close, her presence snaring Trevor's gaze. "Stella would like to say hello."

She gulped. Well, if James went to Charlotte King—and by extension, her father, Richard—for a meeting, she'd at least confirmed King's status within UH. Unfortunately Cole wasn't there to hear the news. Or save her from what was to come. Maybe she could talk her way out of this.

"But there are so many guests. Don't you—" The blonde tried to stop him, but he wasn't about to be delayed.

"Now, Charlotte. Find Richard. I want a meeting *now*. No excuses." James practically snarled like the jaguar inside Stella.

Order delivered, James waved Charlotte off and they returned to their travels to the back of the room. He pulled her to a beige door that blended with the wall until it was nearly invisible. He reached into his jacket and withdrew what appeared to be a magnetic keycard. One swipe of the rectangle along the edge and the panel swung toward them.

"James." She tittered. "Maybe now isn't the time."

"Of course it is." His voice was hard and flat.

Her anxiety increased, and Stella glanced over her shoulder, searching for Cole.

"Come along, Miss Moore." James tugged.

She returned her attention to what stretched out before her—a long, empty hallway. Pristine white walls and sterile tile flooring extended along the passage. It was bright white, glaring fluorescent lighting illuminating the space and leaving not a single shadow.

Most people were afraid of the dark, but it was this *lack* of darkness that frightened Stella. Her jaguar snarled that *it* wasn't afraid of anything. Big cats didn't "do" fear. Slightly distressed, maybe, but not *afraid*. It sniffed. That was for humans.

James tugged her along and pressed a panel on the wall the moment she stepped over the threshold. It sealed the door with a *whoosh* and a *hiss*, locking her in with the shifter-hating human.

Okay, there was nothing to worry about. It was a hallway. A *blah*-looking hallway, but there wasn't anything blatantly threatening. She had her suspicions about his suspicion, that was all. She was fine. *Fine.*

Except the scent of bleach surrounded her. The burning smell scorched her nostrils, and she wrinkled her nose. She parted her lips and breathed through her mouth. Then she had to fight the urge to gag. Sometimes having an inner animal with a heightened sense of smell and taste sucked.

James didn't say anything at first, merely dragging her farther away from the ballroom. The heels of their shoes clicked each time they struck the tile floor, the sounds echoing off the barren walls. The passage curved left before straightening once more, revealing even more of the sterile hall.

"James." She tugged against his hold, and he tightened his grip. Not enough to hurt, but to tell her that he wouldn't be letting go just yet. "I changed my mind. I'm sure Cole is looking for me."

"You wanted to meet the ones in charge, *kitten*."

She swallowed hard, heart thrumming. Yeah, this had been a bad idea. Why had she wanted to play spy again?

"But it's your party. Shouldn't we go back? Won't your guests miss you?" She didn't try to get free, but she did slow her pace. She'd seriously love one of those com things that Cole had. It'd be great to be able to summon the cavalry to save her from this mistake.

He glanced over his shoulder and winked. "There's not a single guest more important than you, kitten."

"More flattery." She forced a grin to her mouth, her lips remaining closed. Her cat stretched and strained against Stella's control. It wanted to push forward, the cat no longer liking this game.

James rubbed her inner wrist with his thumb, tracing small circles on her skin. "It's not flattery if it's the truth."

The hall curved once more, taking a meandering, snake-like path away from the party.

"More flattery?" She laughed, the chuckle sounding fake to her own ears, and she wondered if he sensed her growing nervousness. "Why don't we turn back? I'm sure Cole's looking for me by now. I'm supposed to be *his* date this weekend."

James grunted. "Not too much longer."

He stole a glance over his shoulder, and her breath caught in her throat. Maybe clinging to her cover like a spider monkey wasn't such a good idea anymore. Not with the way James stared at her—as if he couldn't wait to attack.

"James..."

"Just a few more steps. I promise."

Stella shook her head and laughed, pulling against his ever-tightening grip. "It seems like this hallway is going on forever!"

"No, not forever. Just until we reach the restricted area."

"Restricted area?"

James grinned. "You didn't think the highest-ranked members of Unified Humanity would meet and discuss business near the guests, did you?" He shook his head. "We have a private section on the island for a reason—*privacy*."

They finally reached the end of the passage, a smooth wall in their path. James brushed the keycard along the edge just like before. "We've arrived."

# CHAPTER TWENTY-ONE

*C*ole meandered around the edge of the room. Whenever someone tried to drag him into a conversation, he merely tipped his head in acknowledgment and moved on. He feigned calm, pretending not to feel a rising anxiousness in his gut. His tiger experienced the sensation as well, the cat's tail swishing back and forth in agitation.

Something was wrong. Something…He scanned the room again, searching for the cause of his unease, and he soon found the source. Or rather, *didn't*. Stella and James were gone. *Fuck*. When had she disappeared? How long had she been gone?

It didn't matter that Stella was a powerful shifter—that she had an inner jaguar at her beck and call. James had UH on his side. James *was* UH, with their weapons of torture and countless shifter deaths beneath their belts.

His inner tiger snarled, baring its teeth while it attempted to take control. It scraped at his mind, long claws digging into him. It sought to shred Cole's mental bonds, burst free regardless of the consequences. The cat saw Stella as its— theirs—and now she was in danger. It was anxious for a hunt, shaking with the need to burst free and seek out Stella.

Cole passed off his empty glass, freeing his hands, and

continued on his methodical path through the space. The double doors—spread wide for the party—beckoned him, and he took his time as he escaped the crowd. No sense in drawing attention to himself. He stepped into the night, the soft glow of the lamps lining the asphalt path. Deep shadows lined the walkway, and he left the pavement to conceal himself within that darkness.

Hidden from view, he leaned against a tree and crossed his feet at the ankles, appearing relaxed should anyone catch sight of him lingering in the landscaping. Unlikely, but he wasn't alive today because he was unprepared.

His tiger leapt forward the moment he gave way to the beast. The animal overtook Cole's eyesight and then his sense of smell, giving him a deeper understanding of the world around him. He scented perfumes and men's cologne, the stink of liquor and the aroma of human arousal. More than one couple had sex on the brain as they passed him.

Cole would have counted himself as part of that group if he had Stella in his arms. Instead, she was—

The tiger snarled and shoved at him, demanding he do something already.

He tapped the spot behind his ear, drawing Grant's attention.

"Hold on." The words were mumbled low and garbled—not directed at Cole, but at someone else. When he had Grant's attention, the wolf spoke normally. "What's up?"

"Who the hell are you talking to?" He couldn't suppress the hint of growl in his voice, and his inner feline swiped at him. They had to focus on Stella. Nothing else mattered. "Never mind. Where's Stella right now?" He tried to push the growl down, but the animal in his soul fought him.

"One sec. Lemme look."

Now the animal wanted to roar at Cole *and* Grant. Cole for losing Stella and Grant for not paying attention to Stella's movements.

"Find her," he snapped. Because he couldn't, and if she'd been drawn away by James, there was no telling what could happen.

"Did you place the trackers like I said?"

"Yes." He had tucked the small, nearly weightless devices in Stella's clothes. One in each shoe, another in her dress, and a fourth had gone into her panties. She didn't know they were there, but he'd felt their presence was necessary. Now he was glad he'd wired her up.

"I'm tracking her. Gimme a minute."

"If she's alone with Walters, she might not have a minute." A threatening rumble gathered, which he swallowed down.

"I'm getting there," Grant growled back.

"Why the hell weren't you watching the damn screens this whole time, asshole?"

Grant didn't say a word in response. No snappy answer to his question. Just utter quiet.

"What the hell were you doing when you were supposed to—"

Grant cut him off. "Found her."

Yeah, maybe the wolf had found Stella, but if she was hurt because the asshole wasn't doing his job...

There'd be blood spattering the walls, and it wouldn't be Cole's. He wasn't gonna think about why his tiger went from loyal to his teammate to willing to tear the man to shreds over a woman. He wasn't.

"Direct me." Cole stepped out of the darkness and onto the path, tiger coiled and ready to give him strength and speed.

"Follow the path north. She's inside Building A, in the restricted area."

"Motherfucker." He snarled and took off, recalling the island's layout from memory.

While he jogged, he sought her scent, hunting for any recent hints of her presence on the walkway. While this wasn't the *only* way to get to the restricted section, it was the quickest. If they'd gone this way, he should have smelled her already. Her or James Walters.

Yet there was no evidence of either.

"She alone?" Cole veered left at the next fork in the trail.

"Lemme switch to thermal."

Cole tried not to growl—he really did—but why hadn't the asshole already brought thermal online? Seconds ticked by, the click and clack of Grant's fingers on his keyboard warring with the thump of Cole's rapid jog.

The walkway curved left, and the trees formed a canopy above him, blocking even more light. It nearly encased him in utter darkness.

"Dammit, Grant. What's going on?" He cut through the foliage to his right. He should be within twenty feet of one of the walls that separated the two sections of the island.

He raised his arms and leapt, fingers grabbing the edge of the wall. He lifted himself up and threw a leg over, swinging his weight around until gravity took over. He thumped to the ground on the other side of the barrier and dropped to a crouch.

His clothing drew taut across his back, and his slacks squeezed his thighs.

A tux wasn't the best choice when it came to running ops. Not much he could do about it now, though.

"She's got company."

"Fuck," Cole hissed. "How many?"

"One at the moment—I'm guessing Walters—but there's another incoming." More typing. "His heat and the temps around him make me think he's underground."

"You sure it's Walters with her? How do you—"

"Get a move on, Turner." It seemed like Grant had finally gotten a clue, and he'd become equally alarmed. "You've got two humans heading your way."

"God dammit."

Cole made his way to a nearby building, placing his back flat against the exterior. He remained bent low while he peered around the corner, searching for the humans.

"Stay put. I'm tracking them. Move in three...two..." Grant paused. "One. You're clear to the end of that row."

He didn't have to be told twice. He stayed quiet and stuck to the buildings, not stopping until he reached his destination. "Next?"

"Hold it," Grant murmured. "Two coming from the other direction. You're going to dive across the walkway and hide behind a tree. Ready in three...two...*go*."

Cole moved in a single fluid motion, courtesy of his inner cat. Hidden from sight, he let his tiger inch forward even more. His fingers throbbed and stung as his beast's claws emerged. His gums ached as his fangs dropped into his mouth. Skin rippled and burned, his striped fur gradually coming into view.

"Cole, what are you doing?" Wariness filled Grant's tone. Good. It should.

"Nothing."

"Your temp jumped. You either stepped into a sauna or you're shifting. Please tell me there's a self-service sauna in the middle of that clump of trees," Grant begged.

"Nope." Cole rolled his shoulders and loosened his muscles.

"What are you doing, man? You don't need to bust out the claws. She's probably fine. She—"

"She's a shifter. James Walters is one of the top men in UH, and he's suddenly dragging Stella to the restricted area? You think she's fine? You can't be that dumb."

"Fuck. Hold on." Grant's voice went muffled again—as if he was speaking to someone else—only this time Cole couldn't make out the words. "Dammit. I got confirmation: they know what she is. I signaled the team. They're fifteen minutes off the coast and will grab our top suspects. Walters, King, and Stedham will be taken into custody."

"I've got Walters and whoever the hell joins our party."

More murmuring Cole couldn't catch came from Grant. "It's King. Ethan and Birch will go after Stedham. Declan and Pike will meet up with you and lend a hand."

He snorted. "It'll be done by the time they get here."

No way was he letting Walters and King hold on to Stella for that long. No. Way.

"Cole, you should—"

"I'm going in, Grant. Get over it." He crept forward until he reached the edge of the path. Not ten feet away was a familiar door. "Can you get that door open, or am I breaking the glass?"

"Stubborn asshole. Gimme a sec." Grant fell quiet, and Cole counted the seconds as they passed.

Fuck, it was taking forever.

The red light on the keypad by the door flicked to green. "It's done, but you've got night security headed your way. Hold."

Cole vibrated, practically bouncing in place while he waited for the humans to pass.

*C'mon, c'mon, c'mon...*

They soon came into sight, two men who'd be no match

for Cole. His tiger wanted him to take them out—they worked for the enemy. But he kept the beast in check. A fight would just delay him getting to Stella.

Except the choice was taken from him. The first guy glanced at Building A like he probably did every other night. Tonight he spied that green fucking light.

"Hey, that building's unlocked."

"Huh?" The second idiot stopped at his friend's side.

"Yeah, see, it's always red, but—"

Cole didn't have time for this shit, and he sure as hell didn't want the guards calling it in.

He stepped out of the shadows. "Gentlemen," he said. "I've got a bit of a time crunch. Do me a favor and die quickly."

# CHAPTER TWENTY-TWO

*J*ames's "we've arrived" sounded creepy enough without Stella seeing what lay beyond the door.

Her kitty senses went haywire, everything inside her demanding she leave, but her promise to Cole kept her in place. His work was important—no breaking cover even if she ached to rip James apart. She was determined to be a help, not a hindrance.

For the third time, James used his keycard to open a door, after dragging Stella up a sterile white stairwell. The panel swung out into the darkness, and Stella's jaguar lunged against her control. The cat *did not* want to go in there. Period.

They emerged into what sounded like a mostly empty room, their steps echoing off the walls. She squinted into the blackness and let her cat lend its assistance, just enough for her to glimpse the area but not change her eye color. She'd cling to her humanity as long as she possibly could.

"Where are we?" She hadn't meant to sound scared and breathless, but it'd happened.

"Building A, kitten. Don't you remember it?" A soft *click* was followed by flickering lights, and the room brightened. "Oh, that's right." He glanced at her, a dark glint in his eyes. "You didn't make it past the door."

"I was confused, remember?" She smiled and shook her head, pretending she wasn't scared shitless. "I hadn't been trying to break in."

"Hmmm..." That was it. James simply hummed. "This way."

Stella yanked against his grip, keeping to her human strength instead of letting her jaguar have free rein. It'd tear away from him and then keep on tearing until he was nothing but a pile of sludge if the cat had its way.

"Seriously, James. Enough is enough."

She glanced around the area, searching for a weapon of some kind. If she could incapacitate him without using her claws, her cover could stay intact. She'd just be a woman who'd panicked and overreacted.

"Enough? It's not enough. Not nearly."

"James." Her inner animal lent her some strength. She yanked free of his grip and took a step back. "This wasn't a good idea. I'd like to go back to the party *now*."

"There's no reason to get so upset." He backed away, giving her more room to breathe, but it didn't help.

"I'd like to leave." She fisted her hands, hiding the slow, stinging emergence of her jaguar's sharp nails.

"No, I don't think so." He tilted his head to the side, smirk in place. "You wanted to be here and so you are."

He split his attention between her and a nearby bank of stainless-steel cabinets. He opened one after another until he found what he sought. When he focused on her fully, there was no missing the gleam of excitement and the bone-deep loathing in his expression.

And in his hand was a gun.

Stella swallowed hard. "What are you doing? You can't—"

"I can do anything I want." His lips twitched. "Especially when it comes to *you*."

She shook her head, brow furrowed, and took a step away from him. "Me?"

"When you appeared at my little gathering, I became suspicious of you. But, like you said, I need Cole Turner's checkbook." James flashed her that charming smile. "So I insisted you accompany your lover on this little trip."

"And I thank you for the invitation, but I think it's time—"

"Then you decided to poke your nose where it didn't belong."

"I got lost." She'd keep repeating the excuse until he bought it.

"Right. *Lost.*" His bland expression showed he doubted her. "Whatever you'd like to call it, it was enough of a reason to make a few calls." He grinned at her, the smile dark, and it felt like the cold finger of death traced her spine. "I heard back from my contact this evening. Do you know what he said?"

Stella shook her head and released a soft laugh while she pulled her mouth into a smile. "That I'm a poor paralegal who loves Christian Louboutin heels but has a Rack Room Shoes budget?"

"Not quite." James's gaze darkened, eyes nearly black and expression one of fierce longing—for violence. "I discovered you're a jaguar shifter."

She gulped and begged her heart to slow, to suppress her fear so she could make it out of this alive. Panic would only slow her down. It'd force her to freeze in place when she should run. "This is a joke, right?"

"Next you'll tell me that you have no idea what I'm talking about, right?"

"Exactly."

He sighed and shook his head. "It was easy for you to create a new identity in the human world, but not among your own kind. There were traces of your true identity. Ones that couldn't be erased from certain servers." He eased closer, the muzzle of the gun continuing to point at her. "Ella Elizabeth Carrington. Ella...*Stella*. Not very creative, but the years seem to have treated you well." His gaze scraped over her, that glare almost like a physical scouring of her skin. "What's it been...fifteen? Twenty? I'm sure if Madeline were still with us, she'd want me to pass on her love."

"I'm going to kill you," she hissed. She refused to let her fear take hold and used her past grief to fuel her anger. "I'm going to make you suffer like she suffered."

James clucked his tongue. "So cocky while I'm the one holding the gun. We'll sedate you and then bind you until you can't move. What I capture never escapes. There will be no killing...of anyone. At least, not until we're done with you."

Well, Stella would. She shrugged. "So you say."

"So *I know*. Now come on." He urged her on with a twitch of the gun. "Get into the first lab or I'll shoot you and drag you there myself."

The sound of someone's approach—hard heels on tile—came from below her. James's companion?

Then something else caught her senses—grunts and groans from outside, along with a few growls. Those were joined by the all-too-familiar crack of bones and then muffled screams.

*Cole?* She couldn't imagine anyone else on the island starting shit.

"So?" Stella shrugged. "You'll shoot me." She placed

one hand on her waist and eased her weight to the left, hip cocked. "When I shift, every bone in my body breaks and heals within seconds." She smirked. "I'm not too worried about a bullet."

"You should be." He racked the slide, chambering a round. "I have new tricks. These are coated in a drug developed especially for shifters. You won't just get a bullet. You'll get so much more."

She weighed pain and drugs against death at the hands of UH and decided pain and poisoning was the way to go.

"As lovely as that sounds..." A bellowing snarl reached her ears. There was no doubt Cole fought his own battle just outside the building. "I'm going to have to take a hard pass." She wiggled her fingers in a little wave. "Toodles."

Stella spun in place and bolted, searching for the exit as she ran through the building. The *pop* of James's gun boomed through the open space, one shot after another hurting her ears. The wall to her right exploded, a bullet tearing through the tile and drywall. She squeaked and dove left, ducking around a corner.

That didn't deter him though.

Another shot, and this time a desk drawer shattered.

She raced past a familiar door, and it swung toward her as she closed the distance—James's accomplice.

Without thought, she placed her paw on the panel and shoved, sending the door slamming shut. Whoever had approached now tumbled down the stairs. Good. She hoped they broke their neck.

A light came from her right, and she raced for the red glow—an exit sign. The closer she drew, the louder the sounds of battle became. She recognized a familiar voice, a string of curses that could come only from Cole.

A wheeze of relief escaped her. She didn't want to admit

how safe that tiger made her feel. She was being shot at by a homicidal shifter extremist and yet felt *safe* because Cole was near. Cole who fought his own battle to get to her. Violence surrounded them both, and she prayed they'd get out of this alive.

Stella increased her speed as she approached the exit, her cat digging deep and giving her an extra *oomph*. She hit the door with an echoing *thud*, and it blew outward to slam against the exterior wall.

She slid to a stop on the sidewalk and swept the area with her gaze, taking it all in.

Yup, there was a fight. One between Cole and a half dozen guards. Another *pop* came from behind her.

So, they had to face off with a half dozen guards *and* James the Gun-Toting Asshole.

Stella leapt into the fray to help Cole while also making it difficult for James to get a clear shot. Her first opponent went down easy. A kick to his knee and a punch to the temple knocked him out. Cole focused on a target of his own, though he went the deadly route—snapping a neck.

One of the men realized Cole had help and focused on her, an extendable police baton in one hand and a Taser in the other. The human lifted his arm, poised to strike her with the pole, but she reached up and caught it with ease. She halted his attack with her left hand and throat-punched him with her right, then followed that with a quick flick of her claws to rip out his throat. She turned her head and shuddered. It was kill or be killed, but that didn't mean she wanted to watch.

Stella hunted for another human and spied a group surrounding Cole. Three men were left, each focused on attacking the tiger shifter who'd been so good to her.

"Cole!" She ran to him, golden fur emerging from her pores as her beast took over. But she shoulda kept her mouth shut. That one yell was enough to draw his attention from the life-or-death battle, which ended with him... stabbed.

*"Cole."*

# CHAPTER TWENTY-THREE

*C*ole hissed as the sharp blade sank deep into his exposed side. Fuck, knife wounds hurt. The punch that followed wasn't quite as bad, but the kick after *that* made him wheeze.

All because one gorgeous woman had called his name. He'd paddle her ass later for distracting him. As long as they lived through this.

"Grant," he snarled, blocking an attacker's punch and returning it with two of his own. *Jab. Cross.* "What the fuck?"

His words came out a grumbled mess of syllables—his tiger's fangs crowding his human-shaped mouth—but the wolf got the point.

"Five minutes out. They're going to Rendezvous Point C, but you gotta get moving."

Asshole. He talked like Cole stood around getting beat to shit for fun.

One of his opponents spied Stella, and the man spun in place, knife in a white-knuckled grip and tensed to attack.

"Not happening," he growled, snatching the human's shirt.

Stella raced forward, skidding to a stop just out of reach. Before Cole could say a word, bullets sprayed the ground at her feet. He'd find the shooter as soon as he took care of this guy.

Cole grabbed the lapels of the nearest man's jacket and shoved him into his friend. Both men tumbled to the ground—down but not out. That small break was long enough for him to reach Stella. He snared her wrist and hauled her close, then shoved her behind him while the humans recovered. "Stay out of the way."

"You're bleeding!"

Cole grunted. He didn't think he had to reply. The red blood staining his white button-down shirt was pretty fucking obvious.

"You're bleeding?" Grant's rapid typing followed his question. "I've ordered a med team to meet you."

"I'm fine." He thrust the words past gritted teeth.

He wasn't fine. His side burned as if acid had been dumped into the wound. It scorched him through to his bones, and he wondered how far he'd ripped the cut open.

"We need to get out of here." Stella tugged on his arm. "Walters knows what I am."

Cole ducked the guard's next punch and followed it with two uppercuts to the human's torso. Then he straightened and threw a hook that connected with the man's jaw. His attacker's head snapped and down he went, out like a light.

That left him with one.

He ducked a punch and grabbed the human's hand, twisting his arm behind him and holding tight. The man in his grasp screamed, and Cole twisted just a little harder. He hadn't broken the man's arm. Yet.

"Team is close. Move your ass, agent," Grant growled.

Cole was gonna get him for that "agent" remark later. The only one who called them "agents" was Birch, and that was only if they'd fucked up royally.

Cole still had this under control.

Well, maybe not. James Walters burst from the building, gun in hand. Cole quickly spun and used the guard's body as a shield. *One, two, three*...James Walters shot and killed the man in his arms, stepping closer with each bullet.

All right, new plan.

The moment Walters was close enough, Cole shoved the dead body at the Unified Humanity leader. He struggled beneath the deadweight while Cole grabbed Stella's hand and dove into the thick foliage that lined the walkway. He dashed through the trees, running to get deeper within the camouflaging greenery. He couldn't let the humans get him and Stella now.

Walters shot randomly into the darkness, tree trunks exploding to their left and right. No bullets struck them, but they were way too fucking close.

Cole jerked on Stella's arm and shoved her in front of him, forcing her to run ahead so he could shield her with his bulk. He refused to let her be hurt—not if he could help it.

More shots whizzed past...

He grunted with the impact, a bullet slamming into his back near the stab wound. A new edge of pain joined the acidic burning. This one had a sharpness that felt like broken glass flowing through his body.

Cole managed to remain on his feet, continuing to urge Stella on while he struggled for breath. The bullet had to have clipped a lung. He tried to inhale and coughed, and the familiar taste of his own blood coated his tongue.

Normally, he could sustain a lot of damage and his tiger would help him heal almost as quickly as he was injured. Except these wounds weren't normal. A poisoned blade, poisoned bullets...

"Fuck, it hurts," he rasped.

"Keep your ass moving, Cole," the wolf growled in his ear.

"Stabbed and shot, asshole." Snarling at Grant kept his mind off his injuries. "Poisoned." A rough rasp. "Gimme a distraction."

Something to get the UH assholes looking elsewhere.

"Light it up."

Cole stared at the sky, ears attuned to what was to come. It didn't take long for Grant to set everything off in a blaze of fire. *Boom. Boom. Boom…*

The explosions surrounded the island, Cole's little presents scattered around Serene Isle. He waited for the yacht to go. It'd be the largest explosion of them all, and then… The ground shook with the bomb's intensity.

*Ka-mother-fucking-boom.*

But he didn't get a chance to enjoy his handiwork. The feel of that sharpened glass imbedded in his flesh stole more of his strength. A bone-deep numbness crept through him, and he stumbled, grasping a tree trunk to keep from falling to his knees. He grunted with the bright flourish of pain when he hit the ground and winced at Stella's shout. He would do anything to protect her from harm.

"Cole?" Her panicked whisper seemed muffled. *"Cole!"* Stella dropped to her knees at his side. "What's going on?" She shook him. "You can't die on me, Cole."

Cole snorted. She didn't have control over life and death.

"Agent, get your ass up and moving." That rumble didn't belong to Grant but to Birch. The wolf must have patched their team into the com. His voice pulsed with dominance and aggression. It demanded he obey, and Cole was too hurt to give a damn.

"Fuck. Off." He wheezed out a chuckle.

"No, you fuck off," Stella snarled, and the stinging scent of her anger overrode the tang of his own blood.

He coughed, hacking up more blood, and he couldn't stop to tell her his words were meant for Birch.

Grant tried to give him another order. "Get off your ass—"

Stella used her body as leverage to haul him upright. "Tell me the damn exit point or I'll kill you myself."

# CHAPTER TWENTY-FOUR

Stella wouldn't kill him. Not really. At least not yet. Maybe after he was healed. Then it was *on*, and nothing would stop her.

Her blood surged with power and a soul-deep need to keep Cole safe. That rush of adrenaline gave her the strength to duck beneath his biceps and lift him. She grunted and growled, slipping beneath his weight for a moment before she got a good hold on him. The tiger had to have at least a hundred pounds on her. The ass was going on a diet after he recovered.

"C'mon, Cole. Help me out here." She wrapped her arm around his waist and gripped his wrist with the other. "I'm gonna get your ass to your team or die trying."

"No." The sound was so low it was nearly lost in the human shouts.

"You don't get a choice in the matter." Stella held tight and took a step, thankful her jaguar was able to help her. If she hadn't had an inner cat...

"Tell me which way to go." They neared another walkway, the human's yells growing louder with each step. She fought to block out the bellows and gunshots—the sounds of being hunted—so she could hear Cole.

"North."

*North.* Okay, she could go north. If she knew the direction. "Your options are left, right, or straight."

Cole grunted. "Straight."

She spied the path and paused, glancing left and right while listening for any guards. "Can Grant tell us if anyone is coming?"

Because that'd be super helpful.

"Go."

Hopefully that order came from the wolf. She hauled Cole across the asphalt and deep into the opposite side. Not two seconds after they hit the trees, the heavy *thud* of at least ten guards raced past them.

"High five to Grant," she whispered, and moved on.

Stella stumbled over roots and fallen branches, choosing the clearest path, but even that was littered with obstacles. Her toes hit a rock, and she lost her balance, tripping forward. She scrambled to remain upright. Cole's weight shifted, and she gritted her teeth while she battled to hold on to him.

"Have I mentioned that you need to go on a diet?" Sweat peppered her brow, body heating up the harder she worked. "Seriously. Twenty pounds, maybe thirty. Anything would help."

Cole laughed, but it quickly changed to a coughing wheeze.

"Don't laugh at me, asshole." She skirted a large tree stump. "You may be sexy, but I'm serious. Lose fifty pounds if this is going to become a habit."

That was when the wheeze turned into a wet rattle and the scent of his blood grew stronger in her nose. The clouds parted and allowed moonlight to cast a soft glow across their path. Just enough for her to glance at Cole and watch as blood bubbled from his lips.

So not good.

She dragged him another few feet, pausing beside a thick tree trunk, and let his weight gradually slide from her. She lowered him until he sat on the leaves, back resting against the palm tree.

She shook his shoulder. "Cole? Hey, sexy, I need you to shift. Hot stuff, I'm totally down with days of bedroom-boom-boom if you'll just grow some fur, okay?"

Cole's mouth formed one word. *"No."*

She grasped his chin and forced his head up. "Wrong answer. You shift, or we're gonna get snatched up by UH. Personally, that doesn't seem like a good time, but maybe you're into that. Who knows?"

His lips twitched at her comment. So at least his conscious mind was in there despite the pain. Not that it helped if he wasn't going to do as she asked.

"Maybe you didn't know, but..." The heavy tromp of boots warned her that other UH guards were still hunting them. "But the girl is always right in a relationship, and the guy is always wrong. It's a thing."

Stella's cat snarled and growled at her, scraping her from just beneath her skin. The cat's claws pushed against her human confines, forcing red lines to appear along her forearms. The cat wanted *out*. The cat was determined to do what Stella couldn't.

Force Cole's shift.

She mentally shook her head. Cole was so much stronger than her. So proud and fierce. There was no way a jaguar could overpower a tiger. No. Fucking. Way.

The cat huffed, its own version of a laugh, followed by a screeching snarl. No, her jaguar couldn't overpower a tiger in the jungle. But an injured tiger who couldn't carry its own weight? He couldn't help but obey her.

Was this something she wanted to do, though? When he realized what she'd done to him she'd lose his trust.

But he'd still be alive. She hoped.

The stomping steps seemed to draw closer—her time nearly at an end.

Stella leaned forward and spoke against Cole's right ear. "Grant, I hope you're listening and can hear me. I'm going to force his shift." She suppressed the sob tearing its way up her throat. "Otherwise we'll die."

Unified Humanity would see to it.

She released Cole's head and took one shuffling step back. She breathed deep, seeking her center, before she popped the mental lock on her cat's cage. The animal crouched behind its mental bars, claws deep in the ground and muscles taut. It waited to pounce—to burst through Stella's skin. She wrapped her fingers around the lock. She took one more deep breath and held it, steeling herself for what was to come. Then she tore the steel from the latch and allowed the door to swing wide.

The jaguar didn't hesitate to rip Stella to shreds. Her bones snapped and re-formed, her muscles stretched, and her skin burned. Her dress shredded with her changing shape. Couture was replaced by fur. Manicured fingernails were now deadly claws. Milky pale skin now sported deep yellow with black rosettes.

The agony... It stole her breath, set her nerves aflame, and then wrenched a pained yowl from her feline maw. The cat voiced its displeasure.

At being suppressed.

At being attacked.

At its mate's injuries.

She'd examine that last thought later. For now she had a male to manage.

The jaguar crouched in front of the damaged shifter, eyes missing nothing, nose gathering every hint of his scent. Her ears captured sounds she hated. Not the Unified Humanity guards or James Walters. No, it was the deep rattle in Cole. She saw the blood. She scented the poison. She heard his lungs attempting to keep him alive yet failing.

Stella's beast reached out for him, paw to his head, and forced him to look at her. She snarled and snapped her teeth close to his face, threatening the big cat. Next a rumbling growl escaped her chest, giving the tiger another warning. She whacked his head with her right paw and then her left, claws sheathed. For now.

Then one paw went to his chest, large paw flush against his pectoral, and she flexed her toes. Claws appeared for a split second and then sank into Cole's flesh. She released a long, low hiss at the same time, daring the beast inside Cole to stop her.

Tiger eyes flashed to hers, pure amber with wide, dark irises. A sprinkling of orange fur rippled across his cheeks. He gripped her cat's ankle with one large hand and exposed a single fang. His hold tightened, and instead of releasing him, she dug her nails deeper.

*Come on, big kitty. Stop me.*

Cole hissed at her in return, the threatening sound turning into a roar when Stella grasped his calf with another paw. She didn't claw him as deep on his leg, just enough to draw blood and add to his pain.

Sure, hurting him when he was already hurt seemed counterintuitive, but her actions gave him a target. A target a human couldn't defeat with bare hands, but a tiger…A tiger could destroy her.

Easily.

Cole's other hand went to the paw attacking his leg, that grip punishing as well.

"Let me go, Stella." The low growl rumbled through the air. Her cat's first instinct was to obey the stronger predator, but she let his order wash over her and off her back as if it were a suggestion.

She leaned forward, giving her front paws more of her wait. The feline version of "make me."

The orange fur peppering his face spread, gliding over his cheeks and down his neck to disappear beneath the fabric of his dress shirt. She imagined it slithering over his arms, and it finally appeared to cover his fingers.

But that's where the shift stopped.

*Not enough.*

With Cole's gaze locked on to hers, she gave no hint of her next action. She stared at him, cat's eyes holding him captive until she...

She darted forward, ducked beneath his chin, and wrapped her wide jaws around his neck. She growled low, the rumble transferring from her to him. Her fangs dug into his throat just shy of piercing his skin, but it wouldn't take much. She had him—the jaguar victorious over the tiger. Unless the tiger got off his ass.

Holding him in place as she was, her body connected with his, she caught the first hints of his shift. It started with the crack of one bone and the snap of the next. The rip and rending of muscle and tendons while he fought through the pain and threat of death.

She knew it hurt—injuries and poison making the experience a hundred times worse—but at least he'd be alive. His tiger would heal the worst of it.

Stella withdrew her claws and lifted her maw from him, stepping back just enough to give him room to shift.

Then she watched his transition while listening for the humans.

Bloodstained skin became blood-soaked fur. The black and white of his tux ripped and tore at his joints, buttons flying while his transformation destroyed the cloth. He shook and yanked on the jacket, pants, and shirt while he kicked his shoes aside. The tattered remnants of his tux clung to his orange-and-black-striped body.

But at least he was *in* his orange-and-black-striped body.

Cole soon stood on four legs and swung his head toward her, opened his mouth, and hissed at her. If Stella had more sense, she would have been scared. But compared to the mass of UH members hunting them, Cole's tiger was as threatening as a housecat.

Stella snapped her teeth at Cole and hissed in return, then jerked her head in the direction they'd been traveling. She propped him up with her own body, letting him lean his eight-hundred-pound bulk on her hundred-seventy-pound frame. Then wished she could talk to him telepathically. She'd remind him about his diet.

They got moving, their steps slow but steady now. Blood no longer dripped in their wake, but that didn't mean Cole was healed. Moving as fast as they could, they shuffled another two dozen feet until the shelter of trees disappeared. Now they stood in front of the eight-foot-high-wall—a hella-high barrier between them and freedom. She gulped and stared at the top, praying that her jaguar still had enough juice to help her out.

Cole was big. She was small. That wall was high as a motherfucker, and she was not.

The Unified Humanity guys trailing them in the woods seemed to be closing in, and she had to figure out how to get them over this blockade. Then the echoes of pursuit were overwhelmed by a wave of bullets. Someone was shooting from the other side of that wall, the *pop, pop, pop* of guns followed by shouts of agony and fear.

Then...*PraiseJesushallelujahamen*...She heard roars.

Two wolf howls, different yet similar. She doubted Grant would abandon his post handling tech, which meant Pike and Declan were on the way. Scratches and scrapes came from the other side of the wall. The rustling of trees and snapping of branches joined the sounds. After that came a familiar voice from above.

"Someone call for an Uber?" The male's words were garbled, and when she looked up, she saw why—his face was half shifted into a wolf. Declan hopped over the wall as if it didn't exist, and he landed in a crouch at their side. "Damn." The werewolf inspected Cole with a sweeping glance and looked to her. "Can you partially shift and help me get him up and over? Then follow?"

Stella nodded, an odd movement for a cat, and prodded her beast. The jaguar needed to step aside so she could become the horror-film version of a shifter, a perverted mix of beast and woman. She shoved the transition through her body as quickly as she could, some of her fur receding while paws turned into fierce claw-tipped hands. Her snout receded, but fangs remained. Fur shortened but refused to leave entirely.

Now balanced on two legs, she reached for Cole, grasping him carefully. "Be careful. He's been stabbed and shot. The knife was dipped in poison. I made him shift, but..."

Maybe she'd waited too long.

"Pass him up." Another male voice, and she looked up to see Pike peering over the edge.

With her help, the two men maneuvered Cole's nearly

dead weight with ease, getting him up and over the wall in no time.

Then Declan focused on her. "Let's go, kitty. Not leaving your ass behind."

He didn't give her a chance to reply. He simply grabbed her half-shifted ass around the waist and tossed her as if she weighed nothing. She settled on the top of the wall with a grunt, then swung her leg over and hopped down. She landed in a crouch beside Pike and Cole.

Declan soon followed and paused at her side, speaking low. "Grant said we're clear straight to the rendezvous. He'll meet us there."

"Is there a medic for Cole?" Neither side of her could stand seeing the badass tiger hurting.

"Yeah. Got agents waiting." Declan nodded. "Teams Three and Seven are backing us up. Let's move."

She usually wasn't one to listen to orders, but she'd do whatever it took to remain at Cole's side. She wasn't going to examine why the need to stick with him was so strong that the idea of leaving him nearly tore her in two.

Exhaustion pulled at her, the unfamiliar half shift draining both halves of her. As soon as she had clothes, she'd push the cat back and reclaim her human skin. Because she sure as hell wasn't running naked through the forest.

Declan and Pike fisted Cole's fur, propping the large cat up between them. Cole's feet dragged, but he continued to move, his shuffling steps a harsh contrast to the strong male she knew.

The sounds of fighting surrounded them, but the battles were far off, away from their group, just as Declan had promised. Which meant it didn't take long to reach the crowded beach. Men—shifters—in black formed a protective line across the sand, guns in hand and fangs on display.

They were ready to shoot or fight their way across the private island.

They shuffled past the row of barely restrained violence and headed toward the beach. A man came out of the shadows, jogging their way, his stride loose. The glow of the moon illuminated him, revealing that Birch drew nearer.

The moment he was within shouting distance, he issued orders. "You three"—he pointed at Pike, Declan, and Cole—"are in the CRRC with Ethan. I got a medic from Seven with you. Push off as soon as you're loaded."

Stella took a step forward to follow, cat unwilling to let Cole out of her sight. But a touch on her arm had her swinging her attention back to Birch. "You need to either go human or go cat, Stella."

She tilted her head, eyebrows furrowed. She didn't understand what he was talking about until he gestured at her body. Right. She was still half shifted after helping Cole. "Do you have something I can wrap around...?"

Birch reached back and whipped his T-shirt off, handing it over. "Just make sure you shower before you visit Cole. That tiger can be a possessive sonofabitch."

She tugged on the thin black shirt, fighting to ignore Birch's smoky scent. Her cat hissed its objection, hating that they now smelled like the grizzly bear shifter. Well, it was better than strutting around butt-ass naked in front of a bunch of total strangers. The jaguar hissed once again, hating that Stella actually made sense, and then retreated. Fur receded fully, claws slipped back into her flesh, and teeth were blunted once more. Her face returned to its heart shape, no hint of feline jaws in sight. Back in her human skin, she rolled her shoulders and cracked her neck, shrugging and stretching as hairless flesh settled into place.

"Good," Birch grunted. "Let's go. You're with me and

Grant. He's tying down his equipment, and then our CRRC will be ready to move out." He turned away from her and strode across the sand, not even glancing back to see if she followed. Hell yeah she was following. She wanted to watch out for Cole *and* get the hell off the island filled with crazies.

"CRRC?" she called out to the SHOC team alpha.

"Combat Rubber Raiding Craft," he yelled back, but didn't glance her way. Just kept walking toward a small boat.

Birch jogged a handful of steps and joined Grant in shoving a black boat into the water. One that held Cole. Stella kept her eyes trained on the boat as it disappeared into the night, the lack of running lights making it difficult to see.

Birch looked to Grant. "We're taking her on ours. Move your ass."

Once more the grizzly left, now leaving her in Grant's capable-ish hands. She had her doubts after hearing some of Cole's stories. He was a jokester, lighthearted, the funny guy. Would he take this situation seriously?

"This way, Stella." Grant held out his hand, palm-up, waiting for her. "The quicker we load, the quicker we get to Cole."

All hesitation fled, and she placed her hand in his, using his hold to steady herself on the uneven ground. They tromped through the sand, soft granules giving way to damp, compact ground. The wet sand sent a chill racing through her, and the wind whipped and tore at her shirt, threatening to fly high and expose her.

Grant paused beside a black boat much like the one Cole had been in. "In you go. Hold on to me. Don't fall."

The moment a person tells another *not* to fall, they want

to fall. The only thing that saved her was Grant's sure grip. Well, he saved her from getting hurt, but not from flashing everyone behind her.

"Lovely view. Is this Cole's weekend entertainment? Is there a reason she's here?" The sickly masculine voice rolled through her, and Stella shuddered. If mildew and rot had combined, their voice would sound *exactly* like that man's.

She tugged her shirt down to cover her pink bits and turned around once she had her balance. When she did, she discovered two things: a black-haired, dark-eyed stranger dressed much like Birch stood nearby, and that stranger's hand was wrapped around the arm of a restrained James Walters.

# CHAPTER TWENTY-FIVE

$S$tella didn't think Grant would let her tear James to shreds, but that didn't stop the craving for blood. He stood not ten feet from her, his roughed-up body bleeding, while bruises coated his skin in swaths of purple and blue. The stranger holding him captive didn't matter to her—just another SHOC agent—but James was a prize.

"Hartley," Grant murmured, climbing into the boat and moving until he'd positioned himself between Stella and the other guy. "What do you want?"

"Transport to the primary com center. Warn them I've got Walters and I need a room. The director wants me to begin interrogations as soon as we board." Hartley seemed *way* too excited about the prospect of interrogating someone.

"Sure." Grant reached back, and Stella grabbed his hand, allowing him to lead her to a different seat. He dropped his voice when he next spoke. "That's the team alpha for Three. He's a twisted sonofabitch and the director's brother. Sit here. Don't look at him. Don't say a word."

She risked a glance at Grant, and what she saw there made her breath catch. His words hadn't been a request, but an order. A flat-out life-and-death order. There was so

much meaning in his gaze, a warning and a plea in one.
And Stella would listen to him. She'd glanced at Hartley
only once, hardly meeting his eyes, but that'd been enough.
Enough for her to never want to repeat the process. Something dark lurked inside him, something feral and wicked.

Evil.

But maybe that was because he was part of SHOC? Cole
had told her that the men of Shifter Operations Command
did bad things for all the right reasons. All that darkness had
to weigh on a soul. Even if what they were doing was hon-
orable, it still had to tear at their psyche, right?

The boat rocked as Hartley stepped aboard, James tripping after him. The human caught himself on his bound
hands, but only just. His face still struck one of the bench
seats, a new bruise forming with the others.

Hartley hissed and yanked on James, pulling until the
human sat upright beside him. That hiss…She couldn't
smell the other agent, but instinct told her he was a snake
shifter.

She flicked her attention to Hartley's face for a split second, cataloging his features once again. Yeah, danger clung
to him, covering him in an invisible blanket of darkness.

James swayed in his seat, wavering back and forth, as
though he was woozy and unable to sit upright by himself.

"Hartley." Birch snapped out the agent's name as he
emerged from the night.

"Birch." The director's oily lips pulled back to form
a wide smile. Somehow it managed to look more like
a threat than an expression of happiness. "It seems"—
Hartley released James, and the human slumped forward,
a string of drool escaping his lips—"I managed to do what
you could not." He gestured at the human. "I have James
Walters secured. You have an injured agent and wasted

SHOC resources. My team had to come in here and save your asses."

Birch clenched his jaw and fisted his hands, knuckles turning white. That was one pissed-off grizzly.

"Save us? Or are you here to make sure we failed, Hartley?" Grant's voice was smooth, with no hint of accusation, though his words told a different story.

Hartley's stare slithered over her to land on the were-wolf. "You got something to say, Grant?"

Birch stepped forward. "Maybe your big brother didn't share this with you, but our mission objectives stretched beyond the apprehension of James Walters." Birch's eyes went full black, no hint of white surrounding his irises.

Stella watched Hartley out of the corner of her eye, tracing the path of his blood as he flushed red. Anger was carved into his face, and his grip tightened on James.

Before the snake shifter could say anything, Birch leaned to the side to speak to Grant. "Get us moving."

With those three words, Birch bent and placed his hands on the bow. He shoved and roared at the same time, voicing his anger while he got them fully in the water. He soon leapt over the side and joined Stella, Grant, Hartley, and James Walters.

The engine rumbled and transformed into a roar, Grant sending them bouncing over the waves and farther from the shore. The echo of gunshots and screams chased them, the fight still ongoing back on Serene Isle. Though it wasn't so serene any longer, was it?

Worry churned in her gut, the constant ache and edge of panic about Cole that just wouldn't be brushed aside. But they were headed to him. They followed Ethan's path and soon she'd be with Cole. She could hold his hand and *know* that he was still breathing. She refused to examine why that seemed so important to her and her cat.

She split her attention between the human she hated more than anything and the sea beyond their boat. Though with James so close, he stole a little more of her focus.

Another string of drool dripped to soak his pants, and she noticed that his lips were moving as if he spoke. Too bad the boat was too loud for her to hear him. She hoped he was begging for his life or admitting all of his sins. Or maybe praying.

She stared at Walters, eyes focused while she sought to read his lips.

"...he...no warning."

"...relationship not working..."

"...good money...heads up."

"...call bullshit."

The wind buffeted them, the boat jerking sideways for a moment before Grant straightened them out once more. She snatched a safety handle and used it to regain her seat, but when she tried to read James's lips once more she found him slumped over, face hidden. She darted a look at Hartley and met his dark stare. Goose bumps rose on her arms, and more than a hint of fear filled her veins. This shifter—this snake—scared the hell out of her. Scared the hell out of both *halves* of her—human and jaguar alike.

Lights in the distance caught her attention, an expanse of glowing dots along the profile of a yacht. They drew closer with each passing second, the boat's engine straining to push them onward toward the finish line. Cole had to have arrived by then. He was probably already undergoing treatment.

It wasn't much longer before they bumped up against the yacht. Two agents on the launch grabbed the bow and slid them beneath the yacht itself to hide them from view.

Birch grabbed Walters, hauling him from the small boat before Hartley even moved a muscle. Then the director's brother disembarked, straightening his T-shirt and brushing lint off of his camouflage pants once his boots were on the stable surface. While everyone else who'd been on the island was covered in sweat, sand, and dirt, Hartley didn't have a hair out of place.

How had he managed to do that while capturing Walters?

Hartley turned to face Stella and extended his hand as if to help her. She'd rather do anything *but* touch the snake. Thankfully Grant saved her.

"Aw, thanks so much for helping me, Hartley. 'Ppreciate it." Grant grunted as he hefted a case and presented it to the other man, handle first. "These are my babies. Be careful with them." He kissed the sandy case. "Be good, children."

Stella bit her lip and closed her eyes, fighting the urge to laugh. It was just…Hartley looked at Grant as if he were a bug. No, even lower than a bug—slime. And Grant had a goofy yet totally serious expression on his face.

Hartley dropped his hand and spun in place, stomping across the launch area and following Birch, who was still dragging Walters along. When the snake reached Birch, there was a low hiss and a tug-of-war that Hartley eventually won, pulling James up the nearby steps while Birch followed in his wake.

And Stella…

"C'mon, kitty. Let's find a place to put you." Grant jumped onto the dock, and she used his extended hand to balance herself as she joined him. "There's gotta be an empty bedroom somewhere." The wolf smirked at her and waggled his eyebrows. "Unless you want to stay with me."

"Um…"

Grant sighed and shook his head. "You don't know what you're missing. I could show you the moon! The stars! The kitchen!"

That brought a smile to her lips, and she couldn't suppress her laughter. "You're a dork."

"I'm also hungry." He rubbed his flat stomach, the cotton leaving nothing to the imagination. Like the others, Grant was all heavily carved muscle.

*But not as sexy as Cole.*

They tromped up a set of narrow, steep steps, traveling through a maze of hallways and past numerous SHOC agents. It was controlled chaos, the men and women of SHOC working together for a common goal—the safety of shifters.

Grant strode up to a metal desk, legs bolted to the deck, and knocked on the hard surface. "Yo, Meowses. Need a room."

The man at the desk slowly lifted his head, amber eyes narrowed at Grant with the promise of pain. "It's Moses." The *asshole* was implied. Then she was the focus of that intent gaze. "You can do better than him. Hell, I'm gay and we could have a platonic marriage and that relationship would *still* be better than hooking up with him."

"Obviously he's a delicate flower," Grant murmured not so quietly and then spoke to Moses again. "We're not rooming together. She belongs to Cole. I'm just taking care of her until he gets off his ass." He snorted. "I swear, you'd think he got shot or something."

Then Grant winked, flashing her a small grin while they both suffered beneath Moses's glare.

Finally, Moses dug in a drawer and tossed a key at Grant. "Room fourteen. Not far from the med bay."

Grant didn't even say thanks to the agent. He just took off down the hallway. Stella paused long enough to toss out a murmured "thanks" before rushing to catch up. They were back to the unending maze, dodging people while hunting for her room.

And then they'd arrived, a gold plaque with the number "fourteen" etched onto its surface. Grant quickly unlocked the door and pushed it open, glancing around the space before stepping back to let her in.

"There should be some clothes in the dresser. Probably big on you, but at least it'll be better than Birch's shirt. Shower, dress, and while you do that I'll check on Cole. See if there's any news on that front."

She nodded, overjoyed that he was going to do what she couldn't—demand answers. Stella was a nobody as far as most of these agents were concerned. She mattered to only one person—Cole. Though even that wasn't guaranteed. There were so many emotions tied up in the weekend that it was hard to figure out which were real and which were fake.

"Thanks, Grant." She laid her hand on his forearm and gave it a gentle squeeze. "I really appreciate what you did for him—us—this weekend. Thank you for taking care of me when it went sideways."

Grant shrugged. "Part of the job."

Her lips twitched, and she gently shook her head. "It wasn't. Which is why I appreciate your help even more."

"Well—"

A siren screeched through the air, lights flashed, and an unknown voice came over the speakers. "Code Oscar. Time check engineering. Code Oscar. Time check engineering."

*"Fuck."* Grant cursed and pushed her into the room.

"Grant? What's going on?"

"There's a bomb in the engine room, and someone has gone overboard."

Stella froze in place, staring at the werewolf. Then she was staring at a closed door. One that let out an audible *snick* a moment later.

Someone was overboard. There was a bomb on the yacht. And Stella was locked in her room.

# CHAPTER TWENTY-SIX

## GRANT

*G*rant stared at the small screen, the monitor showing Stella still sitting at Cole's bedside. The high-definition camera and sensitive microphones picked up everything in that room—Cole's every breath and Stella's every sniffle.

She'd stayed strong through the evac from Serene Isle to the SHOC yacht. He hadn't liked how Hartley had looked at her, but then other shit had taken precedence. She'd been only a little rattled when Grant had locked her in her stateroom. Of course, when he'd let her out, that'd been a different story.

No one knew how—the investigation was still underway—but James Walters had managed to plant a bomb in engineering and then launch himself over the side. He mentally snorted. Right. *Of course.* The guy who was half-concious, drooling, and barely able to speak was able to put together an explosive device and then jump into the sea and disappear.

He shook his head...*Fucking Hartley.*

When Grant had told Stella, it'd taken every ounce of smooth talking to keep her aboard the yacht. She'd wanted to chase after him. Even if that meant doing something stupid like shifting and diving into the sea to swim after the human. He'd redirected her intense concentration to Cole, her worry for the tiger pushing aside her need for vengeance.

He'd managed to keep her focused on transporting Cole to Birch's vacation cabin at the lake. The team usually used the space to unwind, but it was also a secret place for a team member to rest and recover. Quiet. Solitary. Disconnected from the public.

Grant sighed and ran a hand down his face, rubbing his palm against the whiskers that covered his cheeks. It'd been a rough twenty-four hours, and it didn't seem like the pressure would let up anytime soon. Not until Cole woke. Not until they had James Walters back in their grasp once more.

Movement on the monitor tugged at his attention again—Stella rising to reach over Cole, brush a few strands of hair off his forehead. Then she leaned down, her head near his, and he figured she was doing one of those sweet girlfriend things. A kiss on the forehead or a sweet nuzzle. She retreated and lowered herself to her chair, her fingers clutching his while her unwavering attention remained on Cole's face. They might have played house during the weekend, but at some point it'd turned into more.

Kinda like him and Lottie. A chance meeting. A meal. A kiss beneath the moonlight and...And not worth thinking about. They couldn't have a relationship. He'd never have her sitting at his bedside. He'd never wake to her smile. He'd never taste her lips.

At least Cole would get some of that...As long as he wasn't stupid enough to let Stella slip through his paws.

Grant's wolf told him that *he* was stupid for letting Lottie get away. He'd tried to explain the situation to the animal—about Lottie being a human and her father...

It'd snapped and snarled at him, refusing to listen. It saw Lottie, loved the way she smelled, and wanted her. Full stop.

He took a deep breath and let it out slowly. Grant could commiserate with the wolf, but that didn't mean he'd do anything about his driving need for Lottie. Anything other than fanatically stare at his cell phone, that is. Lottie had his number and had promised to text. Not just about "official" business, either.

They'd already had their first exchange. Two words in total.

Him: *Safe?*

Her: *Yes.*

Now he stared at his cell phone, wishing she'd text him again. Something. Anything. No sooner had the thought crossed his mind than his phone emitted a familiar tone, the default *ping* announcing a new text message.

Grant sprang forward and snatched his phone from the desk, quickly unlocking the device and tapping the text notification. Movement in his periphery drew his attention, and his eyes found Stella once again. She bolted to her feet and darted out of sight, the rapid patter of her feet on wood soon following. In less than ten seconds she slid to a stop in the doorway, hands clutching the doorframe to keep her from falling.

"Who is it? Is it news? Have they found him?" She fired off question after question, hardly breathing between each one.

He didn't say a word. Just held up a finger and returned his attention to his phone. There, in black-and-white, was the proof that the weekend had been more than a fling to Lottie. It wasn't an update on her location or a report on UH happenings after the op last night.

*I already miss our cliff.*

His fingers were poised to reply, but he had to deal with Stella before he could send his message. He didn't need the she-cat getting all up in his business. The situation was fucked enough. He didn't need a crazy jaguar making it worse.

"Grant?" She stepped into the office, bare feet hardly making a sound as she moved closer to him. "Is it done?"

He sighed and locked his phone, not wanting her to see the sender's name. He'd listed Charlotte King as "Lottie" in his contact list, but he didn't want to take the chance.

"No." He shook his head and placed his phone facedown on his thigh. "Nothing yet."

"But…"

Another *ding* and he internally winced. Excitement thrummed in his veins, but instead of the cause being the prospect of finding Walters, he was thrilled that it might be a text from Lottie.

She took another step closer. "Is that them? What did they say?"

"Nosy much?" He quirked a single brow.

Stella didn't say a word at first. Then again, she didn't have to. Her face paled, no hint of a pink flush in her cheeks. Her eyes widened, whites fully visible, and her mouth dropped open. The worst were her tears.

Fuck. He never had dealt with emotional women well. They should have sent Pike to babysit Cole and Stella. He was younger—a charmer. Instead she'd gotten Grant.

A guy who couldn't stop thinking about another woman.

"Sorry." He rubbed his cheek and pinched the bridge of

his nose, releasing a sigh. "I'm really sorry. I'm…" He dropped his hand and shook his head. "You're a civilian, and you're dealing with Cole being injured. I know me being an ass isn't making it better."

She sniffled and squeezed her eyes shut, running the back of her hand across her face. "It's fine." She coughed and cleared her throat before looking at him again. "I'm fine. I just…"

"Want Walters to be found. Want Cole to be okay. We want the same things, Stella. I'm being a dick." Though he was sure his teammates would have used stronger language. "Cole will be just fine. That tiger has lived through worse." He scoffed. "A stab and a couple bullets are nothing. As for the other…"

Grant twirled his phone in his hands, the text message notification filling the screen. Lottie's name was there, bright and bold. He sensed Stella's unease, her fear, and her bone-deep need for vengeance. He'd been listening through Cole's com all weekend, so he'd heard Stella explain why Walters deserved her wrath. Grant agreed with the jaguar.

"We have an inside track on the location for the UH higher-ups." And that was all he'd say about that.

"Inside track? If you have that, why don't you have them in custody?" She crossed her arms beneath her breasts, pushing them up and together. If his mind weren't obsessed with Lottie, he'd appreciate the cleavage Stella sported.

"Sometimes things are hit or miss." Or they don't get a location update and simply receive a sweet note.

"Then your 'inside track' "—she made air quotes—"is useless."

His wolf snarled at Stella's words. Lottie *wasn't* useless. "No. There are times that things change without warning, which can result in a less-than-ideal situation."

"Maybe it's not useless. Maybe they're lying to you. You're going one way and Walters and the rest of UH are going the other because—"

"Stella." He snapped out her name, silencing her before his wolf leapt over the edge. Disparaging Lottie was on his beast's "never, ever do" list. He rolled his head, cracking his neck and embracing the release of tension. "I need you to trust me." He pressed a hand to his chest. "I want this settled just as much as anyone else. I trust my contact. She—"

"She?" Stella pounced on that slip, and Grant moaned.

He dropped his head forward with a sigh, eyes closed while he spoke to himself. *Can't just shut the fuck up, can you? Nooo, you gotta try and smooth shit over. That damned lion has it right. You can't get in trouble if you don't talk.*

"Grant? She?"

Grant lifted his head and focused on the jaguar. "Pull up a seat."

Stella stepped toward a chair, but she kept glancing at the door, lower lip caught between her teeth. She was still worrying about Cole.

He reached over and nudged one of the monitors, changing the angle so they could both see that Cole was still out of it in bed. "You can see him here."

She lowered herself to a heavily cushioned chair, curling up in the seat. "Thanks. So, she?"

"Like a damned dog with a bone." He shook his head. "Yeah, 'she.' I met someone who is well known within the organization but not a participant herself. She agreed to feed me information."

"How is she not a participant? How do you know she's not feeding you bullshit so you guys can just walk into a trap?"

"I…" He wasn't sure how to put it into words. He finally settled for meeting Stella's stare, not hiding behind the blank mask most men used when trying to disguise their feelings. "Have you ever met someone—looked in their eyes—and just…*known*? It doesn't make sense. It's stupid and irrational and crazy, but…"

"But it feels right," she finished for him.

"Yeah," he whispered. "That's it."

"And that's how you felt—feel—about your 'she'?"

He nodded. "Yeah. It sucks and it's inconvenient as hell. She's who she is and I'm who I am. What kind of fucked-up shit is that? But there's no stopping it, and she's as determined to put an end to things as I am."

They were both quiet for a moment, and Grant almost slumped in his chair in relief. If that was the worst of their arguments until Cole woke, he'd count himself lucky. Though just as a hint of happiness emerged, Stella had to stomp all over it.

"You'll let me know when you hear something from her? I don't want to leave Cole, but…" She swallowed hard. "I need to be there. I need to watch Walters be brought in."

"An op really isn't the place for an untrained shifter."

"I was on that island all weekend *with* Cole *while* he was on an op," she countered, and he couldn't call her a liar. "*And*, before any of this began, Cole agreed to let me see this through to the end."

Right. He wasn't sure she was telling the truth. Or she'd misinterpreted Cole's words. Because he'd known Cole for many years, and he wasn't about to tell her that the protective-as-hell tiger wouldn't allow her within a hundred feet of danger. Period.

# CHAPTER TWENTY-SEVEN

$C$ole was pretty damned sure he'd been run over by a truck. A dually, maybe. Or a semi! Something with a fuck-ton of wheels that had rolled over him from head to toe. His bones ached, his muscles throbbed, and even his *blood* pricked him with sharp zaps of pain. Sure, blood hurting wasn't a biological possibility, but he was past logic.

He tensed his muscles, ache increasing in his shoulder and along his ribs. One of his hips throbbed, and he must have taken a kick to the thigh, because it practically screamed in protest with movement. It all hurt—body and mind and soul...

*Soul.* The single word reminded him of something. Of...of Stella. Just thinking her name pulled memories forward. Memories of Serene Isle, of James Walters and Richard King. Thoughts about his attempt to rescue her only to end up needing to be rescued himself. He'd been stabbed and shot.

Stella had gotten him out. Or at least she'd gotten him to the team, who'd gotten him off the island, but what happened to Stella?

His tiger snarled and roared, furious that he didn't know the answer to that question. How could he have lost track of her? He tried to remind the beast that he'd been unconscious, but the cat didn't want to listen to excuses. It wanted results.

Cole took a deep breath and released it slowly, suppressing the pain and gradually clearing his mind. He forced his eyes to open, then squinted against the glaring sunlight. The bright rays filled the room, burning his eyes, and he quickly took in his surroundings. Wood walls. Wood floors. Hell, wood furniture. Country quilts and a rocking chair. Large woven area rug. Tall pines visible through the massive window.

"Aw, shit," he grumbled under his breath, his eyes fluttering closed. He relaxed against his pillow and let the soft surface cradle him. *"Shit."*

Cole hadn't just gotten hurt. He'd been injured bad enough to be taken off active duty. They'd hauled him to Birch's vacation home for recovery, but he knew he wasn't alone. The team wouldn't have just dropped Cole off before going back to work. He had a babysitter somewhere in the house. A babysitter who knew more than him. A babysitter who could probably tell him what the hell had happened to Stella.

He tugged on the quilt that'd been tucked around him, the blanket practically swaddling him like a damned baby. He yanked a little harder, pressure constant as he unraveled himself. Cool air soon reached his skin, and he sighed in relief with the drop in temperature. He got a hand beneath himself, using it to push his upper body off the mattress, then swung his legs over the side of the bed. He paused for a moment, fighting for breath while pain surged.

Maybe finding the babysitter wasn't such a good idea.

Then his tiger caught a scent. One that made it purr and roll around on the ground as if it'd found the source of all catnip in existence. The beast crouched and rubbed its head on his paws, chuffing and begging for attention from the owner of that smell.

*Stella*... Her name echoed in his mind, rolling across his thoughts in time with his tiger's purrs.

*Stella*... That was the scent he'd caught, the sweet muskiness that could belong only to her. And it seemed so close. As if she'd been standing beside him moments ago. But there was no way Birch would have let a civvy invade their space. Right? Logically, that made sense. But sometimes hope wasn't logical, and Cole had a whole lot of hope that he'd find her somewhere in the cabin. Even if he'd never given her a reason to be with him. Even if he'd never given her a reason to stay.

Cole reached for the bedside table and gripped the edge, using it to maintain his balance as he stood. He wavered for a moment, swaying in place until his head cleared of disabling fog. His steps were slow and close together, more a shuffle than a steady walk, but those small strides got the job done. He made his way to the door, pausing to get his bearings before continuing.

The hallway stretched on to his right, long pale planks of wood forming the floor and leading him onward. He eased into the corridor, one hand skimming the wall while he kept moving. He followed that scent, searching for the source so he could appease his cat. Appease his human half, too.

Cole approached one of the other doorways along the hall, his steps growing firmer with every stride. The pain remained, but his tiger pushed past the aches and focused on the one they sought. Stella's scent strengthened the farther he went, and his cat purred with the thought that he'd have her in his arms soon.

Or was it all in his mind?

He shook his head. No, Stella's flavors were too rich, too alluring, for it to be fake. Stella was *here*. Or she'd been here recently.

He rubbed his forehead and cursed the injuries he'd sustained on that damned island. Fuck James Walters and fuck Unified Humanity. The rhythmic rolling *thump* of wheels on wood reached him a split second before a familiar face appeared from inside one of the rooms.

Grant stuck his head out, goofy smile in place. "What's up, slacker?"

Cole lifted his middle finger and flipped off Grant.

"*Nice.* I see that naptime hasn't improved your mood. Are you done being a burden to society or . . . ?"

Cole raised his other hand, flipping him off with both middle fingers.

"I get no respect. I've been sitting here with this bedside-vigil crap, and you're still being a dick." Grant sniffed.

Cole rolled his eyes and shuffled closer to his fellow teammate, not stopping until he gripped the doorframe to Grant's room. He peeked into the space, noted the camera and computer setup the wolf had installed.

"How long have we been here?"

The werewolf shrugged. "About—"

Grant was cut off by the rapid *thud* of bare feet on wood, someone racing toward them as if their life depended on it.

"Who else is—"

Then she swung around the corner, sliding on a thick rug until she nearly lost her balance. She clung to a decorative table, sending knickknacks tumbling to the ground. Thank God Birch had learned his lesson and made sure all of the decorations were plastic. She quickly righted herself and straightened the table before stepping away, and that was when he got her attention.

"Stella." He breathed out her name.

"Cole, you're..."

"You..."

Stella didn't let him say anything else. She raced toward him, and Cole propped himself against the doorframe. One minute his arms were empty and the next he had the gorgeous Stella all over him. Her mouth pressed firmly to his, her tongue lapping at the seam of his lips. He happily opened for her, granting her entrance while he rediscovered her flavors. She clung to his shirt, fingers fisting the material, and he wrapped his arms around her, pulling her even closer. Lush curves cushioned his hard muscles, cradling him in her sweetness and warmth.

So perfect. So beautiful. So...his? Fuck, if only he was so lucky. Stella was the perfect pretty little spotted package.

Cole shifted his hold to her hair, one hand delving into the strands and fisting the mass. He carefully tugged and turned her, tilting her head *just right* so he had the access he craved. Now he was the hunter, the fierce beast that took what he desired.

Their tongues tangled, swirling and lapping at each other while they reconnected. He'd woken alone, but now he was filled with her scent just as his arms were filled with her.

Cole groaned against her mouth, savoring every snippet of her he gathered. He pulled back the slightest bit, a hint of space between their lips that allowed him to murmur, "*Stella.*"

Grant chose that moment to interrupt. "Ew. *Gag.*"

Sometimes it was good to be a shifter—a cat in particular. Situational awareness was an awesome perk as a SHOC agent. It was also pretty kick-ass for a guy who felt the urge to slug his friend.

Cole reached out, his mouth still on Stella's, while his

fist connected with Grant in a solid punch. Knuckles met the wolf's jaw, an audible *crack* splitting through the air, immediately followed by a yelp and the clatter of Grant's chair sliding across the wood.

Stella laughed and pulled away, her smiling lips still so close—within reach. "Did you just...?"

"Punch Grant?" he murmured. "Yes."

And he wasn't going to apologize for it, either. He didn't care if Grant had a sore jaw. Cole had something much more important to focus on—he had Stella in his arms.

# CHAPTER TWENTY-EIGHT

Stella didn't have a chance to laugh again. Not when Cole's lips captured hers once more, his tongue doing that tappy-twisty thing that made her moan. He delved deeper into her mouth, lapping at her lips and arousing her with each stroke. She burned for him, core hot and aching, anxious to be filled.

She absorbed his essence into her very cells, the long, drugging kisses stealing her ability to think. He was fierce in his possession, and she was just as fierce when meeting his passion.

Cole moaned, body trembling and breath wheezing in and out of his lungs in heavy pants. He adjusted his position and leaned away from her. Was he trying to break the kiss?

She slowed their building hunger, gradually ending the meeting of their mouths so she could ease away from him—check on his condition. Then she cursed her own selfish ass. She'd launched herself at an injured guy. Sure, he was a shifter and healed faster than humans, but he was still injured. And she'd tried to climb him like a tree.

"Cole..." she murmured, grabbing his hands when he went to pull her close once more. "We need to stop."

"Hell yeah you do," Grant grumbled, and she whipped

her head around to glare at him. The wolf just sat there in his office chair, rubbing his jaw after Cole's punch and grinning even though he had to be in pain. "I like porn as much as the next guy, but that doesn't mean I want to watch you two go at it."

"Mother Fu..." Cole growled, moving to edge past Stella, his fist clenched and arm stretching out toward the werewolf.

"Hey, calm down." Stella stepped into his path, forming a physical barrier between Cole and Grant. She stroked his chest, palm resting over his heart. The rapid *thud* of his heartbeat pulsed against her palm. She traced small circles on his shirt, petting and stroking him in an attempt to ease his anger. "Grant is just being an ass. No reason to get mad."

"She's right," Grant said, but he must have just taken a bite of something because it came out as, "Sh...ite." Though his next words were clear. The guy must have swallowed. "I'm just being a dick to be a dick."

Cole growled, the vibrating rumble sliding through her, and Stella sighed. They acted like children when they were around each other. Except these grown kids didn't have the "good" part of children. She got the fighting, grumbling, whining, and growling with none of the smiles and playing well with others.

No wonder Birch always had a glare on his face when he spoke with the team.

Cole wavered, body swaying from side to side the tiniest bit, and she grasped his biceps to keep him steady.

"Hey, let's get you back to bed. You just woke up after being seriously injured. You should still be resting. Not..." Getting mauled by a jaguar shifter in heat.

He shook his head once, and then again, hair falling into

his eyes. "I'm..." He reached for the strands and missed. "Fine."

"Uh-huh." She suppressed the urge to snort. Barely. "Humor me, then. Seeing you like that." She shook her head. "I don't want to ever experience that again."

Something in her tone had to have gotten to him. Cole lowered his attention from Grant and stared at her—his gaze intent. Blue eyes turned amber, the tiger peering out from behind Cole's human half. He cupped her cheek, calloused palm rough against her sensitive skin. "I'll *be* fine even if I'm not right now."

"And you won't get better unless you let your body heal." She stepped back and grasped his hand, tugging while she urged him to follow. "So, I vote that you get back into bed."

"With you." Cole's lips twitched, and she had to admit that the idea had merit.

"With me? I dunno..."

"Yes," he hissed, the drawn-out sound completely feline in nature.

"Maybe." She grinned and winked, continuing to back away and toward his bedroom.

*"Yes."* A growl filled his voice that time.

*"Maybe."* Stella grinned even wider, enjoying annoying Cole's tiger.

His next response was a pure snarl from his beast, the animal furious at her teasing. He sped up and she darted away, a tinkling laugh escaping her lips as she rushed into his bedroom. The room smelled like him... and her. They'd shared the space for a full day, him unconscious while she simply stared at his unmoving body. Their combined scent now permeated the space, claiming it as theirs. At least temporarily. Who knew what'd happen once Walters had been handled.

Stella stood beside the bed, watching Cole approach and noticing all the little things about him. Like the way his step still had a small hitch and how stiff he held his upper body. He wrapped an arm around his front, hand squeezing his side, and she frowned.

"You're still hurting a lot, aren't you?"

He shrugged and then winced. "I'll recover. How long have I been out? What happened to the op?"

She didn't reply at first, just focused on caring for him. Once he was close enough, she grabbed his hand and braced him as he sat on the edge of the bed. He groaned as he let the mattress take his weight and then moaned as he moved to lie on his back.

She reached across him, fingers fisting the edge of his quilt before she tugged to draw them over his body. Only to have her progress stopped by Cole—his large hand wrapped around her much smaller wrist.

"Stella?"

"Why don't I leave you alone to rest and we can talk about it later?"

He gave her a bland expression and quirked one eyebrow. "Why don't you get into bed with me and talk?"

"Later."

He shook his head. "Now."

"But..."

Cole changed his grasp, fingers no longer holding her captive but simply cradling her hand. He stroked her palm with his thumb, tracing tiny, soothing circles. "I think this past weekend's events on that island proved that anything can happen at any time." He shrugged. "There might not be a later."

Stella's throat closed up tight, cutting off any chance for her to breathe. Her eyes burned, tears pooling and blurring her vision. She sniffled and wiped her face with her free hand, brushing the first hint of tears aside.

"Fine," she rasped, failing at her attempt to grumble at the big idiot. She tugged on his hold, but he refused to release her. "Let me go and I'll get in on the other side."

"Nope. You'll try to escape." He shook his head, and this time it was *him* who pulled. Pulled her on top of his stretched-out body. He rolled to his right, Stella falling from atop him to land on the mattress.

"Cole!" she squeaked. "I could hurt you."

"You? Really?" Cole snorted while he rolled his eyes. He propped himself on his elbow, wincing with the movement, and she suppressed the need to ask if he was okay. "Sure, my body aches and I wouldn't mind a lazy nap in the sun, but I'm not about to break."

Stella's cat purred at the idea of lying across the sunny porch with Cole in nothing but their fur. Spots and stripes tangled together, warmed by the sun's rays. She breathed deep, pulling his scent into her lungs, and released the air with a satisfying purr. It was so good to have him with her—awake and on his way to being healthy.

"And now that you know I won't break, you can give me a recap."

She closed her eyes and groaned. He just wouldn't give up.

"You shouldn't make sounds like that. It gives my cat ideas." Those words delivered with his husky whisper had her nearly coming right then and there. She managed to suppress her whine, but she couldn't do a thing about the shudder that racked her body.

"That wasn't meant to be sexy," she murmured.

"Everything about you is sexy." She could hear the grin

in his voice and refused to open her eyes. It'd take only one look from him and she'd be putty in his hands.

With a shake of her head, she let her mind drift back to the other night, the events that had brought them to this cabin with Grant leading the way.

"I caught up to you outside Building A. You'd been stabbed with a poisoned knife and, at some point, shot." Cole grunted, and she wasn't sure what *that* meant. She just continued. "We ran through the forest, but your injuries were too much. I tried to get you to shift, but when you wouldn't, I sort of..." She nibbled her lower lip and met his gaze. "I'm really sorry, but I pulled you through your shift."

Cole grunted again. Earlier he was all about talking her around to agreeing with him, and now he wouldn't say a word? What the hell?

"We got to the wall around the restricted section, and Pike and Declan were there to help get you over the barrier. Then we made it to the beach. They took you away with Ethan at that point, so I'm not sure what they did on the SHOC yacht. I hitched a ride with Grant, Birch, Hartley, and Walters."

Cole stiffened, eyes blazing with his cat's amber color, while a pale peppering of fur coated his cheeks. "You met Hartley? We have Walters?"

"Yes...and no." A combination of unease and anger slithered through her blood. She still wasn't sure what it was about he that set her cat on edge, but there was *something* about that snake. "Hartley brought Walters in, but while Grant was showing me to my room, he escaped. Someone set off a bomb in engineering, and they assume he leapt over the side of the boat."

"Wait, *Hartley* captured Walters?"

Stella nodded. "Not a hair out of place, not a wrinkle to be seen in his clothes, and he walked right up to the boat with Walters in cuffs."

"Isn't that convenient?" Cole drawled.

"I thought it was odd. Based on the looks I caught between Grant and Birch, they thought it was suspicious, too. They wouldn't tell me anything, though." And the lack of knowledge was killing her. "I mean, he seemed snakish, and Birch mentioned his big brother, but that was all. I felt dirty just looking at him, and Grant wouldn't let him touch me when I went to crawl out of the boat."

"*Stella*." Cole's tone was harsh, a commanding voice that demanded attention. "Promise me you'll stay away from Hartley."

"I will, but—"

"No." His voice dropped to a deeper growl, more of his tiger emerging. "You don't know what that family is capable of. SHOC does a lot of good for shifters, but that doesn't mean we're good people. Bad things for the right reasons, remember?" She nodded and he continued. "The director of SHOC, Quade, does whatever he needs to do to get things done. He has no heart." He snorted. "I doubt he even has a soul. His younger brother, Hartley, is the same way. Hartley is constantly trying to get on his brother's good side, but no part of Quade is good. They're both dangerous. I don't want you anywhere near them."

"I think he let Walters go."

He pressed a single finger to her lips. "Let it go. Stay away from him. For me. If you see either of them coming, turn around and walk in the opposite direction. I hate that you even shared the same air as Hartley. That family is heartless. Promise me. Promise me you'll leave it be."

Stella nodded, happy to make that promise. It wasn't like

she *wanted* to be around the guy. The look in his eyes, the way he stared at others...He scared the hell out of her. "I promise I won't go near him."

His face relaxed, relief easy to see now that the tension vanished. "Thank you."

Silence descended for a moment, blanketing them in quiet. A quiet occasionally broken by the chirping of birds in the forest beyond the cabin's yard and the rustling of leaves. Stella closed her eyes and bathed in the silence, the soft *whoosh* of their breaths joining nature's symphony.

Cole ran his fingers through her hair, brushing the strands with his blunt digits, and she basked in his gentle attentions. His fingers drifted, tracing the line of her brow and the bridge of her nose, then the shape of her lips and along her jawline. He teased her neck, tickling her with the barely there touch, before going even farther south.

"You're so beautiful. Do you know that?"

Every touch, every caress, brought her nerves to life, sparked a new sensitivity that sang through her blood. Her breath caught as he traced the neckline of her thin shirt, fingers not delving beneath the fabric, and yet he was *so close*. Her breasts ached, her nipples hard and begging to be touched, while her pussy heated with arousal.

He leaned over her, his bulk blocking out the sun peeking through the windows, and whispered, "Everything about you is gorgeous."

Stella opened her mouth to say...something. She wasn't sure what, exactly. She simply knew—*knew*—that being there with Cole was the right answer no matter the question. His scent, his body, his mind...It was all just so *right*.

Cole snared her lips in another of those drugging kisses, his mouth capturing hers in a single swoop. While hc began fiercely, he quickly gentled, his tongue lingering as he gave her long, intoxicating kisses. Kisses that stoked the fires inside her, urging her desire to burn brighter and hotter.

They parted for a breath, and he changed his angle before swooping in once more. He reclaimed her mouth in a delicious, seeking exploration. Her jaguar purred as more and more of his natural flavors invaded her mouth. His heated sweetness filled her, while his musky scent wrapped around her.

Their tongues tangled and danced, urging their need to climb.

Cole was hard against her hip, his arousal unmistakable. His hard, thick length pulsed, and her fingers itched with the need to explore his cock.

To stroke him.

To tease him.

To *please* him. And ultimately herself.

The thought of taking him in her mouth drew a deep moan from Stella's throat, and she was gratified when Cole returned the deep sound.

She wasn't gratified by the next voice in the room. Grant. *"Ew. Gag."*

Cole ripped his mouth from hers, a threatening rumble in his chest, while Stella simply slumped into the bed and closed her eyes.

How had she forgotten about the camera Grant had pointed out? When he'd first told her of the device, she'd been comforted by its presence. It meant Grant was always watching. Now she didn't want Grant seeing a damn thing, but it was obvious he already had.

"Where is it?" Cole snarled. "Where's the camera?"

Eyes still closed, she pointed at the back corner of the room and the small black camera that clung to the wall.

"Do you have my gun?"

She opened one eye. "Gun?"

"*A* gun, then? Doesn't have to be mine."

She opened the other eye and frowned at him. "You want a gun?"

"I doubt you've got an explosive device or two. Or do you?" He looked way too excited about that possibility.

She shook her head. "No. No guns or explosives."

Cole grunted and rolled away from her. "Nothing for it, then."

He didn't even make it upright before the rapid thud of bare feet on wood reached their ears. Soon Grant stomped into the room, headed right for the camera. Reaching up, he grasped the small device and tugged so that it fell into his hand. Then they had his full attention, fierce glare in place while he stomped from the room. Stella nibbled on her lower lip, worried over the anger she'd seen in the wolf's expression, but Cole just laughed and slumped beside her once again.

"Were you really going to shoot out his camera?"

He shrugged. "Or blow it up."

Stella didn't really have anything to say to that. She'd discovered that this SHOC team was a group of violent teens who somehow topped six feet and had been given very, very dangerous toys.

Cole gave the corner one last look before returning his focus to her. "Now, where were we?"

"*We*"—she placed her hand on his chest—"are going to *rest*."

"But we could…"

"Rest."

"Maybe after…"

"Re-st." She made the word have two syllables instead of one.

He huffed out a long-suffering sigh and rolled to his back, eyes on the ceiling. He lifted his right arm and peered at her. "If I'm going to rest, so are you. Get over here."

Stella had no problem following that order. No problem at all.

# CHAPTER TWENTY-NINE

*C*ole took a sip of his coffee, the hot liquid warming him from the inside out. He savored the lightly sweetened bitter brew as it glided over his taste buds and down his throat. It was good to be alive. And not just because he had an excellent cup of coffee in hand.

It had something to do with one particular she-cat. The she-cat that'd spent the last two days in his bed without an inch of space between their bodies. The only way it could have been better was if they'd both been naked, but he'd take what he could get. At least until he talked her around to his kind of sweaty, passionate, mind-blowing thinking. He smiled at the thought of Stella without a stitch of clothing, begging him for more. Yeah, he liked that idea. A lot.

Cole topped off his cup with the nearby carafe and then padded across the kitchen to the opposite counter. He leaned back against the granite's edge and turned his attention to the window. Or rather, the view beyond the window. From his new position, he was able to watch the morning sun rise above the pines. The rays sparkled on the lake's still waters, as if glitter coated the placid surface.

A new day and he was alive and well. A man—shifter— couldn't ask for more.

Except Cole could and would. Living through the op hadn't been enough. Now he wanted even *more*. He just hadn't quite figured out how to get that "more." He had to come up with a plan eventually, right?

Eh, he'd get there. For the moment, he'd enjoy the view. And not just the sunrise, the swaying trees, or soothing lake, either. There was something else even more beautiful than anything that could be found in the wilds of nature—Stella. Stella on the dock that extended into the lake, barefoot, wearing nothing but a pair of tight shorts and a snug shirt and with her hair in a messy pile atop her head. There wasn't a poised and polished thing about her in that moment. No makeup, no flat-ironed hair, and none of that Spanx crap.

Pure woman.

Damn, she was beautiful. His tiger agreed, the beast chuffing and purring. It liked the woman's human shape, and it was anxious to run with her on four paws. It didn't remember being present during their run to safety, and it was still pouting about missing out. The cat snarled, baring its fangs and telling him that tigers *didn't* pout.

Cole snorted. *Right*.

He kept his eyes trained on her, pausing to sip on his coffee now and again, but mainly focusing on the redhead outside. Did the woman know how tempting she was? Especially when she went all twisty and did fucking *yoga*? Some of the poses he recognized—Declan's mate had decided that pregnancy yoga was a thing—while others were new to him. The one that damn near everyone in the world had to know was downward-facing dog. Now Stella had her ass up in the air, hips tilted just right, and Cole could go out there and...

"Da-*yum*." Grant broke into Cole's fantasies. Bastard.

Then the wolf's word—and how he said it—sank into his mind. *"Excuse me?"*

Grant obviously hadn't heard the warning in Cole's tone because the werewolf repeated himself. And then some. "Da-double-*yum*." He shook his head. "I need to take up yoga. *Today*." The werewolf looked at Cole, his smile wide, and waggled his eyebrows. "Think she'll give me a hands-on lesson?"

He'd managed to keep his tiger on the leash until Grant had gotten to the end of his question, but the "hands-on lesson" pushed the cat over the edge. It slipped its leash, baring its fangs and sinking its claws into Cole's mind as it raced forward. The animal was going to take control and bring Grant down no matter what his human half said. Although his human half was just about on the same page as the cat.

Where the tiger yearned to kill the male that threatened to encroach on its territory, Cole-the-human simply wanted to pluck out Grant's eyes. Grant couldn't ogle what he couldn't see, right? It seemed perfectly logical and an excellent plan.

"You want Stella to give you a hands-on lesson?" He managed to keep the anger out of his voice. Barely.

Cole extended his arm and placed his half-empty coffee mug on the counter, the ceramic not making a sound as it touched granite. He had to retain control of his body—movements careful and precise. Otherwise the cat would win and overwhelm him with brute strength.

Grant snorted. "Have you *seen* her?" The wolf chuckled. "Of course you have. You've had her in your bed for days *and* over the weekend." He padded to the coffeepot and snared a mug, filling his cup before going back to his position. The one that let him watch Stella. "I've never been

one to pick up a teammate's ex, but..." He shook his head
and took a sip of his coffee. "Whoo. She's tempting enough
to forget you ever—"

Cole burst into action, striking before Grant realized he
was moving. One hand snared Grant's mug while the other
went to his shoulder. A shove and spin, and then Cole had
the wolf by the back of the neck. He pushed on Grant's
neck, forcing him to bend over while Cole brought his knee
up to strike the wolf's stomach. Air wheezed from his teammate, and while Grant sucked wind, Cole pinned the wolf's
head to the granite counter. Grant continued to cough and
wheeze, so Cole took a moment to place his friend's mug
beside his own.

Hand empty, Cole bent and placed his elbow on the
counter, propping his head in his hand. "Would you care to
repeat that?"

"Uh..." Grant tensed as if he were gonna fight Cole, but
he and his tiger were having none of that.

"I *said*, would you repeat that?" Cole squeezed the
wolf's neck a little tighter, his tiger's claws emerging to
prick his teammate's skin. The tiniest hint of blood snuck
into the air, the scent mingling with the smell of Grant's
unease.

"I was just...you know..." Grant stuttered, rushing
through excuses, and Cole waited. The wolf would get
to denying everything eventually. "She's a grown woman
and...My mama said a woman has a right to choose,
so...*Dammit, Cole*, it's not like you've claimed her. I'm
not stealing her from you. I'd wait until she actually *was*
an ex before I made my move. You're acting like a jealous
boyfriend."

*Boyfriend?*

Cole furrowed his brow, mind replaying that single word

over and over, and that was just enough distraction for his inner cat. The beast pounced, animal's mind overtaking his human thoughts. Fur slipped from his pores while his fangs pushed past human teeth. His bones ached, the tiger wanting to take on more of his feline shape. He managed to hold the animal back enough to cling to two legs and two arms. That didn't keep the tiger from talking, though.

It had one word in mind. *"Mine."*

Grant sucked in a quick breath and tensed within his grip. "Yours? As in your girlfriend? Or your mate?"

The cat spoke through him again, no hesitation in its thoughts. "Mate."

The word reverberated in his head in an unending echo. The tiger was making its feelings *known*. And Cole...Fuck him sideways, he embraced the beast's desires. There'd been something about Stella from the moment he'd caught sight of her in that fucking ballroom. Something about her innocence tempered by her craving for violence that connected with a hidden part of him.

Butter wouldn't melt in her mouth, but watch out because she might stab you with the *butter knife*.

"Does she know that? Or is this the first time you've said the words out loud?"

Cole glared at Grant and wondered if killing Grant because he was annoying would be classified as justifiable homicide. He sighed. Probably not.

Giving his teammate one last squeeze, he lifted Grant's head from the counter and shoved the wolf. "Fuck off."

That just made the wolf laugh. "It is the first time, isn't it? You've been panting after her for a week and you're just now admitting she's your mate? You two alternate between fighting like wet cats and climbing all over each other. It didn't take me long to see that she was it for you." Grant snorted. "I hope I'm not as oblivious as you are when I find my mate."

Cole didn't have anything to say to that, so he just kept glaring.

"So, if you're just admitting it to yourself, you obviously haven't talked to Stella about anything." Grant looked to him, eyebrows raised.

He answered it by quirking one of his. "That wasn't a question."

The werewolf rolled his eyes and shook his head. "You're such an ass. You two need to figure that shit out. Soon." He pointed at Cole. "Because she thinks she's coming along when we find Walters."

"Fuck no." Cole's tiger still spoke, but it wasn't like Cole's human mind disagreed. "It's too dangerous. The weekend on the island was bad enough, but to actively seek him out." Cole shook his head. "No."

"Uh-huh. You're gonna go with the *grunt, grunt* 'me mate, you listen' approach? I'm sure that'll work *juuust fine*."

"It will." Cole nodded to reaffirm his statement. "Mates trust each other. I'm a trained agent; she's not. She trusts me. She'll know that I have her safety in mind and will do what I think is best."

"I'm not sure if you believe what you're saying or if you're fucking with me." Grant narrowed his eyes. "Because it's not about trust. It's about giving her what she needs. She *needs* to be there."

He pinched the bridge of his nose. "Did you spontaneously grow a vagina, or did you find a *Cosmo* magazine somewhere in the cabin?" Grant opened his mouth to reply, but Cole held up a hand, silencing him. "Never mind. Keep it to yourself because I've got this."

"Got what?"

"The mating thing. I can handle it *on my own*. And"—Cole pointed at Grant—"I don't need you hanging around here giving me shit."

"My job is to look after you two."

"Because I was hurt." Cole brought his arms to his sides and flexed his chest and abs. "I'm not anymore. Which means you can leave us alone. As soon as you know where Walters is, send a babysitter for Stella, and I'll hook up with the team."

"Babysitter for Stella?" Grant slowly shook his head. "You need to rethink your plan because it's so full of mistakes, I'd think Pike came up with it."

"I'm not gonna let you goad me by comparing me to some twentysomething newbie baby-agent." Cole crossed his arms over his chest. "I'll make you a deal. As soon as you have a mate of your own, I'll take your advice. Since you don't, I guess I'll just have to make decisions on my own. My decision is that you need to get the hell out of here so I can go claim Stella."

Privately. Loudly. Repeatedly.

Grant shrugged. "Have it your way, but when she tries to blow you up, don't come crying to me."

Grant spun on his heel and left the room on silent feet. Cole snorted and turned back to watching Stella. The morning sun outlined her curves, touching her hair so it looked like living fire and caressing her pale skin until she seemed to glow.

Stella? Blow him up? Grant was an idiot.

# CHAPTER THIRTY

Stella gave her body one last stretch, sinking into the pull on her muscles, and breathed into the pain. She—and her cat—enjoyed the peace that yoga brought to her mind. It forced her to slow and think of her body placement, to forget everything else in her life.

Like Cole Turner—lickable body, seductive smile, and confusing-as-hell tiger.

They'd kissed, they'd touched, and they'd explored each other's bodies with the exception of *one thing*. There had been no home run, no parting of the pink sea or jamming the clam. Which, okay, Cole had almost *died*. She understood that even a shifter needed time to recover.

Her pink taco did not understand.

Wait. She was supposed to be forgetting about her lack of funny business. Maybe it was time to go through her poses again. She began in the mountain pose, then stepped back and adjusted to warrior. From there...

The rumble of a vehicle engine disturbed the morning silence, the deep growl filling the air. She lowered her arms and turned her attention to the cabin, gaze sliding from the building to the gravel driveway nearby. Their SUV slowly backed up along the length of gravel, Grant behind the wheel. He flashed her a small smile and a tiny wave, which she returned even though she was pretty sure Grant had told her they wouldn't be leaving the cabin for a while. Like, not until Walters was located.

But there Grant went, SUV disappearing between the trees. Her jaguar gave her hearing a boost, and she continued to listen until he reached the end of the long drive. She furrowed her brow, trying to think of any reason why the werewolf would leave them. Had his contact sent him a message? Was he off to meet someone and had decided to leave her out?

Asshole. If he—

The dock rocked, large wood platform trembling beneath her bare feet. She looked down at the aged wood and then scanned the water, searching for a cause for the shaking. She didn't see anything, the water clear, with no hint of large aquatic life. A few little minnows, but they wouldn't have shaken the pier. Except then it trembled again. And again. And again. It felt almost like something big and heavy was running...

Stella swung her attention to the shore and gasped. A massive, eight-hundred-pound tiger raced toward her, its dinner-plate-sized paws stomping on the pier, shaking the wood so hard she wondered if it'd survive the shifter's treatment. His black stripes contrasted against the bright orange and splotches of white. Amber eyes met hers, serious and intent, but she sensed the playfulness that lingered as well.

The oversized housecat moved faster, and she was awed by the power the beast held. Layers of thick muscle covered him, and he had four-inch claws at the tips of his paws. Death on four legs. And he was coming for *her*.

That realization had her jaguar purring in response.

Furball forbid his attack spur her into fight-or-flight mode like any normal person. Nope, her kitty wanted to rub all over Cole's tiger. It wanted to get up close and *purr*sonal.

*Lame pun, Stella. Funny but lame.*

The distance between them lessened with each bounding step, the pier shaking harder and harder the closer he came. Any moment now he'd be within striking distance and... And Cole's muscles tensed, powerful body crouching while his nails dug into the aged wood. As a cat shifter herself, she recognized the pose. He was getting ready to pounce.

Stella's cat chirped with the thought, more than happy to get pounced by the big guy. Suddenly it didn't care that he hadn't given them what they craved. The she-cat wanted to rub her scent on Cole, bathe him in her aromas until every bitch within a thousand miles knew that Cole Turner belonged to... She refused to let that thought continue. Especially since she had no idea about Cole's feelings for her.

Cole leapt. Eight hundred pounds launched into the air, front legs outstretched and reaching for her. If she allowed herself to get caught, the big asshole would send her tumbling into the lake. Hell no. With the tiger in the air, she dropped to the wood dock and rolled toward the shore, effectively trading places with the animal. She popped to her feet, and the cat slid across the wood planks, digging his claws in to keep himself from sliding into the still lake.

Stella faced off against Cole, hands outstretched to keep him at bay while she backed away from him. "Cole, what are you doing?"

He chuffed, a feline laugh.

"Bravo to you for laughing at me, but seriously. What the hell?" Another chuff, the tiger slowly padding forward. His strides were longer than her own, bringing him closer instead of her movements keeping the distance the same.

"You know, I was just trying to do some yoga. Can't a girl get her yoga on without being pounced?"

The tiger's gaze slid over her, capturing her from head to toe. He licked his chops, large pink tongue sliding along his snout. His eyes were half-lidded, and then he did some weird thing with his tongue that...

"Ew. Stop that," she snapped. "You're trying to be sexy or something, but you're a *cat*. That's..." She shuddered. "That's gross, not sexy."

Cole straightened and faced her, his tail flicking left and right, betraying his anxiousness. At least she wasn't the only one uneasy at the situation. He attempted to pull off the innocent "I'm made of sunshine and rainbows" look, but she saw through him. There was nothing innocent about the tiger. Nothing at all.

"Cole..." She went back to warning him off. "I don't know what's up with you, but I'm going back into the house and..."

He pounced. The tiger was faster than any eight-hundred-pound beast should be. One moment butter wouldn't melt in his mouth, and the next she had a tiger's massive front legs wrapped around her. He was gentle but firm, his feline hug unbreakable as he eased his weight to his right. She fought his tumble, pulling against his weight, but she was no match for the tiger.

A scream escaped her mouth, the loud screech scaring the birds out of the trees. Then she heard nothing, frigid water rushing over her head, up her nose and into her mouth. The cold enveloped her, soaking her clothes and hair.

Cole released her the moment they struck the water, muscular legs unlocking before he swam away.

As she scrambled for air, her feet struck the silt bottom of the lake and she pushed herself toward the surface. She

heaved in a large breath, filling her lungs in one deep inhale. Flinging her hair out of her face, she wiped her eyes
and then her face before finally searching out the stupid cat.

He was easy to find, the big orange asshole not too
far away and looking pleased with himself. Eyes dancing,
pupils large, and mouth parted with his lips pulled back. Almost as if the tiger *smiled* at her. She'd wipe that smile right
off his snout.

"What. The. Hell?" A clump of hair fell forward, and she
whipped it back again.

More chuffing from the tiger.

Stella pointed at him. "Shift back so I can yell at you."

Except her jaguar didn't want to yell. It wanted to rub
all over the tiger that'd caught them. She was ignoring the
horny bitch for now.

Cole tilted his head to the side as if she confused him.
*Riiight.*

"This is..." She gritted her teeth and glared a little
harder, pulling on her building anger and frustration. "This
is...This is bullshit."

She sighed and turned away from him, plodding through
the water and toward the shore. The lake sloshed around
her, pulling at her as she fought to leave. She trudged onward, not stopping until she reached the dried grass, and
then plopped onto the ground. She faced him, Cole still in
his tiger form while she sat with her knees bent and elbows
propped on them. She crossed her arms and rested her chin
on them, eyes staring at nothing and everything.

"You get that this is bullshit, right?" She couldn't look at
him while she spoke. "You and me? We're together and it's
fake, but then we kiss and then I save you and then we're
together some more but nothing really happens and..." She
huffed. "I'm rambling, but that doesn't change the fact that

this is all muddled and confusing." She turned her head slightly. Just enough to meet the tiger's stare. "And then there's SHOC and UH tied up in the middle of everything."

Cole huffed and frowned, the cat carefully easing toward her. He approached slowly, as if she'd bolt at any moment. The cat wasn't wrong. Even if Stella's jaguar disagreed, she could retain control long enough to put some distance between them. She didn't say anything as he drew near, waiting to see how close the tiger would come to her. The answer was as close as she'd let him. He kept padding nearer, not stopping until she nearly had a tiger in her lap. She parted her legs enough for him to crawl between her thighs and plop his head on her leg.

Cole turned onto his back, cat's eyes focused on hers, and she stared down at the massive beast that could shred her in an instant. Yet she knew he wouldn't. She knew he'd never hurt her. She sank her fingers into his fur, traced his snout and *bopp*ed the tip of his nose. And he... He purred, fierce tiger acting more like a domesticated cat than a highly trained SHOC agent.

"What are you doing, Cole? What are *we* doing?" she whispered, the fight leaving her and exhaustion taking its place.

The tiger stared at her, and his purr stopped for a moment, his eyes never leaving hers, and he... waggled his eyebrows.

*"Seriously?"* Stella *thump*ed his nose, not caring if it hurt. Even her inner cat was annoyed with the tiger now. The jaguar knew what *she* wanted. It started with an "M" and ended with an "ate." The she-cat knew it'd have a fight on its paws since Stella was so twitchy about a relationship with the tiger, but the jaguar was determined.

It didn't remember losing someone she loved. It didn't

recall the utter desolation she'd experienced when her parents had given up. It'd been Stella's human half that'd dealt with that pain. It was Stella's human half that bore the emotional scars of loss. Her jaguar didn't remember nights spent crying. Nights spent so fucking lonely she thought she'd shatter beneath the grief that weighed her down.

Cole jerked away from her hand and sneezed, shaking his head while he brought his paw up to rub the end of his nose. His wiggling gave her the chance to escape, and she hurriedly crawled to her feet. She spun and marched back to the cabin, ignoring the tiger's disapproving roar. It could get as pissy as it wanted. Stella didn't give a damn.

Though she should have at least kept some of her attention on the striped asshole.

# CHAPTER THIRTY-ONE

*T*he tiger's claws dug into the soft dirt and grass, feline body quick to catch up to its mate. He took advantage of the animal's speed, but Cole refused to let the furry pain in the ass retain control.

He flexed and stretched his human consciousness, expanding to shove the big cat from the forefront of their shared mind. He battled the beast, mental arms wrapping around the tiger's chest just before he stood and launched the animal over his shoulder. He body-slammed the idiot feline, distracting it just enough to reclaim possession.

Cole didn't hesitate to take the reins. He secured the tiger with mental chains while his human awareness pushed forward. Between one stride and the next, he went from four paws to two feet as he reclaimed his body. Orange, black, and white fur receded, revealing his tanned skin to the bright sunlight. Paws transformed to feet and hands while his cat's legs returned to their normal human shape. His head narrowed and face rearranged, snout receding while his tiger's fangs shortened and turned dull.

He chased after her, leaves, grass, and dirt stuck to the soles of his feet. The occasional twig dug into his calloused skin, but that small hint of pain didn't matter to him. Not when the only thing that *did* matter was Stella. Stella who continued to stomp toward the cabin.

"Stella." He called out to her, hoping that hearing his voice—instead of the tiger's chuffing—would get her to stop. It didn't.

"Stella! Just a second." He picked up his pace, breaking into a jog to catch her. His cat urged him to pounce again. *Idiot.* Cole shoved the tiger deeper into his mind until its roars sounded more like the cries of a young kitten.

Once he was close enough, he reached out, his touch gentle yet firm when his fingers met her elbow. "Just gimme a minute, Stella."

Stella paused but didn't turn to face him. "What?"

"Uh…"

He stared at the back of her head, at her lopsided, water-soaked ponytail and the random curls that'd fallen free of her hair tie. Her clothes clung to her body, fabric drenched in lake water. Silt and bits of grass peppered her calves, while dirt stuck to the bottom of her feet. Her scent no longer drifted to him on the wind, sweet aroma replaced by the stink of lake water and the decay of vegetation.

She snorted and shook her head, taking a step forward.

He needed to think of something to say. *Fast.* His tiger released a series of chuffs and then a snort, the animal finding way too much pleasure in Cole's failings. The little shit. It'd been the one that had gotten them into this mess, and now Cole had to clean it up.

Cole's mind dove for the gutter, fantasies of getting Stella in a shower and bathing her body flooding his thoughts. But imagining her naked and slick with water wouldn't get him any closer to his goal—mating. Mating a woman he didn't deserve. One who was too good for him but he hoped would accept him anyway.

He moved forward slowly, making sure she heard his approach so she could move if she desired. But Stella remained in place, back straight and body tense. With infinite care, he cupped her shoulders and slid his palms down her arms. He gently rubbed her arms, giving her some of his warmth. He realized now that he'd been an idiot to listen to the cat. What the hell did it know about interacting with his mate's human half? If Stella had been on four legs, the tiger might have convinced her to mate with a playful game. Since she had been in human form, all he'd done was annoy her.

"I'm sorry." He murmured the two words, putting every ounce of tumultuous emotion in the syllables. "That was..." He sighed and dropped his head forward. He curled inward and rested his forehand on the base of her neck. "That was stupid."

"What was stupid?"

"Coming out here as a cat. Shoving you in the lake." She relaxed the tiniest bit, and he risked reaching around her. "Acting like a dumbass when I actually came out here to have a serious conversation. Take your pick."

She snorted and shook her head. "All of the above?"

"I deserve that." He winced and then sighed. "That and more. I..."

Stella slowly turned in his embrace, and he loosened his grip, allowing her to move freely. "You're"—her attention flicked down and then sprang back up to meet his gaze—"*naked.*"

His lips twitched, but he suppressed the smile that threatened to take over. "It was all the cat's idea, I assure you. It thought..." Another sigh. Now that he'd let the tiger's reasoning replay in his mind, he realized how truly dumb he'd been. "It thought teasing and pouncing on you was the perfect way to get your attention." He grimaced. "It was flirting with you, your jaguar."

She quirked a brow, skepticism obvious in her expression. "Flirting?"

"I never said he was the most mature cat."

"And yet you let him have control?" she drawled. "Why did he feel the need to flirt?" She stepped closer, her cold, wet body flush with his. Any hint of arousal due to her nearness vanished when they touched. The cold stomped on his body's responses to Stella's proximity. "What was its endgame—your endgame?"

He slid his arms from around her waist, skated his palms up her biceps, and didn't stop until he reached her heart-shaped face. It was time for Cole to go balls-to-the-wall, rock-out-with-his-cock-out honest. "It wants you for its mate. *I* want you for my mate."

He couldn't blame her for being skeptical. For the little frown on her lips and the wrinkles that formed between her brows. Or the way her eyes narrowed. Not enough to convey anger, but she didn't exactly look happy, either.

He lifted his hand from her cheek and brushed away those little lines between her eyebrows. "I'm sure you doubt me. I haven't given you any reason to think that this was heading in a 'permanent' direction, but..." He ghosted his fingertips over her skin to her hairline and softly tickled the short strands that framed her face. "You want to know what we're doing?" He leaned down and rubbed the tip of his nose against hers. "If I have my way, we're mating."

"Cole..." she whispered, a mixture of hope and heartache in her voice that tore him in two.

"You're mine, Stella Moore, but fair warning...I'm an ass, my tiger is an immature little shit, and I spend my time surrounded by guys with guns who are just as bad or worse." He brushed his lips across hers, teasing them both with the soft caress. "But when I'm not annoying the hell out of you, I'm gonna make you so fucking happy."

Stella's laugh burst from her lips, and she leaned away, letting her delight fill the air. And he held on, his grip sure and steady while she let him take her weight. She trusted him not to let her fall. *Trusted. Him.* No one but his team had ever trusted him so much, and the ties between him and his teammates were forged in blood and sweat.

His connection to Stella...formed the same way. They'd bled and fought side by side to get off that island. She'd stayed by his side while he recovered. Now it seemed she'd forgiven him for being such a hopeless example of a typical male. The operative word, though, was "seemed." He might make her laugh, but she hadn't agreed to mate him. His tiger wasn't letting her go until she agreed, and he didn't give a damn how stalkery that sounded.

Her body trembled with her laughter, wet cloth stroking his, and somehow his cock managed to harden despite the chill from her touch. And not just a little hard, either. This wasn't just a chubby. It was a full-on, soul-deep, raw craving for her.

"What do you say, Stella?"

"You're crazy."

He nodded. There was no doubt about *that*. He was in SHOC, after all. It wasn't like the organization attracted men that were sane. "Yeah, but that's not an answer. Mate me."

At least not the one he wanted.

"Cole, we..."

He kissed her, pressure gentle with lips barely parted. Just enough to capture a quick taste. "Mate me."

"But…"

He went for her again, lapping at the seam of her lips and gathering the sweetness he found there. "Mate me."

"We hardly…"

The next kiss delved deeper, slipping into her mouth and gathering every hint of her taste he could find. He showed her how much he craved her, how badly he needed her, and the depth of his hunger. As quickly as he'd fallen into their kiss, he ended the meeting of their mouths. "From the moment I saw you in that ballroom you were mine. It didn't matter that I was surrounded by humans who wanted to kill me. All I could see was you. All I could think about was making you mine." Voice hoarse, strained by the strength of his emotions, he tried again. "You deserve so much better than a scarred, violent tiger with homicidal tendencies, but I can't stand the idea of anyone else touching you. Mate me."

Stella didn't say a word at first. Her green eyes still remained focused on his, and his gut clenched when he realized that tears spilled over her lashes to form damp trails on her cheeks.

"Stella, I'm—"

She was the one to interrupt that time. She was the one to press a finger to his lips while her mouth formed a wide smile. She was the one to give him the greatest gift he'd ever known.

"Yes."

* * *

Stella was probably stupid for agreeing, but she couldn't have stopped herself had she tried. Her jaguar roared for Cole, and her body ached to become one with his. She forgot about the lake, the water soaking her clothes, and the dirt and grass on her feet. Instead, all she noticed was Cole's scent, his taste, the feel of his bare skin beneath her palms.

He swept her into his arms, his shifter strength easily carrying her up the porch steps and into the house and then farther, to the bedroom they'd shared. Shared, yet they'd never gone this far. She'd never accepted what he offered so willingly. She was more than willing now. She craved his body, his bite. The feel of him piercing her... She shuddered, and her pussy clenched. Arousal burned a path along her nerves, sparking them to life one after another. It raced through her, sinking into her blood and bones.

He reached the bed and lowered her legs to the ground, not even pausing before he grasped the bottom of her tee. But she snatched it from him and he froze. "Stella? I thought..."

She grinned and gave him a quick kiss and a wink. "I've got the top; you work on the bottoms."

She tugged on the wet fabric, pulling until the top whipped free of her head. She reached behind herself and fought with her bra, the hooks determined to clam jam her.

Cole didn't seem to have that same trouble. Her pants fell to the ground without a hitch, leaving her bare from the waist down. "Fuck, Stella. No panties."

He leaned forward and nuzzled her closely cropped curls, breathing deep and then releasing his breath with a slow sigh. "You smell so good." His tongue flicked out, teasing the top of her slit, and she shuddered.

"Cole..." She reached for his shoulders, gripping them so she wouldn't suddenly topple. "You...I'm..."

He grasped her thighs and pushed her until she fell

back against the bed, and then she found him between her legs.

"What are you doing?"

He grinned. "You'll see."

Suddenly she realized her condition, the dirt clinging to her and her body covered in lake water. "Cole, I should shower before—"

Cole pressed his face to her pussy, tongue delving between her sex lips and lapping at her sensitive flesh. He moaned and licked her harder, increasing the pressure of his attentions. She forgot about whatever she'd been saying. This—his touch—was too overwhelming to think beyond the rolls of pleasure he gave her.

He sucked on her clit, flicking the nub and teasing the bundle of nerves. His rapid flicks and rhythmic strokes urged her toward release, giving her more and more pleasure with his every movement.

He moved farther south, circling her core and sliding into her before retracing his path. He made love to her with his mouth, giving and taking pleasure in equal measure.

Stella cupped her breasts and pinched her nipples, enjoying that added sting. With each tug, she rolled her hips, reveling in Cole's intimate attentions. He growled and moaned against her flesh, voicing his pleasure as she took her own from him.

She eased closer and closer to the precipice, all-encompassing pleasure drawing her to the edge. And she wanted it. Wanted to gather every snippet of bliss he was willing to give.

But not like this. She reached down and tugged on his hair, pulling until he finally released her clit. She withdrew one hand and propped herself on her elbow, meeting his amber stare. "I want to come with you in me. Fuck me. Claim me. Mate me."

Those eyes flared brighter—hotter—and she soon found herself in the middle of the bed on her back, legs splayed, with Cole between them. He sat on his heels and stroked his cock, the thick length hard and topped with a droplet of pre-come. He slid his palm from base to tip and back again, tugging on his dick and squeezing the tip.

"Is this what you want, Stella? You don't want to come on my mouth? You want my cock?"

She kept her eyes trained on his hand, unable to tear her stare away. "Yes."

Up and down, then up again. Squeeze. Stroke. Down. Up. Squeeze. She imagined riding him, squeezing his shaft with her muscles and making him shout her name.

He rubbed his thumb across the head of his dick, gathering the bit of moisture, and she licked her lips. She wanted to taste him, to savor him, and Cole gave her the chance. He held out his hand, and she quickly sat up, lips parted.

She sucked his thumb into her mouth, licking and lapping at the digit as if it were his cock. She pretended it was him in her mouth, so she suckled him, teased him, and imagined the feel of his hardness on her tongue. Her pussy clenched once more, her center hard and aching to be filled.

Stella couldn't remain still, too desperate for her mate. She released his thumb with a soft *pop* and moved before he even realized she'd changed positions. He remained sitting on his heels while she climbed atop him, straddled his lap, and sank onto his length.

"Oh fuck, oh fuck, oh fuck..." She took more and more of him in, his cock stroking her inner sheath and stretching her almost to the point of pain. "Fuck, you're inside me."

"Shit. Stella." A claw-tipped hand grasped her hip,

nails digging into her flesh. "Don't stop. Keep taking more of me."

And she did. She lowered her body until their hips met and his cock was fully seated. She rolled her hips and gasped at the pleasure, at the way it made her pussy clench and her body shudder.

"God dammit," he rasped. "You're so wet. So hot."

She rocked her hips back and forth, sliding up and down his shaft until she found a rhythm she liked. Her clit rubbed against him each time she lowered herself, the bundle of nerves singing with each touch. She rippled around him, milking his thick cock and body begging for his come.

Cole's attention transferred to where their bodies met, his gaze unmoving. "Do you know what it's like to see my dick in you? Mine." He growled then, his tiger pushing forward. "My mate."

Stella couldn't do more than pant a single word. "Yours."

He growled again and lifted his hips, meeting her on the downstroke. He slammed their bodies together, flesh hitting flesh in the very best of ways. He wrapped his arms around her, holding her in a cage of his flesh, and then changed their position. Now she lay beneath him, Cole's larger body hovering above hers.

He fucked her then, cock slamming into her with every word. "Mine. Mine. Mine."

And he didn't stop. He kept pounding into her, his growls adding to the ecstasy she found in his arms.

"Yours. Fuck me. Fuck, Cole... Your cock." It was perfect, stretching and filling her in a way that made her want to scream and cry.

She trembled in his arms, the growing pleasure snatching any hint of her ability to control herself.

And still he went on, giving her more and more with every flex of muscle. She met him stroke for stroke, giving them both the pleasure they craved.

"Give it to me, Stella. Come for me."

"Yes," she hissed, unable to stop herself.

Cole changed his angle then, a small lift of her hips and tilt of his and then..."*Fuck*. So good."

The head of his cock skated over her G-spot, stroking her inner walls and urging her to fall over the edge. He wanted her to come, and she wanted to fall apart in his arms.

Again and again and again...Her body shook, nipples hardened, and her pussy now milked his dick in time with his thrusts. Her body craved this male, craved his possession.

"Cole. Gonna..." So close. So fucking close to coming. She could feel the first tingles that announced release.

"Yes. Now. Come for me." Sweat dripped from his brow, proving how hard he worked to give her pleasure, and he somehow picked up his pace again. The bed slammed against the wall, and she had no doubt there'd be damage, but...

Stella lost herself to the spiraling bliss. She embraced it with open arms and leapt off the edge of the cliff. Her body trembled, toes curling and muscles shaking as she screamed Cole's name.

Cole's pace stuttered for a moment, his body jerking and cock twitching inside her before he finally sealed their hips together. His warmth flooded her, and she trembled with renewed arousal. Her first orgasm had barely finished and she wanted more.

While she continued to ride the high of her orgasm, Cole struck. Teeth sank into flesh, sharp teeth cutting through skin and clamping onto Stella's shoulder. He bit hard and deep—his first strike a clean claiming bite. She sensed the tie settling into place, their mating connecting them in a way nothing else could.

He released her wound slowly, careful when he withdrew his fangs and then lapped at the ragged flesh. Instead of rough passion, he gave her gentle healing, touches soft while he cleaned her skin of blood.

Finally he paused and pressed a soft kiss to her ragged shoulder. "Mine."

Cole turned his head and rested his cheek on her arm, keeping her wound in sight. He lowered his weight onto her, pinning her with his bulk, and she welcomed the pressure. She welcomed the feel of his exhausted body atop her. She caressed his sweat-soaked skin, fingers trailing across his shoulders and teasing his neck.

He remained inside her, his hardness continuing even though they'd both found their pleasure. She wiggled her hips, and she smiled when he moaned in response.

"Woman. You're gonna kill me," he growled as if he were angry, and she turned her head and nipped his ear.

"As if little old me could kill you."

"Mmm...It'd be fun trying. I can imagine my headstone: 'Here lies Cole Turner. He died with a smile on his face and his dick in his mate.'" He chuckled. "I think that sounds fantastic."

"I think you really want to die," she drawled.

Stella placed one foot on the mattress and stroked his calf with the other, the need to caress him overwhelming her. That simple movement was enough to remind her of something. Something that hadn't been important when lost in the desire for her mate. Now that her itch was scratched though...

"Hey, Cole?"

"Uh-huh." He pressed a kiss to her shoulder and lapped at her mating mark once more.

"Does Birch have other sheets?"

Cole froze and lifted away from her. Amber eyes met hers, and orange and black stripes slithered across his skin—emerging from his pores. "I have my dick in you."

"Yeah." It was kinda hard to miss. Big and thick and long and...*delicious*.

"Don't say another man's name while *my dick is in you*." He eased his hips back and pushed them forward once more, beginning another round of overwhelming pleasure.

They could talk about Birch and his dirty bedsheets later.

# CHAPTER THIRTY-TWO

Stella woke slowly, body thrumming with the most deliciously wicked hum of pain. She moaned and stretched, legs straight and toes pointed while she lifted her arms until they met the headboard. Muscles she'd forgotten about now throbbed with their strained objection to movement. The skin between her thighs burned, proof that Cole had worshipped her pussy more than once during the night. She was torn between demanding he shave or just enjoying the scrape of his rough cheeks on her sensitive flesh.

Then there was her shoulder... Stella lowered her arms and relaxed her legs while she turned her head to the side. She tipped her head down, and her eyes sought out the scarring he'd caused. There it was, her pale skin now marred with the healing wound—lines and dots of red replacing the white. The pink and red would lessen throughout the day until her mating mark turned into white slivers of a scar.

Any shifter that looked at her—at that mark—would know she was taken.

Her lips twitched, and then the corners of her mouth rose to form a soft, sated smile. Her body had been well used, and she was sore for the most wonderful reasons *ever*. Life was good. Or as good as it could be while a psychopath and his insanely funded terrorist group remained free. Ugh. She pushed thoughts of those assholes—Unified Humanity—to the back of her mind. She didn't need UH raining on her newly mated parade.

She rolled to her stomach and stretched again, a bit of her cat coming through as she sat back on her heels, arms extended in front of her. She wiggled and moaned, sinking into the stretch while letting memories from the previous night flood her. Images of when Cole had kissed her *there* and then nibbled her over *there* and that thing he'd done with his tongue... She moaned again, body heating with a now familiar craving for the big kitty. It was like one bite made her addicted to the tiger. Now that she'd had him once, she wanted him always.

Except... She opened one eye and then the other, turning her head to scan the room for other occupants. Occupants like a specific tiger she wanted to lick from head to toe. Unfortunately, said tiger—and his toes—weren't in the bedroom. Bastard. Here she woke all achy and ready for another round and he'd wandered off. Just see if she lifted her tail for him again. Eh, who was she kidding? She'd totally take another ride on the tiger train. But not until she grumbled a bit about it first.

She closed her eyes and slumped onto the mattress into a boneless heap once again. Tipping her head, she listened to the rest of the cabin, searching for any sounds that might announce Cole's location. At first she heard only the rustle of trees outside, along with the soft twitter of birds. The brush of leaves blown across the yard joined in and then the squeaking chitters of a squirrel came to her.

Lovely to listen to—nature's early-morning music—but not the one she sought. Which meant, *ugh*, she'd actually have to get up and go find him. Then, because he hadn't stayed in bed with her, *nor* did it sound like he was making her breakfast, she'd shove him into the kitchen and put him to work. Sure, there were probably men who said a woman's place was in the kitchen, but they didn't say that after they'd taken a bite out of that woman's shoulder. His ass could scramble the eggs.

Stella rolled from the bed, grabbing a fistful of sheet and dragging it free of the pile as she stood. Another tug and pull and she somehow managed to drape it across her shoulders. A quick tuck and she had a toga—ish. Well, her pink bits weren't exposed, at least. Sure, Grant had left them alone, but there was no telling when the big bad wolf would return.

Flashing him seemed unhealthy. For Grant, not her. Cole might glare at her for flashing his teammate, but he'd probably pop Grant's eyes right out of his head for looking. That shouldn't give her the warm fuzzies, but it did.

With the sheet dragging on the ground, Stella padded from the room, steps nearly silent on the hardwood flooring. Her movements carried her down the hallway, and she continued to scan her surroundings in search of Cole. At the top of the stairs, she paused and tilted her head once more. Eyes closed, she concentrated and sought any clue to her mate's location. *Her mate.* She still couldn't get over that.

The soft *click*—of a door opening? or closing?—and the slide of drawer glides reached her. Faint but present and somewhere downstairs. Opening her eyes, she continued on her trek, heading downstairs and pausing at their base.

*Mmm . . .* She hadn't caught the scent upstairs, but now the roasted goodness of fresh coffee lured her onward. She still heard movement on the other side of the great room, a hallway and several bedrooms opposite her, but . . . *coffee.*

She'd just snag one cup, and then she really would look for her mate. Really.

Stella went left, quickly entering the kitchen and snaring a clean mug off the drying rack. A near full pot of coffee sat on the coffeemaker, and it took her no time to fill her mug. She cradled the now hot ceramic between her palms and blew across the steaming liquid before taking a deep breath. *Perfection.*

She sipped at the hot coffee, careful not to burn her tongue while she savored the first jolt of caffeine. With a hum, she took another bit into her mouth, rolling the dark brew across her taste buds. She moved to the back entrance, French doors barring the entry, and peered into the backyard. A gust of wind blew a ripple across the lake, reminding her of a stone being tossed into the placid waters. A stone or a fully grown jaguar shifter—whatever was at hand.

The sounds from the other side of the house grew louder, a drawer slamming shut instead of merely gliding back into place. She turned, ready to hunt her mate now that she had liquid fortification, but drew up short. She stuttered to a stop and stared at what sat upon the kitchen table. A laptop computer rested on the oak table, the device open and unlocked, displaying the most recent message.

An e-mail.

With an address.

And a single name—Walters.

She glanced at the sender area and saw that it'd come from someone named Grant Bond. She didn't believe that Grant's last name was really Bond, but . . . But could she trust it enough to accept its contents at face value? Had Grant found Walters? Was that his address? Excitement bubbled in her chest, body already preparing for battle by releasing a sudden flood of adrenaline. She'd face off against the human who'd destroyed her family. The human who'd destroyed her *life*.

Well, first she'd find Cole and then she'd look for Walters. It wasn't like she could do anything without the big kitty. This would be their first outing as a mated couple. She doubted most couples kicked off mated life with a hunt, followed by a (hopefully) bloody homicide, but she and Cole had met when Stella had a bomb between her tits. This seemed par for the course.

She took one last sip of her coffee and set it aside, leaving it behind as she continued to hunt for her mate. She drew a deep breath into her lungs and followed his scent and the sounds of his movement on the other side of the house. His steps were heavy now—hard. No longer the soft slap of bare feet on hardwood. There was another sound— fabric rustling.

He'd obviously gotten dressed, so he must have been up for a while. Up and preparing to leave. Eh, she could throw on some clothes and put her hair in a ponytail in a second if needed. She wouldn't be too far behind him if he intended to leave soon.

This hallway was short—shorter than the one upstairs—and she soon found herself in an unfamiliar guest room. Guest room turned armory, anyway. The closet doors were spread wide to reveal a wonderful collection of things that went *boom*. Two gun safes, dark clothing arranged in a neat row, and body armor filled the space, along with just about any ammunition a gun whore would ever need.

And her mate stood in front of it all, black pants tucked into combat boots, leg holsters strapped on with guns secured. She watched as he reached for another weapon, this one a long blade, which he secured to his calf. Next he pulled on his shirt, thick muscles rippling beneath his skin as he tugged the stretchy fabric into place. He followed that with body armor and then another midnight shirt on top. Damn he was sexy.

Stella licked her lips and cleared her throat. "Hey."

Cole didn't stiffen or jolt. So he'd known she was watching. "Hey."

"I missed waking up with you." She moved toward him, not stopping until she reached her mate and pressed her front to his back. She expected a little loving. Maybe him turning around to give her a bit of snuggling. She *hadn't* expected him to continue getting ready as if she weren't even there.

"The team has an op." Curt. Each word bitten off.

"Yeah, I know. I saw the e-mail from Grant."

Cole froze in place, muscles tightening. "That wasn't for your eyes."

"Then you probably shouldn't have left the laptop open and the e-mail on the screen." She drew the words out, fighting not to respond to his level of dickdom with bitchville of her own. "How much time do we have? Who's coming to pick us up?"

She almost asked if she'd get to be a badass secret agent in a helo, but held herself back. Barely. The only thing that kept her quiet was the increasing tension in her mate. With every word, more and more of his muscles knotted until he looked as stiff as a board.

"*I* have fifteen minutes before I'm being relieved."

"I?" She furrowed her brow and stepped away, staring at his back. "You're being relieved?"

He hadn't even stopped to look at her. "Yes."

"To be clear…" She couldn't go to bitchville. They

hadn't been mated long, so she could consider this their first foray into communication. "You're being *relieved*? As in, only you, and 'relieved,' like I'm a *job* of some sort?"

He paused and sighed, dropping his head forward while his shoulders fell. "Stella..."

He said her name in that weird condescending, annoyed, frustrated way. As if *she* was the one in the wrong, or an idiot or...something.

When he didn't say anything for a while, she spoke up. "Yes?"

"You're twisting my words." He finally turned to face her, those blue eyes looking more like a stormy sea than bright skies. "I meant that...Remember, I *was* assigned to watch over you and...If I took you along, you'd be..."

He still hadn't finished a complete sentence, but his half sentences were enough to annoy her.

Stella held up a hand. "We'll move past the 'relieved' comment because we don't have the time for that level of arguing." Though all bets were off once Walters was handled. "Let's, instead, focus on your misbelief that I'm staying here while you go off and do your secret agent thing."

Cole's frown remained in place. His lips didn't even so much as *twitch* with her joke. "Walters is dangerous. You learned that over the weekend. There's no way I'm going to let you—"

*"Let?"* Oh. Hell. No.

"Put yourself in danger by tagging along. I'll handle this. Trust me."

"Tagging along? Like I'm some little girl in pigtails and ruffled socks?" She shook her head. "Trust you? This isn't about trust. This is about getting a piece of the asshole who ruined my family."

"And I'll do that for you. Walters is dangerous."

"*Life* is dangerous. I'm not some weak woman who needs to be coddled. I've been taking care of myself since that asshole took my sister and my parents lost it. I snuck into that man's house with C-4 strapped to my tits, for God's sake." She cupped said tits to emphasize her point. "I'm not an accountant attacking a thug with a ten-key calculator like Declan's mate. I'm an adult. Treat me like one."

Silence stretched between them, the endless quiet broken by the double honk of a vehicle's horn.

"I gotta go." Cole bent toward her, eyes on hers as he drew near. When he would have kissed her lips, she turned her head, accepting a kiss to her temple instead. "I'll see you tomorrow."

He stomped toward the doorway, the echo of his boots thudding against the wood floor, giving her his location as he left the house. His pace remained solid and steady. There was no rushing for her mate. No, just fierce determination that led him from the cabin. She listened to the knob turn, the squeak of the hinges as he opened the door, and the *thump* as it slammed closed once more.

Stella stayed in place, not moving until the roar of an engine reached her, the crunch of tires on the gravel driveway. The rumble faded, Cole leaving her behind to, what? Wait. Worry.

She shook her head. That wasn't her. She didn't sit at home and wring her hands, hoping someone else would solve her problems. Cole could leave her behind, but that didn't mean she'd stay where she was put.

She grabbed a handful of her sheet and swept it behind her as she spun in place. Back straight and filled with renewed determination, she retraced her path with determined strides. She had clothes in the cabin. She'd get dressed and—

The stomp of someone large and heavy climbing the stairs filled the cabin's living room. She froze in place, gaze fixed on the entry. She held her breath and waited, senses heightened with the arrival of this newcomer.

"Yo, Stella? You here?"

She recognized that voice, though the last time she'd heard it she'd been surrounded by gunfire while trying to save a certain tiger's ass. Now maybe he could help her *kick* a certain tiger's ass.

"Yeah. I'm here. One sec," she called out, and went to the door to let him in, except it swung open to reveal Pike.

Stella stared at Pike. Pike stared at Stella. So she kept staring at Pike, narrowing her eyes the longer they kept their gazes locked, until finally Pike gave in with a roll of his eyes. He sighed, shoulders slumping and head bowing while he tucked his hands in his pockets.

"You're not gonna make this easy, are you?"

"Nope."

"You're gonna make me betray my brother-in-arms, aren't you?"

"Yup."

"He's gonna want to kick my ass, isn't he?"

"Oh yeah." She grinned then, smile widening.

"Grant said you wouldn't take Cole's shit. And as much as I'm enjoying the view…" Pike leaned out the front door and retrieved a black bag. "He packed you a bag. Same shit the team wears, just smaller." The wolf looked her up and down, his expression telling her that he was imagining her without the sheet. "And curvier. Sometimes the buckles can be a little confusing. Do you want some help?" His lips quirked in a little smirk, and he winked. "You know, one teammate helping another."

Stella rolled her eyes. "Down, boy."

# CHAPTER THIRTY-THREE

*T*he darkness was a welcome partner, the shadows enveloping Cole in a concealing embrace. It hid the rest of the team, too. Each of them hunkered down, motionless among the trees and undergrowth. They surrounded the property, the sprawling ranch-style home dead center and enclosed by forest on three sides. Not the smartest hideaway for a human on the run from shifters. The feral parts of themselves called the untamed wilds home and found comfort in nature. *This* was their playground.

Cole remained motionless beneath the bushes, protected from the wet ground, dry leaves, and sticks by his dark clothing. Handgun snug against his palm, he was poised to shoot anyone who stood in their way. SHOC Team One had a mission. In truth, they had two missions—one handed down through SHOC's hierarchy and another agreed upon between his teammates.

Director Quade wanted Walters *dead*.

Cole's team wanted the human dead, too. But first they wanted *information*. Walters had gotten off the SHOC yacht somehow. They wanted to know who'd helped him, the name of his contact within SHOC. Because, sure as shit,

Walters wouldn't still be alive if he hadn't had help from someone in the organization.

Cole voted for Hartley. Birch picked Quade. A joking Grant nominated their cafeteria woman at headquarters.

"Explain to me again why couldn't I bring snacks?" Grant's voice was low but crystal clear. The modified coms the wolf had spread through the team were a work of art. And an artful pain in the ass. They couldn't even mumble insults anymore. The device was too good at picking up every syllable no matter how quiet.

"Seriously. I'd even take a protein bar right now." Grant gagged. He was surprised they couldn't hear the wolf's stomach grumbling across the coms. "And you know that shit causes 'digestive issues.'"

Birch sighed, but he didn't say a word.

Ethan grunted. "There's nothing wrong with protein bars. You had 'digestive issues' after dinner at Declan's last month."

"It was the bad spinach," Declan mumbled. "It must have been tainted with salmonella. Everything else was perfect, and you know it. I already told Abby not to serve green shit to carnivores."

Cole snickered. He couldn't help it. "Perfect. Sure. Remind her to defrost the turkeys before baking them. They might actually cook through, and then we won't be forced to touch raw poultry because you ordered us to be nice to the pregnant woman."

Grant spoke again. "Beef is better anyway. Even raw."

Birch sighed, and Cole imagined the grizzly rolling his eyes. "Focus."

Focus. Right. They had a job. Observe. Kidnap. Question. *Then* report.

"It wasn't like anyone was sick for long," Declan grumbled once more, not letting the topic drop. "Your beasts handled it."

Grant's low growl traveled over the com. "Just because my wolf eliminated the infection doesn't mean I had a good time worshipping the porcelain—" He cut off. "I have contact. Southern wall. Two heat signatures. Fur on two legs and fur on four legs. Fur on two is a big mofo. Probably male."

Not the most private code words, but they got the point across. They had two shifters—their higher temperatures identifying them easily—on approach. One walked on two legs in its human form while the other sported paws.

"Identity." Birch didn't ask; he demanded.

"Working." The click and clack of keys came over the com, Grant's fingers flying across the keyboard. "Declan, they're coming right up your ass."

"Birch, we thinking friend or foe?" Cole wondered if the SHOC traitors were taking a walk in the woods and right into their hands.

"Not sure. Grant?" Birch barked out the word like a wolf rather than a bear.

*"Working."* The werewolf snarled and then grumbled. Probably forgetting about the tinkering he'd done to their coms. "Don't you think I'd fucking tell you who it is if I fucking knew?"

No one replied to that one, though he was sure Ethan had a response on the tip of his tongue. The lion liked poking the wolf. A thing about cats and dogs that the "king of the jungle" enjoyed.

Ignoring it all, Cole spoke to the other wolf on the team. "Dec, you smell anything?"

Declan grunted, and Cole was glad he'd spent so much time with Declan during their last big op. The one that had included Declan finding Abby and mating her.

*Mating*... That simple word reminded Cole of Stella... and the situation he'd left in that cabin not so long ago. He wrenched his thoughts from that direction and refocused on the here and now. He'd fix his relationship with Stella later. He *had* to. He couldn't live without her.

Cole shook his head and thought of the tone of Declan's grunt. The wolf didn't smell anything. Yet. "You see anything, then?"

The next grunt said that Cole was an idiot *and* an asshole.

"You don't have to be a dick just because you haven't been laid in a while, fucker." More than one snigger followed Cole's words.

"Declan, they're twenty yards behind you. They'll be ten yards west of your position when they come even with you." Tension thrummed in Grant's voice.

"Orders?" Ethan was on the opposite side of the house, taking up the north position. If he broke cover, he had a clear line of sight to take out the two newcomers. Bullets or sedatives, either worked. Right now the two strangers were stomping in the middle of their shit, and they had the potential to fuck it *all* up.

"Hold." Birch's voice was flat—unemotional.

Everyone fell silent, the only sound coming across the com was the tap of Grant's fingers on his keyboard. Not even the whoosh of breathing could be heard—as if everyone held their breath and waited for the outcome.

The wind picked up, tree branches rustling with the random gusts. The scents of the forest wrapped around him, and he imagined it enveloped the others as well. Leaves rustled and ghosted across the yard, while sprinkles of dirt danced through the breeze. The scent of birds and squirrels teased his nose, and he knew a rabbit's burrow was no more than sixty feet west.

His tiger snarled at him—demanding he focus on the op. It was the first time the beast had bothered to make a sound since he'd left Stella. Immediately after it'd broken the quiet, it went back to hiding itself from his human side. The cat was *pissed* that they'd left Stella behind. Even more pissed at how Cole had talked to her.

He'd apologize tomorrow. After the op was done and he was sure Walters was no longer a threat. When he was sure she was safe.

He'd ask Declan for tips. The mated wolf would know how to do the apologizing shit. With Abby pregnant and emotional, the wolf was apologizing for something *constantly*. Yeah, he'd ask Declan tomorrow. Tonight...

Another gust of wind whipped through the area, drenching him in the scents in the area. Scents like...

Cole growled. "Mother—"

"—fucking," Declan finished.

Then Birch. "Sonofabitch."

"Hey, I identified the guys in the woods." Grant followed that with a stilted laugh. "Buuut, from the sound of things, you did, too."

Yeah, Cole had. He'd know that sweetness anywhere. Honeysuckle. Strawberry. Then that something extra that was pure Stella. He imagined Declan scented his younger brother, Pike. The wolf had been tasked with watching Stella, and the kid enjoyed creative interpretation of orders.

He could just hear Pike's voice now. *I'm watching her, aren't I? Watching her join the op.*

Cole closed his eyes for a moment and breathed deep, drawing Stella's scent into his lungs until he was filled with her aroma. Until she permeated every cell in his body. The stink of betrayal and rage didn't taint her flavors any longer. Now she was consumed by anticipation, excitement, and an edge of worry.

He opened his eyes and glanced around the area while he beckoned his tiger to come forward. The asshole could be pissed at him later. Right now he needed his cat's vision to spy Stella. Grumbling with every step, the animal padded forward, and Cole's eyes burned—his vision transforming within moments. The world around him transitioned, colors leaching from the forest while his eyesight focused. His view sharpened, eyes able to pick out details that'd been mere blurs before.

"The dynamic duo are almost to the tree line." Grant tried to joke, but his voice was flat, the words not lightening the mood a bit.

Cole turned his head and zeroed in on the edge of the yard, the bushes that swayed and the tall trees that grew along the trimmed border. He watched the area, gaze unwavering while he waited for her to come into sight.

"And the party is officially crashed." Grant again. His words meaning that Pike and Stella had arrived, but there was no hint of his jaguar mate. He didn't expect to see Pike. The man knew to come to an op wrapped in black clothing—easily blending into the scenery. Cole *should* see Stella's golden fur and dark spots. Yet he didn't.

Then the clouds drifted onward, revealing the full moon that hung in the sky and allowing the soft glow to bathe the area. That was when he spied her eyes, the reflective orbs seeming to float in the middle of the blackness.

"I have eyes on them." Cole's voice came out as a growl, his tiger pushing forward harder and harder as he processed what he saw. "She's in Grant's new tech."

"The fuck?" The surprise in the techy werewolf's voice was real. So, he hadn't given up his toys willingly.

"Define." One word from Birch. The bear always managed to say a lot with so little.

*Tell me what the fuck you're talking about before I lose my shit.*

Cole's tiger shoved at him, demanding he shift and chase his mate down—keep her safe while the op continued. "Remember how Grant designed a spandex suit that should cover us from head to tail and still keep our dicks covered if we were on two legs?"

"The Green Man outfits?" Disgust laced Ethan's voice.

Grant sighed. "We're not in the middle of an episode of *It's Always Sunny in Philadelphia* and none of us are Charlie Kelly. They're *not* 'Green Man' outfits."

Declan coughed. "Green Man." Then coughed again.

Cole didn't say anything else. Just kept staring at Stella's black-clad, shifted form. At least until the soft glow of the moon gradually waned. That's when Stella pulled her attention from him and let it drift across the yard. It paused near the house, then continued to the sky—the moon. A moon with dark clouds easing to block the minimal light it shined down on the world.

"Don't do it, Stella," he murmured, hoping his cat's growl marred the words enough that the others didn't understand his warning.

Because he already knew what she was gonna do. And it was gonna get her ass killed.

"Who's doing what?" The crunch of leaves accompanied Declan's question, the wolf moving beneath his cover.

"Update." Birch's voice didn't have any hint of tension, which meant the bear was pissed as hell. The quieter and more controlled he sounded, the more furious he truly was.

"Still stationary," Grant reassured their team alpha.

*Stationary, but not for long.*

The largest collection of clouds continued their gentle drift across the sky, blanketing more and more of their surroundings in utter blackness. If his team was going in, they'd need to wait until *everyone* was covered by the shadows—from Ethan, around the half circle, and all the way to Declan.

Unfortunately, Stella wasn't part of his team. She was one pissed-off jaguar with a vendetta pushing her onward. Stella's attention lowered from the sky, her gaze now watching the progress of that darkness as it crept across the yard. It'd already passed Ethan, Birch, and Cole. It'd even overtaken her. But she remained in place until...

Cole stared at the home, recalling the list of plans they'd created when designing their attack. Including the one that Ethan had proposed. The one that included a lion shifter doing *purr*kour and bouncing between the house exterior and a tree until he landed on the roof.

Birch had stared at Ethan and shaken his head. Just because Ethan looked at memes on his damned phone didn't mean he could *become* a meme by doing parkour when shifted. No one was going to record him and put that shit on YouTube.

Well, by the way Stella stared at the tree growing near the house, it seemed that Ethan would get his purrkour after all. It would just be a jaguar instead of the king of the jungle.

Stella jolted forward before any of them could react. Before Cole could warn Birch and a new plan could be organized. A bolt of black cat raced across the distance toward the corner of the house. No windows at that juncture and a big tree ten feet from the roofline. She performed the maneuver with ease. Leap at the wall, spring off the brick to the tree, then the wall and tree once more, before silently landing on the shingle roof.

If she weren't putting herself in danger and destroying the op, he'd be fucking proud of what she'd just done. She hadn't made a sound. Hadn't triggered any lights or alarms.

"And that, gentlemen, is how it's done." *Pike.* The cocky sonofabitch that Cole couldn't wait to pummel. He could practically see the wolf's smile.

"I'm gonna kick your ass." Cole's tiger was on board with that idea. It wanted to take control and destroy the younger wolf, teach him to fuck around with another male's mate.

"Does she know this plan, Pike?" Birch's voice vibrated through their coms.

"Yeah. She's got a pack strapped to her chest. She knows the layout of the house."

"And how to disarm the security system?" Their team alpha's voice carried a heavy dose of skepticism.

"Stella built *bombs*. I think she can cut a coupla wires," Pike drawled.

Yeah, Cole would have agreed with the younger wolf *if* the house's alarm hadn't chosen that moment to go off. "Fuck."

# CHAPTER THIRTY-FOUR

*U*sing the home's exterior wall and a nearby tree to reach the roof had all been part of the plan. Stella had even enjoyed the strain on her muscles, her body performing in a way she'd never tried before. Plus, it'd gotten her closer to Walters. Once on the roof it was a quick, *one, two, three* and...she woulda been in like Flynn.

Except the night's plans had been discussed with Pike while Stella had been human. She'd been on two legs with pale skin instead of spotted fur. She'd given the werewolf assurances while she had hands instead of paws. She'd promised she'd follow his orders to the letter.

Then she'd shifted.

As soon as her jaguar took possession of her body, the battle began. Stella's desires struggled against the cat's instincts—the feline craving the blood of its enemy. Her human half wanted James's life to end quickly. His death was the point of the exercise. The jaguar wanted to play with its prey. It wanted to hear the screams and watch as life bled from his body. It wanted him to suffer as she suffered. Pain was its goal. Death would be the result. The cat had full control and its own plans in mind. It didn't care about her promises to Pike or that Cole's SHOC team lurked in the shadows.

She'd scented Walters the moment her paws hit the shingle roof, the dark, coarse surface providing additional friction. His stink teased her nose for a moment—no more than a second—before the cat overwhelmed her with its craving. She'd raced across the roof, nails scraping the shingles as she hunted the source of that aroma. She drew closer with every stride, and then frustration joined the cat's craving.

Entering the home silently required hands, but the jaguar refused to relinquish its hold. Which was why her front paws morphed into a perverted version of human hands, the fingers long and crooked with thick, dark nails at the tips.

With the house's floor plan in mind, she leapt for the edge of the roof. Arms outstretched, she twisted in air, body contorting so she could grasp the fascia. Momentum carried her onward, and she stretched out her legs, bracing to collide with the window. Grant's suit protected her body from the glass, shards bouncing off the fabric.

She'd landed just inside the room with a low *thump* and dropped into a crouch, cat's eyes scanning her surroundings. Within a heartbeat, the alarm sounded, but the cat hadn't cared.

Now they had to deal with what the cat wrought. The jaguar re-shaped her body, returning to full cat instead of the twisted in-between form. But with those changes, Stella managed to grasp some control from the cat—enough to insert logic and caution into the beast's instinctual drive.

The alarm continued to blare, the piercing screech bouncing off the walls and crowding her ears. She fought past the pain from that sound and sought out other noises. Noises that belonged to James Walters. The male was somewhere in the house, and Stella would find him. His scent was light in the room, the space appearing unused and the air stale. A guest room, then. She padded forward, covered paws crunching over the shattered glass as she headed for the open door. A sliver of light shone through the narrow crack, leading her onward.

Stella nudged the door with her nose and drew air into her lungs. The stink of James Walters was sharper outside the room, and his scent beckoned her. She prodded the door once more, pushing until her shoulders made it through the doorway and she spilled out onto a balcony that overlooked the first floor. Carpet lined the walkway, the wall to her right and a railing and spindles to her left.

Nowhere to hide, but there was nothing to mar her visibility, either. It made it easy to see lights flickering on down below. The rapid progression of lights was soon followed by utter silence. One that didn't last long. Soon there was the rapid *thwap* of bare feet on tile flooring—someone running.

Stella peered over the edge of the walkway, eyes on the shadows that danced across the first-floor wall. Then there were more noises—some she could identify and some she couldn't. A voice—murmurs and the occasional shout. She recognized that voice. She also recognized that she didn't hear anyone else. At least, not yet. She was sure it'd get loud when Cole's SHOC team breeched the home. She had to act before they could intervene.

She swept the first floor with her gaze, eyeing the furniture that was scattered around the entry. She backed away from the edge until her ass met the wall, and then, in two giant steps, she leapt. She flew over the banister, body twisting as she fell. She landed on a thin area rug that slid sideways, and she dug her claws into the woven floor covering.

She heard nothing after she landed. No running. No

murmurs. She wasn't even sure her prey *breathed*. But even if he didn't make a sound, she could still find him. Her jaguar hunted by smell and sight, not sound. And the smell filling her nose ... It was exactly what she craved. He was close, contained in the house with nowhere to run—nowhere to hide.

Glass upstairs shattered, and her ears twitched, one turning toward the source of the crash.

"Who's there? What do you want!" Walters's voice was harsh and rough, almost strained.

Did he really have to ask who'd come for him? The human couldn't be *that* dumb, could he?

"Take anything! I won't call the police!" Apparently, he could be that dumb. He obviously thought he was dealing with a simple breaking and entering.

Stella licked her snout, tongue sliding over her left whiskers and then her right. She wanted to do some breaking, all right.

A heavy *thud* came from one of the rooms upstairs and then the snap of wood from the other side of the house—first floor. Cole's team was coming in and, dammit, he'd ruin her fun. He wouldn't let her toy with her prey. Hell, he wouldn't let her *have* her prey. So she left her spot in the entry and padded through the house, breathing deep with every step. Walters's scent permeated the whole house, but she followed the strongest trail and the brightest lights.

She turned left and then right, heading down the hallway toward an open arch. She spied a refrigerator through the opening, which meant she was about to enter the kitchen. Walters probably had probably gone for a knife. Not that it'd do much against Stella. She had her own knives, sixteen to be precise. Long. Sharp. Deadly.

She paused near the edge of the kitchen and drew in

another lungful of air, searching for any hint of gun oil or ammunition. She could handle hand-to-paw action, but no one wanted to tangle with a gun. Thankfully, it didn't smell like Walters had a projectile weapon.

Stella slowly eased around the corner, body moving like water, movements slow and sensuous. The space wasn't large—there wasn't even an island in the middle of the kitchen—and it took no time to find the man she sought. He had enough of a brain to have snatched a knife from the block, and he now clutched the handle.

"Oh fuck," he rasped.

*Oh fuck, indeed.*

"You...You're..." He swallowed hard and didn't say anything else, just stared at her with wide, scared eyes.

Stella hissed, mouth stretched wide to show off her fangs. He was a scared little boy when he didn't have security and weapons at his disposal. There were no men in white coats with sedatives on standby. Just him. And her.

She moved nearer, prowling and pacing across the kitchen but never losing sight of the trembling human. Her cat wanted him for a midnight snack. He stank of fear and sweat, and the feline wasn't looking forward to listening to him beg for his life. He'd probably piss himself, and *then* where would she be? She preferred to go with the "one bite and he's dead" approach. Her human half...Well, it seemed her human half wanted to see the blood and hear his cries.

Maybe a bit of both?

Stella darted forward, claws outstretched, and she batted at James Walters. Her nails sliced through cloth and flesh, leaving four shallow furrows across his thigh before he could react.

His pain-tinged cry echoed through the house, while the coppery scent of his blood filled the air.

"Stay back!" he sobbed.

As if she'd listen.

She leapt toward him again, this time going for his arm, mouth open and saliva dripping to the tile. Fangs sank through flesh and struck bone, so she added pressure, not stopping until his forearm snapped. The knife clattered to the ground, bouncing on the bloodstained tile.

His whiny shout scraped at her ears, the piercing cries clawing at her eardrums. *What a little bitch.* The only break in those sounds were the rapid *thuds* of boots throughout the house. All headed in her direction. It seemed that Cole's team wasn't trying for any kind of stealth. They were in a hurry. Probably to stop her. But she refused to be stopped. James Walters had to be killed.

Stella paced in front of Walters once again, scanning his body for her next target. He'd curled in on himself, forming a tiny ball tucked against the corner of the cabinets. He clutched one arm, cradling the damaged limb, while blood flowed freely from the wound in his thigh. If she went at his head, she could...

"*Stella,*" Cole hissed, and she turned one of her ears to listen to him. She wouldn't turn her back on Walters. He might still have a trick up his sleeve.

"Help me! This animal—"

Stella growled, the deep rumble beginning in her chest and vibrating through the air. Walters snapped his mouth closed.

"Stella, back off." Cole again, issuing orders as if he had a right.

She whipped her head around for a split second to hiss at her mate.

"You've got guns. She's a wild animal! Shoot her!"

Oh, James was cruising for a crushed skull.

She curled her lip and batted at him with claws retracted. He cried out again, and she almost rolled her eyes. What a whiny bitch.

"Wild animal? Seriously?" Cole snorted. "You guys hear that? Mr. James Walters, bigwig for Unified Humanity, thinks Stella is a wild animal."

He racked the slide on one of his weapons. It sounded like a handgun to her, but what did she know? She had eyes on Walters and was the first to see his reaction to Cole's statement. She got to see his face pale and his mouth drop open, observed the shudder that traveled through his body. She was the first to taste a new scent that wafted off the human. Unfortunately, it wasn't fear.

"I bet Stella's a wildcat in bed. Maybe that's what he means?" She recognized Pike's voice and decided she'd teach him some manners once she was done with Walters.

Then came the *thwap* of bone striking flesh, followed by Pike's grumbled "You didn't have to hit me."

"Yes, I really did," Cole drawled.

Maybe she wouldn't have to teach Pike anything, but she did still have to handle Walters. She stared at the human and tipped her head to the side, wondering if she could hold him still and bite off his fingers one by one. Her mouth wasn't exactly shaped to make the process easy, and she'd probably have to sit on him, but maybe...

"Why aren't you doing anything?" Walters spoke through gritted teeth.

"Well..." Cole's slow steps echoed in the kitchen, and she spied her mate gradually coming into view in her peripheral vision. He leaned against the granite counter and crossed his arms over his chest, gun still clutched in one hand. "The thing about it is, I don't really want to."

"Cole..." Birch's voice held a warning tone.

Cole grunted. "I can disagree with an order and still carry it out." He cleared his throat. "As I was saying, I want to let her have at you."

Stella liked the sound of that and took a step forward, tail flicking and twitching with excitement. *Bite, bite, bite…*

"*But*"—her mate's voice filled the room—"my mate isn't a killer. Not like me."

She wasn't? Actually, she was pretty sure she wanted "killer" on her résumé. Really. She glared at him out of the corner of her eye and huffed. James Walters had destroyed her family. He, in turn, needed to be destroyed. *One plus one equals dead, dead, dead.*

His voice softened. "Stella, step away from him. Let the team handle this."

She blew air out of her nose in a feline snort.

"This isn't you. Step away from him."

She curled her lip and exposed a single fang. She'd bite him if he kept trying to stop her.

"You aren't this person." His voice lowered further, and he dropped into a squat. "Killing another being changes something inside you. I promised you once, and I'll repeat my promise. I'll do this for you, Stella. I'll make sure you get your justice. Let my tiger carry the weight of his death."

Tail still whipping back and forth, she gave Cole more of her attention, staring at him and weighing his words. But she wanted him dead *now*.

The sound of creaking leather and metal sliding on metal broke the quiet, and she spared a glance for the others in the room. The whole team other than Grant filled the kitchen, and she figured the wolf was probably in some com center offsite. Now they stared at her, guns pointing at the floor and fingers nowhere near the trigger. They watched and waited, much like Cole. Waited to see what she'd do.

She turned back to Walters, meeting his eyes and staring the human down. His complexion had lightened further, skin waxy and peppered with sweat.

"Come on, sweet. Let us take him in." A large hand stroked her head. The fabric of her skintight suit blunted the sensation, but it couldn't block his scent. Cole touched her, stroked her in an attempt to calm her raging beast.

"Oh God." Walters chuckled, the laughter coming out in harsh breaths. "You're... You are, aren't you? You're all shifters." He sneered and shook his head. "He told me this place was secure. I wouldn't be found, he said." Walters grimaced. "And here you are. *Abominations*."

Stella flexed her claws, aching to scratch that smirk right off his face, but Cole's touch stopped her.

"Keep laughing, asshole." She could hear the smile in Cole's voice. "Just keep laughing. Laugh all the way to headquarters and right into your cell."

Walters snorted, and he shook his head. "You think you'll get me to your little SHOC headquarters? Not likely."

Stella wondered how the human knew about SHOC. Then again, a man had to know his enemy, and UH had been trying to get rid of shifters for a long time.

"And why is that?"

The human smiled wide, exposing bright white teeth, and his smile reminded her of a great white shark...just before he eats someone. "A mutual acquaintance made sure I got off that boat. You think he'll let you walk me into your headquarters? I'm untouchable. You won't hold me for long. Somehow, some way, they'll get me out, and I'll disappear."

Well, the pain she'd caused Walters had at least loosened his tongue a bit. Cole had said he was concerned there was a mole inside SHOC, and Walters had basically confirmed that suspicion. Cole trembled, and she swung her attention to her mate, worried that he'd gotten hurt somehow. But he wasn't trembling. No, he was laughing.

"I figured I'd probably *drag* you into headquarters personally." Cole shrugged and turned to his team alpha. "Actually...You know, Birch. He's human, and they're fragile little fucks. I think Mr. Walters needs medical attention. Maybe from our satellite compound about twenty minutes north of here. And since it's just a quick stopover, we don't have to give anyone a heads-up, right?" Cole dropped his voice and leaned toward Walters. "Maybe he gets talkative, and he tells us everything." Cole looked at Birch again. "What do you say?"

Birch grunted. She wasn't sure what that meant, but Cole must have because a wide smile spread across his face. He was one happy tiger.

# CHAPTER THIRTY-FIVE

Stella still hadn't shifted by the time Cole walked her back to Pike's SUV. He held the back door open, and the sleek jaguar leapt into the vehicle before he nudged it closed. A double thumping knock on the door signaled Pike he could take off. Then Cole was alone, waiting for his team to haul a still-breathing Walters to their panel van. He stomped across the leaf-strewn grass, the crunch of dead leaves accompanying his every step.

Grant swung the van's side door open, its light popping on to reveal the interior. The wolf didn't say a word, simply held out his bag of Doritos.

Cole grunted and stuck his hand in, snagging a handful and chomping down the snack. His cat told him it would have preferred them chomping on Walters. Yeah, well, him too.

Then came the *pop* of a soda can, and Grant's hand appeared once more, offering him a drink. They exchanged low grunts, silent guy speak for "thanks" and "you're welcome." The fucker was a pain in the ass and liked to tweak Cole's tail, but he knew enough to be silent when it was needed.

Cole needed it now. Needed it because he'd just sent

his mate off with another male while he'd vowed to stick around and end Walters's life. When all he wanted was to wrap his arms around Stella and hold on tight.

It was good to have a team who got him—didn't think of him as the rich asshole playing at soldier.

The rustle of brush and the snap of twigs announced the team's approach, movements loud and peppered with groans and moans. Soon the group came into sight, team members clothed in head-to-toe black, while Walters stumbled along with them. Blood soaked Walters's pants leg, bright red against his torn khakis. Stella had gotten a good swipe in, at least. He limped, steps stilted, and the only thing keeping him upright was Birch's tight hold, though one look at Walters's face showed he was disgusted by the contact.

*TFB, motherfucker. Too fucking bad.*

They drew near the van, and Birch released the human with a small nudge, sending Walters careening into the side of the vehicle. His head struck metal with a low *thump*, and he slumped to the ground, one hand clutching his skull.

"Oops," Birch drawled, then focused on Grant. "Any chatter?"

"No, sir. All's quiet."

"Damn." Birch sighed.

Yeah, Cole didn't like quiet, either. There should at least be local traffic. If no one was making a sound, there was a reason.

Like their mole pulling strings and hoping to catch Team One doing something they shouldn't.

Now he was being paranoid, right? A glance at his teammates told him that they were having the same thoughts. All right, then. They'd be paranoid together.

"Time for a trip, Mr. Walters." Birch grabbed the human

once more, using his bear's strength to pick Walters up like a toy and toss him into the van. Walters whined and groaned as he rolled across the floorboard.

"Hey, no blood on the equipment, man," Grant grumbled, scooting away from the human, then gathering his electronics and moving them away from Walters. "Blood and electricity don't mix."

Cole just snorted and shook his head, following Walters into the vehicle, with Declan right behind him. Birch hopped into the passenger seat, their master of transportation at the wheel. Though Ethan whined like a bitch whenever they took the van on an op.

Why take a van when they could take a Porsche?

Except this time Ethan kept his trap shut. The lion just tugged on his seat belt and got the van moving. They whipped around with a quick U-turn and crept along the darkened suburban streets. Small back roads led them through the countryside, civilization thinning the farther they got from town.

Still quiet. No joking. No laughter. Shit was heavy, the scene they'd just left weighing on them all. Stella hadn't been able to speak in her jaguar form, but there was no missing the pain she held in her feline heart.

His mate had been broken, shattered by the confrontation. But he'd gotten her to walk away. Now he had to keep his promise. He'd finish it.

Cole must have zoned out, because when he came back to himself, they were pulling between two tall trees, the underbrush hiding what was probably a path at some point. The gravel remained buried beneath the encroaching forest, crunching under their tires. The van swayed back and forth, bouncing over the drive and hitting damn near every pothole.

The trees and brush enveloped them, darkness swallowing their black van as if it were part of the scenery. Soon the trees gave way to a larger open space, a squat cabin in the center of the overgrown clearing. The place looked half dead, the roof caving in and more than one window missing. But it wasn't the outside that mattered. Nah, it was what remained buried beneath the small building that they'd come for.

A secluded, insulated space to have a private *conversation* with Walters.

Cole's tiger rumbled and rubbed against his mental walls. The cat wanted out, anxious to keep their promise to Stella. *Soon.*

Birch didn't have to issue orders—this was something they knew by heart. Grant packed up his most important equipment, while Ethan secured the van. Declan scanned their surroundings, the wolf ready to shoot at anything that moved. Cole did the same, palming his nine-millimeter while his tiger lent its assistance. Birch was the one who hauled Walters out of the van, dragging him by his collar across the yard.

Walters struggled to find his feet, cursing and fighting the bear's grip, but if a grizzly didn't want to let go, it wasn't going to let go. The human should just accept his fate and get real talkative, real fast.

They picked their way through the abandoned cabin, wood floor groaning with their weight. Small rodents scattered, shadows scurrying across the small space as they delved deeper and toward the back corner.

"Grant." Birch growled the wolf's name, and their tech genius moved forward, dropping to the ground near a trapdoor hidden in the waste. "Get us in undetected."

Grant lifted the panel of wood and brushed away errant flakes of dirt. He tugged a cord out of his pocket and connected it to a small computer. Once the screen flickered to life, he murmured, "Hello, beautiful."

Sometimes Cole thought the werewolf loved electronics more than the ladies, but in times like this, that was a good thing.

Cole moved to a nearby window and scanned the rough clearing, searching for any followers. Declan did the same, peering out the front entry while Ethan took a side. Birch kept Walters upright, and the coppery scent of the human's blood soaked the air. It overwhelmed the cloying flavors of decay, dampening all other aromas.

"We need to get him taped up before he bleeds out." Cole stated the obvious, getting nothing but a grunt back from his team alpha.

"He'll stay alive long enough to answer questions," Ethan murmured, the golden-haired lion's attention still on the darkness beyond the cabin.

"That's all that matters." Declan's voice floated across the shadows.

"Come to Papa, baby girl," Grant whispered, fingers flying over keys. He punctuated his next words with harsh taps of the keyboard. "Who's." *Tap*. "Your." *Tap*. "Daddy." *Tap*.

A soft *beep* broke the quiet, a small light flashing green from his corner.

"And we're in with no one the wiser. Saddle up, gang." The wolf hurried to pack up his toys, carefully tucking his tools away as if they were made of glass.

Things moved fast then, the team peeling away from their positions and crawling into that hole—Birch leading the way. Soft lighting illuminated the abandoned satellite base, the reserve batteries at least giving them a little visibility. Cole brought up the rear, tugging the thick metal door back into place and locking it. With a double tap to the door, he turned and followed his team deeper into the winding halls.

Five shifters, one human, none of them authorized to do a damned thing in this place, but then again, they didn't care.

*Time to do bad things for the right reasons.*

Cole only had one reason tonight—Stella.

Up ahead, Birch kicked in a door and shoved Walters forward, the bear following him in and then slamming that same door shut behind him.

"Hey," Cole called ahead. "What the fuck?"

Declan glanced back and tipped his head toward the room their team alpha now occupied. "Boss man wants first crack."

Cole's tiger snarled, not liking that the bear had gone first. Sure, he submitted to the grizzly—the bear his alpha within SHOC—but his beast craved the violence against their human captive.

And his beast wouldn't be denied.

The rest of the team remained outside the room, forming a line in front of the window with its one-way mirror. But Cole? Fuck it. He went inside. He stepped in softly, and then just as softly nudged the door closed. He focused on the bleeding man in the center of the room, Walters slumped in a dust-covered chair—skin pale and slicked with sweat, taking shallow breaths.

Cole joined his team alpha, mirroring the bear's position—legs braced shoulder-width apart and arms crossed over his chest. Birch slowly turned his head, near-black eyes focusing on him, and his team alpha quirked a single brow.

A silent *"what the fuck?"*

He returned a raised brow of his own. *"I'm not moving."*

Walters shifted in place, the chair creaking beneath his weight, which drew their attention back to him. He remained slumped in his seat, elbow braced on the other arm and palm cradling his head.

"You're all so fucked." Walters chuckled, the laugh turning into a moan. "*So* fucked." The man flashed a crazed smile, his wild-eyed expression adding to his twisted appearance. "You have no idea what you've done."

Cole came forward, steps deliberate and pace slow. "Why don't you tell us, then? 'Cause from where I'm standing, I've got a kill order with your name on it. No questions. No debates. Just a bullet to the brain and my job is done."

Walters scoffed. "Not likely."

"Aw, now, that's just not right." Cole looked back to his boss. "I think he called me a liar. Am I a liar, Birch?"

"Nope." The grizzly shook his head. "Seems our fearless leader decided Mr. Walters can best serve our purposes by taking a permanent nap."

That had the human freezing in place. "What are you talking about?"

Cole shrugged. "SHOC wants you dead. You've done enough over the years, and now it's time to pay." He grinned, his tiger's fangs pushing through. "And I'm looking forward to taking my pound of flesh."

"Wait a minute." Walters shook his head. "This isn't... This isn't supposed to happen. I'm protected. I'm *safe*, God dammit."

"Safe?" Cole chuckled, the sound evil even to his ears. "Hear that, Birch? He's safe." His next movements came in a blur, hand flashing to his side to withdraw a blade. Then he pressed the sharp tip beneath Walters's chin. "Feeling safe now?"

Walters swallowed, that pointed tip slicing through his skin. "You don't want to do this."

"Don't I?" He pressed the point a little deeper into the human's flesh. The scent of Walters's blood teased his nose, and his tiger roared for more. This man had hurt his jaguar mate. He'd taken something from her she could never get back. "It's pretty clear that you're no longer needed by SHOC. Maybe it's time to cleanse your soul before you meet your Maker, huh?"

"Nah. Our Mr. Walters doesn't have a soul. Do you, James?" Birch's measured steps echoed off the walls. The grizzly stopped at Cole's side. "You got something else, though." His boss crouched at Cole's side. "You got someone inside SHOC, and you're gonna gimme his name."

"Why should I?" Walters's voice was reedy and thin.

"Bleeding out isn't a fun way to die. My boy Cole can make it quick."

Cole's tiger snarled. It didn't want the human's death to be quick. It wanted it drawn-out, nice and slow and painful as hell. Fur rippled along his arms in a wave of orange and black, the cat making its displeasure known. He wouldn't let it out though, wouldn't turn his boss into a liar by acting without authorization.

"It just takes a name." Birch pulled away, standing tall once more. "The name of your contact and you can die nice and clean."

"No." Walters tried to shake his head, but he froze with a low hiss as the blade dug into his flesh. "No. I'll give you what you want, but I want out."

Cole chuckled, the cat's growl adding to the dark sound. "After everything you've done to our people." He shook his head. "You're dying, James Walters. You and all your little friends. The only thing open to negotiation is how long it takes." He lifted his free hand into Walters's view and let the tiger roll forward. He shifted his fingers into claws, the dark nails emerging from his human nail beds. "I can snap your neck, or I can carve the name of every shifter you've ever harmed into your skin with these. You'll die"—he sliced through Walters's shirt, leaving shredded fabric in his wake—"eventually."

Personally, Cole voted for taking his time with the human. A very, very long time.

"No way. If I'm going to reveal him, I want my freedom."

At least they'd confirmed the UH contact inside SHOC was male.

"I'm not hearing a name, Mr. Walters." Birch drawled the words.

"I—"

A knock cut off whatever Walters might have said, Ethan nudging the door open and interrupting their interrogation. "Boss, Grant's got a visitor on his camera, and Declan has him in his sights."

"Identity?"

Cole kept his gaze on Walters while the other two talked, watching for any change in his expression.

"Our good old boy from Three—Hartley—and crew, if I know the ass." Ethan's distaste for the snake shifter was obvious in his voice. "Hold. Declan spotted someone else." The seconds ticked past, Cole not letting his attention wander. "Our illustrious director showed, too."

Cole learned a couple things right then: (1) he wasn't gonna get his blood-soaked fun and (2) James Walters knew both Hartley and Quade.

# CHAPTER THIRTY-SIX

*C*ole was one antsy-as-hell tiger. Not that he'd admit that shit to anyone. He was a big, badass tiger—a fucking *SHOC agent*. Those kind of shifters didn't worry about seeing their mate after they'd left her behind for an op. Well, he'd tried to leave her behind, but the woman was...fucking amazing. He'd wanted to keep her safe by excluding her from the op, but she'd shown up anyway and then had gotten a bit of revenge on James Walters. Then he and the guys had gotten a little more.

He smiled with that memory, hearing James Walters's screams while they ensured his need for medical attention had been fun. Though that smile turned into a frown as some of the un-fun events pushed forward. Like the fact that Team Three showed up at the satellite base to pick up the human even though no one had reported that they'd had Walters in custody. Conveniently, the director had "changed his mind" about killing Walters. Uh-huh.

Further proof that there was a mole in SHOC. One that had the ability to move teams around like chess pieces. Birch had always been good at chess, and Grant was a smart fucker. They'd figure it out and let the rest of the team know who they needed to hunt.

At the moment they were regrouping—taking a break after this last hunt. Between the weekend on Serene Isle and then continuing the hunt for Walters on dry land, they were due a week of decompression time. Then they'd be back on call.

Now, standing at the edge of the forest that surrounded Birch's lakeside cabin, Cole wished they were already back at work. It'd give him an excuse to stay away a little longer. Just enough time to figure out what the hell he was gonna tell his mate.

*Hey, babe, the thing about it is...*

He sounded like a chick. Plus, he never called Stella "babe." Shit. He ran his hand through his hair, fisting the strands and tugging in the hopes that the slight sting would help him think. It didn't. Cole sighed and leaned against one of the thick pine trees. He'd had two days to figure shit out and hadn't. So. Fucked.

"You're so fucked." Grant followed his words with a low chuckle.

Cole stiffened, but he remained silent. He wasn't about to let the wolf know he'd surprised him. "Grant," he drawled. "How it's hanging?"

"They're swinging a little to the left." Grant's steps were loud, shoes crunching over dead leaves, pine needles, and twigs. "But I know you didn't come here to talk about my balls." The wolf leaned against a nearby tree, back against the bar. "You're here to see the woman who's holding yours."

He turned his head and glared at his teammate. "She's *not* holding my junk."

Grant shrugged. "Then why are you still standing out here like a ball-less wonder?" He jerked his chin toward Birch's cabin. "Go inside."

"I will."

"Before she's ninety?"

Cole curled his lip. "Fuck off."

"Nah, no fucking for me. Isn't that why I got shipped here to babysit? Because your woman couldn't wrap me around her pinkie? You know, like she did with Pike."

He snorted. "Pike is in so much shit for bringing her on the op. When I left, Birch was sitting on his front porch with a tall glass of sweet tea. He told Pike to run—"

They finished together. "—until *my* balls are sweating."

"He even brought out a little battery-powered fan to keep himself cool. Last I saw, Abby was giving him a fresh glass of tea and there wasn't a drop of sweat in sight."

He grinned at the memory. Not just because Pike was getting run into the ground. He also recalled the curve of Abby's pregnant stomach. He mentally replaced Stella with Abby, her belly filled with his child. He didn't care if they had a jaguar or a tiger as long as the baby was healthy. Of course, getting her pregnant required his presence, and he was still standing at the tree line. He had a big dick, but it wasn't long enough to impregnate her from that distance.

Grant grunted. "Hopefully, Pike learns something."

"Unlikely." Cole shrugged. "The kid's young."

"We were all young once. He hasn't been shot and he hasn't had an op go sideways on him. He'll get there."

It was Cole's turn to grunt. "What makes you sure the kid can learn? Can change?"

Grant pressed his lips together, attention moving from Cole to the placid lake. "Anyone can change and learn from their mistakes. Even if someone has been wrong their whole life, they can still open their eyes and realize they fucked up. Sometimes it takes some training. Other times it takes a helping hand."

Cole quirked an eyebrow. "We still talking about Pike? Because it doesn't sound like we're talking about Pike."

The wolf returned his attention to Cole. "Fuck off."

He just snorted. "Right. So, we're not talking about Pike."

The werewolf crossed his arms over his chest. "Why don't we talk about *you* and Stella, then?"

He glared at his teammate. "Stella and I are fine."

"Uh-huh. That's why you're still out here and she's still in there. She knows your ass is here. You get that, right? She's your *mate*, motherfucker. Even if she hates you right now, she'll get over it." Grant lowered his voice, but Cole still heard his next word. *"Eventually."*

"I was an ass."

"Uh-huh."

"I shouldn't have left her."

"Nope."

"I broke my promise."

"-ish. You broke-ish your promise." Grant shook his head. "None of us could have known that our mole would find him so quick. We didn't even check in at the satellite base just so we could keep Walters's captivity on the down low, but Team Three still showed up before we got our hurt on. Not your fault, man."

"Whatever." Cole's tiger disagreed. It still raged in the back of his mind, snarling, pushing, and prodding him to go hunt Walters once more. The next time they got their paws on him, he'd be dead.

"God, you're gonna be fucking stubborn, aren't you?" Grant clicked his tongue. "What the hell is it with you mated guys?"

"I will put a bomb in your truck if you don't shut the fuck up."

"You blow it up, you bought it. My insurance company isn't going to pay for any more 'mysterious incidents.'" Grant even did air quotes. "They've already paid for three totaled trucks."

"They weren't all my fault." Cole pointed at Grant. "Ethan drove the last one off the overpass."

Even Grant smiled and chuckled a little at that one. "The tree frog wasn't even *inside* the cab—it was on the windshield. But there he is screaming like a girl and running off the road." He shook his head, his laughter dying off, but then his mood quickly changed. "You're trying to distract me, aren't you?"

"I have no idea what you're talking about." Which was a lie, but whatever.

"Uh-huh. Nut up or shut up, Cole." Grant pointed at the cabin. "Go in there and apologize to your mate for being a dick. Give her the shitty news about Walters. Then kiss and make up."

Cole rolled his eyes. "Yeah, yeah."

"If you don't"—the wolf pushed away from the tree and prowled forward, slowly closing the distance between them—"I'll call your *mother*."

His breath caught, his heartbeat stuttering. "You wouldn't."

"Fuck yeah, I would."

"That's cold, man." He stared at the ground, shaking his head. "Ice cold."

Grant shrugged. "I bet your bed is, too. It'll be even colder if your mother finds out you got mated and didn't tell her. You know she'll have the family jet on its way here within thirty seconds of my call. *Then* she'll be in your shit until you agree to a froufrou mating party. A party your mate might plan, but you know your mother. She'll move into your house at headquarters just so that she's on hand to 'help.'" The wolf grinned. "Tell me I'm wrong."

Unfortunately, Grant *wasn't* wrong. He'd seen his mother do the same to his siblings. He and Stella needed to present a united front if they were going to survive his mother's passion for parties. Cole got money from his father's companies. He got his strategic planning, surveillance, and interest in explosives from his mother. (His mother was never happy with "off-the-shelf" fireworks.)

It was time for him to get over his crap. Cole straightened and shoved Grant back. "Go eat something, Grant. I got shit to do."

"You mean a woman to do?"

"I will punch you in your suckhole so hard you'll be eating through a straw for a week."

Grant smiled wide and gave Cole a two-finger salute. "And that's my cue to leave. Good luck."

\* \* \*

Stella sensed Cole's presence, something inside her connecting with her mate and announcing his nearness. She couldn't pinpoint his location. She simply knew he was coming closer. Her jaguar purred, anxious to reconnect with their other half while Stella's human mind balked at his arrival. Just because she'd left James Walters in Cole's hands two days ago didn't mean she wasn't still pissed at the tiger. The old pain of being left behind reared its ugly head once more.

The feline in her mind hissed, baring its fangs and snarling. It didn't like Stella's attitude. Cole had come for them; their mate was near. She should run to the tiger and leap into his arms, then lift her tail and... She cut off the cat's line of thinking. That really wasn't happening. The beast hissed again—louder and longer this time.

She simply shook her head and sighed. She'd been having this same argument in varying degrees for two days. The cat told her that it was determined to win. It was the jaguar's turn, dammit. Stella brushed off the beast. It was funny to joke about taking turns over inconsequential things, but this was their *life*, their *future*. The animal assured her that it was right and Stella was wrong. Full stop.

She rolled her eyes. She wasn't going to continue the argument. *Full stop*. She sneered at her inner beast. The cat was not amused. But Stella was, so she counted it a win.

The closer Cole moved, the stronger his pull, the connection almost like a physical rope stretched between them. His every step felt like a tug on the line, making her uncomfortable yet excited at the same time. Was she ready for this confrontation? Not really, but they were mated. She couldn't just ignore the male.

So she rose from the living room couch and closed her eyes for a moment, sensing Cole's direction. She was pulled toward the back of the house and through the kitchen, onward to the back door. The smooth lake spread out before her, but that wasn't what snared her attention.

No, it was the single male who stood in the middle of the backyard who had her focus. He remained in place, those blue eyes turning amber while she stared at him. He wore his typical off-duty uniform—worn jeans and a thin T-shirt—and had his hands tucked in his pockets. Because he was nervous? Unsure? Nah, that couldn't be it. Cole Turner was one of the most self-assured shifters she'd ever met. He made decisions and took action without a hint of hesitation.

And yet he hadn't budged an inch. He remained right

there, sun slowly casting him in shadow as it sank toward the horizon. The longer she stared, the more Stella's cat reacted to his nearness, the beast pushing forward and demanding a larger presence. It wanted to be part of the reconnection, dammit. She couldn't find a reason to deny the jaguar as long as it understood she *was not* getting her fur on in the near future. After that escapade during the op, she'd kept the bitch under lock, key, and concrete block.

Her jaguar purred as she released the heaviest of her mental locks and then padded forward. Stella's eyesight changed, the brighter colors fading as the cat infused her eyes. Now the beast urged her to move again. All she had to do was step out the door and... And if the cat didn't shut up, its furry ass would spend the rest of its life inside a soundproofed mental cage.

Stella turned the doorknob and nudged the back door open. A breeze off the lake ruffled her hair and caressed her skin as she stepped outside and then let the door slam shut in her wake.

Cole still hadn't moved.

Barefoot, she padded across the wood porch and slowly descended the warped stairs. The grass at the bottom of the steps was cool on her soles, and her feet sank into the plush yard. That put her and Cole on even ground, facing each other across the yard's expanse.

She could go to him. Run into his arms and drag him to bed and never talk about him breaking his promise. Or they could argue it out and solve future problems before they cropped up by setting expectations. Her mother had always told her: *When you first mate, don't start doing anything for him that you're not willing to do for the rest of your life.*

She sure as hell wasn't going to teach him that running

off and leaving her behind when he said he wouldn't was gonna fly.

Stella moved forward a couple steps before she spoke. "What are you doing here, Cole?"

"You're here." Cole gave her one of those hangdog puppy faces. The jerk.

She went ahead and took another step so she wouldn't have to yell quite so loud. "Yeah. I'm here because this is where you *left* me, remember?"

"Stella..." His shoulders fell, and this time he eased closer to her. "You can't expect me..." He pulled one hand out of his pocket and ran his fingers through his hair. "I know more about certain things and..." He sighed and just looked at her once more, no longer trying to justify himself. Instead, he gave her two simple words. "I'm sorry."

She narrowed her eyes. Getting an apology was way too easy. "For what?"

"Huh?"

"What are you sorry for?"

"Uh..."

"Cole." She didn't know what else to say after his name. Seriously? He was going to apologize but not know *why*?

"I'm sorry I stopped you from getting vengeance." He took a step closer. "I'm sorry I left you behind." And another. "I'm sorry I broke my promise." Then another. "I'm sorry I tried to protect you when you don't need it." A fourth step. "I'm sorry I can't even entertain the idea of you getting hurt." He took a fifth step, so only a few feet separated them now. "I'm sorry I love you, Stella Moore. Because if I didn't love you so much, I wouldn't have broken your heart."

Stella didn't hesitate. She launched herself at Cole, her matc's arms catching her with ease. Those strong arms wrapped around her, embracing her in a blanket of comfort and love.

Love. Holy shit. Love.

She pressed her mouth to his, tongue sliding between his lips as she dove into a passionate kiss. Cole's tongue tangled with hers, his deep moan vibrating through her body. He moved his hands, palms cupping her ass while they continued to explore each other. It'd been only a couple of days, but she'd missed him. Missed his scent and taste. Missed the heat of his body next to hers. The kiss gradually slowed, and she pulled away from his mouth, resting her forehead on his as she fought to catch her breath.

"Cole." She whispered his name and nothing else, simply enjoying the feel of it on her tongue.

"I'm sorry," he whispered back, and she shook her head.

"No. Don't apologize anymore. You..." She pulled back and met his stare. "You love me."

He nodded. "I do."

Stella nibbled her lower lip and stared at her mate, at the thin scars that peppered his face and neck, at the evidence of his violent life. He was dangerous. He had a dangerous job. And he had...her heart. She could live through anything, but she couldn't live through *not* having him.

"I love you, too." She leaned in and brushed her lips across his, flicking his lower lip with her tongue. "*But* if you try to pull something like that again..."

"Stella, I can deal with a lot, but the thought of you getting hurt..." He shook his head. "I just couldn't bring you along. It...My tiger wouldn't allow it, and my human half agreed." He gradually loosed his hold, and her legs lowered to the ground. He brought his hands to her cheeks. "I joined SHOC to keep others safe, and no one is more important to me than you—you and the family we'll have. *Nothing*.

I'll stand between you and pain. I'll protect you when others fail. I'll fight for you, Stella, but you can't ask me to put you at risk. You can't."

She grasped his wrists, sliding her palms along his forearms and feeling the strength that lurked just beneath his human surface. Tears blurred her vision, the depth of his feelings washing away any lingering heartache over his actions.

She sniffled and smiled at her mate. "You shouldn't count your cubs before they're conceived, big kitty."

Cole grinned. "I'll take whatever you'll give me, Stella. Wanna start on those cubs?"

"I want to start on our life. I want everything. *Now*." And when she said "now," she meant the moment she could drag his furry ass inside.

# CHAPTER THIRTY-SEVEN

*C*ole couldn't help but stare at Stella. They'd come together so many times during the night—both of them covered in the scent of each other—and his body stirred again. He wanted her beneath him, above him, or even against the wall. He wanted to get as close to her as he could and bury himself inside her. And dammit, those few thoughts had him hard again. His tiger urged him to pull her into his arms, make love to her, and fill her with their cubs. He pushed against the cat and sent it to the back of his mind. The asshole needed to give a woman a chance to get pregnant. The cat sniffed and flicked its tail, turning its back on him.

At least it'd leave him alone while he stared at his mate. Her auburn hair was spread across the pillow, the red contrasting against the white pillowcase. Her pale skin glowed in the morning's early rays of sun. The brightness streamed through the parted curtains and window sheers, giving them light to see by. The sheets shielded her from view, but he knew every dip and hollow of her body. He'd kissed and tasted every inch more than once during the night and it still wasn't enough. Not nearly.

Stella simply, utterly stole his breath. He didn't know

what he'd done to get a mate who was so beautiful inside and out, but he would never let her go.

She sighed, the sheet inching down her body to reveal one nipple, the nub bright red in the light of day. He winced and examined her with his gaze. Her skin glowed red, proof of his unending need. He'd shave before he took her again. Otherwise she'd end up with even more beard burn.

Stella opened one green eye, her attention drifting across the ceiling and then over to him. "M-m-morning."

"Good morning." He leaned down and kissed the tip of her nose. "Sleep well?"

She snorted. "Didn't sleep at all."

"You complaining?" He quirked a brow.

"Hell no." She grinned at him. "Let's shower, maybe get some breakfast, and then we can work at getting dirty again."

He hummed and leaned over once more, brushing his lips across hers. "Unfortunately…"

Stella moaned—and it wasn't a sexy moan. "You have an op."

"Not quite."

She turned her head and glared at him. "Just explain. If I have to drag it out of you, I'm going to bite you." She opened her mouth and clacked her human teeth together while she stretched toward him. "Nom, nom, nom…"

Cole laughed and shook his head. "I've never been into biting, but if you want to give it a try…" He kissed her, a hint of tongue along with the caress of his lips. He explored the opening of her mouth, taking gentle pleasure from his mate. "I'm down for getting bitten if you need to sink your teeth into something." He nuzzled her neck and breathed deep, savoring their combined scent on her skin. "Wanna bite me? Wanna claim your tiger?"

Stella moaned, and the musk of her arousal crept into the air. Yes, she very much wanted to claim her tiger and Cole couldn't wait.

Except he had to. Otherwise he'd get so distracted by her, he'd forget what he'd come in to say. He nibbled her neck, nipping her throat before gently biting her shoulder. A reminder of what they'd already shared.

He released her and lapped at the indentations he'd made. "We'll get to that later. For now…" He sighed. "We've gotta get on the move and head to headquarters."

"Headquarters?" She wrinkled her nose. "Do we *have to*?"

"Yup. I want you in my house—in my bed. And that's at headquarters. The guys and I have houses right next to each other. You can meet Abby and hang out with her when we go on ops and do girly shit together."

"And the reason we have to go *now*?"

Cole winced. "Can you just trust me and listen?"

She raised an eyebrow. "Not so much, no."

"Fine," he grumbled. "Grant got some new intel from *somewhere*. The guy is being a sneaky fuck. He spends more time staring at his cell phone than Ethan now." Cole shook his head. "Anyway, he says we need to talk and make some plans."

"Can you be a tiny bit more specific before you haul me God knows where?"

"But you're going and you're not going to give me a hard time?"

"Not give you a hard time? Have you met me?"

Cole grunted. "Met you. Loved you. Fucked you."

"You say such the sweetest things," she drawled. "I don't know how you've stayed single all this time."

He narrowed his eyes. "I think you're joking, but…"

She flicked his chest, and he jerked away from the sting. "Ouch. Play nice or I won't tell you the good news."

At least he thought it was good news. He was about to make her dreams come true—he hoped.

"Walters confirmed King is the brains behind UH, and Grant has his location. We'll cut the head off the beast and let the organization fall apart. That'll leave us focusing on the mole."

"And that's why we have to leave now?"

Cole nodded and stroked her hand with his thumb. "Yeah. We need to make plans and requisition equipment. That sort of thing. King's in a highly protected compound."

"Sounds dangerous." Her voice softened, and he didn't like the way her face paled.

"It is, but I've trained for this. The whole team has. My brothers sit behind a desk, but I've had a gun in my hand as long as I can remember." He kissed her forehead, her nose, her cheeks, and then her mouth before retreating. He dropped his voice and altered his accent. *"I have a very particular set of skills..."*

"Asshole." She shoved his shoulder, and he rolled away only to return to her. "You can't start quoting movies when I tell you I'm worried."

Cole dropped his voice to a whisper. "I'll always come back to you, Stella. They can beat me. They can stab me. They can shoot me. But they can't stop me from coming back to you."

Drops of moisture filled her eyes, tears gathering, and dammit, he hated tears. Which was why he leapt into revealing his surprise.

"Besides, if I'm not with you, how can I pay for that shifter program you want to set up? I thought we'd name it Finding Home." He stared into her eyes, and he realized he could get lost in their depths. "Shifters who lose someone don't just lose a mother, a father, a sister, or a brother. They break like your family did. If home is where the heart is, and the loss of someone breaks that heart ... well, they sorta lost home, huh? I thought that with my money, you could help people find home again. So no one has to suffer like you did." Cole shook his head. It sounded better in his mind when he was trying to figure shit out. Out loud it sounded dumb. "Never mind. That was—"

Stella shoved him then, her shifter's strength and surprise rolling him to his back before he realized she'd moved. She climbed atop him, straddling his waist while she pinned him with her hands on his shoulders.

"I love you, Cole Turner. I loved you when I thought you were an asshole, and now ..." A single tear landed on his chest, the warm liquid sliding over his skin. "I don't know what to do with you."

He reached around her, pulling her down until their chests touched and he could meet her gaze. "Just love me. Forgive me when I'm an ass." He grinned. "But just be my home while you help others find theirs, huh?"

"Always."

Look for Grant's story and the next high-adrenaline Shifter Rogues adventure in **WOLF'S HUNGER,** coming in Summer 2019.

# ABOUT THE AUTHOR

Celia Kyle is a *New York Times* and *USA Today* bestselling author, ex–dance teacher, former accountant, and erstwhile collectible doll salesperson. She now writes paranormal romances for readers who:

1) Like super-hunky heroes (they generally get furry)
2) Dig beautiful women (who have a few more curves than the average lady)
3) Love laughing in (and out of) bed.

It goes without saying that there's always a happily-ever-after for her characters, even if there are a few bumps along the road. Today she lives in central Florida and writes full-time with the support of her loving husband and two finicky cats.

Learn more at:

Twitter: @celiakyle
Facebook.com/authorceliakyle
CeliaKyle.com

# *Fall in Love with Forever Romance*

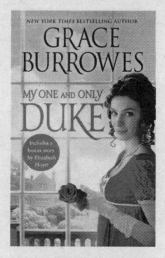

**MY ONE AND ONLY DUKE**
**By Grace Burrowes**

A charming Regency romance with a Cinderella twist! When London banker Quinn Wentworth is saved from execution by the news that he's the long-lost heir to a dukedom, there's just one problem: He's promised to marry Jane Winston, the widowed, pregnant daughter of a prison preacher. Also includes the novella *Once Upon a Christmas Eve* by Elizabeth Hoyt, available for the first time in print!

# *Fall in Love with Forever Romance*

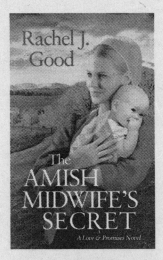

### *THE AMISH MIDWIFE'S SECRET*
### By Rachel J. Good

When *Englisher* Kyle Miller is offered a medical practice in his hometown, he knows he must face the painful past he left behind. Except he's not prepared for Leah Stoltzfus, the pretty Amish midwife who refuses to compromise her traditions with his modern medicine...But one surprising revelation and one helpless baby in need of love will show Leah and Kyle that their bond may be greater than their differences.

# Fall in Love with Forever Romance

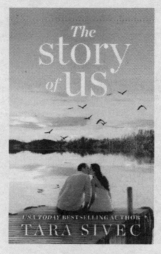

**THE STORY OF US**
By Tara Sivec

Don't miss this heartbreaking novel about love and second chances from *USA Today* bestselling author Tara Sivec! One thousand eight hundred and forty-three days. That's how long I survived in that hellhole. And I owe it all to the memory of the one woman who loved me more than I ever deserved to be loved. Now, I'll do anything to get back to her...I may not be the man I used to be, but I will do whatever it takes to remind her of the story of us.

# Fall in Love with Forever Romance

### TIGER'S CLAIM
### By Celia Kyle

Two big-cat shifters go undercover as a couple in love to take down an organization that wants to kill all of their kind. But to survive among so many enemies, they absolutely *cannot* fall in love...

### THE CAJUN COWBOY
### By Sandra Hill

With the moon shining over the bayou, this Cajun cowboy must sweet-talk his way into his wife's arms again...before she unties the knot for good!